Jean-Christophe Grangé

THE STONE COUNCIL

Translated from the French by
Ian Monk

THE HARVILL PRESS
LONDON

First published with the title
Le concile de pierre by Éditions Albin Michel, 2000

First published in Great Britain in 2001 by
The Harvill Press
2 Aztec Row
Berners Road
London N1 0PW

www.harvill.com

1 3 5 7 9 8 6 4 2

A CIP catalogue record for this book is available from the British Library

This edition is supported by the French Ministry for Foreign
Affairs, as part of the Burgess Programme headed for the French
Embassy in London by the Institut Français du Royaume-Uni

ĭi institut français

This edition has also been published with the financial assistance
of the French Ministry of Culture

ISBN 1 86046 864 0 (hardback)
ISBN 1 86046 865 9 (paperback)

Text designed and typeset in Minion
at Libanus Press, Marlborough, Wiltshire

Printed and bound in Great Britain by
Butler & Tanner Ltd at Selwood Printing, Burgess Hill

For Virginie Luc

I
First Signs

CHAPTER 1

Diane Thiberge had just 48 hours, not a minute more.

From Bangkok airport she was to reach Phuket via an internal flight, then head straight north to Takua-Pa, on the edge of the Andaman Sea. There, she could get a short night's rest in a hotel, before setting off northwards once more at five o'clock the next morning. By noon, she would be at Ra-Nong, on the Burmese border, where she would dive into the mangroves to collect what she was after. Upon which, she would simply have to repeat the same journey the other way round and catch the international flight to Paris the next evening. The time difference would play in her favour, as she would gain five hours over the time in Paris. She could then appear back at work on the morning of 6 September 1999. As fresh as a daisy.

But then the Phuket flight was delayed.

And nothing turned out as planned.

With her stomach in a knot, Diane rushed to the toilets. She felt a wave of nausea run over her, and said to herself: "It's just the jet lag. It's got nothing to do with my project." The next moment, she was sick, vomiting until her guts were burning in her throat. Her blood was hammering in her arteries, her forehead was icy cold and her heart was racing somewhere, everywhere, in her chest. She stared at herself in the mirrors. She was ashen. Her blond wavy locks looked more than ever out of place in this land of smooth, thin brunettes, and her size – her huge height that had given her such a complex during her adolescence – seemed even more grotesque.

Diane damped down her face, cleaned the nose-stud that decked her right nostril, then adjusted her tiny pair of hippy glasses. She went back into the transit lounge, floating in her tee-shirt like a ghost. The air-conditioning felt ice-cold.

She looked up again at the departure board. No news of Phuket. She idled around for a moment, then her eyes were drawn by the warning signs in Thai and English that were plastered up all over the lounge: anybody arrested carrying hard drugs in Thai territory would be sentenced to death by hanging. At that moment, two policemen passed behind her. In khaki uniforms. With the criss-cross butts of their rifles. She bit her lip. Everything seemed hostile in this fucking airport.

She sat down and tried to stop herself from trembling. For the thousandth time that morning, she ran through her itinerary. It just had to work. This was her choice. Her life. There would be no going back to Paris empty-handed.

Finally, at 14.00, the Phuket shuttle took off. Diane had lost five and a half hours.

But now she would really encounter the tropics. Relief surged over her. Bluish clouds stretched away into the distance. Patches of silver lit up the sky. Beside the runway, pale trees swayed, while the dust was being blown about in piercing swirls. But more than anything there was the smell. The odour of the monsoon, scalding, suffocating, saturated with fruits, rain and decay. The headiness of life when it overcame its own limitations and turned to decomposition. Diane closed her eyes in delight and nearly fell down the step ladder fixed to the side of the plane.

16.00 hours.

She ran over to the car-hire counter, grabbed the keys from

the receptionist's hand and rapidly found her vehicle. On the road, it started to rain. First a few drops, then a real downpour. The drumming on the bonnet was deafening. The windscreen-wipers were powerless against that red-brown mud. Diane drove on, her face up against the windscreen, fingers clutching the steering-wheel.

18.00 hours. Just before nightfall, the rains died down. The landscape glittered in the dusk. Gleaming paddy fields, dark houses standing on piles, golden buffalo with tapering horns. Or else carved temples with rolled-up roofs. But always the sky, streaked with lightning, marbled with darkness, which was now rolling down to her right in a languid blush.

She got to Takua-Pa at 20.00 hours. Only then did she wind down. Despite the delay, despite the rain, despite the panic, she was still on time.

She found a hotel in the centre of town, near a high water tank, and ate dinner below its canopy. Spicy prawns and white rice. She felt a lot better. The rain which had started falling again covered her entire body with a cool, healing halo.

That's when the girls appeared. Little girls with too much make-up, squeezed into leatherette miniskirts and dressed in tiny tops. Diane watched them. They looked ten, twelve at the most. They were like cases of indecent exposure on high heels. At the back of the room, big blond guys were already nudging one another. They were Germans, or Australians, as massive as bulls. Suddenly, Diane sensed some sort of hostility being directed against her, as though her presence were putting a block on whatever business had brought that little crowd together.

She felt the bile bite into her throat. Even then, at the age of 30, she could not imagine a sexual act without being over-whelmed by a feeling of utter disgust and nausea. She ran back to her room without turning round and without feeling the

3

slightest compassion for those tiny children who were to be given over to male desire.

Lying under her mosquito net, she thought over her plan once more. Just before going to sleep, in her mind's eye she saw the warning signs at the airport, the police uniforms and the butts of the rifles. She felt as though she could hear the clanging of distant bolts, and the whirring of an even more distant helicopter . . .

At five o'clock the next morning she was up. Her malaise had vanished. The sun was shining. The window was overflowing with exuberance, like the porthole of a ship open on a storm of vegetation. Diane felt strong enough to overturn the entire jungle if she had to.

She headed off again and reached Ra-Nong before noon, just as she had planned. She took in the view of the sea. It seemed more like a scattering of marshlands amid the tangles of trees growing in the water. Somewhere, amid that watery maze, lay the border with Burma. A fisherman nodded and wordlessly agreed to guide her there. They slipped down at once into the dark waters. In the heat, the light, the walls of greenery that slipped by and the noise of the spluttering motor, Diane took in each sensation stoically, her throat dry, her skin white hot.

An hour later, they had reached a spit of sand with concrete buildings standing on it. Grey stone on dull earth. She set foot on the sand and felt a girlish surge of triumph. She had made it. There wasn't a single place on the planet that she couldn't have reached . . .

Indifferent to the midday blaze, a group of children were playing around in front of the dispensary. Diane stared at their black mops of hair and their dark eyes below the slight shelter of their lashes. She then went into the main building and asked for Teresa Maxwell. She was soaking with sweat. She felt as though she had just passed through a mirror. A mirror she had worn down by dint of dreaming.

An old woman arrived, wearing a navy-blue sweater from which a large white collar emerged, like two slices of pie. Below her short grey hair, her broad kindly face seemed to be frozen into an expression of constant wariness. Diane introduced herself. Mrs Maxwell led her to the back of a fretwork hall and into an office that lacked any furniture barring a wobbly table and a couple of chairs.

Diane produced her application file, reduced to the bare minimum amount of paper.

"You didn't come with your husband?" Teresa asked her suspiciously:

"I'm not married."

Her face tensed. The woman was looking at the ring in her nose.

"How old are you?"

"Thirty."

"Are you sterile?"

"I don't think so."

Teresa flicked through the file. She muttered: "What the hell do they think they're doing in Paris?" Then went on, louder, staring at Diane:

"You just don't have the right profile, young lady. You're beautiful. You're single. What brought you here?"

Diane sat up at once. Her voice was husky. She hadn't spoken for two days:

"Listen, it took me two years to track this place down. I had to fill in form after form after form. I was questioned. People vetted my past, my income, my private life. I had to have medical and psychological tests. I had to take out new insurance policies, go to Bangkok twice and spend a small fortune. My application is now perfectly in order and totally legal. I've just travelled nearly ten thousand miles and I've got to be back at work the day after tomorrow. So, can we now please get down to business?"

A burning silence settled into that bare room. Suddenly, a smile flickered across the old woman's wrinkled face:

"Follow me."

They crossed a room full of fans. Net curtains fluttered over the windows and a smell of phenol hovered in the air, as though blown in on the waves of fever. Between the metal beds, children of all ages were playing, screaming and running, while their supervisors were trying to control the situation. It was as though the force of childhood were struggling against the sluggish atmosphere of convalescence. Then terrible details emerged. Infirmities. Atrophy. Scars. Diane's eyes fell on a baby with no feet or hands.

Teresa Maxwell commented:

"He's from Southern India, from the far side of the Andaman Islands. Hindu fanatics mutilated him after killing his parents. They were Muslims."

Diane felt her nausea rising again. At the same time, a ridiculous thought crossed her mind: how could this woman stand wearing a pullover in such heat? Teresa walked on. They went into a second room, with more beds and with coloured balloons floating in the air. The woman pointed to a cluster of young girls, all lying on one bed:

"They're Karens. Their parents were burnt to death last year in a refugee camp. They . . ."

Diane squeezed her arm so tight that her finger joints whitened.

"Sorry," she whispered. "But I want to see him now."

The old woman smiled joylessly.

"But, he's here."

Diane turned round and, in an alcove in the room, finally

came face to face with what she had been struggling to find all her life: a little boy, all on his own, playing with some crepe paper ribbons. She recognised him at once, from the Polaroid snap she had been sent. His shoulders were so slight that it almost looked as though the wind was helping him wear his tee-shirt. His face, which was far paler than the others, wore an expression of intense, deep concentration, which seemed almost frantic.

Teresa Maxwell folded her arms.

"He must be about six or seven. But we don't really know. In fact we know nothing about him, where he's from, what happened to him. We suppose he must have escaped from a camp. Or else his mother might be a prostitute. He was found in Ra-Nong, among the usual crowd of beggars. He speaks some sort of lingo that nobody round here understands. We finally managed to make out two syllables, which he keeps repeating: 'Lu' and 'Sian'. So we called him 'Lu-Sian.'"

Diane tried to smile, but her lips refused to move. She had forgotten about the heat, the fans, her nausea. She pushed aside the balloons, which were still fluttering around, knelt down beside the child and remained still for a moment, to admire him. Then she whispered:

"So it's Lu-Sian, is it? Then I'm going to call you Lucien."

CHAPTER 2

Diane Thiberge had been a normal little girl.

A keen child, who had gone about everything in an applied, enthusiastic and highly concentrated manner. While playing, she looked so serious with her head down that adults hesitated

before interrupting her. She watched television with such concentration that it was as though she were trying to force the
pictures into the back of her eyes. Even her sleep looked like
an act of will in which her entire being was involved, as though
she had sworn to herself to emerge from the folds of her duvet
the next morning livelier and brighter than ever.

Diane grew up full of trust. She let herself be rocked to
sleep by the stories children are told at nightfall. She saw her
future through the deceptive, tinted spectacles of cartoons,
pastel books and puppet shows. Her heart was a feather bed
and her thoughts crystallised like April snow around secure
happiness. She knew that there would always be a Prince
Charming to whisk her away, or a Fairy Godmother to wrap
her up in starlight when it was time to go to the ball. Somewhere, everything had already been written. She just had to
wait for it to happen.

And so Diane waited.

But it was another force that bore her away.

At the age of twelve, she began to feel vague desires rise
inside her. Her body seemed to be swelling, filling with confusion. Her light aspirations had been replaced by dark, menacing
impulses, which pierced her chest with a mysterious pain. She
told her friends. They just giggled and shrugged, but Diane
realised that they, too, were experiencing the same sensations.
The only difference was that they had decided to hide behind
their experiments with make-up, or the smoke of their first
cigarettes. But Diane was not one for such stratagems. She
wanted to see her adolescence face to face, whatever the truth
turned out to be.

What is more, a terrible lucidity now gripped her. She felt
able instantaneously to unmask the lies and half-truths of the
people around her. More importantly, the adult world fell
crashing from its pedestal. The men and women that had been

pointed out to her as role models now seemed weak, compromised, insidious hypocrites.

And especially her mother.

One morning, Diane declared that the woman she had been living with alone, since she had been born, did not love her and never had loved her. No matter what Sybille Thiberge said or did, her daughter no longer swallowed her act of being the model mother. On the contrary, she became increasingly wary. Her mother was too blond. Too beautiful. Too sensual. Diane went over and over those details that seemed to her to typify her mother's artificial, self-obsessed nature, and her powers of seduction. The way she would mince about as soon as a man had buttered her up a bit. That extravagant laugh she had whenever there was a male prowling round the place. Everything about her was put-on, calculated and affected. She was just one big lie, and the life they shared was pure deceit.

The proof came when the accident happened in June 1983. Diane was going home on her own from the wedding of her godmother, Isabelle Ybert. Meanwhile, Sybille had decided to go off with her new lover. "The accident". The term was not exactly right, but that was how Diane always mentally referred to what happened to her in the back-streets of Nogent-sur-Marne. Even today, she refused to remember. It was just a crack in time, in which distant lights and willow leaves glittered, and where, just by her, the heavy breathing from behind a balaclava could be heard . . . But, whenever she ended up wondering if anything really had happened, all she had to do was touch the tiny scars in the swollen flesh beneath her pubic hair.

The teenager had no idea how such a nightmare could have turned into reality. But she was sure of one thing – it was all her mother's fault. Because of her selfishness, and her complete lack of interest in anything unrelated to the muscular buttocks and sharp lust of her lovers, who formed a sort of evil circle

9

around her. Wasn't that the reason why she had had to go home on her own? Hadn't she quite simply been abandoned? That attack was a piece of hard evidence. The proof she needed.

Diane was 14. She said nothing to Sybil. Her vengeance seemed richer, more elaborate, if her mother remained completely ignorant of her tragedy. She nursed her wounds on her own and locked her pain up in her heart. All she did was demand to go to boarding school as of the beginning of the next school year. Sybille put up a little token resistance, then agreed to her request, no doubt delighted at this chance of getting rid of that silent, gawky girl who would soon start over-shadowing her own charms.

And silent Diane certainly was. It was because she always thought things over. She was learning from her experiences. The real world was thus nothing but violence, betrayal and evil. Life was based on an irrepressible force, a hard kernel of hatred, which seized the slightest chance to surge up in all of us. Diane decided to study that power. To learn about how violence structured the world. To observe and analyse it.

She made two resolutions.

The first was that after school she would devote herself to studying biology and ethology – the science of animal behaviour. And she had already chosen her specialised field. She would study predators and, in particular, the hunting and combat techniques that allowed big cats, reptiles and even insects to lord it over their territories and to survive thanks to their destructive power. It was her way of plunging into the heart of violence. A natural violence, freed of any conscience, or any motivation other than the simple logic of existence. By introducing her own accident into a broader, more universal logic this was perhaps also a way to justify and lessen its horror.

So much for her brains.

For her body, Diane chose *Wing-Chun.*

Literally, *Wing-Chun* means "eternal spring", and it is the most effective of the Shaolin schools of boxing. Its technique is based on close combat, and tradition states that it was invented by a Buddhist nun. At the start of the 1983 school year, Diane enrolled in a specialised club, near her boarding school, in the Fontainebleau region. By the end of the first year, she was displaying exceptional promise. By then, she was already nearly six feet tall but weighed barely eight stone. Despite her lanky build, she was as supple as an acrobat and extraordinarily muscular.

Her teachers noticed her abilities and suggested giving her more advanced lessons, including an initiation into *wou-te* ("virtue" or "martial discipline"). Diane refused. She was not at all interested in philosophy or cosmic energy. All she wanted to do was to forge her body into a weapon so as never again to be a little girl who can be jumped.

Her masters – wise and stuffy Asians – were rather put out by her aggressive answers. But they knew that they had a champion on their hands and, with or without the philosophy, this was a rare opportunity.

The training built up. One competition followed another. In 1986, while still at school, Diane Thiberge won the junior French championship. In 1987, she won the silver belt in the European finals then, the next year, the gold belt. Her victories were devastating. The judges could not believe their eyes and the crowd was rather disappointed. Close and bent over, her eyes fixed on her hands, Diane did not give her opponents a chance. They were still looking for an opening, when suddenly they found themselves laid flat out, shoulders pinned on the mat.

Nothing seemed to stand in the way of this young athlete. But, in 1989, Diane gave up competition. She was nearly 21 and, miraculously, neither her face nor body had ever been seriously marked. Sooner or later, her luck would run out and, in any case, she had already achieved her goal.

She had become what she had been determined to become. A thoroughly dangerous young lady whom you approached at your own risk.

CHAPTER 3

At the time, Diane Thiberge used to listen to Frankie Goes to Hollywood on her tiny personal hi-fi, with the bass turned up full. She loved that group because it was a mixture of several, apparently irreconcilable, trends made into one magical blend.

Firstly, it was group of hard-nuts from Liverpool. Then, it was a post-disco group, which had worked up a sense of rhythm and beat fit to enchant anyone who set foot on a dance-floor. Finally, they were gay. And that was the craziest part of it. That succession of cries, of barbaric beats and harsh slogans was produced by a load of screaming queens who looked like they had come straight out of Louis XIII's court. This factor gave them a quite unbelievable lightness, mobility and agility. For example, the fifth member of the group did not play an instrument. He hardly even sang. He just danced. He was the "movement" man at the back of the stage, rolling his shoulders in his leather jacket. Yes, Frankie really was a magical group, and Diane was under their spell.

But the fever of student nights went no further than her Walkman. She did not go out, did not dance and met nobody. She applied herself entirely to her ethology books, each evening revising the works of Lorenz or Von Uexküll while swallowing a takeaway burger in her bedsit in the Cardinal-Lemoine quarter of Paris.

But, that night, she was resolved to act.

Nathalie – the little bitch in the biology class who managed to get her claws into every hunk the university had on offer – was throwing a party, and Diane had decided to go.

It was now or never.

She just had to find out.

Later, Diane would often go over her memories of that crucial night. Her arrival in the block of flats on Boulevard Saint-Michel. The silence of the vast staircase with its velvet carpet. Then the deep thudding, as though entirely formed of bass-lines, coming from the upper floors. She tried to calm her racing heart, which was beating in off-time to the rhythm, and gripped the icy bottle of champagne that she had bought specially. The booming behind the large door of varnished wood sounded strong enough to knock it off its hinges. "No-one will hear me," she said to herself, as she rang the bell.

Almost at once, the door opened on a tidal wave of music. She immediately recognised the voice of Holly Johnson, the singer with Frankie, who was yelling: "RELAX! DON'T DO IT!" This was a good sign. Her favourite group was welcoming her to the ordeal. An over-made-up brunette with bony features was flapping around in the doorway. Nathalie the Gorgon, as large as life.

"Diane!" she yelled. "I'm so thrilled you could come!"

As the girl sized her up, she smiled back at the lie. Diane was wearing a black cardigan with mother-of-pearl buttons and dark, cotton leggings – a young woman's uniform of that time. All of this was enveloped in a huge padded coat, which was also black.

"So you've come with your pyjamas and duvet, have you?" Nathalie giggled.

Diane fingered the girl's black taffeta dress.

"Well, it is a fancy-dress party, isn't it?"

Nathalie burst out laughing. She took the bottle of champagne and shouted:

"Come in! Put your stuff in the room at the end of the corridor."

Inside, the party was in full swing. After taking off her coat, Diane took up position beside the food table, the inevitable place for people who know no-one. She had sworn to herself not to touch a drop of alcohol, whatever might happen, in order to remain completely clear-headed. But, after an hour's thumb-twiddling, she was already on her third glass of champagne. She sipped slowly, while glancing round at the dance-floor. The ritual had begun.

If Diane had little experience of parties, she did know the cycles involved. Preliminaries started at midnight. The girls danced, spinning around, putting on a display, exaggerating the flicks of their hair and the swaying of their hips, while the boys stayed in the background, looking on, grinning and breaking the ice with jokes . . .

At two o'clock, things got livelier. The music became more frantic. Alcohol chased inhibitions away. Everything and anything could be hoped for. The boys went into action, exchanging remarks over the heads of the crowd, hunting for their prey. Once again, it was Frankie that was pushing them into a frenzy. "Two Tribes". An anti-war song of revolt, borne up by a wild beat, which Diane knew down to the slightest note, the slightest riff.

This time, she let the music take hold of her. She moved in among the others, placing her big feet as carefully as she could. She noticed some people looking round towards her. Diane could hardly believe it. Although shier than most, she knew that more than anything she intimidated others. Generally speaking, her beauty, wavy locks and great height were enough to keep any suitors at bay. But, that evening, some foolhardy boys dared to chat her up.

She now felt her body dissolve in light twirls, gliding above the rhythm and drifting above the others. It was at that moment that a guy grabbed her arm and tried to make her bop. On every dance-floor in the world, there is always someone who stubbornly tries to make complex moves to the simplest beat. Diane pulled back at once. Her partner pressed his point. Threateningly, she raised her palms. No, she wasn't going to dance rock-and-roll. And no, people didn't just grab her hand like that. Nobody ever grabbed anything of her at all. The young man burst out laughing and vanished into the crowd.

For a moment, she stayed there, frozen, staring at her hand as though it had been burnt by the contact of flesh. She staggered, stepped back, then let herself slide down the wall. She blindly found a half-empty glass on the floor and knocked it back in one. Then she clung on to it, without moving an inch. Sadness overwhelmed her. What had just happened reminded her of the cruel truth. She was never going to be able to tolerate the slightest touch of skin. The slightest caress. The slightest contact. She had a phobia of flesh.

At three o'clock, the music became more esoteric, with Laurie Anderson's "O Superman". A strange lullaby punctuated by a sighing incantation. Time for the last chance. In the half-light, all that was left were a few lonely ghosts, swaying to the rhythm of the track. Stubborn hunters, or else worn-out girls refusing to admit defeat.

Diane studied their sagging faces and uncertain motion. It was like looking at a battlefield, covered with the wounded and dying. She went to get her coat, then discreetly slipped past the food table with its scattering of empty bottles. Her mind was already out of there. She was imagining the cold air, which would sober her up and allow her to take a good long look at her failure.

It was at that moment that she felt arms clamp round her waist.

As tense as a bow, she spun about, leaning back on the table.

Three boys were standing round her, their breaths stinking of drink.

"Hey, look guys. Looks like we're not out of luck yet . . ."

One of her aggressors stretched out his hands towards her again. Diane dodged past him with a swing of her hips and went back to the table. She dropped her coat, found another glass and pretended to drink. For a moment, she thought they had gone, but then she felt alcoholic breath on her neck. The glass smashed between her fingers. One shard had lip-stick stains on it. She pressed her palm down on it and felt the glass cut into her flesh.

"Get lost," she murmured.

Behind her, the boys were chuckling.

"Come on now, it's no time to play at being choosy."

Hot tears ran down under her horn-rimmed glasses. She distinctly felt herself think: "Don't do it." But one of the drunks was now making sucking noises by her ear, while whispering about fanny, snatch and cunts. "Don't do it," she repeated to herself. But she had just taken off her glasses and was now tying her hair in a bun behind her head. By the time she had finished, one of them had slid a hand under her cardigan. She felt the warmth of his fingers brush against her breasts, while he was sniggering:

"Don't tempt me, darling. You . . ."

The snap from his jawbone drowned out "The Art of Noise".

He was flung back against the fireplace, cutting his face open on its marble edge. Diane had unleashed an elbow attack – a *jang tow*. Once again, she thought: "NO!" But her hand had already slammed into her second opponent's ribcage, smashing it in one blow. He fell down on to the table, which buckled under him with a swoop of the tablecloth and a crashing of broken glass.

Diane did not move. *Wing-Chun* is based on a complete economy of movement and breath. The third bastard had vanished. Only then did she notice the terrified faces and the embarrassed whispering around her. She put her glasses back on. She felt flabbergasted – but not by the violence of what had happened or by the scandal of it all. But by how calm she was.

To her right, she heard Nathalie's voice screeching:

"Are you . . . are you crazy, or something?"

Diane turned slowly round towards her hostess and said:

"I'm sorry."

She crossed the room, then yelled again over her shoulder:

"I'm sorry!"

Boulevard Saint-Michel was just as she had hoped.

Empty. Icy. Deserted.

Diane walked through her tears, feeling both horrified and liberated. She now had the proof she had been looking for. She now knew that her entire life would be like this: outside of society, away from everyone else. Then she thought once more about how it had all begun. That terrible event that had broken the most natural of impulses in her, and drawn up an invisible, incomprehensible and above all inviolable prison around her body.

Once more she saw the willow trees and the lights.

She tasted the grass in her mouth and felt the breathing from the mask.

In a shudder of hatred, she also saw her mother's face. A world-weary smile played around her lips. That night, she no longer had enough energy to detest anybody. She reached Place Edmond-Rostand, whose fountain was sparkling with light, with, to her right, the pleasant greenness of the Jardins du Luxembourg. Spontaneously, she leapt up and touched the leaves of the trees that were hanging over the black and gold railings.

She felt so light that she thought she would never fall to earth again.

All of this took place on Saturday, 18 November 1989. Diane Thiberge had just celebrated her twentieth birthday. But she knew that she had said farewell to innocence for ever.

CHAPTER 4

"Do you need anything?"

"No, thanks."

"You're sure?"

Diane looked up. The air-hostess, with her blue uniform and crimson smile, was staring down at her kindly. That was the last straw. She was struggling to cut up the fritters from the "kids' menu" which had been given to the little boy shortly after take-off from Bangkok. She felt the plastic knife and fork bend in her fingers and the food squash flat beneath her nervy gestures. It was as though everyone were staring at her, taking in her clumsiness and nerves.

The hostess moved on. Diane offered another mouthful to the boy. He refused to open his mouth. Totally at a loss, she blushed horribly. Once again, she thought of the spectacle she was making of herself in front of the other passengers, with her red face, dishevelled hair, and her dark-eyed little boy. How many times had the hostesses seen the same carry-on? Western women, trembling, out of their depth, bringing home their destinies with their hand baggage.

The figure in blue tried again. "How about some sweets?" Diane forced herself to smile. "No, thanks. Everything's fine. Really." She tried a couple more spoonfuls then gave up. The child's eyes were fixed on the screen, where cartoons were being shown. She told herself that one failed meal was not the end of the world. She pushed the tray to one side, then put the headphones over Lucien's ears. She hesitated. Should she set them on English? Or French? Or just on music? Every single detail plunged her into a pit of doubt. She opted for a music station and carefully adjusted the volume.

The atmosphere grew more sleepy in the aeroplane. The meal trays were being taken away and the lights dimmed. Lucien was already dozing off. Diane laid him over the two empty seats to his right, then she settled back beneath the usual plaid blanket. Usually, this was her favourite moment during long-distance flights: with the cabin in darkness, the screen shining far away, and the motionless passengers with their headphones on, curled up like cocoons under their covers ... Everything seemed to be floating, hovering between sleep and altitude, somewhere over the clouds.

Diane leant back on her headrest and forced herself to stay still. Little by little, her muscles relaxed and her shoulders slumped down. She felt calm running once again through her veins. With her eyes closed, she projected on the dark screen of her eyelids the various steps that had led her here – to this watershed in her existence.

Her sporting triumphs and her worldly success were now distant memories. Diane passed a PhD in ethology in 1992 on "The Predatory Strategies and Organisation of the Hunting Grounds of the Large Carnivores in the Mara National Park, Kenya". She had then worked for a few private foundations, which spent large amounts of money studying and protecting natural environments. Diane had travelled in sub-Saharan Africa, South-East Asia and in India, particularly in Bengal, where she took part in a project to save the tiger of the Sundarbans. She had also carried out an acclaimed year-long study of the habits of Canadian wolves, which she had followed and observed all on her own as far as the North-West Territories near the Arctic Circle.

Her existence now was devoted to study and travel, as a solitary nomad, getting as close as possible to nature, and this was in fact more or less what she had dreamt of when she was a child. Despite everything, despite her traumas and secret agonies, Diane, with her strong independent streak, had managed to build a sort of personal happiness.

And yet, in 1997, she saw that a point of no return was approaching.

She would soon be 30.

This meant nothing in itself. Especially for a woman like Diane: her wiry build and life in the open air had preserved her well from the passing of time. But, from a biological point of view, the "3" digit marked a turning point. From her studies, she knew perfectly well that it is from this age that the womb begins its imperceptible decline. In fact, contrary to the customs practised in industrialised countries, the female sexual organs were designed to function early – as with those teenage African mothers, aged 15 at most, that she had seen so often. Turning 30 reminded her symbolically of one of her deepest secrets: never would she have a child. For the simple reason that she would never have a lover.

But she was not prepared to renounce motherhood as well. She started to look for an answer. She bought specialised books and plunged intensely into the red night of assisted insemination technology. Firstly, there was artificial insemination. In this hypothesis, she would have to go for an IWD (insemination with donor). The sperm would come from a specialised sperm bank and be injected either through the neck of the womb, or directly into the uterus during the most favourable part of the menstrual cycle. This meant doctors penetrating inside her with their cold, pointed, jagged instruments. The substance of an unknown man would inveigle its way into her womb and melt into her physiological mechanisms. She pictured her organs – uterus, Fallopian tubes, ovaries – reacting, waking up at this contact with the "other". No. Never. To her mind, this would have been a sort of clinical rape.

She investigated a second technique: *in vitro* insemination. This meant removing eggs, then artificially fertilising them in a laboratory. The idea of this distant operation, in the icy mists of a sterile room, appealed to her. She read on: one or several embryos would then be placed in the woman's uterus via the vagina. Diane came to a halt and, for a second time, understood how foolish she had been. What did she imagine? That the entire pregnancy would take place in a test-tube behind a misted-up window? That she could watch the embryo gradually forming, like a disembodied mutant?

Her stubborn phobias stood there as an unscalable wall between her and any way of having a child. Her body, her uterus, would remain for ever alien to such events, to such wonderful changes. Diane entered a period of deep depression. She stayed for a while in a rest-home, then took refuge in the villa belonging to Charles Helikian, her mother's husband, on the slopes of Mont Ventoux, in the Lubéron.

It was there, in that marvellous sun trap full of crickets, that she made a new resolution. Given that she had to drop the idea of anything organic, she might as well consider adoption. In the end, Diane preferred this idea, which was a real moral commitment, and not just some frustrated attempt to mimic nature. In her situation, this was the most logical and honest approach.

As far as she herself was concerned. And as far as the child who would share her existence was concerned.

In autumn 1997, she made a few initial inquiries. They tried by every means to talk her out of it. In theory, full adoption was open to single people. But in practice, it was extremely difficult to obtain the agreement of the Social Services in a context which might imply that she was homosexual. Diane refused to give up hope and drew up her application. There then followed long months of appointments, procedures and tests which seemed to be going round in circles for ever.

Almost a year and a half after her initial application, no progress had been made. Her stepfather then volunteered to help, saying that he could pull a few strings for her. Diane flatly refused. That would mean that, however indirectly, she was letting her mother interfere in her life. Then she changed her mind. Her obsessions and anger should not be allowed to get in the way of such a vital project. She never found out how Charles Helikian did it, but one month later, she obtained the agreement of the Social Services.

All she had to do now was to find an orphanage that would agree to provide her with a child – Diane had always imagined that it would be a little boy from a far-off country. She consulted countless organisations that ran reception centres in the four corners of the world and started to feel lost again. So Charles acted as an intermediary once more. Being something of a philanthropist, he made large donations to the Boria-Mundi Foundation, which financed several orphanages in South-East Asia. If Diane agreed to apply to this foundation, then the final steps would be soon over.

Three months later, she went to the orphanage in Ra-Nong, after two successive trips to Bangkok to see to the administrative formalities. Charles had looked after choosing her son and had taken into consideration the fact that, unlike most adoptive

mothers, Diane wanted the child to be at least five years old.
Generally, women chose new-born babies, because they imagined
that they would adapt more easily to their new surroundings.
Diane disliked this line of thinking. It even revolted her. The
idea that some orphans were deprived of everything and,
what is more, had the misfortune of being too old, or having
been abandoned too late, naturally attracted her to such
waifs . . .

Beside her, the little boy suddenly started. Diane opened her
eyes to find the cabin flooded with sunshine. She realised that
they were about to land. In a panic, she hugged her child and
felt the landing wheels touch down on the tarmac. But it was
not the tyres that were burning up on the runway, it was her
own dreams that were now rubbing up against reality.

CHAPTER 5

Among other resolutions, Diane had decided to maintain her
usual hours of work right from the word go. She wanted Lucien
to get used to their routine as quickly as possible. Right then,
she was busy writing a report on "the circadian rhythms of the
large carnivores in the Hwange National Park, Zimbabwe". She
had to get it finished quickly, so that she could apply for more
funding from the International WWF, which had already
contributed to her mission in southern Africa. So, she went each
morning to the ethology laboratory at the University of Orsay,
where she had been given a small office near the library so
that she could check her scientific data.

To mind her child, Diane took on a young Thai girl, who
was studying at the France–Asia Institute, spoke perfect French

and seemed to be a model of sweetness and kindness. The first week, the new mother kept her promise. She left at 9.00 in the morning, and came back at 6.00 in the evening. But, as of the following Monday, her resolution started to crack. Each morning, she left a little later. Each evening, she came back a little earlier. Despite her decision, she started to spend more and more time at home – as though in a season of love, whose days were gradually lengthening.

She felt totally happy.

Her anxiety at being an adoptive mother shrank while the boy's smiles broadened, and while his childish vivacity overcame her initial fears. By means of expressive gestures, laughter and grimaces, he succeeded in making himself understood, and effortlessly slid into his new role as a city dweller. Diane nodded her head, replied to him in French and tried to hide her stupefaction as best she could.

She had imagined this little fellow for so long that she had forged an image of him from her own dreams. But now the child was really there, and everything had changed. He was a real little boy, with a real face, and real moods. Everything she had imagined fell apart before her very eyes. It was as if Lucien had pulled himself out of that imaginary straitjacket that she had invented, and was now offering her the fullness and diversity of his self, which was so unexpected, surprising and always absolutely right, because it was absolutely true.

Bath time was magical. Diane never tired of observing his tiny body, the whiteness of his back, the bone structure of that bird-like form, so full of energy and lightness. She admired his milky skin, which verged on perfection, and was so unlike that of the other children she had seen in the orphanage, with blue veins and light organs beating beneath it. She thought of a chick, whose life-filled form was rubbing against its thin egg.

Another moment of pure contemplation came at bedtime, while Diane read the child a story in the half-light of the room. Lucien always fell asleep quickly, and then it was Diane's turn to be rocked by the tiny sensations she felt under her fingers. The subtle warmth of his skin. That imperceptible movement of breathing. And that hair, which was so fine that it seemed to call for particular attention from her fingers, as though it had a secret aptitude for being caressed. Where did such hair come from? From what forest of genes? From elsewhere. That was the word which always came to her lips in the darkness. Elsewhere. Each trait, each feature of that body reminded her of the child's distant origins, while also seeming to draw him nearer to her, to unite him with her Parisian loneliness.

Lucien's personality loomed up, like a glass construction which, each day, gradually revealed its architecture, its nooks, its summits. She had always imagined that Lucien would be turbulent, agitated and unpredictable. But he turned out to be quite disconcertingly calm and graceful. Despite his wild appearance – he ate with his fingers, did not want to wash, hid whenever someone came by – he in fact always acted with a deep sensitivity that charmed her. Why deny it? Lucien was exactly like the child she would have liked to have had.

Diane discovered that all these forms of wonder came together when Lucien sang and danced; she therefore encouraged him to do so as much as possible. This was how her adopted son chose to express himself at the slightest pretext, either from a taste for this kind of game, or from a natural gift. Once she had discovered this enthusiasm, she bought him a bright red cassette recorder, with a lemon yellow microphone made of plastic. Each time, the boy recorded himself, sometimes accompanying himself on improvised drums. The key moment in the performance was a special dance. Suddenly, one of his legs rose up at a right angle, while his hands fingered an imaginary veil. Then his entire form started to rotate in quite a different manner. Hunched over and curled up, his little body opened up and rippled to the rhythm like the wings of a beetle.

It was during one of these wild performances that Diane finally dared to congratulate herself. Never had she imagined such total happiness. In just three weeks she had arrived at a calmness and balance that she thought would take years to achieve. For the first time in her life, she was doing something right about her personal life.

At that moment, she noticed the red digits marking the date on her quartz alarm clock.

Monday 20 September.

Everything might well be going perfectly, but this was one date that she could no longer put off.

Dinner at her mother's.

CHAPTER 6

The reinforced door opened to reveal her slender figure.

The lights in the hall made a glowing halo around her chignon, just above the nape of her neck. Facing her, Diane remained on the threshold, as stiff as a rake. She was holding the sleeping Lucien in her arms. Sybille Thiberge whispered:

"Is he asleep? Come in. Let me see him."

Diane cautiously stepped inside, then came to an immediate halt. She had just heard the murmur of conversation from the living-room.

"Aren't you alone with Charles?"

Her mother pulled an embarrassed expression.

"Charles had an important dinner this evening, and so . . ."

Diane spun round towards the staircase. Sybille grabbed her arm, with that blend of authority and gentleness that she relished.

"Where do you think you're going? Are you crazy?"

"You told me this was going to be a quiet family dinner."

"There are obligations that one just cannot avoid. Now, don't be silly. Come on in."

Despite the dimness of the light, Diane could clearly make out her mother's form. Fifty-two years old and still that look of a Slavic Barbie, with her blond eyebrows and flowing golden locks, like on a Soviet propaganda poster. She was wearing a Chinese dress – shimmering birds on a black background – which hugged her firm, curvaceous figure. A slit revealed her perfect breasts, untouched by surgery, as Diane knew. Fifty-two years old, and this creature still had not lost a single ounce of her sensuality. Diane suddenly felt scrawnier and gawkier than ever.

Her shoulders slouched, she allowed herself to be led inside, only pointing to Lucien and whispering:

"Just mention him over dinner and I'll knock you into the middle of next week."

Her mother nodded, ignoring the violence in her daughter's voice. Diane followed her down the long corridor. She passed through the huge rooms she knew so well without paying any attention to them, or to the exotic furniture casting its angular shadows on the kilim rugs, laid out as though they had floated down from the heavens. Modern paintings zig-zagged along the impeccably white walls with their daring colours. And, in the corner of the coffee tables, stood pale, discreet lamps, like sentinels over all this opulence.

Sybille had prepared a painted wooden bed in a bright bedroom, full of silk and tulle. Diane suddenly feared that her mother was going to ham up her new role as a grandmother.

But she opted for a provisional truce. She congratulated her on the decoration and carefully laid Lucien down in the bed. For a fleeting moment, the two women stood together, looking down at him.

Back in the corridor, Sybille immediately returned to her usual tittle-tattle: social niceties and what mustn't be mentioned over dinner. Diane was not listening. Before entering the living-room, the little blond woman turned round and inspected her daughter's clothes. Her face filled with consternation.

"What's the matter?" Diane asked nervously.

She was wearing a short jumper, baggy cotton trousers that swayed on her hips, and a jacket of black synthetic feathers.

"What's the matter?" she repeated. "What's wrong?"

"Nothing. I was just saying to myself that I'd placed you in front of a minister. A government minister."

Diane shrugged.

"I don't give a toss about politics."

Sybille simply smiled and opened the living-room door:

"Be provocative, funny, dumb. Do what you want. Just don't make a scene, OK?"

The guests were sipping at their reddish ochre drinks in armchairs of the same tint. The men were greying, old and garrulous. In the background, their wives were engaged in word-less combat, gauging their respective ages, like a set of crocodiles in a pit. Diane sighed. This was going to be one hell of a boring evening.

And yet, she found her mother's little eccentricities rather amusing. For example, Led Zeppelin was humming away in the background – her mother had listened to nothing but hard rock and free jazz since her wild youth. On the laid table, she also noticed the strange fibreglass cutlery – Sybille was allergic to metal. As for what was on the menu, she knew that the main course would be a sweet and savoury dish garnished with honey, which her mother served with absolutely every-thing.

"My baby! Come and say hello!"

Smiling, she walked over to her stepfather, who was holding out his arms. Small and stocky, Charles Helikian looked like a Persian king. His skin was dark and he wore a beard along the line of his jawbones. His frizzy hair ringed his bald crown, like storm clouds strangely matching his dark eyes. "My baby!" That was what he still called her. Why "baby", given that Diane was 30 years old? And why was she *his* baby, given that she was already a 14-year-old adolescent when they had first met? It was a mystery. She gave up trying to under-stand the vagaries of language and gave him a friendly wave of her hand, but without leaning over to him. He did not press the point, knowing that his stepdaughter was not one for effusive behaviour.

Dinner was served. As always, Charles led the conversation with consummate ease. Quite unexpectedly, Diane had imme-diately adored her mother's umpteenth lover, who had then rapidly became her official stepfather. In his professional life, he was highly distinguished. He had begun by opening a company psychology practice, then started giving far more discreet counselling to big bosses and political figures. What sort of counselling exactly? Diane had never really understood what he did. She had no idea if Charles simply chose the colour of his clients' suits, or whether he actually ran their companies for them.

In fact, she could not really care less about his job or his success. What she liked most about Charles were his human qualities – his generosity and humanistic convictions. As an old leftist, he scoffed at the contradictions his wealth and social standing presented. While living in a sumptuous flat, he still continued to express his altruism, and to defend people's rights and social equality. He had no qualms about praising the "classless society" or the "dictatorship of the proletariat" even though they had sparked off most of the 20th century's worst cases of genocide and oppression. In Charles Helikian's mouth, these tarnished terms recovered all their power. Firstly because of his artful manner – but then also because, at the bottom of his heart, he still had his unbroken faith, sincerity and charisma.

Diane felt a tinge of secret regret for those ideals that she had missed out on and which had inspired her mother's generation. She was like someone who never smokes, but who appreciates the refined scent of tobacco. Despite the massacres, the oppressions and the injustices, she had never managed to free herself completely of her fascination for revolutionary utopias. And when Charles compared socialism to the Inquisition, explaining that people had made off with the finest of all our hopes and turned it into a death cult, she listened to him with gaping eyes, like the serious little girl she had once been.

That evening, conversation turned around the huge, brilliant, endless possibilities for communication with the Internet. Charles did not agree. Beneath the charm of new technology, all he could see was a new means of alienation, encouraging us to consume more, and also lessening our contact with reality and human values.

The guests around the table nodded vigorously. Diane observed them: these bosses and politicians presumably cared as little as Charles in fact did about the Internet being used as a tool for alienation. They were just enjoying themselves, listening to unusual opinions expressed with such fervour, letting themselves be cajoled by this cigar smoker who reminded them of their youth and of the rage they still pretended to sympathise with.

Suddenly, the minister addressed her directly:

"Your mother tells me that you're an ethologist."

The man had a crooked smile, a hooked nose and eyes that shifted about like Japanese seaweed.

"Yes, that's right," she murmured.

The politician smiled round at the other guests, as though applying for their indulgence.

"I have a confession to make," he said. "I've no idea what that means."

Diane looked down. She felt herself blush. Her arm was stretched out obliquely, against the corner of the table. She explained in a neutral tone:

"Ethology is the science of animal behaviour."

"And which animals do you study?"

"The big cats. Reptiles. Raptors. Predators, mainly."

"That's not a very . . . feminine field."

She gazed up. Everyone was staring at her.

"That depends. Among lions, only the female hunts. The males stay with the cubs to protect them against attacks from other prides. The lioness is without doubt the bush's biggest killer."

"That all sounds rather depressing . . ."

Diane sipped her champagne.

"Not at all. It's just one side of life."

The minister chuckled.

"You mean the eternal cliché about life feeding off death . . ."

"Like any other cliché, it's proved to be true a hundred times a day."

Silence followed her reply. In a panic, Sybille broke out in a peal of laughter.

"And it certainly won't stop you from enjoying the dessert!"

Diane looked daggers at her, but then noticed a nervous tic on her mother's face. The plates were passed round, then the dessert spoons. But the politician raised his hand:

"Just a minute."

The table instantly froze. Diane realised that during the entire meal he had never stopped being a minister so far as everyone else was concerned. Staring intently at her, he asked:

"And why that gold ring in your nose?"

Diane opened her arms, as though gesturing to show how obvious the answer was. Her beaten-silver rings glittered in the candlelight.

"To melt into the crowd, I suppose."

To his right, the minister's wife leant over between two candles.

"We are apparently not from the same crowd, then."

Diane emptied her glass. It was then that she realised that she had drunk too much. Articulating carefully, she addressed the politician:

"Of all the species of zebra, only a few are still widespread. Do you know which ones?"

"No, of course I don't."

"The ones whose bodies are entirely covered with stripes. All the others have vanished. Their camouflage was not enough to create a stroboscopic effect when running in the plains."

The minister sounded surprised:

"What's that got to do with your nose-ring? Whatever do you mean?"

"I mean that, if it's going to work, then a camouflage has to be complete."

She stood up, revealing her pierced belly button, which also contained a gold lateral stud, from which a gleaming ring was suspended. The man smiled and shifted around on his chair. His poker-faced wife disappeared back into the shadows. An embarrassed murmur ran around the table.

Diane was now in the hall. Lucien was still asleep in her arms, rolled up in a woollen blanket.

"You're crazy. Absolutely crazy."

Her mother was muttering, while adjusting her hairdo. Diane opened the door.

"What did I say wrong?"

"These are important people. They put up with having you at their table and you . . ."

"You're wrong about that, mother. I put up with them, not the other way round. You promised me a quiet family dinner, didn't you?"

Sybille shook her head in disbelief. Diane went on:

"Anyway, I can't imagine what else we'd have found to discuss . . ."

Her mother was fiddling with her golden locks.

"We have to talk. Let's have lunch."

"That's right. Let's. See you around."

On the landing, she leant against the wall and stayed there for a while in the darkness. At last she could breathe. She felt her child's warm body and this contact was enough to reassure her. She made another resolution. She absolutely had to keep Lucien away from this artificial world. And, even more so, away from her own anger, which was even more absurd than these high-society dinners.

"Can I see him?"

Charles was standing in the brightly lit doorway. He came over to look at the sleeping face.

"He's lovely."

She smelt his male odour – a mixture of expensive aftershave and cigar smoke. She was starting to feel uncomfortable.

Charles ran his hand through Lucien's hair.

"He'll end up looking like you."

She started going downstairs and murmured:

"Right. I'll walk down. I can't stand lifts."

"Wait."

33

Charles suddenly grabbed her arm and dragged her face towards his mouth. She pulled back, but it was too late. His lips had brushed against hers. In a flash, her guts knotted in an uncontrollable spasm of disgust.

She backed down the stairs, her eyes staring out of their sockets. On the landing, Charles remained motionless. His voice was now a mere whisper:

"Good luck, my baby."

Lighter than a spider, Diane fled downstairs.

CHAPTER 7

The lights in the underpass flowed past her more swiftly than a cataract.

Diane thought of a science fiction film. Chases in brightly lit tunnels. Weapons firing blinding beams. She was driving, her foot down, in the left lane of the ring-road. Alcohol was still clouding her thoughts.

It felt as if her sole contact with reality was the steering-wheel she was holding. She was driving a Toyota Landcruiser. This huge four-wheel drive all-purpose vehicle had come her way after one of her missions to Africa. It was now an old wreck, topped by barred fairing, that had trouble reaching 75 miles an hour. But Diane had grown attached to it.

She emerged from the underpass, back into the rain which drummed down on to the metal bonnet. Instinctively, she glanced at Lucien in her rear-view mirror, which she had adjusted so that she could keep an eye on him. The child was sleeping motionlessly in his raised seat.

She concentrated on the road. As usual, she had taken the

34

ring-road at Porte d'Auteuil and was now heading for Porte Maillot. This did take her a little out of her way, but Diane always avoided the rambling maze of the 16th *arrondissement*. Her stepfather had tried to explain the direct route to her a thousand times. And a thousand times her mind had refused to grasp those twists and turns. Charles would then give up with a roar of throaty laughter.

Charles.

Whatever had that kiss meant? She chased the thought away, as though spitting it out, and leant over her wheel to get a better view of the street through the pouring rain. Why had he done that? Was it another one of his eccentric quirks? One of the attitudes he liked to strike? No, it wasn't. That kiss had not been part of his usual carry-on. It meant something quite different. And it was the first time that he had ever held her like that.

The pouring rain pounded in waves against the windscreen. Visibility was nearly down to zero. Diane tried to increase the speed of the wipers. In vain. She glanced at her rear-view mirror. Lucien was still asleep. The orange gleam from the sodium lights was making stripes across his still face. This vision reassured her. Her destiny lay with that little boy. He had given her an unsuspected strength. Nothing else now mattered in her life.

When her gaze drifted back to the road, it was filled with terror.

A juggernaut was bursting through the sheets of rain, lurching across all four lanes, as though totally out of control.

Diane braked. The truck hit the central safety barrier, smashing into its metallic strips with a screeching crunch. The cabin bounced back violently, while the container swung across the entire width of the roadway. The front of the truck spun round again through a 270° angle, hitting the barrier once more, this time with its right-hand side. The metallic screeches rose up again through the downpour, mingling with the explosion of sparks, while the monster's headlamps played into the darkness.

She wanted to scream, but the cry stuck in her throat. She braked again, but instead of slowing down, she went into an uncontrolled acceleration. Diane was paralysed. Her car was now skidding at full speed, its wheels blocked, having entirely lost its grip on the tarmac. The juggernaut jack-knifed violently.

Her Toyota was now just a few yards from the monster. She braked again. By short shocks, she tried to stop her car from aquaplaning. Nothing doing. She kept going faster and faster. This fragment of time seemed to be going on for ever.

Suddenly she saw herself hit the steel wall. She seemed to picture herself bursting through the impact. Passing through the metal and coming to rest inside the structure of the truck. She saw herself dead, crushed, smashed into a mess of blood, flesh and iron.

The scream finally burst from her throat. Frantically, she turned her wheel to the left.

The car hit the smashed barrier. The impact took her breath away. Her head hit the rear-view mirror. She blacked out as, at that very moment, a gleam of astonishment rose up inside her. Time passed. A pause, with no shape nor succession. Diane coughed, hiccupped, spat out some bloody phlegm. Vaguely she understood – her body understood: she was still alive.

She opened her eyes. The transparent form coming towards her was her own windscreen, compressed by its distorted surround. She tried to move her head, and set off a shower of glass. The nape of her neck was trapped by the covering of the boot, which had been torn off and had landed on her shoulders, like a yoke. Through the pain, Diane felt further panic rise inside her. Something did not fit. Her windscreen had not smashed. So where was this glass coming from?

Her first conscious thought was for Lucien. In agony, she

turned round and stared speechlessly. His seat was empty.

In his place on the back seat were thousands of translucent shards and traces of blood. The rain was pouring in through the broken window and soaking the fabric of the seat, which was printed with tiny teddy bears. With her flayed hands, Diane blindly felt for her glasses. They were dotted with starbursts, but confirmed the horror: the boy was no longer in the car. The collision had sent him flying through the side window.

Diane managed to undo her safety belt. She pushed her shoulder against her smashed door and inched her way out. At once she collapsed into a puddle, tearing her coat against the jagged safety barrier. Despite her hazy wits, she felt the damp grass beneath her and smelt the scorched grease. She got to her feet and limped over to the roadway. Headlamps were criss-crossing the night. Horns were blaring out in a thunderous din. She could see nothing clearly. Apart from pools of petrol on the road, which formed iridescent gleams in the lights, like scraps of a fallen rainbow.

She staggered on, taking in odd details of this apocalypse. The overturned juggernaut, jack-knifed across the width of the ring-road. The bright company logo on the tarpaulin, upon which the downpour drummed. The driver, tumbling out from his cabin, his head in his hands, his fore-arms streaming with blood. But she could not see Lucien. Not the slightest trace of his body.

She approached the truck once again. Then suddenly stopped. She had just noticed one of the boy's shoes – a red trainer – then, in its wake, a few yards further on, the inevitable form. He was there. At the point of articulation, below the system that connected the container to the truck, stuck down under the torn cables and jets of steam. She could now make out every detail. His little head lying in a dark puddle, his tiny body half hidden under the metal, his fleece jacket soaked with petrol and rain ... Diane summoned up all her strength and went over to him.

"Don't ..."

A hand was holding her back.

"Don't. Don't look at him."

Without understanding, Diane looked round at the man. Another voice rose up to her left:

"There's nothing you can do, Madame."

Every sound melted into the beating of the downpour. She did not understand what they meant.

"I saw it all ... Jesus Christ," another voice said. "It's incredible that you've escaped in one piece ... You must have been saved by your seat-belt ..."

This time, Diane grasped what was being implied. She pulled herself free of the hands that were gripping her and headed back to her car. She walked round it, leant on the seething bodywork until she reached the rear right-hand door of the Toyota. With all her strength, she wrenched it open. Then she stared carefully at the raised seat that was scattered with powdered glass.

The polycarbon strap was lying, intact, beside the seat.

Diane had not done up the buckle of Lucien's seat-belt.

She had inadvertently killed her child.

The storm seemed to break out afresh in her belly. Lightning. A pit of electricity.

The ground rose; it was her falling to her knees.

She did not have a thought left, no consciousness, nothing. All she could sense was the hammering of her rings mixing blood with rainwater as she beat her face with her two fists.

CHAPTER 8

The room in intensive care consisted of three glass walls opening out on to a corridor, which was itself streaked by the translucency of other rooms. Diane was sitting in the darkness. In a white coat, with a paper hat and mask, she stood perfectly still facing the chrome-plated bed. As though under its control. Controlled by that arch of metal striated with cables and equipment, below which Lucien lay.

An intubation probe, connected to an artificial respirator, was stuck into the child's mouth. Along his right hand, the tube led up to electronic drips which, as they had explained to her, meant that the dose he received could be controlled down to the last millilitre per minute, 24 hours a day. On his left arm, a catheter recorded his blood pressure, while a clamp that gleamed like a ruby in the darkness gripped one of his fingers to gauge his response to "oxygen saturation".

Diane knew that there were also some electrodes somewhere beneath the sheets which were following his heartbeat. Nor could she see – which was just as well – the two drains stuck under the large dressing on his head. Instinctively, her eyes fell on the screen that hung up to the left of the bed. Wave patterns and figures stood out on it in a fluorescent green, constantly recording the comatose boy's physiological activity.

As she stared at them, they made Diane think of a chapel. Of a place of mourning and fervour, with the pale light of icons, ciboria, candles . . . The shining curves of those quartz figures were her candles. The votive offerings in which she had placed her hopes and prayers.

She was now spending practically her entire time in that room in Necker hospital's children's neurosurgery unit. Since the accident, she had hardly slept or eaten anything. Nor had she taken any tranquillisers. All she did was to run over and over her slightest memories – each minute, each detail which had come after the collision.

The arrival of the first emergency vehicle broke her fit of despair.

Only then did she stop hitting herself and look up at the truck which, sirens wailing, was breaking through the crowd of stationary cars. Red. Chrome. Flanked by metal instruments. The firemen leapt out equipped for a blaze, while another vehicle, marked with the city police's logo, was already arriving down the hard shoulder. The police officers concentrated on the traffic. Dressed in fluorescent orange oilskins, they stood as signposts along the roadway, signalling to the cars to take the right-hand lane – the only one that was not blocked by the truck's container.

Diane was now on her feet again, by her Toyota. The firemen roughly pushed her to one side and immediately hosed down her car with carbonic foam. Desperate, she now felt surrounded by a growing horde of motorists, murmurs, and the rustling of the rain. But all she could hear were her own words, hammering away at her conscience. "I've killed my son. I've killed my son . . ."

She turned round towards the truck and, among the hooded figures crossing amid the lights from the underpass, she noticed a man in leather moving away from the precise spot where her child had come to rest. Instinctively, she went over to him. The fireman had dived into the cabin of his vehicle to use his radio. When Diane was a just a few yards away from him, she heard him yell into his transmitter:

"Yes, it's the accident unit here, by Porte de Passy . . . Where the hell are the medics?"

She walked though the fine needles of the rain. The man was shouting:

"There's a victim . . . A kid . . . Yes, he's still breathing, but . . ."

The fireman did not finish his sentence. He threw down his transmitter and rushed over to the van that had just emerged through the sheets of water. Diane saw the letters gleaming on the bodywork: SAMU de Paris, SMUR, Necker 01. All the circuits in her body switched over. A second before, she had been floating, frozen, empty, as though dead. Now her heart leapt as she observed each detail. The ambulance men, with their heavy kitbags, were running across the roadway. A hope. There was hope.

Trailing them, she managed to outflank the row of police officers. She sneaked in as close as possible to the cabin of the juggernaut. A large pool of petrol and oil had spread out over the tarmac, refusing to mix with the rainwater. The orange vapour from the lamps crossed its surface. All the men were bent over the same area. Diane could no longer see her child.

She went nearer and forced herself to look. She was trembling, but an inner strength was controlling her body, forcing it to stay observant. At last, she made out the tiny figure. Her legs gave way under her when she saw the wound to his skull, swimming in a dark flood. Amid the torn-off clumps of hair, she noticed a crescent of red, naked, open flesh. She fell on one knee and, once on the ground, came across a man bent double under the chassis of the truck, just by Lucien's body. He was bawling into his transmitter:

"OK. There's a cerebral contusion. And it's definitely bilateral. Yeah. I need a paediatrician at once. At once, you hear? Have you got that?"

Diane pursed her lips. The words burned into her flesh. The doctor emerged from under the cave of steel. A white coat was sticking up from below his parka.

"Yes, in a coma . . . Glasgow . . ."

With lightning speed, he opened the child's eyes, then touched his neck, feeling it with his fingers.

"Four."

He half-opened the eyes once more.

"I confirm that: Glasgow on four. Has the paediatrician left yet?"

Then, rapidly examining Lucien's right arm, he added:

"I also have an open fracture on the right elbow. (He fingered the child's bloody hair.) A wound on the scalp. Not serious. End of report in ten minutes."

Beside him, a male nurse was ripping open the Velcro fastenings of a backpack, while a second one was slipping folded blankets between the body and the twisted metal. Firemen were holding up plastic sheets to protect them from the rain. Nobody had apparently noticed Diane.

The doctor was now massaging Lucien's jaws, while cautiously uncovering his neck. One of the nurses slipped a surgical collar under his neck. The doctor snapped it shut with a single gesture.

"OK. Let's intube him."

A translucent tube appeared in his hand, which he immediately slid into the half-open mouth. The second nurse was already placing a catheter in Lucien's left hand. These men seemed to be running on reflexes acquired from a long experience of emergencies.

"What the hell do you think you're doing here?"

Diane looked up. The medic did not give her time to reply, as though he had guessed the answer through the rain, from the expression in her eyes – had read her distress in the gold gleams of her irises.

"How old is he?" he asked.

She muttered something incomprehensible, then started again,

42

louder, talking over the rain as it beat on the tarpaulin.

"Six or seven."

"What do you mean *six or seven*?" the doctor yelled. "Are you taking the piss?"

"He's an adopted child. I . . . I've just adopted him. A few weeks ago."

The man opened his mouth, hesitated, then decided not to reply. He undid Lucien's jacket and pulled up his sweater. Diane felt as though she had been punched in the guts. His body was black. It took her a moment to realise that it was not blood, but only oil. With a compress, the doctor was cleaning the thorax. Without looking up, he asked:

"Any past history?"

"Sorry?"

He stuck some adhesive patches on the boy's chest.

"Any illnesses? Health problems?" he murmured.

"No."

He placed the electrodes on to the patches.

"Has he been vaccinated against tetanus?"

"Yes. Two weeks ago."

He handed the wires to the second nurse, who immediately plugged them into the rear of a box covered with black cloth. The doctor was now slipping a tensiometer over the boy's biceps. A bleep sounded. The man passed some more cables to the nurse, who connected them to another unit.

A fireman appeared under the sheeting. He was wearing massive canvas gloves and a hooded parka. Behind him, a truck was slowly reversing towards them. On its side was written: DISINCARCERATION. Other figures approached, holding barbaric tools plugged into pneumatic cables, pushing hydraulic jacks on trolleys, while others still, equipped for fire fighting, stood round the cabin in an arc, holding their hoses and extinguishers. A casebook operation was in progress.

"Ready?"

The doctor, his face streaked with sweat, did not reply. Further rips of Velcro could be heard. A screen appeared between the nurse's hands. Green lights shone out from it: peaks and troughs, figures. For Diane, it was as if the impossible were coming true. The language of life was wavering across that monitor.

Lucien's life.

The fireman yelled:

"Are you ready or what?"

The doctor looked up at the padded fireman.

"No, we're not ready. We're waiting for the anaesthetist."

"Impossible." He pointed at the petrol glistening on the ground. "In one minute's time, we'll all be . . ."

"Here I am."

Another person had just slipped below the sheeting. Hirsute, pale, in an even worse state than the first doctor. The two medics had an obscure conversation, full of abbreviations and acronyms. The anaesthetist bent down over Lucien and opened his eyelids.

"Shit."

"What?"

"Mydriasis. The pupil's dilating."

The two men fell momentarily silent. The fireman spun round. The mechanical equipment was still approaching inexorably.

"OK," the anaesthetist said at last. "General anaesthetic. PentoCelo. Where's the radio?"

While the first doctor and the nurses busied themselves, the second medic grabbed the transmitter and took over relaying information:

"New report on the emergency patient. Get the neurological theatre ready. There's a high possibility of epidural haematoma. I repeat: an EDH in one of the hemispheres!" A pause. "We've got a neurosurgical lesion *and* a cerebral contusion . . ." He paused again. "But I don't fucking know! All I can see is that mydriasis has already set in. Shit, it's a kid. Not even seven. Daguerre. Get Daguerre on the case! And no-one else!"

The fireman reappeared. The emergency medic nodded curtly to him. A few seconds later, a different organisation was already in place. The nurses were wrapping the child up in felt covers and cloth pads. Further on, the blades of the jacks were being slipped under the truck's chassis.

"You'd better go now," the first doctor whispered to Diane.

She looked at him vacantly, then nodded, in exhaustion. The last she saw of Lucien was his body encased in boards and blankets, with padded goggles over his eyes.

A shrill whistling noise started up in the room. Diane jumped. Almost at once, a nurse appeared. Without looking at her, she hung a fresh pouch of sodium chloride on to the metal frame and plugged it into the drip.

"What's the time?"

The nurse turned round. Diane asked again:

"What's the time?"

"Nine o'clock. I thought you'd gone home, Madame Thiberge."

She answered with a vague shake of her head, then closed her eyes. But her eyelids were aflame, as though she was not permitted the slightest moment of rest. When she opened them again, the woman had gone.

Once more, her memories dragged her away from the present.

"Are you sure you wouldn't prefer to come into my office?"

Diane looked at Dr Eric Daguerre, as he stood near the panel of the x-ray screen. On the lit glass plate could be seen the x-rays and scans of Lucien's shattered skull. The images were reflected on to the surgeon's face.

She shook her head, then asked in a neutral tone:

"How did it go?"

The operation had lasted over three hours. The doctor stuck his hands into the pockets of his white coat.

"We did everything we could."

"Please, doctor, can you give me a straight answer?"

Daguerre never took his eyes off her. Everyone had told her: he was the best neurosurgeon in Necker hospital. A virtuoso who had already brought back dozens of children from the distant shores of irreversible coma. He cleared his throat:

"Your child was suffering from an epidural haematoma. A pocket of blood in the right hemisphere." He pointed out the region on one of the x-rays. "We opened the temple in order to reach the haematoma. We then removed the blood clots and coagulated the entire region. It's what's called haemostasis. We then closed up, after leaving a drain to remove any remaining blood. In that respect, everything went perfectly."

"What do you mean 'in that respect'?"

Daguerre leant over towards the illuminated panel. It was impossible to guess how old he was – somewhere between 30 and 50. His keen features were extremely pallid, but this did not make him appear sickly. On the contrary, it gave him a sort of illumination. A decisive clarity that beamed out from his entire face. With his index finger, he tapped on the shots of the brain.

"Lucien is also suffering from a second traumatism: a bilateral contusion that we can't do much about."

"You mean parts of his brain have been damaged?"

The surgeon gestured vaguely.

"It's impossible to say. Right now, we're faced with quite a different problem. The brain, like any other part of body, has a tendency to swell up after receiving a shock. But the skull is closed. It doesn't allow the slightest swelling. If the brain

46

presses too hard against the bone, it can't do its job properly any more. And brain death is the result."

Diane leant against the desk. The blue reflections from the negatives glimmered in the surgeon's face. The heat in that room, heightened by the rays from the neon lights, was unbearable.

"Can't . . . can't you do anything?"

"We've placed a second drain in the skull which allows us constantly to monitor the pressure of the brain. If it rises again, then we'll open the channel and remove a few millilitres of cephalo-rachidian fluid. It's the only way to soothe the organ."

"But the brain won't go on swelling for ever?"

"No, it won't. The fits will quieten down, then stop altogether. So we have to deal with them until things go back to normal again."

"Doctor, can you give me an honest answer? I mean, is there any chance that . . . that Lucien will pull through?"

Another vague gesture.

"If the intracranial pressure goes down quickly, then everything will be fine. But if the swelling goes on for too long, then there's nothing we can do. Brain death will then be inevitable."

Silence. Daguerre concluded:

"We'll have to wait and see."

For nine days, Diane had been waiting.

For nine days, she had ended up going home each evening, replacing one form of solitude with another, in the flat on Rue Valette, near Place du Panthéon, which was now in such a mess that it mirrored her own abandon.

She walked across the main courtyard of the university hospital. The campus was like a town, with its buildings, shops and chapel. During the day, there was a deceptive busyness about the place which made you forget its true purpose – care, sickness, the struggle against death. But at night, when silence and solitude descended on them, the buildings recovered all of their deathly gloom and seemed more than ever dominated by fear, illness and annihilation. The young woman took the last path that led to the main gate.

"Diane."

She stopped and squinted.

Among the spherical lamps on the lawn, her mother's form stood out.

CHAPTER 9

"How is he?" Sybille Thiberge asked. "Can I go and see him?"

"Do whatever you want."

The little figure, her head still topped with its overly blond chignon, gently replied:

"What's wrong? Is it because I'm late? Were you expecting me earlier?"

Diane stared into space, far away beyond Sybille. Finally, looking down on her mother from her great height, she said:

"I know what you're thinking."

"And what's that?"

Imperceptibly, Sybille's voice had risen a tone.

"You think that I should never have adopted him," Diane declared.

"But I was the one who advised you to do it!"

"No, it was Charles."

"We discussed the matter together."

"Who cares? You think that not only would I have been incapable of bringing him up properly, or of making him happy, but now I've actually killed him."

"Don't say things like that."

"But isn't it true?" Diane suddenly yelled. "Who forgot to do up his belt? Someone else maybe? Who hit the safety barrier?"

"The truck driver had fallen asleep. He admitted that afterwards. It's not your fault at all."

"And what about the drink? If Charles hadn't been around to hush up the results of the breathalyser, I'd probably be behind bars right now!"

"For heaven's sake, not so loud!"

Diane bent over and touched the dressings on her forehead and temples. She felt faint. Hunger and fatigue had unbalanced her. She headed off towards the main gate without even saying goodbye to her mother then, all of a sudden, she turned back and said:

"I want you to know something."

"What's that?"

Two nurses passed by, pushing a bed. A body could just be made out, under a blanket, connected to a drip.

"I want you to know that everything's your fault."

Preparing for conflict, Sybille crossed her arms.

"How very facile," she said.

Diane raised her voice once again:

"Didn't you ever wonder why I was in such a state? Why I'd made such a mess of my life?"

Sybille's tone became ironic:

"No, of course I didn't. I've been watching my daughter sinking for the past 15 years, and I don't give a damn. I've taken her to see every psychologist in Paris, but that was only to save face. I do my best to talk to her, to get her to break her silence, but that's only to assuage my own conscience." She was now yelling. "I've been trying to find out what's wrong with you for years! How can you say that?"

"It's the story of the mote in your neighbour's eye," Diane sneered.

"What do you mean?"

"That misery begins at home."

They fell silent again. Branches were rustling in the darkness. Sybille kept fiddling with her chignon – a clear sign of her uneasiness.

"You've gone too far now, my dear," she said decisively. "Explain yourself."

Diane felt dizzy. At last, the past was going to be revealed.

"It's because of you that I'm the way I am," she whispered. "Because of your selfishness, because of your profound scorn for everything apart from yourself . . ."

"How can you come out with such things? I brought you up on my own, I . . ."

"I'm talking about the deep truth. Not the superficial part you play."

"What do you know about my deep truth?"

Diane felt like she was on a burning tightrope – she went on:

"I can prove what I'm saying."

A moment's pause. An alert. Sybille's voice wavered:

"You can . . . prove it? Prove what?"

Diane tried to speak calmly; she wanted each syllable to hit home.

"It all happened at Nathalie Ybert's wedding, in June 1983."

"What did? I've no idea what you're talking about."

"You can't remember? That doesn't surprise me. We spent all month getting ready for it. We didn't speak about anything else. Then, as soon as we got there, you pissed off somewhere. You just dumped me there, with my dress, my little shoes, my little girl's illusions . . ."

Sybille sounded incredulous:

"But that's all ancient history, I can hardly remember . . ."

Something snapped in Diane's body. She felt tears welling up in her eyes and stifled them at once.

"You dumped me, mother. You went off with some guy . . ."

"With Charles. I met him that evening." Her voice was rising again. "So you expect me to sacrifice my entire private life to you?"

"You dumped me. You quite simply dumped me!" Diane repeated doggedly.

Sybille seemed to hesitate, then she opened her arms and walked towards her.

"Listen," she said, changing her tone. "If that business hurt you, I'm sorry. I'm . . ."

Diane leapt backwards.

"Don't touch me. Nobody touches me."

At that moment, she realised that she was not going to tell her about the accident. That truth would not cross the barrier of her lips. She declared:

"Just forget it."

She felt stronger than steel, surrounded by a force field. This was the sole advantage to be gleaned from her old wound: her sorrow and anxiety had been slowly transformed into a cold fury, into self control. She nodded towards the paediatric surgery block, and the pale light from the windows of the intensive care unit.

"If you have any tears left, shed them for him. Bye."

When she turned on her heel, it seemed to her that the rustling of the trees had wrapped her up in a cloak of evil.

CHAPTER 10

Other days and nights followed.

Diane lost count of them. Her daily routine was marked only by Lucien's fits in the intensive care unit. Since her latest argument with her mother, there had been four more mydriases. On four occasions, the boy's eyes had stared fixedly, showing that the end was near. Each time, the doctors had used drains to remove a few millilitres of cephalo-rachidian fluid and had calmed the brain down. They thus succeeded in avoiding the worst.

Her life was suspended on the doctors' lips. She read things into their slightest word, the slightest inflection of their voices, and she hated herself for this dependency. Her mind contained nothing but questions, which constantly came back to torment her, like a searing lance. She slept in dribs and drabs, absent-mindedly, so much so that she sometimes even wondered if she was alive or just dreaming. Her health was failing – and yet she still refused to take any medication. In fact, such mortification finally inebriated her, stunning her like a religious trance, and allowing her no longer to see reality face to face: all hope had gone. Lucien's life now depended on a batch of machines and unfeeling technology.

To end it all, they would simply have to turn off the switch.

That day, at around three o'clock in the afternoon, it was her own body that lost its grip. Diane fainted on one of the staircases in the paediatric unit and fell down the steps on her back. Eric Daguerre gave her an intravenous jab of glucose and told her to go home and sleep. And no arguing.

Nevertheless, at about ten o'clock that evening, Diane shoved open the door of the medical unit. She was obstinate, crazy and ill – but she was there. She was full of some vague premonition. The last hour had chimed. It seemed that each detail confirmed what she thought. The heaviness of the atmosphere inside the building. The flickering neon lights on the ground floor. The vacant stare of the nurse she bumped into and found decidedly odd. They were all signs, presages. Death was lurking there, just near, by her side.

When she reached the second-floor lobby, she spotted Daguerre and saw that her intuition had been right. The doctor came over to her. Diane stopped.

"What's happening?"

Without answering, the doctor took her arm and led her to a row of chairs fixed against the wall.

"Sit down."

She slumped down, murmuring:

"What's happening? Is it . . . is it all over?"

Eric Daguerre crouched down to face her.

"Calm down."

Diane had her eyes open, but couldn't see him. She saw nothing but nothingness. It was not even a vision, it was the absence of any vision, of any perspective. For the first time in her life, Diane could no longer project herself into the next moment, or envisage the second that was to follow this one. She realised that she already belonged to the world of the dead.

"Diane, look at me."

She concentrated on the surgeon's bony features. She still could not see anything. Her consciousness was no longer analysing the images that were being captured by her retinas. The doctor grabbed her wrists. She let him – she was too weak now for her phobias.

"While you were at home, this afternoon," the man murmured, "Lucien suffered two more mydriases. In under four hours."

Diane was frozen. Her limbs had been strapped up and

immobilised by fear. After a minute's silence, the surgeon added:

"I'm sorry."

This time, she stared straight at the doctor and fixed him through the veil of her anger.

"He isn't dead yet, then, is he?"

"You don't understand. Lucien has had the symptoms of brain death six times now. He can no longer regain consciousness. And even if such a miracle happened and he did start to wake up, the after-effects would now be too serious. His brain must have been damaged, you do see that? You don't want him to live on as a vegetable, do you?"

Diane stared at Daguerre for a few seconds. She was suddenly struck by the medic's good looks. Her voice cracked with anger:

"You want him to die, don't you?"

The doctor stood up. He was trembling.

"You can't say that, Diane, not to me. I've been struggling day and night to save these kids. I belong to life." He pointed at the glazed corridor behind the glass door. "We belong to life, all of us! Don't ask the dead to exist among us."

She threw her head back and closed her eyes. Her skull hit the wall. Once, twice, three times. The heat was suffocating her. The whiteness of the strip-lights was burning her irises through her eyelids. She felt her body collapse, opening out into a black hole, sucking its consciousness down through the gap.

And yet, with a final effort, she got to her feet. Without saying a word, she grabbed her bag and headed towards the intensive care unit.

The unit full of tiny motionless bodies.

On the other side of the door, all was quiet.

Not a sound, not a whisper came from the line of dark, translucent rooms, lit only by their glittering machines.

Diane slipped into Lucien's room, pulled off her glasses and slumped to her knees. With her head in the sheets at the bottom end of the bed, she burst into tears. With unhoped-for violence. Since the accident, it was the first time that her body had allowed her this relief. Her muscles relaxed, her nerves loosened. Her sobbing was suffocating her, her sorrow was choking her, but at the same time she felt liberation welling up, a dull pleasure, like an evil bloom announcing peace at last.

She knew that she would not survive Lucien's death. That child had been her last chance. If he died, then Diane would give up living. Or else her sanity would fall to pieces. One way or another, she would take the plunge.

Suddenly, she felt a presence close to her. She raised her eyes, which were stinging from the salt of her tears. Without her glasses, she could not make out a thing. But she just knew that somewhere, in the darkness, someone was there.

Then, softly, mysteriously, a voice said:

"I can help you."

CHAPTER 11

With a sweep of her sleeve, Diane dried her eyes and grabbed her glasses. A man was standing in the room, a few feet from her. She then realised that he must have been already there when she came in. She desperately tried to think straight.

The man came over to her. He was huge, almost seven feet tall, and wearing a white coat. His thick neck was topped by a head that was just as massive, decked with a white mop of hair. The pale light from the corridor fleetingly lit his face. His skin was red, his vague features like those of a broken statue. His face gave off a sort of gentleness. Diane noticed his long, upturned eyelashes. He repeated:

"I can help you." He turned towards the child. "Or help him."

His voice was calm, matching his appearance, and he had a slight foreign accent. In just a few seconds, Diane had overcome her surprise. She noticed the badge, pinned on his white coat.

"Are you . . . are you on duty here?" she asked.

He stepped forward. Despite his bulk, he made no sound when he moved.

"My name's Rolf van Kaen. I'm a head anaesthetist. I come from Berlin. From the Charity Children's Hospital. I'm working on a Franco-German development scheme with Dr Daguerre."

His French was fluent, as smooth as a pebble left too long in a pocket. Diane got up, then sat down on the only chair. She perched there clumsily. There were no nurses in the corridor.

"What . . . what are you doing here? I mean . . . in this room?" she asked.

The doctor seemed to be thinking over his answer, weighing each term precisely:

"You were told this evening about how your child's condition had worsened. I myself read the results." He stopped, then went on. "I think you have been fully informed. So far as western medicine is concerned, there's no more hope."

"What do you mean, *western medicine*?"

Immediately, Diane was sorry she had asked. She had reacted to the man's words too hastily. The German went on:

"We could try a different technique."

"What sort?"

"Acupuncture."

Diane spat through her teeth:

"Don't take me for a fool and piss off! Jesus Christ! Get out before I throw you out!"

The anaesthetist did not budge. His monolithic bulk stood

out against the gleaming windows. He murmured:

"I'm in a delicate position here, Madame. I don't have much time to convince you. And your son has even less time . . ."

Diane noticed a natural, spontaneous tone in his voice, which touched her. It was the first time that a voice had mentioned without fear or embarrassment her mother-child relationship with Lucien. The doctor continued:

"You know what's wrong with your son, don't you?"

She looked down and stammered:

"Flows of blood which . . ."

"Are choking his brain, that's right. But do you know where these flows come from?"

"It's because of the shock. The shock from the accident. They're set off by the haematoma and . . ."

"Of course. But the deeper reason? What sets off the flow? What force pushes the haemoglobin towards the brain?"

She remained silent. The doctor took another step forward.

"What if I told you that I could act on that very motion? That I could calm down the impetus?"

Diane forced herself to speak calmly, in order to try to get this over with quickly:

"Look, I'm sure you mean well, but my son has had the best possible care here. I don't see how . . ."

"Eric Daguerre works on life's mechanical phenomena. But I can act on the other side of these mechanisms. On the energy that sets them in motion. I can reduce the force that is drawing your son's blood towards his brain and is gradually killing him."

"Bullshit!"

"Listen to me!"

Diane jumped. The doctor was almost screaming. She glanced over at the corridor. Nobody. This floor had never seemed so deserted to her, so quiet. She was starting to feel vaguely scared. The German went on, more calmly:

"When you look at a river, you can see the water, the foam, the weeds among the waves, but you can't see the most important part: the current, the movement, the life of the stream . . . Who would dare claim that the human body doesn't work in the same way? Who would dare deny that, beneath the complexity of blood circulation, heartbeats and chemical secretions, there is just one current which makes it all work: our vital energy?"

She shook her head. The man was now just a few inches away from her. It was almost as if they were conversing in a confessional.

"Rivers have their sources, their underground networks, which we can't see. Human life also has its secret origins and its water-tables. There is an entire hidden geography which eludes modern science, but which lies inside our bodies."

Diane remained motionless, her face bent down into the shadows. What this man did not know was that she had heard all this before. How many times had she listened to her *Wing-Chun* masters going on about *chi*, vital energy, the *ying* and the *yang* and all that crap! She had never fallen for it. On the contrary, her victories in competition seemed to show how empty their arguments were. You could be a Shaolin prize fighter without giving a damn about its values. And yet, his voice was wheedling its way into her consciousness:

"Acupuncture is part of traditional Chinese medicine. It's thousands of years old, and isn't based on beliefs, but on results. It must be the world's most pragmatic form of medicine, because no-one has ever been able to explain how it works. Acupuncture acts directly on the network of our vital energy – what we call meridians. Madame, I beg of you, please trust me. I can stop the contusions your son is suffering from. I can slow down the flows of blood that are killing him!"

58

Diane looked at Lucien's form. His tiny body wrapped up in bandages, plaster and cables. He seemed crushed, controlled by hostile machinery – already buried in a complex, futuristic tomb. Van Kaen whispered on:

"There's not much time left, Madame! If you don't trust me, then trust the human body." He straightened himself and turned towards Lucien. "Give him everything you still can. Who knows how he might react?"

Diane tore at her hair – she was dripping with sweat. In her skull, her certainties and convictions were being smashed to pieces, like crystal glasses hit by the right note.

A dry rasping sound filled the room. It took Diane a moment before she realised that it was her own voice:

"OK, OK, go on. Try your funny business. Make him come back!"

CHAPTER 12

When the phone first rang, Diane realised that she was dreaming. She saw the German doctor pushing back the sheets, then undoing Lucien's dressings. He pulled out the wires, the electrodes, then released the arm from its plaster cast. The child was now naked. Only the bandage on his head and the drip still connected him to western medicine.

At the second ring, she woke up.

In the silence that followed the electronic peal, she was struck by a bolt of lucidity. Her dream had been no dream. Or, at the very least, had been modelled on reality. She could distinctly remember Rolf van Kaen's form, as he fingered, massaged and smoothed out each of Lucien's limbs, his attentive face bent down. At that moment, Diane had the impression that the acupuncturist was "reading" that tiny, pale body. He was deciphering it, as though he possessed a secret code, unknown to the other doctors. A silent dialogue now began between that white-haired colossus and the unconscious child, on the verge of death, but still apparently able to whisper a few secrets to the initiated.

Van Kaen had got out his needles, then placed them across Lucien's epidermis. As he stuck them into the child's torso, arms and legs, their points seemed to light up in the green glow of the monitor screen which was overlooking the scene. At the foot of the bed, Diane was paralysed. That frail body, as white as chalk, bristling with needles glimmering like fireflies in a dark glass cage . . .

Third ring.

Diane opened her eyes. In the half-light, she could see the reproductions of paintings that decorated her bedroom: Paul Klee's pastel squares and the more vivid geometry of Piet Mondrian. She looked down at the bedside table. The red figures of the alarm clock said 03.44. She now felt even surer. Five hours earlier, a mysterious doctor had given her son an acupuncture session. Before going, he had simply said: "This is just the first step. I'll be back. This child must live, you realise that?"

Fourth ring.

Diane felt for the phone and lifted the receiver.

"Yes?"

"Madame Thiberge?"

She recognised the voice of Madame Ferrer, one of the night nurses.

"Dr Daguerre asked me to contact you."

Her voice had a totally neutral tone, but Diane still detected a slight hesitation. She groaned:

"So it's all over?"

There was a brief silence, then:

"No, Madame, quite the opposite. There seem to be signs of remission."

Diane felt an indescribable wave of love come over her.

"A sign that he's waking up," the nurse went on.

"When?"

"Three hours ago. I noticed that his fingers were moving. I called in the duty doctors so that they could see for themselves. They are adamant that Lucien's showing signs of regaining consciousness. We called up Dr Daguerre. Then he told me to call you."

"Have you told Dr van Kaen?" Diane asked.

"Who?"

"Rolf van Kaen. The German doctor who works with Daguerre."

"I've no idea who you mean."

"Never mind. I'm on my way."

The atmosphere in Lucien's room was the mirror image of a wake. Around the body, people spoke in hushed voices, but their whispers were full of joy. And if the room still lay in darkness, their faces were lit with delight. There were five doctors and three nurses. None of them was wearing a mask and, in the heat of the moment, the housemen had nearly forgotten to put on their white coats.

But Diane was disappointed. Her child still lay in the same position, inert, in the pit of his stainless-steel bed. She had been so excited that she had almost been expecting him to be sitting up with his eyes open. But the doctors reassured her. Given their observations, they were thrilled, now they could hope for the best.

She looked down at her son and thought about that mysterious giant. She noticed that the dressings were back in place, as well as the plaster cast, the electrodes and sensors. No-one could have suspected that that German had stripped this tiny body in order to converse with it. Once again, she saw the green tips as they moved up and down in time with Lucien's breathing and those powerful fingers twisting the minuscule needles into his flesh.

"I must see him," she said.

"Who?"

"The anaesthetist from Berlin who works here."

There were startled glances, and an embarrassed silence. One of the doctors went over to her and murmured, with a smile:

"It's Daguerre who wants to see you."

"You remember what I told you, Diane. No false hope. Lucien may well come out of his coma, but still have irreversible brain damage . . ."

The surgeon's office was completely white, as though it had been irradiated with light. Here, even the shadows seemed less dark and heavy than elsewhere. Sitting in front of him, Diane butted in:

"It's a miracle. An unbelievable miracle."

Daguerre's face tensed. He kept fiddling with his pencil in a way that seemed to channel all of his nervous energy.

"Diane, I'm delighted for your child," he replied. "What's happening is absolutely . . . incredible. That's true. But, I must insist on the fact that we should not count our chickens before they're hatched. If he regains consciousness other serious traumatisms might appear. And it's not even certain that he will wake up fully."

"It's a miracle. Van Kaen has saved Lucien."

Daguerre sighed:

"Tell me about him. What did he tell you exactly?"

"That he came from Berlin and that he was working with you."

"Never heard of him." Daguerre was becoming annoyed. "How come the nurses let this lunatic into intensive care?"

"There weren't any nurses."

The surgeon looked increasingly rattled. The eraser on his pencil was now hammering regularly.

"And what exactly did he do to Lucien? Standard acupuncture treatment?"

"I've no idea. It was the first time I'd seen anything like it. He took off all Lucien's bandages and stuck needles into various parts of his body."

The surgeon could not help sneering. Diane stared daggers at him.

"You shouldn't laugh. I repeat: he saved my son."

The smile faded. The surgeon now adopted a semi-calm, semi-irritated tone – as though trying to reason with a child:

"Diane, you know who I am. In neurological terms, only a dozen other people in the world know the human brain as well as I do."

"I don't doubt your experience."

"Listen to me: the brain is an incredibly complex system. Do you know how many brain cells there are?"

Without waiting for her to answer, he continued:

"A hundred billion, and they're linked up by myriads of connections. If a machine like that starts up again, then it's because it's decided to do so on its own. Believe me, it's your son's own body that did the work. Do you follow me?"

"That's easy to say with hindsight."

"You're forgetting that I operated on your son."

"Sorry."

Diane continued more softly:

"Please forgive me. But I'm certain that that doctor played a part in Lucien's recovery."

63

Daguerre at last dropped his pencil and put his hands together. He adjusted his tone to match Diane's:

"Look. I'm not a narrow-minded doctor. I've even worked in Vietnam."

He smiled to himself – at his past, his old dreams.

"After qualifying, I did a little humanitarian work. And I studied acupuncture while I was abroad. Do you know what it's based on? What its famous network of points is?"

"The man spoke of meridians . . ."

"Yes, and what are meridians in physical terms?"

She fell silent. She tried to remember what the German had said exactly. Daguerre answered the question for her:

"Nothing at all. Physiologically, meridians don't exist. People have tried tests, x-rays and scans. Nothing has ever come of their analyses. Contrary to certain claims, acupuncture points don't even correspond to particular regions of the epidermis. In modern physiological terms, the acupuncturist sticks his needles in randomly. It's all hot air. Pie in the sky."

Van Kaen's words came back to her. She cut him off:

"The doctor also spoke of a vital energy that circulates around the body and . . ."

"And this energy can be got to like that." He snapped his fingers. "From the surface of the skin? And only Chinese practitioners have discovered this underground network? That's absurd."

There was a knock at the door. Madame Ferrer came in.

"Doctor, we've found the man who broke into the unit," she declared, a little out of breath.

Diane's face lit up. She turned right round, one elbow on the back of her chair.

"Have you told him about Lucien? What did he say?"

Madame Ferrer ignored her questions and looked back at the doctor.

"But there's a problem."

The surgeon picked up his pencil again and twiddled it around his index finger, like a majorette's baton. He tried to sound light-hearted:

"Just one? Are you sure?"

The nurse did not even attempt to smile.

"He's dead, doctor."

CHAPTER 13

Diane was now waiting on the second floor of the Lavoisier block. According to the signs, she was in the corridors of the genetic research unit. Why had they brought her here? Why genetics? It was a mystery. She stood with her arms crossed behind her, leaning against the wall and wavering between the thrill caused by Lucien's remission and the utter stupefaction triggered by van Kaen's death. It was half past five in the morning and nobody had yet said a word to her. Not the slightest piece of information about how he had died. Nothing about how the body had been discovered.

"Diane Thiberge?"

She turned towards the voice. The man walking towards her was well over six foot tall. His build immediately reminded her of the German giant. In the end, it was not so bad to be among people of such dimensions.

"My name's Patrick Langlois," the new arrival immediately added. "I'm a police lieutenant."

He looked about 40. His face was dry, furrowed and unshaven. Entirely dressed in black – coat, jacket, turtleneck sweater and jeans. His hair and bristles were greying – like steel prickles.

Add the red rings around his eyes and you have a portrait in cold colours. A walking Mondrian – black-grey-red – with a lanky figure and a devilish grin.

"I'm from the murder squad," the man said.

Diane trembled. He raised his hand to calm her.

"Don't panic. I'm here by mistake."

Diane would have liked to remain silent to show that she was in command of the situation, but she could not help asking:

"What do you mean, 'by mistake'?"

"Look." He placed his palms together, as though about to start praying. "First things first, OK? You're going to start by telling me exactly what happened last night."

Diane rapidly summed up what she had experienced over the past few hours. With his tongue slightly sticking out to one side, the officer noted down her answers on a spiral-bound notepad. His expression looked so out of place on his harsh features that she thought he was messing about and pulling a silly face on purpose. But his tongue retreated as soon as he had finished writing.

"That's amazing," he said.

With his notepad still in his hand, he began to simulate a pair of scales and his voice took on a commanding tone:

"On the one hand, life returns, on the other, death strikes . . ."

Diane stared at him dumbfounded. The policeman grinned at her, as though joy were constantly about to break out over his face.

"Maybe I should cut the gushes of lyricism."

"You should with me, in any case."

Langlois shrugged.

"Very well. Then let's just say that I'm delighted for your son."

"Can you tell me how van Kaen's body was discovered?"

He seemed to hesitate. He ran his hand through the bristles

of his hair, glanced up and down the corridor, then said as he set off towards the lift:

"Come with me."

They went out into the cool dawn air, walked round the building and headed towards the adjacent block. The village of Necker was starting to wake up. Diane noticed some large trucks parked in the central alleyway, from which emerged huge trolleys stacked with thousands of stainless steel-covered meals. She was surprised to discover that the hospital had its meals delivered.

The lieutenant guided her towards another building. The only lights that were on were in the basement. They went through the main door and came across several uniformed policemen. Here, the usual whiff of chemicals had been replaced by the smell of food:

"The hospital kitchens," Langlois pointed out.

He indicated a half-open door, then went through it. Diane followed. They went down a narrow staircase until they reached a large room in the basement, its walls painted blue. Packaging lines lay at either side of the huge empty space.

"This is how we see things so far," the policeman explained as he walked on. "At about half past eleven last night, the man who called himself van Kaen went with you as far as the entrance to the intensive care unit. He then walked round the block, crossed over the courtyard and slipped into the kitchens here. At that time of night, there aren't many people around. Nobody noticed him."

Langlois kept walking. With a sweep of his hand, he pulled aside a curtain of plastic strips.

"He crossed this room . . ."

This time, the concrete walls were coloured orange. Massive ovens topped by outsized hoods gave off a silvery gleam. He pulled back a second curtain.

" . . . and then headed for the cold store."

A green corridor lay before them, with a series of chrome-plated doors. The cold intensified. The strip-lights on the ceiling looked like horizontal stalactites. The bleak, coloured atmosphere of the place was reminiscent of a giant set of children's building blocks.

The officer stopped in front of one of the panels, which was mounted on a lateral steel rail. Above it, to the right, was marked: 4th Range. Two policemen in uniform parkas were on guard. Flecks of ice clung to the rims of their caps. Diane was now feeling more and more confused. Langlois lifted up the yellow ribbon across the metal door.

He removed a key from his pocket and slipped it into the high lock.

"Van Kaen selected this particular cold room."

"Did . . . did he have a key?"

"He had the same key as this one. He must have stolen it from the kitchen manager's office."

Diane was devastated. And she still had not asked the million dollar question: "how did he die?" The lieutenant pushed aside the steel bolt. When he was on the verge of opening the door, he turned towards her and leant back on the metal surface.

"I must warn you first that it's not a pretty sight. But it isn't blood."

"What on earth do you mean?"

He grabbed the vertical handle, bent over and pulled the door open along its rail. A wave of even colder air hit their faces. He repeated:

"Just remember what I told you: it isn't blood."

He beckoned to her to follow him. Diane stepped forwards then stopped at once. Opposite a line of grey plastic racks, the white concrete wall had been sprayed red. Purplish blotches were stuck all over it, crimson lines ran across it and the unmade

68

floor was covered with brownish stains as far as the threshold. This room, which measured 15 square feet, and was full of plastic cases, appeared to have been the scene of a terrible massacre. But the most surprising and revolting part of it was the heavy smell of fruit that was hanging in the air.

Patrick Langlois took down a vacuum pack from the top of one of the stacks of crates and handed it to Diane.

"Cranberries." He made as if to read the label on the bag. "Red fruit. Imported from Turkey. After administering his treatment, van Kaen came here to pig out on cranberries."

Convincing herself that she was trembling only because of the cold, Diane walked further into the room.

"What . . . whatever does it all mean?"

The lieutenant smiled apologetically.

"Just what I've told you. After the acupuncture session, van Kaen's first thought was not to leg it, but to come in here and scoff bags full of cranberries." He glanced round the room. "And scoff them in the wildest way you can imagine."

"But . . . but what did he die of?" she stammered.

Langlois tossed the vacuum pack back on to the crate.

"Indigestion, I should think."

He glanced at her, then corrected himself:

"Sorry, it isn't funny, really. In fact, we don't yet know what he died of. But it was certainly from natural causes. Or what I call 'natural'. From our initial examination, the body has no trace of any wounds. Perhaps van Kaen died of a heart attack, a burst blood vessel, or some other condition. I really couldn't tell you."

Langlois pointed at the half-open door. There was an oppressive silence.

"All of which explains why the kitchens have been quarantined. Imagine the effect of finding a corpse, perhaps carrying a disease, slap bang in the middle of them. After all, this is where they cook the kids' dinners. By deciding to come and die here, our German has let all hell loose in Necker."

Diane leant back against one of the racks. The smell of sugary fruit was starting to get to her.

"Can we go now?" she mumbled. "Really, I . . . I can't stand any more . . ."

The chill light of dawn revived her spirits a little, but it took her several minutes to recover the use of words. She finally asked:

"Why are you telling me all this?"

Langlois raised his eyebrows in surprise.

"Because you're at the heart of the whole business! If there hasn't been a murder, then there has been the illegal practising of medicine, intrusion into a hospital, probable use of an assumed identity . . ." He pointed with his index finger. "For all of which, you are our plaintiff."

Diane felt calmer now. She found enough strength to say:

"You don't seem to understand, lieutenant. That man, who-ever he really was, whatever his motivation was, saved my son's life. And by doing so, he also saved mine. So who cares how he did it? The only thing that I regret right now, that really makes me sorry, is not being able to thank him. You do under-stand that? And I don't think that your investigations are going to help me do so."

Langlois gave a world-weary gesture.

"But you do see what I mean. There are several mysteries in this business. In my opinion, this is only the start. In fact, I . . ."

The shrill sound of a pager started up. The lieutenant removed a tiny screen from his belt and read the message on it. He then handed it to Diane and said:

"What did I tell you?"

CHAPTER 14

Diane knew that all this was really happening, but she perceived it with such incredulity that she managed to keep a distance and not be absorbed totally into insanity. Later, she would sort the whole thing out. Later, she would find an underlying logic. But right now she took each new fact, each new piece of information, with the distracted powerlessness of a dreamer.

Langlois led her back to the Lavoisier block. This time, they stayed on the ground floor. Diane immediately recognised the room they were heading for: the Computerised Tomography Scanner, where Lucien had been given his initial tests.

Diane hesitated on the threshold – she sensed that, if she went inside, she would be assailed by terrible memories. But the policeman firmly shoved her in and closed the door behind them. The horror she had feared did not materialise for the simple reason that the room's atmosphere had totally changed.

It was now racked with nervous energy. In front of the control panel, which was topped with monitors and x-ray plates, two men in leather jackets were hammering at their computer keyboards and bringing coloured images up on to their screens. On the other side of the glass panel, figures were moving about in the soft light, fiddling with the chrome-plated controls on the imposing ring of the scanner. Others were unplugging cables on the floor, turning off suspended monitors, or readjusting strange tubes and optical instruments. Apparently, they did not want anyone to know they had even been there.

None of them was wearing a white coat.

Diane noticed other strange details. They all looked under 30, and most of them wore automatics on the belts, in holsters with Velcro fastenings.

Policemen.

She now understood why she had been made to wait on the second floor of the building: this is where the police had set up their HQ. And, for a few hours, they had taken over all this medical imaging equipment.

"Do you know what palaeopathology is?" Langlois suddenly asked her.

Diane turned towards him. Wearily, she replied:

"It's an archaeological technique, which consists in placing a mummy, or any other organic remains, into a scanner, an IRM or other piece of imaging equipment, in order to evaluate the inner parts without damaging them. It's become possible to do virtual autopsies on people who died thousands of years ago."

Langlois grinned:

"You're great."

"I'm a scientist. I read learned journals. But I don't see what . . ."

"We've got a whiz-kid in this field in our pathology unit. He can probe a mummy's guts without undoing a single one of its bandages."

Diane glanced in panic through the glass. She made out a form under a sheet, lying inside the machine. Staring at the coverings, she murmured:

"You mean you've scanned van Kaen's body . . ."

"The necessary machines were to hand." He grinned again. "That's the good part about finding corpses in hospitals."

"You're crazy."

"In a hurry, more like. Thanks to this equipment, we've been able to carry out a virtual post-mortem on van Kaen. We'll now hand him over to forensics. They'll be none the wiser."

"What sort of a policeman are you?"

Langlois was about to reply, when the door separating the two compartments opened.

"We got it wrong."

The lieutenant spun round towards the young man who had just come in. With his wiry fair hair, grey tint and burnt-out eyes, he looked like a stubbed cigar. He repeated:

"We got it wrong, Langlois."

"What?"

"This is a murder. An unbelievable murder."

The lieutenant glanced across at Diane. Reading his thoughts, she said:

"You've been trailing me around after you. Now it's time to accept your responsibility. I'm not moving from this room."

For the first time, the officer's face stiffened, then immediately relaxed. He wiped his hands over his face, as though slipping his devilish mask back on.

"You're right." He turned back to the pathologist. "Explain yourself."

"When we started the tomographic sections of the torso, we expected to find traces of necrosis there, super-abundant cardiac enzymes or some other sign of an infarct . . ."

"Cut the crap. What did you find?"

The pathologist's face fell. But, at the same time, there was something tough and untouchable about him. His eyelids flickered rapidly, then he dropped his bombshell:

"The guy's heart exploded. There was so much blood concentrated there that it blew the tissue to pieces."

Langlois flushed, revealing for the first time his true nature as a hunter.

"Jesus Christ. But you told me there was no sign of any wounds."

The doctor looked down. Beneath his blond curls, a smile flickered over his face.

"There isn't. It all happened on the inside. Inside the body."

73

He pointed at the computer. "You've just got to see the images."

Without even looking at them, the lieutenant yelled at his men:

"Right! The lot of you! Out of here!"

The compartment emptied. The pathologist set the programme running, then handed smoked-glass goggles to Diane and Langlois.

"You've got to wear these. It's 3-D software."

Following the two men, Diane slipped them over her own glasses and discovered the sinister sight on the screen: a relief image of Rolf van Kaen, bare chested, hairless, cut off at the navel.

Sitting in front of the monitor, the doctor started his presentation:

"Here's a 3-D reconstruction of the victim."

The torso rotated round then returned to its starting point in a regular motion, as though it was part of a computer graphics display.

"As I told you," the young scientist went on, "we first concentrated on the cardiac region. It took us 40 seconds of tomographic downloading to recreate a 3-D version of ..."

"OK, OK, just get on with it."

The doctor typed on his keyboard.

"And this is what we found ..."

From the shoulders down, the digitised flesh gradually vanished. Firstly, the arteries jutted up, then an entire section of organs and fibres, reddish lumps and intertwining blue labyrinths. It was all still spinning round, like a ghastly roundabout. Diane was disgusted – and, at the same time, fascinated.

It took them barely a second to grasp what the doctor wanted to show them: the heart was a motionless explosion of blood and tissue. A black stain spreading among the twisting veins and pulmonary air-cells. He said:

"I'll isolate it."

He pressed another button, thus wiping out everything that was not part of the organ in question. The exploded heart appeared, standing out perfectly against the grey screen. It looked rather like coral, with brownish branches and petrified stalks. A proliferation of pure violence.

"How the hell did that happen?" Langlois asked in a hoarse voice.

The pathologist's tone changed, as though he was now more distant, coming from the heart of cold analysis:

"Physiologically speaking, it's quite simple. All you have to do is bend the aorta to stop the blood from leaving the heart. A bit like with a hosepipe, if you see what I mean. Then what happens is that the blood keeps pouring in from the veins and lungs, swelling the heart until it reaches bursting point."

He pressed some buttons on his keyboard. The other organs and blood vessels reappeared on the screen.

"You can clearly see the pressure point here." He clicked with his arrow. "And here." Another click.

Langlois sounded dumbfounded:

"But how could anyone get to that artery inside the body?"

The pathologist stopped what he was doing and turned round, crossing his arms as though barring the way against the fear and nausea that were rising inside him.

"That's the really crazy part. The killer stuck his hand into the victim's innards, then worked up to the aorta. Look."

He swivelled back towards the monitor and pressed his keyboard once more. Van Kaen's torso fitted itself back together, his entrails sliding in below his gleaming, grey skin. The image focused on the axis of his sternum, at the top of the abdomen. A tiny incision appeared.

"There's the wound," his voice went on. "It's so small that

no-one noticed it under the body hair during the external examination."

"That's where the murderer slipped in his hand?"

"Definitely. The wound is under four inches long. But if we take into account the skin's elasticity, that's enough for someone to slide their arm inside. So long as it was someone small. Measuring no more than about five feet, I'd say."

"But van Kaen was a colossus!"

"In that case there were several of them. Or else the victim was drugged. I don't know."

Leaning over the screen, Patrick Langlois asked:

"And was he still alive while he was being gutted?"

"Yes, he was alive and conscious. The way his heart exploded proves that. While the vicious bastard was ferreting around in his innards, the heart speeded up and started pumping away like a mad thing. The blood saturation must have been quick and extremely violent."

The lieutenant murmured:

"I was expecting problems, but nothing like this . . ."

At that very moment, the two men seemed to remember Diane's existence. They both turned round in unison. Langlois said:

"Sorry, Diane, really I am . . . Diane? Are you OK?"

She looked petrified behind her dark goggles, eyes fixed on the monitor. In a mechanical voice, she pronounced:

"My son. I want to see my son."

CHAPTER 15

She knew this park as well as her own dreams. As a child, she had spent whole afternoons by the fountain, surrounded by those green paths. And yet, she felt no particular nostalgia for the Jardins du Luxembourg. She simply felt that it brought her peace of mind.

The miracle had now happened over 48 hours before. And Lucien was still showing signs of remission. Yesterday, he had moved the index and middle fingers of his right hand several times. It even seemed to Diane that, when she had been there, he had lifted his right wrist. Medical tests had shown that the signs of cerebral contusion were fading. Meanwhile, his physiological functions were taking over again. Even Dr Daguerre seemed now to admit that the boy was on the road to recovery. He had mentioned the possibility of removing the drains in a few days' time.

Diane should have been thrilled. And yet a shadow hung over her happiness. There was now a murder, carried out with an unfathomable violence; those images on the computer screen that had devastated her. How could such an atrocity have happened? Why should the man who had saved her son have been condemned to die like that, just a few hours after treating him?

"Mind if I sit down?"

Diane looked up. Lieutenant Langlois was standing in front of her, looking just as he had done the day before yesterday. Black coat, black jeans, black tee-shirt. She supposed that he must have several copies of this outfit like so many corpses in his wardrobe. What is more, he did not smell of aftershave, but rather of the dry cleaner's. In reply, she stood up:

"Let's go for a stroll instead."

The officer nodded. Diane headed for the upper terraces. Three lanes of lawn rising with a slight gradient.

He said in a jovial tone:

"It was a good idea to meet here."

"Yes, I like it. I live nearby."

They walked up the stone steps. The day was overcast and the pathways almost deserted. The trees seemed to welcome the cool wind into their branches with delight, like a woman holding her skirts over a subway vent. The policeman breathed in deeply then said:

"I thought such a thing would never happen to me."

"What?"

"Chatting up a pretty girl on one of those benches."

"Hah hah hah . . ." Diane went, looking half amused and half offended.

All of the pressure and danger seemed to have vanished from both of their hearts and minds. With a tinge of disgust, she was thinking about how terribly selfish the living are when it comes to the dead. Now, the bright green leaves, the freshness of the wind and the far-off cries of children made up her entire present – and the memory of van Kaen was fading away against that reality. The lieutenant was saying:

"When I was a boarder at the police academy, I used to get away each weekend to attend philosophy lectures at the Sorbonne. Then, in the evening, I'd come here to the Jardins du Luxembourg. In those days, I felt like I'd escaped from the natural disaster of being unemployed. But then I found myself up against an even worse catastrophe."

"What was that?"

He opened his hands.

"The indifference of Parisian girls. I used to walk along here and peer at them out of the corner of my eye while they were sitting on their iron benches, reading, and acting all hoity

78

toity. And I'd say to myself: 'what on earth can I think of as an opening line? how on earth can I chat them up?'"

Diane smiled, a fine line on her lips, shaped by the breeze.

"And so?"

"So, I never found the answer."

She leant her head to one side and adopted a confidential tone.

"Now you could always produce your police card."

"Good idea. Or else turn up with a squad and chuck them all in the prison van."

Diane burst out laughing. They were heading towards the gate leading to Rue Auguste-Comte. On the other side, smaller, more secretive gardens could be seen. Langlois went on:

"How's Lucien?"

"Better and better. Movements in all four limbs have been noticed."

"That's absolutely fantastic."

She interrupted:

"Life . . . then death . . . As you yourself pointed out."

Langlois grinned. His wicked looks gave him a sort of boyish charm. He continued in a more serious tone:

"I wanted to give you the latest. We've identified our mysterious doctor. Van Kaen was his real name."

Diane tried to hide her impatience:

"So who was he then?"

"He told you the truth: he was head of the anaesthetics department in the paediatric surgery wing of the Charity Hospital. An enormous place, a bit like Necker. He was also Professor of Neurobiology at the University of Berlin. Van Kaen organised symposiums about neuro-stimulation and its connections with acupuncture. He was a bit of a star, apparently."

Diane pictured that fair-headed giant, standing in the half-light of the room, and his hands turning the needles in her son's flesh.

"Where did he learn his acupuncture?" she asked.

"I don't know exactly. But he spent nearly the whole of the 1980s in Vietnam."

Still walking, the lieutenant had removed a cardboard folder from his pocket, which he occasionally consulted.

"Van Kaen was an East German. He came from Leipzig. That's why he was able to stay over there. Vietnam was completely closed at the time."

"You mean he was able to go to Vietnam because he was a Communist."

"That's right. In those days, it was far easier for an East German to get a job in Ho Chi Minh City than to go shopping in West Berlin."

Patrick Langlois flicked through his notes.

"There's just one mysterious period in his life. No-one knows where he was between 1969 and 1972. When the wall came down, he returned to Germany and set up home in West Berlin. He soon made a name for himself and became part of the former Federal Republic's intelligentsia."

Diane returned to the present.

"You don't have a lead on why he was murdered?"

"We don't have a motive, that's for sure. He was universally admired. Except for the fact that people found him a bit odd."

"How do you mean, odd?"

"He was a real ladies' man. Apparently, each spring he started trying to pick up the nurses in strange ways."

"How?"

"By singing. Opera arias. Word has it that his voice bewitched the entire female staff of the hospital. He was a real Casanova. But I don't think this was a jealousy killing . . ."

"So what do you think?"

"This was a settling of old scores. Westerners getting their revenge for their families that had been abandoned in the East,

80

something along those lines . . . But in this case, van Kaen had already made a break by going to live in Vietnam. And nothing proves that he had had much to do with the Communists in power. All the same, I'm following up this lead."

They walked through the tall gate into Rue Auguste-Comte, then went into the gardens of the Observatoire. Cramped by the surrounding buildings and roofed over by branches, this park seemed to be curled up in its chill shadows.

"In fact," the policeman went on after a moment's pause, "what interests me as much as the murder is *why* he came here to treat your son."

Diane started.

"You're trying to connect this murder with Lucien?"

"Of course not! But his intervention is part of the puzzle . . . And it could help us to learn a bit more about him."

"I don't see how."

Langlois adopted a reasoning tone.

"Here we are with a famous doctor, highly reputed in his country, who suddenly abandons his department, rushes to Berlin airport to take the first flight to Paris – we've managed to piece together his various movements – then, once he's landed at Roissy, he heads straight for Necker, procures a fake badge, steals some keys, takes the precaution of bleeping all the nurses in Dr Daguerre's unit so he can slip into intensive care more easily . . ."

The silence of the corridor came back to her. So van Kaen had done all that? The lieutenant continued:

"And why? To use a mysterious technique on Lucien, who was in a critical state. This man was a saviour, Diane. And the person he saved was your son."

She listened in silence. Langlois's questions echoed her own doubts. Why had this German become interested in Lucien? Who had told him that his condition was now critical? Had

81

someone in the hospital helped him? As though mentally following Diane's thoughts, the lieutenant asked:

"It wasn't someone you know who contacted him, was it?"

She shook her head at once and he nodded in agreement. She supposed that he must have already checked that possibility. Opening the gate of the third garden, he went on:

"We're questioning the staff at Necker. The medics and the nurses. Maybe one of them knew him. Either personally, or from his reputation. Meanwhile, the German police are checking all his calls and messages. One thing's for sure: he was told just after Lucien's last attack, when the French doctors had given up all hope."

They were still walking beneath the quiet shadows of the trees. Their steps were accompanied by a slight crunching from the gravel under their feet.

"And do you have any news about the murder?" Diane asked.

"No, I don't. The physical autopsy confirmed what the virtual one had told us. This murder was quite unbelievably violent. It's like something . . . sacrificial, maybe. We've looked to see if there have been any other similar cases in France. There haven't, of course. So we haven't got a single clue, not a single lead, nothing. The only fresh piece of evidence that was turned up by the post mortem was that van Kaen suffered from a strange deformity."

"What's that?"

"He had an atrophied stomach, which meant that he had to chew his food thoroughly before swallowing it. That explains all the stains we found on the walls in the cold room. When van Kaen was attacked, he spat out all the fruit he still had in his oesophagus."

Diane felt as though the words leaving Langlois's mouth were penetrating directly inside her, slipping under her skin, like tiny crystals of fear. An occult reality was taking over her existence, gradually evolving into an utter nightmare.

They had just reached the Observatoire fountain: eight stone horses were rearing up in the roaring foam. Each time she came here, where the trees opened to the winds and the air became laden with drops of water, she experienced the same sadness and emptiness. But today that feeling was particularly strong.

Langlois approached her, so as to be heard over the rippling of the fountain:

"I've got one last question, Diane. Could your adopted son have originally come from Vietnam?"

She turned slowly towards him and seemed to see him from a distance, through a veil of tears. She felt neither let down nor shocked. She had quite simply discovered at last why they had taken this morning stroll. When she did not answer at once, Langlois seemed to be irritated by her silence, or perhaps by his own question. He said, more loudly:

"Van Kaen spent ten years in Vietnam. It's something we can't overlook! Who knows, maybe Lucien comes from a family he knew over there?"

She was now frozen. He asked, in an authoritarian tone:

"Answer, Diane. Could Lucien be of Vietnamese origin?"

She stared again at the dripping horses. Drops were stinging her face and a fine mist was covering her glasses.

"I've no idea. Anything's possible."

The lieutenant's voice dropped a tone:

"Could you find out? Ask the people at the orphanage?"

Diane let her stare drift into space. Beyond the Boulevard Port-Royal, a sky of storm clouds was laying out its dreary colours. She remembered with nostalgia the monsoon clouds that gave off real flashes of mercury.

"I'll phone them," she said at last. "I'll see what I can do to help you."

CHAPTER 16

On her way home, Diane's mind filled with the most improbable suppositions. On Boulevard Port-Royal, she convinced herself that Lucien really was Vietnamese. On Rue Barbusse, she told herself that he was no longer an anonymous child. Rolf van Kaen had known his family. For some strange reason, the child had been abandoned and, for some even stranger reason, this German doctor had been told that he was living in France. On Rue Saint-Jacques, she imagined that he was the hidden son of some important figure, who had contacted the acupuncturist as a last resort. As she walked on, Diane lost all control of her thoughts. The entry code of her apartment block stopped this train of fantasy in its tracks.

She was now back in the calm atmosphere of her home. The familiar sensations of her small three-room flat calmed her down. She sat there contemplating the white walls, the mahogany parquet and the long, spotless curtains that seemed to be keepers of the memory of sunny days and rain. She breathed in the smell of wax and the stench of bleach, which had lingered there since she had spring-cleaned the place. The morning after that miraculous night, Diane had tidied and scrubbed down the entire flat, wiping out the slightest trace of her misery and the abandon of the past two weeks. This odour of cleanliness reassured her and made her more resolved.

She looked at her watch and calculated what time it must now be in Thailand. Noon in Paris, so 5.00 p.m. in Ra-Nong. She found her "adoption" files, then sat down on the floor in her room, back against the bed. In a further attempt to remain calm, she concentrated her breathing low down in her belly, just a few inches above her navel – a classic relaxation technique used in *Wing-Chun*. When the air had dissolved into her blood and flowed towards that mysterious point, when calm had filled her like a soothing void, she knew that she was ready.

She picked up the phone and dialled the number of the Boria-Mundi Foundation's orphanage. After a few wavering rings, a nasal voice replied. Diane asked to speak to Teresa Maxwell. After a good two minutes' wait, a "hello" rang out, like a door slamming on her fingers. Diane asked, more loudly than she meant to:

"Is that Mrs Maxwell?"

"Speaking. Who's calling?"

It was a bad line. And the principal's voice even worse than usual.

"This is Diane Thiberge," she replied. "We met about a month ago. I came to your centre on the fourth of September. I'm the one who . . ."

"The nose-stud?"

"Yes, that's me."

"What can I do for you? Is there a problem?"

In her mind's eye, Diane pictured once again that good-natured face and those inquisitive eyes. Without a moment's hesitation, she lied:

"No, not at all."

"How's the boy?"

"Fine."

"Are you ringing to give me his news?"

"That's right. Or, rather, not entirely. I'd like to ask you a few questions."

The only reply she got was the crackling of interference. She continued:

"When we met, you told me that you didn't know where the boy was from."

"That's right."

"You don't know his family?"

85

"No."

"You never saw his mother."

"No, never."

"And you have no idea of his racial origin? Or why he was abandoned?"

After each question, Teresa Maxwell marked a slight pause that was laden with hostility. She asked in turn:

"Why all these questions?"

"But . . . I am his adoptive mother, after all. I have a right to know, so I can understand him better."

"Something's wrong. You're hiding something."

Diane imagined that little boy in his bandages, plugged into those machines and drips. Her throat in a knot, she found the strength to say:

"No, I'm not concealing a thing! I just wanted to know a bit more about him, so I . . ."

Teresa Maxwell sighed and replied in a slightly less aggressive tone:

"I told you everything I know when we met. Kids are found wandering through the dusty streets of Ra-Nong, with no parents, no-one to care for them. When one of them is in a really bad way, then we pick him up, that's all there is to it. And this was the case for Lu-Sian."

"What was wrong with him?"

"He was dehydrated. And suffering from malnutrition."

"How long had he been in the orphanage when I came to fetch him?"

"For about two months."

"And you hadn't found out anything about him?"

"We don't run investigations."

"No-one came to visit him?"

The crackling started up again even more loudly. Diane felt as though she was being torn away from her source of information. But the harsh voice was still there:

"Watch out, Diane."

She started. The voice suddenly seemed nearer. She stammered: "W . . . why?"

"For yourself," the principal murmured. "Beware of this wish to know more, of digging into Lu-Sian's past. He's now your son. And you're his origin. Don't go back beyond that point."

"But . . . why ever not?"

"It won't get you anywhere. It's an obsession among adoptive parents. There always comes a time when you want to know, when you start searching and rummaging around. It's as though you want to occupy that mysterious time before you existed for your child. But these children do have a past, and you can't do anything to change that. It's their little mystery."

There was nothing Diane could add to that. Her throat was too dry. Teresa went on:

"You know what a palimpsest is?"

"Uh, yes, I think so."

That did not stop Teresa from explaining:

"It's an ancient manuscript which monks in the Middle Ages scratched clean so that they could use it for their own writings. One document is thus covered over by another text, but the older words are still lurking in its depths. That's what an adopted child is like. You're going to bring him up, teach him all sorts of things, inculcate him with your culture, your personality . . . But, beneath it all, the ancient manuscript will still be there. He will always have his own personal origins. The genetic legacy of his parents, of his country. The few years he spent in his original environment . . . You'll have to learn to live with that and respect his mystery. It's the only way you're going to be able to love your son."

Teresa's brittle voice had become softened by tenderness. In her mind's eye, Diane saw the orphanage again. She smelt its scent, felt its warmth, sensed its atmosphere of convalescence. The principal was quite right. But then she did not know about the true reason for these questions. And Diane wanted accurate answers.

"Just tell me one thing," she said in conclusion. "In your opinion, could Lucien . . . I mean, is it possible that Lucien might be Vietnamese?"

"Vietnamese? Good lord! But why on earth should he be Vietnamese?"

"Well . . . Vietnam's not far and so . . ."

"No. It's completely impossible. I know because I speak the language, and Lu-Sian's dialect was completely different."

Diane murmured:

"Thank you. I'll . . . I'll call you back."

She hung up and let the principal's words echo inside her, as in a nave of ice.

At that moment, a distant memory came back to her.

It had happened in Spain, during a reconnaissance mission in Asturias. In an idle moment, Diane had visited a monastery. It was a harsh, grey building that still lived in an age of meditation and stony whispers. In the library she came across something that fascinated her. A parchment had been hung up on steel wires in a showcase. Its uneven, rosy appearance made it look organic, almost alive. It was covered in cramped but regular Gothic letters, with just an occasional gap left for a delicate illumination.

But the fascinating part lay elsewhere.

At regular intervals, an ultraviolet neon light shone down on it, revealing the dark red letters of another fluid hand. The traces of an older text, from Antiquity. Like a print left at the heart of the manuscript.

Diane now understood. If her son was a palimpsest, if his

past was a sort of half-erased text, then she still had some scraps of it. Lu. Sian. And the handful of other words which the child had kept on repeating during the three weeks they had spent together in Paris. Those words that Teresa Maxwell did not understand.

CHAPTER 17

One of the offices of the National Institute for Oriental Languages and Civilisations was on Rue de Lille, just behind the Musée d'Orsay. It was a vast, sombre and stuffy edifice, marked by that feeling of majesty which Diane always sensed in the fine buildings of the 7th *arrondissement.*

She crossed the marble hall, then entered the maze of stairways and classrooms. On the first floor, she located the office covering the languages of South-East Asia. She rapidly explained to the secretary that she was a journalist and that she was researching an article on the peoples of the Golden Triangle. So could she possibly meet Isabelle Condroyer?

She had found the name in an encyclopedia entry about ethnology and apparently this woman was the greatest expert on the ethnic groups of the region.

The secretary answered with a smile. Diane was lucky: Professor Condroyer had just finished giving a lecture in the Institute itself. All she would have to do was wait for her in Room 138 on the ground floor. The professor would be informed.

Diane went straight down to the classroom. It was a tiny room on a mezzanine, with small, barred, laminated windows looking out at ground level on to the inner courtyard.

The small desks, side by side, the blackboard and the smell of varnished wood reminded Diane of her own studies. Still acting like a solitary student, she sat down at the back of the room and, almost despite herself, was flooded by memories of university.

When she thought about that period of her life, what struck her were not the hours spent in lecture halls, but the trips that had marked the final years of her PhD course. She had never been very studious. Nor had she been attracted by analysis and theory. All Diane liked doing was fieldwork. Functional morphology. Auto-ecology. Topography of habitats. Population dynamics ... These terms and disciplines had been mere pretexts for her to travel – to watch, to observe, to learn about wildlife.

Ever since her first trip, Diane's sole objective had been to understand the barbarity of hunting and the violence of predators. It was an enigma that obsessed her and that could be summed up as the snapping of jaws on to living flesh. But perhaps there was nothing to understand – just something to feel. When she observed big cats on the look-out, crouching in the bush, so motionless that they almost totally merged into the surrounding vegetation, almost vanished into the texture of the moment, Diane numbly felt as though, by concentrating hard, she too could become that predator, that look-out, that moment. It was now no longer a question of understanding animal instincts. She had to slip inside. She would then become that blind impulse, that destructive motion governed by its own logic ...

The door suddenly opened. Isabelle Condroyer wore her cheekbones like other women wear high-heels. Beneath her short-cropped brown hair, her eyes slanted slightly, but their irises were tea-green. Two almonds, still fresh, among the foliage. A drop of Asian elixir had slipped into that woman's blood, giving her, instead of the charm of an exotic kitten, the hardness of a mountain. A high-altitude ruggedness. Diane stood up and walked over to her. The professor immediately asked:

"My secretary tells me that you're a reporter. Which paper are you on?"

Diane noticed that the ethnologist's red blouse was too tight. It flared out into rather indiscreet openings. She forced a smile to her lips:

"Um . . . In fact I only said that so I could meet you."

"I'm sorry?"

"I need some information. Some highly urgent information . . ."

"You are joking, aren't you? Do you think I haven't got better things to do?"

For a moment, Diane felt like replying in the same tone, but she changed her mind. One combat technique consisted in using the speed of your adversaries against them. But she decided to use the sensitive touch to cool down this woman's hostility.

"I've just adopted a child," she explained. "From near Ra-Nong, in Thailand. I suppose you know the region I mean. The child is about six or seven years old."

"So what?"

"So, he comes out with a few snatches of sentences. I'd like to know what language he speaks, what his dialect is."

The ethnologist put her bag down on the table facing the lines of desks. She crossed her arms. The openings of her blouse were now gaping ever larger over the bright splash of her bra. Imperturbably, Diane went on:

"We've just been in a car crash. He nearly died. He's unconscious, but the doctors think that he'll probably come round."

The woman's expression changed. She seemed to be wondering if she was face to face with a complete lunatic, or whether anybody could have made up such a story. A good lie began to take root in Diane's mind:

"Here's the situation. The doctors think that it would be a good idea if we spoke to the boy in his own language when he wakes up. He's only been in Paris for a few weeks, you see what I mean?"

This sounded so likely, that she even wondered for a second if it was not true and whether they should look into the possibility. The professor's tone softened:

"Your story is a bit . . . Well . . . What's his present condition?"

"A few days ago, he seemed doomed. But now the doctors are more optimistic. There are signs that he's coming out of the coma. But there might be after-effects."

Isabelle Condroyer sat down. Her face was still just as hard, but her hostility had gone. She was now quite simply serious. She murmured:

"But if he can't speak, then how do you expect me to . . . ?"

"He kept on repeating the same words. Especially these two: Lu-Sian . . ."

"You have no other information about his ethnic origins?"

"None, nothing except those words."

The ethnologist stared long and hard at her. Diane was wearing a waisted, natural-coloured fitted coat, shards of quartz as a necklace and a grey pencil to keep her bun in place.

At last, doctorial and cold once more, she said:

"Do you know how many languages and dialects are spoken in the Andaman region?"

"Not exactly."

"A good dozen."

"But I'm talking about a tiny area. A pinpoint on the map. The orphanage is at Ra-Nong and . . ."

"What with the population shifts caused by the fighting in Burma, wars and drug dealing, migrations from the Golden

Triangle and India, this brings the number of languages up to at least 20. And probably more like 30."

"No, all I've got are those two words, but you must know specialists for each language. I could . . ."

The scientist was now sounding a touch exasperated.

"But a few odd vocables are no use! Especially when relayed by you. In the Thai language alone, the same word can have different meanings depending on which syllable is accentuated, whether the word itself comes at the beginning or end of the sentence . . ."

Outside, dusk was setting in. The laminated pane was glowing a fiery red. It was as though the woman's anger had distilled its flame into the glass. She abruptly concluded:

"I'm sorry. Without the pronunciation your request is pointless. I can't help you."

Diane grinned. She raised a triumphant finger.

"That's what I thought you'd say."

From her bag, she produced a bright-red tape recorder: the karaoke toy Lucien had used to record his own songs. Diane had realised that it would be impossible to identify a dialect without the right accent and pronunciation. That was when she remembered her son's cassette.

Diane pressed "play". Suddenly, Lucien's nasal tones filled the russet-shaded room. His jolting, slightly guttural syllables rose up like childish bubbles in the silent evening. Isabelle Condroyer was visibly staggered.

Diane had won. But she did not savour her victory. Her child's voice surprised her, too. She had not listened to his cassette since the accident. This modulation that was now occupying all of the available space, lining it with Lucien's presence, his face, his airy gestures, had cut through her like a knife. A second later, her sorrow welled up, freeing itself in a flood bursting up towards her eyes.

She lowered her head and hid her face in her hands. She did not want to cry. She doubled over, while that voice continued to rise up in the purple light of the classroom.

Suddenly, there was silence.

Diane looked up. The ethnologist had realised what was happening and had just turned the machine off. Diane opened her mouth to speak, but the professor had already got to her feet and had laid her hand on her shoulder. Her voice, which had been so harsh and brittle just a few seconds before, now whispered:

"Leave the cassette with me. I'll see what I can do."

CHAPTER 18

Hands together.

This was the *Wing-Chun* technique that Diane was best at and the fastest at. It was a technique in which the adversary was so close that you had to attack him or else dodge his assaults while remaining in constant physical contact. Punches. Elbows. Cuts from the hand. The violence rained down with no way to run or pull back – it was as if you and the enemy had been soldered together.

Normally speaking, such body to body contact would have disgusted Diane, but this was a fight, and combat did not act as a red rag for her phobia. On the contrary. Touching people this way gave her a dull sort of pleasure. As though, inside her, she were relishing the inversion of a caress into a blow.

What is more, Diane had a secret. The reason why she was so good at this form of close combat was that she was short-sighted, and her best chance of winning was to keep her adversaries always near to her, in a field of vision in which she could make out the slightest detail. In this way, she had transformed a handicap into a strength, learning to fight close up, relying entirely on speed and taking such terrible risks that her enemies were completely confused.

That evening, the training session at the Maubert-Mutualité dojo was a perfect way for her to work off the day's emotions. After phoning Teresa and meeting the ethnologist, Diane had gone directly to the hospital. Lucien was undergoing some tests, and she had not been allowed to see him. Her first reaction had been to get angry, but then she realised that good news lay behind this ban: Dr Daguerre was planning to take the drains out the next morning.

However, on going home, Diane still had not managed to savour the relief. Van Kaen's murder was beginning to swamp everything else – even her son's recovery. She could not get that horror out of her mind. The hand twisting its way into his entrails. The cranberries splattered over the walls. The gleaming screen that had revealed the acupuncturist's desecrated innards. Everything mixed together in her mind. Mentally, she no longer managed to make a distinction between his death and her son's recovery.

What is more, the paediatric block was now being watched by uniformed police officers. When she had asked Madame Ferrer why they were there, the simple answer had been "security", and Diane understood that the secretary was merely repeating what she had been told. What security? Against what danger? Was a killer still at large in the corridors of Necker hospital? Rather than wear herself out on conjectures, she decided to turn back to the sweat and the blows of the dojo. Hands together. One way of getting rid of her anxieties was as good as another . . .

*

95

When she got home she had a hot shower then listened to her answering machine. Always the same calls – the eternal litany of friends and acquaintances asking for news and repeating their words of comfort. There were also some messages from her mother. But, each time she recognised that loathed voice, Diane pressed "next".

She went into the kitchen. Her hair unkempt and her cheeks flaming, she made some strong black Darjeeling, then placed the teapot on a tray, with some biscuits and yoghurt – her diet consisted almost entirely of dairy produce and biscuits. Then she made herself comfortable in her bedroom with the books she had bought that afternoon.

There was one lead left to explore. Her ideas were indirect, unfocused, but she just could not get the question of acupuncture out of her mind. She wanted to understand it, to grasp exactly what van Kaen had done to Lucien's body. A vague suspicion told her that this technique was directly linked to all the other events of that fatal night.

An hour's read was enough to confirm several points.

Firstly, Eric Daguerre was right. Physiologically, an acupuncturist did not stick his needles into any particular points. No special nerves, muscles or cutaneous zones that were highly sensitive – or, at least, not always so. Never had the physical existence of meridians in the body been proved. All that studies had shown was that the needles sometimes caused secretions of endorphins – hormones that act as a natural pain killer. Other research had revealed the electric properties of certain points. But none of these observations could be generalised, and they were mere epiphenomena when compared with the prodigious results obtained by van Kaen.

But the German had also been right. According to Chinese medicine, acupuncture made use of a mysterious entity, which practitioners called "vital energy", and which the anaesthetist had compared to a sort of primitive force, or a prime mover. And why not? Despite her strict rationalism and scientific education, Diane was prepared to admit just about anything when it came to Lucien's recovery. It was clear that the acupuncturist had influenced the boy's physiological functions at a level which western medical techniques could not reach.

Diane read on. What interested her now was the geography of those mysterious forces. The German had spoken of a "water-table" and claimed that this energy ran through the body like "streams", following the underground topography of the meridians. For several hours, Diane studied these complex flows and their interactions.

The strangest thing was that this energy seemed to be at once inside and outside the body. The technique did not consist in warming up, soothing or awakening any given meridian, but rather in balancing its current with outside forces. In other words, those needles acted like tiny relays with the universe, thus "harmonising" the organism with a supposed cosmic force. Diane stopped reading. She found such concepts and vocabulary off-putting – it all reminded her of spiritualist jargon, of manipulative speeches aimed at lost souls looking for their guru. And yet she could still remember those glistening green needles that had stuck up over her child's body. At that moment she too had thought of them as communication channels, aerials turned towards some mysterious, indescribable force.

Diane switched off the light and thought things over. Reading about Chinese medicine had told her nothing of interest in terms of the investigation, except the following idea: perhaps her son had been more sensitive to acupuncture than other people because of his cultural heritage. Perhaps there was a sort of genetic adaptation that had allowed his body to react so strongly to the technique. But what did she really know about the laws of atavism? Wasn't it mere hypothesis? In any case, it could give

97

her no precise information as to where Lucien had been born.

Once again, she ran through van Kaen's actions. A sentence came back to her. Something she had not paid attention to during the torments of that night, but which now had a special ring to it. Before leaving, the doctor had said: "This child must live, you realise that?" At the time, she had taken this as a statement of the acupuncturist's determination. But it could also be interpreted to mean that, for some strange reason, Lucien absolutely had to survive, come what may.

The German had spoken as though he were in possession of a secret, some hidden reality concerning her child. Perhaps he was from some exceptional background, as Diane had fondly imagined that afternoon. Or else he had some physiological particularity. Or some mission, some task that Lucien was to carry out when he was older . . .

She was starting to fall back under the spell of absurd hypotheses. But at the same time, like an echo, she could still hear the tone of the doctor's voice. She had felt the extreme tension, the undercurrent of anxiety, which he had done his best to conceal during the session. That doctor knew something. Lucien was not just any child. And Langlois, with his detective's flair, had sensed that too. That was why he was so interested in Lucien and where he had come from.

Now submerged in craziness, Diane saw a further possibility.

Such an overpowering reason to save a child could also be a very good reason to kill it . . . What if van Kaen had been murdered precisely because he had woken the boy up?

What if Lucien was in danger?

She came to a halt. One last conviction had completely taken her breath away.

And what if that danger had already struck?

What if that accident on the ring-road had not been an accident at all?

98

II
The Watchers

CHAPTER 19

Monday 11 October.

Diane was driving along the slopes of Mont-Valérien in Suresnes.

She had crossed the American cemetery, full of white crosses, then passed over the green hills that overlook the Bois de Boulogne. This was not the right way and she must have taken a wrong turning somewhere around Pont de Saint Cloud. She drove her hired car down Rue des Bas-Rogers and back into the greyness of the town. The rain fell on the dull drabness of the suburbs, with their dreary avenues and prim little streets. A tedium that weighed down on your shoulders.

Diane was now totally absorbed in her investigations. She had spent the weekend checking a few points, but it was only now that she was going to enter the heart of the matter. She sped under a massive granite aqueduct, passed the roundabout which proudly welcomed her to the Belvédère district, then on her right she spotted Rue Gambetta. Dominated by the railway line, the street was full of houses cramped up against each other, looking as if they would exist for ever.

Number 58 was a dirty, run-down three-storey building with a brick façade and black iron balconies. Diane quickly spotted a place to park and went inside. She found herself in an ancient hallway, with filthy letter boxes and a shadowy stairwell. Even the dustbins fitted in with the overall scene – they lurked in a musty, stinking, shabby area beneath the stairs, which seemed to sum up the building's entire history.

She tried the light switch, but soon realised that nothing was going to happen. She then went over to the list of tenants, displayed on a piece of mouldy cardboard, and in the dim daylight found the name she was looking for – the name that she had managed to drag out of Patrick Langlois last night by calling him at his home.

The steps creaked, the banisters were greasy – the list of expected sensations continued. Diane was wearing a long petrol-blue raincoat, which squeaked at every step she took. Tiny drops of rain were dripping from her shoulders, and their presence reassured her. She reached the second floor and rang at the left-hand door.

No answer.

She rang again.

Another minute went by. Diane was about to retrace her steps, when she heard a toilet flush.

The door finally opened.

A young man was standing at the entrance. He was wearing a shapeless, colourless hooded tracksuit top. Diane could not make out his face in the shadows. All she could see was that he looked younger than she remembered – 30 at the very most. Thinner, too. But what caught her attention more than anything was the smell of hemp that was wafting through the half-open door. She had obviously caught him while he was getting stoned. Hence the flushing toilet. She asked:

"Are you Marc Vulovic?"

The shadowy face did not budge an inch. Then a nasal voice said:

"Who's asking?"

Diane fiddled with her glasses. His heavy cold confirmed her worst fears. It was not only cannabis that he was doing.

"I'm Diane Thiberge."

No response. She then added:

"You do know who I am, don't you?"

"No."

"I was driving the Landcruiser on the night of the accident."

Vulovic said nothing. A minute ticked by. Or just a few seconds. Diane was so nervous she no longer knew. In a hollow voice, he said:

"Come in."

Diane walked across the cramped hall, its walls covered with CDs and videos, then to her right she saw a kitchen decked with formica and lino. The man motioned to her to go in.

The dull daylight filtered in through the grey net curtains. There was a sink and a water heater, like two pale stains submerged beneath a heap of dirty crockery. And the smell of drugs in the air. Diane went over to a chair by the half-open window. She sat down quickly, setting off a further series of glints from her raincoat.

The man followed her, selecting a stool at the other side of the table. His face was long and dry, sticking out from under his hood like a yellow root. His hair was fair and bristly, and his wispy goatee looked liked corn fibres. His bandages had already been removed. The only traces he had left were a few brownish scabs on his forehead and over his eyebrows. Head down, he murmured:

"I meant to come to the hospital, but I . . ."

He trailed off and looked up. His green eyes were like small portholes looking out on to an icy sea. He asked:

"He's . . . I mean, is the child . . . ?"

Diane realised that no-one had given him any news.

"He's better now," she murmured. "We'd given up all hope, but he's making a recovery. So let's leave him out of this, OK?"

Vulovic vaguely nodded his head, and looked at her uncertainly. His body was twisted and his shoulders hunched – a drug addict imprisoned in his own private hell.

"What do you want?" he asked.

"I just want to go over the exact circumstances of the accident. To find out what happened to you while you were driving."

A twitch crossed the driver's face. Mistrust gleamed in his eyes. Diane did not give him the chance to answer back.

"You said that that evening you'd come from the truck park on Avenue de la Porte d'Auteuil. What were you doing there? Having a rest?"

The man smiled despite himself. A wicked look gleamed in his eye.

"You've never been round there? I mean, in the evening?"

Diane imagined a bland avenue, stuck between the ring-road and Roland Garros stadium, that led directly to the Bois de Boulogne. Suddenly, she could picture the scene as it must be at night time and she understood what her own demons had been hiding from her – whores. He had quite simply gone looking for a whore.

He nodded, as though having followed Diane's train of thought.

"It's what we all do before setting off. I was on my way to Holland. To Hilversum. A 24-hour round trip."

Diane went on:

"OK. As a matter of fact I read the vigilance statistics. Eighty per cent of heavy goods vehicle accidents caused by the driver going to sleep occur between eleven at night and one in the morning. But according to the same set of figures, they never happen on the ring-road. The proximity of Paris seems to 'wake up' the drivers. If you'd just been . . ."

"You joined the force or something?" he suddenly cut in aggressively.

"All I want is to understand. To understand how you could have fallen asleep at midnight, when you'd just seen a prostitute and were about to set off on a 24-hour trip."

Vulovic squirmed. His hands were shaking above the table. Diane controlled her own nerves and adopted a different approach.

"What do you take to stay awake?"

"Coffee. From a thermos flask."

Diane twitched her nose – a silent allusion to the smell in that stinking kitchen.

"You smoke, too, don't you?"

"Just like everyone else."

"I mean, you smoke dope."

The man did not answer. She pressed on:

"It never occurred to you that it might screw you up completely? Might put you to sleep?"

Vulovic stretched his neck. A network of veins was beating in his throat.

"All drivers take stuff to keep going. And we all have our own recipes, see what I mean?"

Diane leant over the table. His tough guy act did not impress her. She got more personal:

"And you're not doing anything harder?"

The truck driver sank back into his usual silence. Diane insisted:

"Uppers, coke, heroin?"

Crooking his head, he stared at her. Beneath his eyelids, there were two iron spheres, gleaming like ball-bearings. A smile slowly sketched itself over his lips.

"Right. I see where you're coming from. You want to fuck me up, don't you? Get me sacked. Get my licence taken away. I already risk going down, but that's not good enough for you. You want to get me slammed up right now, and for a good long stretch."

Diane gestured to stop him.

"All I want is the truth."

"The truth!" Vulovic yelled. "But it's written there in black and white in the police report! They breathalysed me. Did tests at the hospital. But they found nothing! I was fucking straight! I swear to you, at the moment of the accident, I was fucking straight!"

He was telling the truth. She had already been told about the tests.

"All right," she went on. "So why do you think you fell asleep that night?"

"I dunno. I can't remember a thing."

Diane sat up.

"What do you mean, you can't remember a thing?"

He hesitated. Sweat was pouring down his face. He mumbled:

"Honestly . . . However much I think about it, the last thing I can remember is Porte d'Auteuil, and then nothing . . . I don't even know if I had a fuck or not. I must have been all in. I dunno. The next thing I remember is the crash."

Diane sensed some hidden truth. A terrifying reality, which she had half suspected and which was now crystallising. She asked:

"And nobody got at your coffee?"

"What are you on about? Who'd do a thing like that?"

"Did you speak to anyone in the truck park?"

He shook his head. His hood was soaking with sweat.

"This is getting us nowhere. I can't remember. For fuck's sake, it was an accident. What's the point of all these questions? Even if I thought that what happened was weird too."

Diane pulled her chair over. Despite her damp hair, and the rain on her neck, her skin was burning.

"Can't you understand how important this is for me? Try to remember!"

Vulovic opened a drawer in the kitchen table. He removed his joint-rolling kit: cigarettes, OCB skins and a lump of dope in aluminium foil. While sticking together two papers, he said:

"The door's that way."

With a swift gesture, Diane swept all his makings on to the floor. He leapt to his feet, his fists raised.

"Watch it, bitch!"

Diane flattened him against the wall. She was taller than him. And a thousand times more dangerous. She smiled to herself. In the end, that was how she preferred things. She preferred to have this creep who was capable of trying to beat her up. She preferred it to be a bastard who had been chosen as the instrument to kill her child. She spoke very slowly:

"Listen good, fuck face. For nine days, my boy's brain kept swelling and drowning in its own blood. For nine days, I followed this dance with death. Even today, we don't know what state he'll be in when he wakes up. Maybe he'll be normal. Or maybe he'll be a bit slower than the others. Or maybe he'll just be a vegetable. Then picture to yourself what sort of life the two of us are going to have."

The driver lowered his head. He was melting between her hands. She let him slump on to the stool. She leant down, still speaking clearly and calmly:

"So if you reckon that there was anything remotely odd about the lead-up to the accident, if deep down you've got the slightest suspicion, then, for Christ's sake, it's time to come out with it."

Looking down, his face running with sweat and tears, he whispered:

"I dunno ... I dunno ... I kind of feel like someone did something to me ..."

"What do you mean?"

"I dunno. I fell asleep just like that. As though ..."

"As though what?"

"As though I was under control . . . That's what it felt like."

Diane held her breath. Before her lay a gulf of darkness, but this was also a ray of light. An idea formed itself, clear and precise: one way or another, this person had been influenced. Her first thought was hypnosis. She did not know if something as complex as this was possible, but if it was, then there must have been a pre-programmed signal to set the trance off.

"Were you listening to the radio?"

"No."

"Do you have a Walkman?"

"No!"

"Did you see anything by the road?"

"No, I didn't!"

Diane pulled back a little. A retreat that meant she could get an even stronger grip.

"Did you tell the police about this?"

"No. I'm not sure really. Why would someone do that to me? Why organise all this?"

Vulovic had more to say. Somewhere inside him, a knot of fear was beating. Finally, he murmured:

"When I think back, there's just one possibility I can see . . ."

"What's that?"

"Green."

"The colour green?"

"A khaki green. Like . . . like a soldier's uniform."

Diane stopped to think. For the moment, she had no idea what use could be made of this clue, but she sensed that it would lead her little by little to the truth. The man was sobbing, his hands clenched over his temples.

"Jesus . . . Your little boy . . . I think about him every night . . . I'm sorry. Jesus, I'm so sorry! Forgive me!"

Motionless, Diane simply said:

"There's nothing to forgive you for."

"I'm Orthodox," he went on. "I pray to Saint Sava for him, and . . ."

"I repeat, there's nothing to forgive you for. It probably wasn't your fault."

The truck driver looked up. Tears were blurring his eyes.

"What . . . what are you on about?"

Diane murmured:

"I don't know what I'm on about. Not yet."

CHAPTER 20

In the middle of the morning, there did not appear to be anything special about the truck park on Avenue de la Porte d'Auteuil. The buildings of Roland Garros looked like the outskirts of a forbidden city. As for the ring-road, its hum could be heard coming from behind the parapet, but it could not be seen. And yet, as soon as Diane parked, she could immediately imagine the heady atmosphere that must reign there during the night. The flesh lit up in the headlamps, the prowling cars, the cabins of the parked lorries in the background, dark and locked up as instincts were being released. She shivered. She could almost sense those nocturnal desires, see them float and mingle together over the tarmac, like crouching, menacing beasts.

She removed her watch, clipped it over her steering-wheel, switched it over to its stopwatch function, and pulled off. She drove back up the avenue, then turned right, passing by Square des Poètes and the greenhouses of Auteuil, before reaching Porte Molitor. Her speed was reasonable, about what a truck would be doing in the middle of the night. Finally, she came to the ring-road and headed in the direction of Porte Maillot / Autoroute Rouen.

Two minutes, 20 seconds had gone by.

Still in the right-hand lane, Diane accelerated. Luckily for her, the traffic was light – as light as it had been that night. Fifty-five miles an hour. It was the first time that she had been back on the ring-road. Her hands gripped the steering-wheel tightly to stop other thoughts from troubling her.

Porte de Passy. Three minutes, 10 seconds. She accelerated again. Sixty miles an hour. Marc Vulovic's juggernaut could hardly have been going any faster than that. Four minutes, 20 seconds. She entered the tunnel at Porte de la Muette.

She remembered the streams of light, and how her mind had been addled by the champagne.

She emerged back into the open air.

Half a mile further on, she drove into a second tunnel.

Five minutes, 10 seconds.

When Diane saw the last tunnel before Porte Dauphine loom up, she knew that she was entering a new reality. And that her own guilt feelings might have a secret to whisper to her . . .

About a hundred yards from the concrete opening, she closed her eyes and swerved violently to the left. She heard tyres screeching and horns hooting. She opened her eyes again just in time to brake next to the metal barriers that separated the two sides of the ring-road.

She snapped off the stopwatch.

Five minutes, 37 seconds.

She was now at the exact scene of the accident. The crash barriers had been changed, but the cracks in the stone at the entrance of the tunnel, which had been caused by the truck's container, could still be seen.

Five minutes, 37 seconds.

That was the first half of the truth.

She slipped back into the traffic stream and waited for Porte Maillot, before leaving the ring-road, driving back across the square and turning back on to it in the opposite direction. She then kept going as far as Porte Molitor. Turning off the road once more, she took Boulevard Suchet, before slowing down in front of number 72 – her mother's address. She was expecting another fit of nausea, another upsurge of memories. But none came. She tried to remember where she had parked that night. Details began to clarify in her mind: it had been on Avenue du Maréchal-Franchet-d'Espérey, just by the Auteuil racetrack.

She headed off towards the avenue, stopped somewhere near the place where she remembered parking, then set off her stopwatch once more. She drove up the tree-lined street then, a few hundred yards further on, she turned right into Square de la Porte-de-Passy. Exactly as she had done on that fateful night. She then turned on to the ring-road.

A glance at her watch – two minutes, 33 seconds.

Diane intentionally stuck to the average speed of the Toyota Landcruiser: 75 miles per hour. Porte de la Muette. Four minutes.

Above the rim of the ring-road, she spotted the streamlined buildings of the Russian Embassy.

Four minutes, 50 seconds.

The blocks of the University of Paris IX.

Five minutes, 10 . . .

Then, at last, the entrance to that terrible tunnel. This time, Diane put her warning lights on and stopped on the hard shoulder. No crashing about and no skidding. But her hands shook when she looked at the face of her watch: five minutes, 35 seconds.

She could not have imagined a closer synchronisation. Both from the parking lot on Avenue de la Porte d'Auteuil and from Avenue du Maréchal-Franchet-d'Espérey it had taken her exactly five minutes, 35 seconds to reach the scene of the accident. So, if Marc Vulovic had been "programmed" in some way, this would mean that he had set off at exactly the same moment as that at which Diane and her son had got into their car, and they had thus coincided at the entrance to the last tunnel before Porte Dauphine.

The idea of a trap now seemed increasingly likely to Diane. A trap based on sleep, the rain and a juggernaut skidding at full speed. But such an ambush required the presence of a look-out in front of the building on Boulevard Suchet, waiting for her departure, and some other person who, by using hypnosis or some other technique, had "switched on" Marc Vulovic at the same moment. The two men could have communicated by walky-talkies, or quite simply by using mobile phones. So far, there was nothing impossible about it.

There was then the problem of making him fall asleep, which had to occur at the precise moment when the truck was passing her car. And it was here that the trap now seemed feasible to her. If she was right, the killers had worked out the moment when the truck and the Landcruiser would meet. So all they then had to do was to arrange for a signal to be made at that place, thus making the driver fall asleep . . .

Diane closed her eyes. A dull excitement rose up inside her as she heard once more the furious roar of the traffic on the ring-road. Perhaps she was going crazy, perhaps this was a complete waste of time, but she now knew that however unlikely it might sound, such an ambush was possible.

But there was one remaining factor, without which the entire set-up would have been impossible. A detail that, right from the start, had not gelled. Diane switched on her indicator and slipped back into the traffic.

She rapidly changed up and headed off towards Porte de Champerret.

CHAPTER 21

"If you want to piss someone about, young lady, then you'll have to wait for the boss."

Diane could see the workshop of the car pound as she gazed through the office window. The walls were so black that they seemed to soak up all the lighting from the ceiling lights. Further off, there was a clacking of iron equipment. Greasy jacks were screeching somewhere, like tortured lungs. She had always felt a strange aversion to garages. For the cold draughts that chilled you to the bone. That stench of oil that hung around your nostrils. Those grubby hands wielding sharp, cold instruments. A place that was so hard, so dark, that hands were washed not with water, but with sand.

Behind the counter, the fat man in the blue overalls was repeating his leitmotiv:

"Authorisations aren't my department. You've got to see the boss."

"When will he be back?"

"He's at lunch. He'll be back in about an hour."

Diane made a show of looking put out. In fact, she had made a point of waiting for it to be noon before turning up, in the hope of coming across some underling like the one she was now talking to. This was her only chance to get near her own car, given that it had not yet been officially examined. She sighed:

"Look. My son's in hospital. He's seriously injured. I have to go back to see him, but before that I've got to pick up the MOT certificate, which is still in the car!"

The mechanic shuffled about. He did not seem to know how to get out of this situation.

"Sorry. No-one can open your car before the inspector's been round. It's because of the insurance."

"But it's the insurance broker who wants the certificate!"

The man hesitated again. A throbbing truck pulling a damaged car surged down the slope, just a few yards from the office. Diane was now feeling decidedly sick. The man finally sighed:

"OK, got the keys?"

She rattled them in her pocket. He murmured:

"Number 58. On the second floor under ground in the car park at the back. Get a move on. If the boss comes back while you're still there . . ."

She slipped between the vehicles that bordered the front of the car park and crossed the workshop. Then she passed the dark walls, avoiding the pools of oil and hydraulic ramps. In this semi-darkness, the glow from the neon strip-lights seemed to harbour some hidden, esoteric meaning – utterly alien to the light of day.

She went down a gently sloping ramp and into a second car park. The cars looked like cold monsters, sleeping their metallic sleep. Diane felt increasingly ill at ease. Grease oozed under her feet. A smell of oil and burnt petroleum stuck in her throat. She watched the half-erased numbers go past on the ground with mounting apprehension. The very idea of facing her smashed Toyota was knotting her guts. But there was one detail that she just had to check.

The safety belt.

Her child had been flung from his seat because the belt had not been done up. The killers, if killers there were, must have counted on the crash being as lethal as possible. So how could they have known that Diane would not protect her child by strapping him into his seat?

The Toyota Landcruiser was there, just a few yards away. Diane spotted its crushed bonnet, its buckled windscreen and its left wing that had been pressed into violent folds. She had to lean against a pillar. She bent double, thought she was going to be sick, but then, little by little, her blood gathered in her lowered forehead, giving her a sort of balance, an unexpected stability. Gathering her strength together, she went over to the rear right-hand door of her car.

Digging around in her bag, she produced a halogen torch, switched it on, then pulled open the metal panel. Another shock. Black, dry blood on the edges of the child's seat. Tiny pearls of glass scattered over the back of the car.

Two contradictory images became superimposed in her mind.

She could see the woven strap and the metal buckle lying beside Lucien's seat. The belt had clearly not been fastened. But, mentally, she could also see herself doing up the safety harness after she had sat Lucien down. This was not the first time. Over the last few days, and despite all the indications to the contrary, she had been growing more and more certain, more and more convinced, that she had fastened the belt. But now that she was staring at the inside of her car, there seemed to be no room for doubt.

So how could these two versions of the truth co-exist? She slid her torch between her teeth and got into the car. She examined the safety system closely. Perhaps it had been sabotaged, a strap had been cut, or a rivet sawn through . . . No. Everything was perfectly intact. She slid on to the back seat. It was covered with cardboard boxes containing photocopied studies, plastic cases with marking clips and a khaki duvet that dangled down to the floor. All of these things had been thrown back against the seat at the moment of impact. She looked at them, picked them up, pulled them to one side. She found nothing.

She searched on. With one knee on the cushions, she slipped her head over the back of the seat towards the boot. The force of the impact had torn off the composite covering. She remembered it hitting her in the back of the neck. Leaning over the space, she beamed her torch around. More boxes, an old canvas bag, hiking boots, a parka soaked in petrol. Nothing odd. Nothing suspect.

And yet, ever so slowly, a thought started to form in her mind. A possible explanation, which she could not exclude. She turned off her lamp and leant back against the front seat. To check her supposition, she would now have to question the only witness she had.

Herself.

She would have to awaken her own memories in order to dredge up one fact, one detail that would prove if she was or was not going crazy, and if this business really had crossed the border of the possible.

And there was only one technique that would allow her to make such a plunge.

And only one man who could help her.

CHAPTER 22

On the other side of the marble hall, the restaurant opened out into a large room of white pillars and dark velvet hangings. A few tables stood in semi-circular niches. A lacquered piano glittered in the half-light, dusky paintings gave off gilded reflections and, through the tall bay windows, the gardens of the Champs Elysées complemented this luxurious setting with their delicate shrubs and white façades. It was a day when the stormy sky was diffusing a smooth, pearl light that perfectly matched the softness of the room lit by shaded lamps. A specific sort of silence was added to this economy of colour and light: a murmur punctuated by tinkling crystal, the clatter of silver and starched laughter.

Diane followed the head-waiter. As she walked, she felt a few fleeting stares. Most of the customers were men wearing dark ties and dull smiles. She was no fool. She knew that behind that genteel atmosphere and those peaceful faces the secret heart of power was beating. This restaurant was one of those prestigious places where, each day at noon, the political and economic destiny of the country was decided.

The head-waiter drifted away, leaving her in front of the last alcove, just beside the bay windows. Charles Helikian was there. He was not reading a newspaper. He was not in conversation with another businessman at a neighbouring table. He was waiting for her. And this seemed to occupy him completely. Diane silently thanked him for this sign of respect.

On leaving the car pound, she had phoned up her stepfather on his mobile – only at most a dozen people in Paris had that number. She had insisted that they see each other as soon as possible. Charles had answered with a laugh, as though giving in to a child's whim, and had suggested that they meet here, where he was to have lunch with one of his clients. Diane just had time to rush home, remove the stench of cannabis and oil from her hair, before re-emerging wrapped up in devil-may-care indolence, as was expected of her.

Charles stood up, then guided her to the sculpted wall seat. Diane removed her raincoat. She was now wearing a black sleeveless stretch dress that was so simple it did not seem to possess a single stitch. A gleaming pearl necklace adorned her collarbone, perfectly matching her pair of earrings. Diane, dressed to kill.

"You're . . ."

"Superb?"

Charles smiled. Diane proffered:

"Fabulous?"

The smile broadened. His immaculate teeth glistened across

his face. She went on:

"Bewitching? Sexy? Spellbinding?"

"All that and more."

She sighed and clasped her long fingers beneath her chin.

"So why is it that I'm the only one in the world who thinks I'm plain and gawky?"

Charles Helikian produced a cigar from his inside pocket.

"Well it certainly isn't your mother's fault, in any case."

"Did I say that?"

The brown leaves crackled between his fingers.

"She told me about your . . . little chat."

"She shouldn't have."

"We have no secrets. Ever since the accident, she's been calling you, leaving messages and . . ."

"I don't want to speak to her."

He looked at her gravely.

"You're behaving in a ridiculous way. Firstly, you refuse her sympathy. And now that Lucien's better, you're becoming even more silent and aggressive, I . . ."

"Let's drop the subject, shall we? I didn't come here to talk about her."

Charles raised his palm, like a white flag. Then he called for a waiter and ordered. Coffee for him. Tea for her. In a harsh tone, he asked:

"Well, you wanted to see me. And it sounded urgent. What do you want?"

Diane glanced round at him. The recollection of that kiss rose up inside her. She started to feel slightly sick, and her cheeks flushed. To drive away this malaise, she tried to concentrate on what she had to say:

"Once when I was with you, you talked about hypnosis. You said that it was a technique you sometimes used when treating your clients."

116

"That's right. When they have stage fright, or elocution problems. And so?"

"You said that hypnosis was an almost limitless way of exploring memory."

Charles replied ironically:

"I sometimes play at being a specialist."

"I remember it all distinctly. You explained how, thanks to hypnosis, people can use their own mind like a camera, zooming in on their memories. You then added that, even if we don't realise it, we all keep in our subconscious the slightest detail of everything we've ever experienced. Memories that will never come back to our conscious minds but which are there" – she pointed her index finger towards her temple – "inscribed in our heads."

"I must have been on good form."

"I'm not joking. From what you said, hypnosis can allow us to relive each moment of our past and to stop at any given moment and focus on a particular detail. To use our own minds like a video recorder. To pause, then zoom in on a selected element in an image . . ."

Charles's smile vanished.

"What's on your mind?" he asked.

Diane ducked the question.

"You also mentioned a psychiatrist," she said. "According to you, he's the best hypnotherapist in Paris. A specialist in this sort of technique."

He repeated, a little louder:

"What's on your mind?"

"I want his address."

The waiter laid a heavy silver tray on the table. The black gleam of the coffee. The delicate flush of the Earl Grey. The colours harmonised subtly, while the odours circled around the delicate ritual of service. The man in white vanished.

"Why?" Charles asked at once.

In a calm voice, Diane hit him with the truth:

"I want to relive the accident under hypnosis."

"You're crazy."

"You're starting to sound like my mother. That's what she always calls me."

"What would be the point?"

She pictured once more Marc Vulovic's vacant gaze, and herself timing the distances. She thought once more about her idea: an attempted murder disguised as an accident, organised by several men. But she simply replied:

"There's something about the accident that doesn't gel."

"What? Whatever do you mean?"

She replied, articulating clearly:

"The safety belt. I'm sure I fastened it."

Charles looked almost relieved. He adopted a reassuring tone:

"Listen, I quite understand why this is getting to you, but . . ."

"No, you listen to me."

Diane stuck both elbows on the table and leant over.

"Do you seriously think that I'm nuts?"

"Not at all."

"You know that I've already been treated on several occasions for mental problems. After all, it was you who helped me to gloss over my stays in clinics for the adoption application. And so, I'd like to have your opinion of me today. Do you think I've been totally cured?"

"Yes."

There was a hint of uncertainty in his reply.

"Yes, but?"

"You're still a bit . . . odd."

"What I want from you is a straight answer. Do you think that I'm still suffering from the after-effects of my traumas? Or do you think I've found a new mental balance?"

Charles first took a drag from his cigar.

"Yes," he said at last. "You're completely cured. And perfectly balanced. You're the opposite of being eccentric, or lunatic. You're extremely down to earth. Pragmatic. Even a little obsessive when it comes to sorting things out correctly. A true scientist."

For the first time, Diane smiled. She knew that he was being sincere. She went on:

"So how do you then explain why I forgot to fasten the boy's seat-belt?"

"We'd had a few drinks, it was late, we . . ."

Diane slammed her fist on the table. The cups clinked. The last customers looked round at them.

"Lucien is my final resolution," she yelled. "He's the best thing I've done since I've been old enough to make decisions. And a couple of glasses of champagne were enough for me to forget to take the simplest of precautions? Am I supposed to have dumped him on the back seat like a sack of potatoes?"

Charles gripped hold of his cigar.

"You shouldn't let all this get to you. It's time to turn over a new leaf. You . . ."

Diane grabbed her coat.

"OK. I thought I could count on you. I was wrong. I guess I'll just have to find one in the phonebook."

"His name's Paul Sacher."

Charles produced a large pen, topped with ivory, and noted down the address and telephone number on the back of one of his calling cards.

"He's very much in demand, but if you say I told you to call, then you'll be able to see him right away. But watch out. He's a bit of a ladies' man. When he was a teacher, he'd always make off with the prettiest girl in the class. The other students just had to shut up and look on. He's a real leader of the pack."

Diane slipped the card into her pocket. She did not thank him. She did not even grin. Instead, she declared:

"There was something else about that evening that could well have put me out."

"What was that?"

"The fact that you kissed me on the staircase."

Charles Helikian's eyebrows rounded in a sign of indecision. He stroked his beard.

"Ah yes, that . . . ," he murmured.

Diane was staring at him.

"Why did you kiss me?"

The businessman was almost squirming in his pricey suit.

"I don't know. It was quite . . . spontaneous."

"What? Charles Helikian? The great psychology consultant? You can do better than that!"

He was looking increasingly embarrassed.

"No, honestly. It was in the heat of the moment. There was the child asleep. And you standing there, stiff and stoical in the shadows. And that evening when you'd been so different. So . . . free. I just wanted to wish you good luck. That's all."

Diane picked up her bag and got to her feet.

"And you were right to do so," she concluded. "Because I reckon I'm going to need all the luck I can get."

She spun round, leaving the Persian King in his alcove. In a few strides she crossed the empty restaurant. All that now shone in the penumbra were the gilded tables and windows splattered with rain.

"Diane!"

She had already reached the marble hall. She turned round. Charles was running after her.

"For heaven's sake! What are you up to? You haven't told me the whole story."

She waited for him to catch up with her before repeating:

"I just want to know. To sort out the problem of the safety belt."

"No," he replied. "You want to relive that accident because you think that it was not an accident."

Diane just could not help admiring his skill as a psychologist. He had read her mind as though her thoughts were written all over her dress. He had been able to follow her ideas even when they passed beyond the limits of the rational. She nodded:

"You're right. I think that the crash is linked to the murder of van Kaen. How could I avoid that? It just can't be a coincidence. I'm convinced that Lucien is at the heart of something quite incomprehensible."

"Good God . . . ," Charles whispered.

"Just don't tell me that I'm crazy."

The matt colour had drained from his face.

"And so you think the accident was . . . attempted murder?"

"I don't have all the necessary information yet."

"What information?"

"Just be patient."

Diane spun round again. He grabbed her arm. His lashes were fluttering like a butterfly's wings.

"Look. We've known each other for 16 years. I've never dabbled in your upbringing. I've never interfered in your relationship with your mother. But this time, I just can't let you go off the rails. Not this much."

She grinned insolently at him, like a cheeky little girl.

"If it's all just in my mind, then there's nothing to be worried about."

"Listen, you little fool, you might well be playing with fire here, and you don't even realise it!"

He was yelling. To her left, Diane noticed some waiters

standing gawping. It must have been the first time that they had seen Charles Helikian in such a state.

"You don't know what you're doing," he went on, returning to his habitual tone. "Let's suppose ... And this is just a supposition ... Let's suppose that you're right. Well in that case, you mustn't get involved. It's a matter for the police."

Without giving her the chance to respond, he asked:

"And this belt business? How can that be a clue? It wasn't locked. The expert's report was categorical about that. So what on earth can ..."

"I'm certain I locked it."

A cloud passed once more over Charles's face.

"And then? Maybe it was Lucien who ..."

"Lucien was fast asleep. I was keeping an eye on him in the rear-view mirror."

"So what's your theory then? That it opened all on its own?"

Diane went over to him. Charles only came up to her shoulders. She whispered to him, in a confidential tone:

"You know the saying, when you've run out of possible explanations, then only an impossible one is left."

Charles looked at her. Her forehead was shining and her eyes staring darkly.

"An impossible one? Like what?"

Diane leant even further over. She pictured the inside of her car: the blood, the glass, the shadows, the creased duvet. Her voice was smooth and languid, and at the same time tinged with fear:

"Something impossible, such as Lucien and I not being alone in the car."

CHAPTER 23

Outside, the gardens of the Champs Elysées were veiled in rain and light. The downpour was emphasising the brilliance of the sunbeams that were intermittently breaking through the cloud cover. The boughs were rustling in the wind, a gently swaying green mass in the downward slant of the rain. On the doorstep, Diane put on her sunglasses and hesitated.

She was devastated by the fact that she had revealed her theory. That she thought that a man had been hiding in her car, presumably under the duvet or else in the boot, and that he had unfastened Lucien's belt while they had been driving along the ring-road. A sort of kamikaze set to remove all protection from her son and ready to die in the crash if necessary.

Of course, it did not make any sense. Who would have taken such a risk? Who would be ready to sacrifice himself in the jaws of his own trap? What is more, after the accident, not the slightest trace of another passenger had been found. And yet, Diane just could not get the idea out of her mind. The doorman came up to her and nervously proclaimed:

"Your car will be here any minute, Madame."

But the tone of his voice and the expression on his face told a different story.

"What's going on?" Diane asked.

The uniformed man looked with desperation towards the car park.

"It was your friend. He said he'd deal with it."

"What friend?"

"The tall man who was waiting for you. He said that he'd drive it up, but . . ." He cast panicked glances in all directions. "I . . . I can't see where . . ."

Diane spotted the car about 30 yards away, parked below a lime tree. She strode across the gravel drive. She recognised the figure of Patrick Langlois, reflected into the curve of the windscreen, while he was struggling with the ignition key. She knocked on the window. He jumped, then smiled sheepishly, before opening the door.

"I forgot that these hire cars have codes. Sorry. I wanted to give you a surprise . . ."

Diane did not know if she was angry or not.

"Move over," she said.

The giant wriggled with some difficulty into the passenger seat. She got in and asked:

"What the hell are you doing here? Are you having me followed?"

The policeman looked offended.

"I sent one of my men to pick you up for lunch. When he got to your place, you were on the way out. He just couldn't resist following you, then he called me."

"So why didn't you come into the restaurant?"

He pointed at his turtleneck.

"No tie. A lack of foresight and planning."

Diane smiled. No, she definitely was not angry. The police officer then added:

"I know. I should have got my card out. And forced my way through."

She giggled. When she was with this apparently carefree man, she felt lighter, clearer, as though cleansed of her worries. But then Langlois pointed at the restaurant and asked:

"Do you get on well with your stepfather?"

Diane did not like the tone of the question.

"What do you mean by that?"

He drummed his fingers on the window and gazed absent-mindedly out at the gardens.

"Nothing. It's just that I see so many things." His eyes were smiling. "In my work, I mean."

Diane, too, stared at the gardens. The shower had chased away the passers-by, the mothers with their children and the stamp dealers. All that was left was a gleaming landscape, alive with reflections. Still puddles. Waves of green. Stone façades, polished by the rain. It reminded her of a beach at low tide. She suddenly felt a need for softness, convalescence, confectionery and mint sweets. She asked:

"Why did you want to see me?"

The police file materialised in his hands.

"I wanted to tell you the news. And to discuss my theory."

He rummaged through his notes. Apparently, Langlois was part of the school of new fogies that refused to accept the influence of technology on daily life. The sort of person capable of glorifying ring-binders or refusing to have a mobile phone. He finally said:

"This whole business is getting increasingly weird. First, there's the violence of the murder. The killer's apparent strength, but at the same time his supposed build: five feet at the most. Then there's another mystery, of a purely anatomical sort."

Langlois came to a stop. The rain was hammering out a light saraband. Diane nodded to him to go on.

"We don't know how the killer managed to locate the aorta while blindly feeling his way through the entrails. According to our pathologists, not even an experienced surgeon could pull that off . . ." He paused for breath, then pressed on. "All of which makes for a lot of impossibilities. So I decided to change targets. It occurred to me that it might be a rite, some sort of sacrificial technique used in Vietnam, for instance."

"And what did you find out?"

"Nothing tangible to begin with. At least, not in South-East Asia. But an ethnologist at the Musée de l'Homme pointed me towards Central Asia – Siberia, Mongolia, Tibet and North-West China . . . So I looked up a few other specialists. According to one of them, there is a technique practised in that region which might match the way our murderer proceeded."

"What do you mean? A way of sacrificing people?"

"No. Far more humdrum than that. It's the way they kill livestock. They make a slit under the ribcage, slide their arms in, then the twist the animal's aorta with their bare hands."

Something clicked in Diane's mind, triggering a series of vague recollections. Langlois went on:

"According to my ethnologist, this technique was widely used in, for example, Mongolia. It's the best way to kill a sheep or a yak without losing a drop of its blood. In cold climates like that, they try to get every scrap of energy possible from their animals. Apparently, there's also some kind of fear of blood. A taboo."

Diane asked sceptically:

"So the killer's from Central Asia?"

"Maybe. Or he might just have lived there and learnt their customs. According to the pathologists, we're not very different from sheep. Anatomically I mean."

"This all sounds a bit vague," she murmured.

"It does to me, too. Except for one thing."

She turned round towards him. He handed her a photocopy of a form, written in German, on the headed notepaper of a travel agency.

"Rolf van Kaen was about to go to Mongolia."

"What?"

"The BBK is continuing with its investigations in Germany. They checked all the doctor's phone calls. Van Kaen had been making inquiries about flights to Ulan Bator, the capital of . . ."

" . . . the People's Republic of Mongolia."

The policeman glanced with surprise at Diane.

126

"You know it?"

"Only by name."

"Our acupuncturist had also been asking about internal flights to a small town in the far north of the country . . ." – he checked his notes – ". . . called Tsagaan-Nuur. Apparently, the only thing that he hadn't decided was his departure date. So, the technique used in the murder can be seen as a link. A tenuous one, admittedly, but a link all the same . . ."

Langlois came to halt, then softly asked:

"And how about you? Do you have any news for me?"

She shrugged and looked back towards the gardens. The rain was now pouring down the windscreen in a glittering flood.

"No. I phoned the orphanage. They know nothing."

"Is that all?"

"I gave a cassette of Lucien singing in his native language to a specialist. There's a chance she might be able to identify the dialect."

"Good idea. Anything else?"

Diane thought of her own theory of a contrived accident, a kamikaze murderer who had hidden in her car.

"No, nothing else," she replied.

Langlois asked:

"Why did you want the truck driver's address?"

She jumped slightly, but forced herself to remain impassive.

"I just wanted to talk to him. To give him news of Lucien."

He sighed. The rain punctuated the long succeeding silence with its metallic drumming.

"People always look down on our experience."

Surprised, she looked round at him.

"Why do you say that?"

"I'll tell you what I think: you're carrying out your own investigation."

"That's what you asked me to do, isn't it?"

"Don't take me for an idiot. I'm talking about the murder of van Kaen."

"Why would I do such a thing?"

"I'm starting to get to know you, Diane. And, to be honest with you, I'd be surprised if you weren't . . ."

She remained silent. The officer's voice became more serious.

"Be careful. We haven't uncovered a tenth of this business yet. It could blow up in our faces at any moment. And in a totally unexpected way. So just don't play at being Miss Sherlock Holmes, OK?"

She nodded like a crest-fallen child. Langlois opened the door. A blast of rain blew into the car. He concluded:

"Next time, let me invite you to lunch."

He got out of the car and added:

"We cops know the best fast food joints in Paris. You do realise that there are milkshakes and milkshakes, don't you? It's a whole new world of subtleties."

Diane forced herself to look cheerful.

"I'll try and live up to the honour."

Langlois was still bending over, with rain drops beating on his back.

"And don't forget: don't act crazy. No schoolgirl heroics. As soon as anything untoward happens, you call me, OK?"

Diane nodded with a parting smile but, when the door slammed, it sounded to her like the closing of a coffin lid.

CHAPTER 24

She looked at him as a source of light, but through his own shadows.

His dressings had been altered. They were tighter and less thick. The bandage round his head was now a simple twist of lint. The drains had been taken out, presumably that very morning. This was a decisive step. Lucien was no longer in danger of haemorrhaging.

She went over to her chair and, with the tip of her index finger, stroked his forehead, the sides of his nose and the corners of his lips. She remembered their first evenings together, with her whispering stories to him as in the darkness her hand idled over his relaxing features and the form of his languid body, slowly rising and falling as he breathed. Once more, she felt ready for that delightful excursion, along those tiny peaks and mysterious depths . . . With delight, she sensed life beating, becoming stronger, affirming itself throughout that bandaged body.

But one agony can lead to another. Now that he was out of real danger, Diane felt fresh troubles arise. In the same way that the body begins to experience pain when the main contusion has faded away, she discovered new degrees in her sorrow. She felt each of the child's wounds and bruises as though they were in her own body, with a raging powerlessness at his destiny. Diane was gripped by a new form of despair – pain by proxy.

But, above all, what she could not get out of her mind was the certainty that, somewhere around them, danger lurked. It was becoming an obsession. And she knew that she would never be able to face the future if she did not help to solve these mysteries. That is why she felt ever more determined. That is why she had just made an appointment with Paul Sacher, the hypnotherapist, at 6.00 that very evening.

Suddenly, she noticed the clip chart fixed to the end of the bed, which showed the daily doses of medication and Lucien's temperature curve. She grabbed the graph paper. The pencil mark indicated that there had been three peaks since 11.00 yesterday evening and 3.00 that afternoon. And not just any sort of peak. All three of them exceeded 104°.

Diane picked up the phone and called Eric Daguerre. He was operating. So she tried Madame Ferrer. One minute later, her grey hair could be seen in the corridor through the glass panels. Not giving Diane time even to open her mouth, the nurse said:

"Dr Daguerre asked me not to tell you about it. He thought there was no point worrying you."

Diane was furious.

"Really?"

"These rises in temperature lasted only a few minutes. It's a benign reaction."

Diane brandished the graph.

"What's so benign about 106°?"

"Dr Daguerre thinks that they're just after-effects caused by the shock your child received. An indirect sign that his metabolism is returning to normal."

Diane nervously bent over and tucked Lucien in.

"If there's the slightest change, you'd better tell me! Is that clear?"

"Yes, of course. But, really, there's absolutely no danger."

Diane smoothed down the blankets and straightened Lucien's white gown. Suddenly, she laughed aggressively, on the verge of tears:

"No danger, eh? But I suppose Dr Daguerre still wants to see me?"

"As soon as he's finished operating."

CHAPTER 25

"Everything's fine, Diane. Believe me."

It was the worst start she had ever heard anyone make.

"What about his temperature?"

Eric Daguerre carelessly swept away her question with the back of his hand. He was standing behind his desk in his white coat.

"That's nothing. Lucien's condition is still improving. All the signs point to a recovery. This morning, we took out the drains. He can change wards soon."

There was a false ring about his casualness. Diane stared at his glistening eyes. The anarchists in *Anna Karenina*, who threw bombs at princes, must have had eyes like that.

"So, why did you want to see me?" Diane asked.

The doctor slipped his hands into his pockets, then stepped towards her. All day and all night, his office was lit at the same intensity.

"I wanted you to meet Didier Romans," he said at last. "He's an anthropologist."

Diane then deigned to turn round and look at the third person in the room, whom she had hitherto ignored. He was younger than Daguerre. Dark, slim and stiff as a ruler, he was wearing glasses in black lacquered frames over his utterly unexpressive face. He was reminiscent of an equation, or some abstract formula.

The doctor went on:

"Didier's an anthropologist, in the modern sense of the term. He specialises in biometry and in population genetics."

The man with the closed face nodded. A timid smile inched on to his features, then fled again at once. Daguerre asked Diane:

"You know what that is?"

"Just about, yes."

Daguerre grinned at the other scientist.

"Didn't I tell you that she was something else?"

His jolly tone was sounding more and more forced. He went on:

"I told Didier about Lucien. And I asked him to carry out a few tests."

Diane stiffened.

"What sort of tests? I hope you didn't . . ."

"No, not medical tests. We simply compared a few of your child's physiological characteristics with other, more general criteria."

"I beg your pardon?"

The anthropologist butted in:

"My speciality is polymorphism, Madame. I work on the characteristics of the various peoples of the world. In each ethnic group, certain traits occur more frequently than in others. Even if they can't be found in all of its members, there will still be an average frequency which will allow us to draw up a general portrait of the group."

The doctor sat down and took up where the anthropologist had left off:

"We thought that it would be of interest to compare Lucien's physiological characteristics with the averages of the peoples in the region where he came from. This method might give us an idea of his exact origin."

Diane's anger went up another notch. But it was directed against herself. Why hadn't she thought of that? She had contacted the orphanage. She had submitted his words to a specialist. She had tried to get a better understanding of the technique that had saved him. But it had not occurred to her to study another, outward sign – his body. That body which must

132

have some physiological traits which, no matter how slight they were, would point towards one particular ethnic origin.

She calmed down, turned to Romans and asked:

"And what did you find?"

The anthropologist produced a wad of paper from his bag.

"Let's start with his height, if you wouldn't mind. When he was admitted you stated that he was probably about six or seven years old. But, an examination of his dentition reveals that he still has nearly all of his milk teeth. This means that he must be nearer five."

He turned to a second document. Diane recognised the admission sheet that she had filled in on the night of the accident.

"Here you wrote that Lucien presumably belongs to one of the ethnic groups living on the shores of the Andaman Sea."

In response, she motioned vaguely with her hands.

"I really don't know. According to the head of the orphanage, the few words he used weren't Thai, or Burmese, or from any other local dialect."

Romans glanced over his glasses, then murmured:

"But you think that he does come from that part of the world which includes, say, Burma, Thailand, Laos, Vietnam and Malaysia?"

Diane hesitated.

"I . . . well, yes, of course. I have no reason to think other-wise."

The anthropologist's stare dropped like a guillotine.

"If we concentrate on those regions that border the Andaman Sea," he said, "and even if we extend our search to the Gulf of Thailand and the China Sea, all we find are tropical or forest-dwelling groups."

He glanced back up at Diane.

"Eric tells me that you're an ethologist. So you know that

the natural habitat has a profound effect on its inhabitants' physique. In forests, men and animals are far smaller than in other environments, for example, the plains."

She stared back at him. Glasses against glasses. Romans looked back at his notes.

"The height of the inhabitants of the intertropical forests of South-East Asia currently ranges from four feet to four feet eight. We can thus deduce that, at the age of five, the children from these families are about two foot tall."

His eyes rose above his glasses once more.

"Do you know how tall your son is, Madame?"

"Over three foot, I think."

"Three feet, two inches, to be precise. In other words, a good 14 inches above average. But then, Lucien might just be very tall for his age."

"Go on."

Romans turned over a fresh sheet.

"Let's turn now to his skin pigmentation. There have been many studies of the skin colours of the world's peoples, even if such a criterion is hard to define – and dangerous to use, as I'm sure you can imagine. In general, such luminosity is measured using a technique called reflectometry. We project a light beam on to the subject's epidermis then measure the photons that are reflected back. The paler the skin, the more photons bounce off it."

Diane was now champing at the bit. She was beginning to see where Romans was heading.

"We performed this test on Lucien," he went on. "And we obtained a result of between 70 and 75 per cent of reflected light. In other words, his epidermis sends back almost all of the beams. His skin is extraordinarily pale and quite different from darker, intertropical shades. To give you a rough idea, the average rate in the Andamans region is 55 per cent."

Diane pictured the extreme pallor of her son's complexion –
that diaphanous body with its fine interlacing of veins when she
was giving him a bath. How could such marvellous traits now
turn out to be sources of distress? The anthropologist went on,
turning over his pages:

"Here's a further study. This time on Lucien's physiological
mechanisms. His blood pressure. His heart beat. His rate of
glycaemia. His lung capacity . . ."

Diane interrupted him:

"And you have statistics for each of those criteria?"

The anthropologist could not resist treating himself to a
smile of pride.

"And for many more besides."

"And you've compared them with those of my son?"

He nodded.

"One of Lucien's results is quite unusual. Despite the fact
that he's convalescing, we still managed to measure his lung
capacity. And his is quite incredible. Now, as you probably
know, a person's lung capacity is directly linked to the altitude
of his habitat. Mountain people have more powerful lungs,
and a greater concentration of haemoglobin, than people living
in valleys, for example. It's a way of adapting to their natural
environment."

"And so? What are your conclusions, for heaven's sake?"

The scientist nodded again.

"In every field, Lucien's results are typical of life at high
altitudes, and are quite different from those associated with
peoples living by the sea or in forests."

Silence was beating in Diane's head. A closed silence, which
could be resolved neither by words nor by suppositions. Didier
Romans's monotonous voice droned on:

"If we put together the three results concerning his height,
his pigmentation and his physiological capacities, then we arrive

at an equation pointing towards the plains, a cold climate and high altitudes . . ."

Diane whispered numbly:

"Is that all?"

The man picked up his wad of papers.

"There's another 50 or so pages of it. We've studied everything: blood group, tissue groups, chromosomes, and so on. Not one single result – I repeat not a single one – fits with the averages found in the area around the Andaman Sea."

Diane whispered:

"Then I suppose your results point to a different origin?"

"Turko-Mongolian, Madame. Your son has all of the typical characteristics of the Siberian peoples of the Far East. Lucien is a child not of the tropics, but of the taiga. He must have been born several thousand miles away from where you adopted him."

CHAPTER 26

It took Diane over 20 minutes to find her car.

She crossed Rue de Sèvres then went into Rue du Général-Bertrand. She then took Rue Duroc and Rue Masseran, before venturing into Avenue Duquesne. She was out of breath and her heart was jolting irregularly. She tried to think. In vain. There were too many questions – and no answers. How had a Turko-Mongolian child ended up in the hot dust of Ra-Nong, on the Burmese border? How had a man like Rolf van Kaen been informed of the child's condition – while he was apparently preparing to visit that very part of the world himself? And how could a little five-year-old boy, wherever he came from, inspire the sort of schemes and diabolical machinations that Diane was starting to suspect?

She finally spotted her car near Place de Breteuil. She got inside, as though it was a shelter. Her thoughts seethed through her mind. Dull thundering that resulted in nothing.

And yet, through that storm, she could see a glimpse of light.

There was a way to take another step towards the truth. In her mind's eye, she saw once more that Spanish monastery – the alternating ultraviolet beams that intermittently revealed the palimpsest's hidden text. She, too, possessed a system that could show up Lucien's hidden side. She grabbed her mobile and called Isabelle Condroyer, the ethnologist whom she had asked to identify her son's mother tongue.

The scientist recognised her at once.

"Diane, is that you? It's far too early to hope for a result yet. I've contacted several researchers specialising in South-East Asia. We're going to organise a meeting and play the cassette, we'll . . ."

"I have some news."

"What news?"

"It'll take too long to explain, but it now seems highly unlikely that Lucien originally comes from the tropical region where I adopted him."

"What's that?"

"He must be from Central Asia. Somewhere in Siberia or Mongolia."

The linguist grumbled:

"But that changes everything . . . That isn't my speciality at all. Nor of the people I work with."

"But you must know other linguists who work on that region?"

"Their lab is in Nanterre University . . ."

"Can you contact them?"

"Yes, I know one person there in particular."

"Good. I'll be counting on you."

Diane hung up. The rhythm of her thoughts eased off slightly. She looked at her watch. It was half past five. The time had come.

Time to plunge into herself.

To relive the accident on the ring-road down to its slightest detail.

CHAPTER 27

Paul Sacher looked about 60 years old. He was tall, scrawny and dressed in an elegant, almost eye-catching manner. He was wearing a grey moiré suit, which gleamed like the blade of an axe. Beneath it could be seen the dark sheen of a black shirt and the shimmering cut of his silk tie. His face was pleasant: straight features, accentuated by wrinkles, but bearing all of the indolence and pretension of high breeding. Under his bushy eyebrows, his green eyes sparkled, rimmed with black and with an almost glassy transparency. But the most astonishing part of his appearance were his sideburns – his cheeks were covered with frizzy whiskers, straight out of the 19th century, emphasised by the tight curls just by his temples. They gave him the look of some forest beast, thus increasing the strange impression created by his presence.

Diane felt a giggling fit coming on. The man in the doorway looked like a hypnotist from an old horror film. All he had missing was a cloak and a silver-tipped cane. He just could not be a serious practitioner, or the psychiatrist that Charles sent his most important clients to see. She was so surprised that she did not hear what he said.

"Pardon?" she stammered.

The face smiled. The whiskers rose up.

"I made a simple request for you to enter."

To cap it all, he had a stage Slavic accent, and rolled his r's like an old coachman in the mists of Walpurgis Night. This time, she backed off.

"No thanks," she said. "In the end, I really don't feel up to . . ."

Paul Sacher grabbed her arm. The softness of his voice partly made up for the brutality of his gesture.

"Come in, do. I don't want you to have come all this way for nothing . . ."

"All this way." That was not how Diane would have described the 400 yards she had walked to his practice on Rue de Pontoise, just above Boulevard Saint-Germain. She tried to keep a straight face, suddenly afraid that she might offend this man who had accepted to see her on the very same day that she had called him.

On entering his office, she felt slightly relieved. No black curtains. No exotic knick-knacks or sinister statues. No smell of incense or lingering dust. Just plain pale yellow walls, white woodwork and austere, modern furniture. She followed him down a corridor, through a waiting room and into his consulting room.

The room, with its glass desk and perfectly arranged bookshelves, was bathed in late-afternoon sunshine. Once inside she could easily picture politicians or captains of industry sitting there, eager to sort out their stress problems.

The man sat down and smiled again. Diane was beginning to get used to his silvery garb and guru stare. She no longer felt like laughing and, instead, experienced a slight sensation of dread at Paul Sacher's powers. Could he really help her to plumb her memory? Was she really going to give up her mind to him? The doctor rolled out a few deep syllables:

"You seem to find me amusing, Madame."

Diane swallowed her saliva.

"Um, how can I put it? I just wasn't expecting . . ."

"Such a picturesque personage?"

"No, in fact . . ." She finally smiled. "I'm sorry. I've rather had my fill for one day, and . . ."

Her voice trailed off. The doctor picked up a black resin paperweight and started fiddling with it.

"Looking like an old sorcerer puts me at a disadvantage, young lady. And yet, I am in fact a rationalist. For nothing is more rational than the technique of hypnosis."

It seemed to Diane that his accent was growing less guttural, or maybe she was just getting used to it. His charm worked like ripples on water – in concentric circles. She now noticed the framed photos lined up on the walls: group shots with Sacher lording it over the others as the sovereign professor. Each time, he had the most ravishing student by his side, wrapping him up in a look of utter adoration. Charles had called him "a real leader of the pack".

"So how can I help you?" he asked, gently putting down the paperweight. "I don't need to tell you that Charles told me that you would be phoning."

She stiffened.

"What did he tell you?"

"Nothing. Except that you mean a lot to him. That you're someone . . . who must be looked after. I repeat my question: how can I help you?"

"First, I'd like to ask you a detailed question about hypnosis."

"Fire away."

"Is it possible to condition somebody so that they do something against their will?"

The man leant his elbows on the chrome-plated armrests of his desk chair. He had several rings on his fingers, decked with turquoises, amethysts and rubies.

"No, it isn't," he replied. "Hypnosis never violates the conscious mind. All of those tales of pre-conditioned killers and raped women are pure urban legends. Patients can always resist. Their will remains unaffected."

"Or else . . . to make someone go to sleep? Could your technique be used to knock someone out?"

Sacher curled his lips, and his whiskers followed this upward shift.

"That is quite a different question. Sleep is a state of abandon that is quite close to the hypnotic trance. Yes, it is certainly possible to do that."

"And could you do it from a distance?"

"What do you mean, 'from a distance'?"

"Could you programme a subject so that he fell asleep some time after the session of hypnosis, while you were no longer present?"

He nodded:

"Yes, that is possible. You would just have to repeat the signal which had been agreed on."

"What sort of signal?" she asked.

"I'm sorry, but I don't really see what you're driving at."

"What sort of signal?"

"Well, it could be a key word, for instance. During a session, a word is lodged in the subject's subconscious mind which is then associated with the state of sleep. Later, you would simply have to pronounce the word in question to set off the reaction."

She remembered what Vulovic had told her: "When I think back, there's just one possibility I can see . . . Green . . . Like a soldier's uniform." She asked him:

"Could it be a visual signal?"

141

"Indeed."

"Like a colour?"

"Yes. It could be a colour, an object, a gesture, anything in fact."

"Then what would the subject remember afterwards?"

"That depends on the depth of the work during the hypnosis."

"Could he forget everything?"

"Yes, after very deep hypnosis. But you're now drawing near to the confines of our profession. We have a strict code of ethics, and . . ."

Diane was no longer listening. She felt, in her heart of hearts, that she was now nearing the truth. It was possible that some-one had hypnotised Marc Vulovic in the truck park on Avenue de la Porte d'Auteuil and that a signal had later set off a state of suggestion. This then led her to van Kaen, a manly colossus who had let someone rip open his belly without putting up the slightest resistance. Had he been hypnotised too? The man went on:

"From what Charles told me, I thought you were more interested in having a session of . . ."

"That's right. I do want to enter into a state of suggestion."

"With what in mind? Your questions seem distinctly odd. Generally my patients have problems giving up smoking, or have an allergy . . ."

"I want to relive an episode in my life."

The man smiled. He was back on familiar territory. He settled into his chair, leant his head to one side – like a painter scrutinising his model – and asked:

"What sort of episode? Something that happened a long time ago?"

"No. The event took place just over a fortnight ago. But I think that my subconscious is hiding certain details from me. Charles told me that you could help me remember them."

"No problem. Just give me the overall context and . . ."

"Wait a second."

Suddenly, Diane panicked at the idea of opening her mind to this man. To put the moment off, she said:

"First, can you tell me . . . about your technique? How are you going to go back into my memory?"

"Don't worry. This is going to be teamwork."

"But teamwork is based on trust. Tell me exactly how you're going to get inside my head."

Sacher sounded reluctant.

"I'm sorry, but I can't do that."

"Why?"

"The more you know about the method I'm using, the more resistance you will put up."

"But I came here of my own free will."

"I'm talking about your subconscious. About that subconscious mind which is apparently holding back certain information from you. If you provide it with weapons to defend itself, then it will use them, believe me."

"But I can't . . . I can't just give up my mind like that."

The psychiatrist remained silent. He seemed to be weighing up what was at stake for Diane. He grabbed the paperweight again, then put it down and mumbled:

"Hypnosis is simply an extremely intense form of concentration. We're going to talk our way through physical sensations – the circulation of your blood, for instance – which will gradually capture all of your attention. Apart from those sensations, you'll forget everything. You'll have just a distant impression of your immediate surroundings. This sort of 'disconnection' sometimes occurs in our daily lives. For example, when you're studying a subject very closely, then your mind can be entirely absorbed by your work. If an insect stings you, you don't even feel it. You're in a hypnotic, or trance-like state. It is also what happens during religious ceremonies that feature physical ordeals. The brain no longer 'receives' messages of pain from the body."

"And it's because of such a state that you can lift unconscious blocks?"

"Yes, that's right. Because it isn't the subconscious that erects them, but the conscious mind. And when you reach a certain level, reason no longer comes into play. It's then a private chat between the subconscious and the hypnotherapist."

Diane thought about her adolescent accident. She had spent part of her life erasing her memories, or rather transforming them into a locked room. She asked:

"How far back can you go like that?"

"There's no limit. You'd be astonished by how many patients have turned back into babies on this very chair. They start babbling. Their eyes become unsynchronised, like a baby a few days after being born. You can even go back further."

"Further?"

"As far as the memories we all have buried in us of our previous lives."

Diane tried to laugh.

"Sorry. But I don't believe in reincarnation."

"I'm not talking about memories of particular existences. What I mean is that natural memory which all of us inherit. In some ways, genetics is just a form of memory. The recollection of our evolution, buried deep in our flesh."

"That's just a figure of speech. What I'm talking about are concrete memories."

"But they can be concrete! Let's take the example of swimming babies. If you put a new-born baby into water, then it instinctively closes its vocal cords. Where does such a reflex come from?"

"From its survival instinct."

"When only a few days old?"

Diane blinked. The hypnologist went on:

"That reflex goes back to time immemorial, when mankind was not yet mankind, but an amphibious creature. In a certain way, when the child touches the water, it remembers that time. Or to be more precise, its body remembers, independently of its mind. Who knows if hypnosis is not capable of bringing even more precise memories of that sort back to our consciousness?"

Diane was feeling increasingly ill at ease. She was no longer sure if she wanted to stay there and take the plunge. Another factor was also disturbing her. Night had fallen, and the room was now submerged in shadows. But the hypnotist's eyes seemed to be shining even more brightly. It even looked as though his eyes were sending off the sort of reflections that are produced by certain nocturnal predators, such as the wolf, that have silver discs between the retina and the sclera that amplify light. Sacher had just that silvery stare . . . She had made up her mind to leave when he said:

"And now, why don't you tell me about the scene you want to relive?"

Diane reasoned with herself. She pictured herself working up her resolution in the hospital room just a few hours before. She slumped back into her chair and calmly announced:

"On Wednesday, 22 September, at about midnight, I had a car accident along with my adopted son on the ring-road, near Porte Dauphine. I survived unscathed, but my son was in a critical condition for two weeks. I think he's out of danger now, but . . ."

Diane hesitated.

"I'd like to recall the minutes leading up to the crash," she finally added. "I want to relive it down to the slightest gesture and detail. I want to be sure that it wasn't my fault."

"Because of bad driving?"

"No. The accident happened because a truck skidded across from the other side of the road. There was nothing I could do. But . . . I had drunk a little. And I want to be sure that I really had fastened the boy's safety belt."

Another moment's hesitation, then:

"When we crashed, the belt wasn't done up."

Sacher crossed his hands on the glistening desk and leant over towards Diane. His irises were glowing more than ever, in symmetrical beams.

"If the belt was unfastened, then that means you didn't do it up, doesn't it?"

"I'm *sure* that I fastened it. And I want to prove it here, under hypnosis."

The doctor stopped to think. He was clearly as surprised as Charles Helikian.

"Let's suppose that you did do the necessary," he said. "How do you then explain that the belt was undone when you crashed?"

"I think someone unfastened it while I was driving."

"Your son perhaps?"

She had to say it. She had to reveal her theory. She whispered:

"I think it was a man. A stowaway passenger in my car. I think that the accident was prepared, organised then carried out down to the slightest detail."

"You are joking, aren't you?"

"OK, let's say I'm joking. Now hypnotise me."

"But it's ridiculous. Why would someone have gone to such lengths?"

"Hypnotise me."

"Someone took the risk of being there in the car with you when it crashed?"

Diane realised that she would get no result here. She picked up her things and got to her feet.

"Wait," he commanded.

Paul Sacher gestured courteously towards the armchair. He was smiling affably at her, but Diane noticed that he was trembling.

"Sit down," he said. "We'll start right away."

CHAPTER 28

The first sensation was of water.

Her mind was floating in a liquid environment. She felt like some forgotten package in the submerged hold of a cargo ship. Or the kernel of a fruit in over-ripe pulp. She was now drifting in the midst of her own skull.

The second sensation was that there were two of her.

Or a double.

As though her consciousness had split into two separate entities, one of which being able to observe the other. She dreamt – and could contemplate herself dreaming. She concentrated – and could, from a distance, watch herself concentrating.

"Can you hear me Diane?"

"Yes, I can."

The submersion into the hypnotic trance had been instantaneous. Paul Sacher had first asked her to concentrate on a red line painted on the wall, then to feel the weight of her limbs. In a flash, Diane had plunged into a state of intense consciousness. She could feel the inertia of her hands and feet. The mass of her members, which seemed to be getting constantly heavier, while her mind rose up and freed itself.

"We're now going to talk about the accident."

Her back straight, her hands on the armrests of the chair, Diane nodded.

"You're coming out of your mother's apartment block. What time is it?"

"About midnight.

"Where are you exactly, Diane?"

"I'm standing in the porch of number 72, Boulevard Suchet."

The pattering of rain. Translucent lines. Thousands of notches in the black surface of the road. High façades of glittering stone. Bluish street lamps, exhaling mists like eager mouths.

"How do you feel?"

Her eyes closed, she smiled without answering.

Champagne in her blood stream, like underground rivers laughing at the rain outside. Diane can hear the light, heavy drops dripping on to her neck. She feels good. She feels woozy. She has forgotten her anger during dinner. Charles's kiss. She is wrapped up in the moment.

"Diane, how do you feel right now?"

"I feel fine."

"Are you alone?"

The warmth of the child in her arms crystallises. The heat from his neck, the fluidity of his body. The calmness of his sleep which the rain cannot break.

"I'm with Lucien, my adopted son."

"What are you doing now?"

"I'm crossing the boulevard."

"What's the traffic like?"

"The street's empty."

"Where's your car parked?"

"By Auteuil racetrack."

"Can you remember the exact address?"

"Avenue du Maréchal-Franchet-d'Espérey."

"Give me some more information. What make is your car?"

"It's a four-wheel drive. An old model. A Toyota Landcruiser from the 1980s."

"Can you see it now?"

"Yes."

A few yards away, the car stands out in the downpour. Diane now seems disturbed by a premonition. She feels bad, full of remorse. She is sorry that she drank so much. That she obeyed that ritual which she in fact loathes. She would like to return at once to a perfect lucidity, to control completely each second in order to protect her son.

Sacher's voice echoed in the room, sounding at once distant and near:

"What are you doing now?"

"I'm opening the door."

"Which door?"

"The rear right-hand door. Lucien's one."

"And then?"

Diane fell silent. Before she had time to define her thoughts, her body provided her with an answer – clear sensations, which were almost too vivid.

The rain sweeping down her back. The heat escaping from the front of her jacket. Her body bending down with Lucien towards the interior of the car.

The hypnologist's voice grew louder:

"Tell me what you're doing, Diane."

"I'm putting Lucien into his car seat . . ."

"This is a very important moment, Diane. Describe precisely each gesture you make."

A short sound snaps between her fingers. The "click" of the belt. She at once experiences that subtle, secret, selfish delight that rounds off everything she does, no matter how trivial, when it comes to protecting her child.

A few seconds passed. Diane's voice finally said:

"I'm . . . I'm fastening his belt."

"Are you sure?"

"Absolutely certain."

Sacher's tone grew deep and persuasive:

"Pause for a moment over that memory. Observe the inside of your car very carefully."

The part of Diane that was still conscious realised that its mental camera had started to turn. She was now looking round inside a memorised image.

The dark interior of the car. The worn upholstery cluttered with various objects. A wrinkled khaki duvet drooping down to the floor. The boot covering swamped with old magazines. The metal doors with no upholstery or fabric . . .

She could quite literally focus on her memory, shift around in it and zoom in. She could examine details that she had not noticed at the time, but which her memory had absorbed unbeknown to her.

"What can you see, Diane?"

"Nothing. Nothing special."

Paul Sacher's silence was tense. Diane vaguely felt that the psychiatrist was on tenterhooks. He asked:

"Shall we go on?"

"Yes, let's go on."

His tone sank into neutrality once more:

"Now you're driving on the ring-road."

She nodded.

"Answer aloud, please."

"I'm driving on the ring-road."

"What can you see?"

"Lights. Waves of lights."

"Be more precise. What can you see exactly?"

On either side of her, lights rush past below their metal shields. Diane can almost see the texture of the laminated windscreen, lit by the incandescence of the orange sodium.

"Rows of neon lights," she murmured. "The lighting in the tunnel. It's dazzling me."

"Where are you now?"

"I'm driving past Porte de la Muette."

"Are there any other cars on the road?"

"Not many."

"Which lane are you driving in?"

"The fourth lane. On the far left."

"What speed are you driving at?"

"I don't know."

The voice pressed her again:

"Look at your dashboard."

Diane looked at the speedometer inside her memory.

"At 120 kilometres per hour."

"Good. Now, what about the road around you. Can you see anything in particular?"

"No."

"And you never look back, towards your son?"

"Yes, I do. I've even adjusted my rear-view mirror so I can see him."

"Is Lucien still asleep?"

The slight dark figure in the car seat. The intensity and depth of his sleep. Dark hair mixed with the shadows. His mop making for a peaceful crib.

"He's fast asleep."

"He's not moving."

"No."

"There's no movement at the back of the car?"

Diane peered round in her rear-view mirror.

"No, nothing."

"Turn back to the road. Where are you now?"

"I've just reached Porte Dauphine."

"Can you see the truck yet?"

A stab of fear in her flesh.

"Yes, I . . ."

"What's happening?"

In the torrential rain, the lines on the ring-road are shifting out of axis. No, it isn't the lines, it's the truck. The truck has just left its lane – it seems to be dragging the entire road in its wake. No indicators. No signal. It swerves through the streaming rain and lights . . .

Diane sat up. Sacher's voice went up a tone:

"What's happening?"

"The truck. . . It's . . . It's . . . swerving left."

"And then?" the hypnologist asked.

"It's now in the fourth lane."

"What are you doing?"

"I'm braking!"

"And what happens then?"

"My wheels get blocked on the rain puddles. I'm skidding! . . ."

Diane screamed. The power of this memory was tearing her apart.

The truck hits the crash barrier. Then pivots in a crashing of steel. The cabin spins, splashing its headlamps over Diane's bonnet.

"What can you see?"

"Nothing, I can't see a thing any more! There's mist all around me. I'm braking . . . I'm braking!"

The juggernaut wobbles under its own weight. A strident hissing of steam. The screeching of brakes. Scraps of iron shooting up above the mayhem . . .

Diane felt a hand grip her shoulder. Sacher's voice was now close by:

"And what about Lucien, Diane? Have you no time for Lucien?"

"Of course I have!"

Her memory returned with crystal clarity. Just before the impact, just before hitting the barrier at full speed, Diane had turned round towards her child.

The frail, sleeping face. Then suddenly the eyelids opening. Jesus! He's waking up. He's going to see what's happening . . .

"Tell me what you can see!"

"He's . . . He's waking up. He's woken up!"

Sacher was now yelling:

"Can you see his belt? Is it still fastened?"

The child's frightened face . . . His gaping eyelids . . . His pupils dilated with terror . . .

"Diane! Look at his belt! Is Lucien taking it off?"

"I CAN'T!"

Diane could no longer take her eyes off Lucien's expression. Sacher's voice crept in amid the terror:

"Look at the road, Diane! Look back at the road!"

Instinctively, she spun round. A scream rose up in her throat. A cry so strong that it threw her from the chair:

"NO!"

She crashed into the window blinds. Sacher ran after her.

"What can you see Diane?"

She yelled again:

"NO!"

"WHAT CAN YOU SEE?"

Diane could not reply. The psychiatrist's voice changed registers. Calmly, but icily, he ordered:

"Wake up."

She trembled, shot through with spasms, bent double on the floor by the blinds.

"WAKE UP! I ORDER YOU TO WAKE UP!"

Diane flipped into full consciousness. Her eyelids fluttered. One of the slats must have cut her head. Blood was pouring down her face, forming a smooth stream with her tears. Sacher was leaning over her.

"Calm down now, Diane. You're here, with me. Everything's fine."

She tried to speak but her vocal cords refused to function.

"What did you see?" the doctor asked.

Her lips twitched. Not a sound emerged. The psychiatrist asked again, his voice full of kindness:

"Was there a man in your car?"

She shook her mane of hair.

"No, not in the car."

The psychiatrist looked stupefied. Diane opened her mouth, but her words disintegrated in her throat.

Then a final vision burst into her mind.

At the very moment when she turned back to the road, she had seen him. To the right, about a hundred yards off, among the shrubs alongside the ring-road, a man was standing in the rain. Draped in a long khaki-coloured greatcoat, with a hood covering his bony features, he was pointing his index finger towards the juggernaut, as though this trivial gesture had set off the entire fury of the accident.

And Diane was sure that she had recognised that green coat. It was an anti-radioactive parka used by the Russian army.

CHAPTER 29

"More like that?"

The analyst added jutting cheekbones to the photofit. Diane nodded. It was midnight. For almost two hours, she had been working with an expert physiognomist at police headquarters at Quai des Orfèvres on drawing up a portrait of the ring-road killer. Despite Paul Sacher's urgent questions, Diane had left him and gone straight to the police station after her hypnosis session.

"And what about his mouth?"

Diane watched differently shaped lips parade in front of her on the computer screen. Fleshy pulp. Compressed ovals. Upturned corners. She settled for thin straight lips with deep furrows.

"And his eyes?"

Another parade started on the monitor. Diane picked diamonds with low eyelids and dark bluish irises – heavy bottles of ink, like those that clunk about in children's satchels. It was of course ridiculous to be that precise about a face she had seen from a distance of over 100 yards. And yet, she could have sworn that the killer's eyes, and all the other details she had selected, had really been like that.

"How about his ears?"

"He was wearing a hood," Diane replied.

"What sort of hood?"

"A rain hood, drawn tightly round his face."

The technician sketched in a dark shadow around the features, which perfectly reproduced a fabric cowl. Diane drew back slightly and screwed up her eyes. The face was now shaping up. A tall, bare forehead. Flint cheekbones bordered by wrinkles. Dark bluish eyes with an agate-like gleam below their drowsy eyelids. Diane scrutinised it, looking for something monstrous, a gleam of cruelty – but she had to admit that it was strikingly good-looking.

Suddenly, Patrick Langlois arrived. He glanced at the screen then looked at Diane. A worried crease was furrowing his brow.

"He looked like that?" he asked.

Diane nodded. The lieutenant stared dubiously at the portrait. At ten that evening, he had agreed to return to his office and call in a physiognomist to draw up the portrait. He sat down on a corner of his desk, clutching his inevitable cardboard folder.

"And you say that he was wearing an army greatcoat?"

"That's right. A Soviet one. With anti-radioactive fibres."

"How can you be so sure?"

"Five years ago, I went on a mission to Kamchatka in the extreme eastern part of Siberia. We were in a military camp and, quite by chance, I witnessed a nuclear alert drill. I saw their coats. They're done up diagonally and the collar snaps shut . . ."

The lieutenant gestured to her to stop. He asked the analyst to print the portrait, then stood up, before saying to Diane: "Come with me."

They walked through corridors dotted with half-open doors and dim skylights. She noticed various palely lit offices and messy dens with officers in them still at work.

Langlois unlocked a door that was covered in felt. He went inside and turned on a halogen lamp. The office was like a bailiff's lair, full of ancient paperwork and scraps of worn leather. He pointed at a chair, then sat down at the other side of the desk. He tapped his fingers for a while on the wooden surface before looking up at her.

"You should have told me, Diane."

"But I wanted to be sure."

"And I did tell you not to play at being Miss Sherlock Holmes."

"But you also told me to investigate Lucien."

He twitched his shoulder to readjust his coat, then declared:

"Let's sum up the situation. In your opinion, your accident was in fact attempted murder. Is that right?"

"Yes."

"The truck driver was put to sleep by remote control, by some exterior force or other . . ."

"By hypnosis."

"OK, by hypnosis. So how did they manage to make the crash happen at that precise point, when you were arriving in the opposite direction?"

"I timed the routes. The truck was coming from a truck park on Avenue de la Porte d'Auteuil, just by the Bois de Boulogne. All it had to do was set off just before I did. Given our respective speeds, it was easy to calculate where we'd meet up."

"But how did they make the driver fall asleep just at that moment?"

"It's possible to condition people so that they will suddenly fall asleep at a predetermined signal."

"And what was the signal this time?"

Diane wiped her hand over her forehead.

"The driver remembers the colour green. Maybe it was the military greatcoat. The man in the parka at the entrance to the tunnel . . ."

The lieutenant was still staring at Diane. His dark eyes were gleaming below his grey fringe.

"So, in your opinion," he went on, "the killers were working as a team."

"Yes, I reckon so."

"Like some sort of military operation?"

"That's a good way of putting it."

"And this whole operation had been organised just in order to kill your adopted son?"

She nodded, but suddenly gauged the absurdity of her version of events. Langlois leant towards her and pinned his eyes straight on her.

"And, in your opinion, why did they want to kill him?"

She pulled at some loose tresses and said:

"I don't know."

Langlois slumped back again into his chair and adopted a different tone, as though starting a fresh chapter:

"And now you tell me that Lucien isn't from Thailand. That he's in fact from Siberia or Mongolia. So how did he end up on the shore of the Andaman Sea?"

"I don't know."

After a moment's pause, Langlois declared in an embarrassed voice:

"Diane, I don't know how to put this, but . . ."

She raised her eyes at him over the curve of her glasses.

"But you think I'm crazy."

"You haven't got the slightest proof for all this. Not a single clue, nothing. It might all be just in your head."

"What about the driver? He doesn't understand why he fell asleep and . . ."

"What did you expect him to say?"

"And what about that man? The one with the protective parka? I didn't invent him, did I?"

The lieutenant tried a different approach:

"If I accept your version, was it the same people who killed Rolf van Kaen?"

She hesitated again.

"Yes, I think so. Maybe they were punishing him because he'd saved Lucien."

"And who told the acupuncturist about the accident?"

"I don't know."

"The BBK officers still haven't found the slightest trace of a call or a message about your son. Van Kaen seems to have been called in by the Holy Ghost."

What could she say to that? Langlois let her remain silent for a while, then softly added:

"I've been investigating you."

"What do you mean?"

"I've phoned round your colleagues, family, the doctors who treated you."

Diane spat out:

"How dare you?"

"It's my job. You're my only real witness in this whole case."

"Bastard."

"Why didn't you tell me that you'd had several courses of psychotherapy, hospitalisations and rest cures?"

"What am I supposed to do? Wear a badge?"

"I could have asked you this before, but ... why did you adopt Lucien?"

"Mind your own business."

"You're so young, and ..."

His face twisted into an embarrassed smile, making his wrinkles multiply.

"OK ... and so beautiful. That's what I was going to say." He twiddled his thumbs. "I always have problems saying that kind of thing. Diane, why did you apply for adoption? Why didn't you try instead to ... you know, find a husband, start a family, that kind of thing?"

She crossed her arms without answering. Langlois bent over and joined his hands as if to pray, like the first time they had met at the hospital.

"According to your mother, you have problems having ... stable relationships."

He let this observation float for a moment, then pressed on:

"She says you've never had a real boyfriend."

"Am I having therapy here or what?"

"Your mother ..."

"Fuck my mother."

The lieutenant backed his chair against the wall, leant his foot on the wastepaper bin and smiled.

"That's what I thought you'd say ... What about your father?"

"What are you after?"

Langlois shifted position and hunched himself up again.

"You're right. I should mind my own business."

Without drawing breath, Diane said:

"I never knew my father. In the 1970s, my mother lived in a

community. She picked some bloke in the group and got herself pregnant. They'd agreed to it. He's never tried to see me. I don't even know his name. My mother wanted to bring a child up on her own. To avoid the trap of marriage, and being a slave to a macho . . . All the ideas of the period. She was a real feminist."

She then added:

"Some people are love children. But I was a lust child."

A smile flickered over the lieutenant's face, that hint of irony that Diane so liked. The expression got to her because she knew that she was looking at forbidden territory. She suddenly felt she had been imprisoned in a glacier, walled up in a prison of frost. He must have sensed that sadness. He put out a hand towards her, but she dodged it.

He froze, let a few seconds go by, then launched into his conclusion:

"Diane, does the word 'tokamak' mean anything to you?"

She did not even try to hide her surprise.

"No. What is it?"

"It's an abbreviation. It means: electric magnetic chamber. It's Russian, in fact."

"Russian? So . . . why are you telling me this?"

Langlois opened his folder. A fax lay on top. Diane noticed the Cyrillic characters and a hazy identity photograph, made even hazier by the ink of the fax machine.

"You may remember I told you that there was a sort of black hole in van Kaen's past . . ."

"Yes, between 1969 and 1972."

"Exactly. Today, the BBK opened a safe deposit box which our doctor had at the Berliner Bank. This was all it contained."

He waved the photocopy.

"They're Soviet identity papers, which show that during the period in question, he worked in a tokamak."

161

"But . . . what is it?"

"It's a revolutionary research project. A nuclear fusion lab."

Diane immediately thought of the killer's anti-radioactive parka. She said:

"You mean nuclear *fission*, don't you?"

The lieutenant grinned fleetingly in admiration.

"You really are extraordinary, Diane. You're right. I did a bit of checking: normally, the activity in power stations is based on the fission of atoms, but the technique in question here is quite different and uses fusion. It's a direct imitation of what goes on in the Sun, and it was invented by the Soviets in the 1960s. It was an incredible project, involving the construction of massive furnaces that could be heated to 200 million degrees Celsius. I don't need to add that all this is a bit over my head."

"So what's the connection with what happened today?" Diane asked.

He turned the photocopy towards her and stared at her blandly.

"The tokamak where van Kaen worked was TK 17, the largest one the Russians ever built. The site was a complete secret. And guess where it was? In the far north of the People's Republic of Mongolia, on the border with Siberia. At Tsagaan-Nuur, just where our medic had decided to go."

She stared at the inky document, just making out the features of a young van Kaen, with a serious stare, on the dark photo. Langlois was thinking out loud:

"Why did he want to go back there? I've not the slightest idea. But it's all part of an overall pattern. That much is obvious."

There was a knock at the door. It was the IT engineer. Without a word, he placed several copies of the photofit portrait on the desk, then vanished. The lieutenant observed the face for a moment, then said:

"Let's see if your guy is on record. I don't expect he will be, but let's try anyway. At the same time, we'll start investigating the Turko-Mongolian communities in Paris. Check their entry visas and so on. That's one piece of good news, because there can't be that many of them."

He stood up and looked at his watch.

"Go and get some sleep, Diane. It's past one in the morning. We'll increase the guard on Lucien's room. Don't worry."

He took her to the door. Leaning on the jamb, he added:

"To be frank, I don't know if you're crazy or not, Diane, but this story is certainly far crazier than you'll ever be."

CHAPTER 30

White rooms. Pastel pictures. The red light on the answering machine.

Diane crossed her apartment without switching on the lamp. She went into her bedroom and slumped down on to the bed. The red gleam from the answering machine beside her was beginning to look like a bright beacon across a stormy sea. She remembered having turned off her mobile just before the hypnosis session. Maybe someone had been trying to get hold of her all evening?

She pressed "play" and listened to just the final message:

"This is Isabelle Condroyer. It's nine o'clock. I've got some great news for you, Diane! We've identified Lucien's dialect! Phone me back!"

The scientist then announced her mobile and home numbers. In the darkness, Diane memorised the latter and dialled it. After several rings – it must have been two o' clock

163

by then – a husky voice answered:

"Yes?"

"Hello. It's Diane Thiberge."

"Diane, ah yes . . ." She seemed to be dredging herself up from her dreams. "Have you seen what time it is?"

Diane had neither the strength nor the desire to apologise. "I've just got back home," she said. "And I'm too impatient."

"Of course, of course . . ." The voice was regaining its clarity. "We now know which dialect your son speaks."

Isabelle paused to get her ideas together, then explained:

"It's a Samoyed tongue, which is spoken only in the region around Lake Tsagaan-Nuur in the far north of the People's Republic of Mongolia."

Her child came from the same area as the nuclear laboratory. What did it all mean? Diane was incapable of thinking straight. Isabelle Condroyer went on:

"Diane, are you listening to me?"

"Yes, yes I am."

The ethnologist went on, with excitement now breaking into her voice:

"It's absolutely incredible. According to the specialist I consulted, it's an extremely rare dialect, spoken by a tiny ethnic group called the Tsevens, who are on the verge of extinction."

Diane was as silent as the grave. The scientist asked once more:

"Are you listening, Diane? I thought you'd be delighted to . . ."

"I'm listening."

"Then there are the two syllables which your son kept repeating on the cassette – Lu and Sian. My colleague is adamant that these two phonemes form a word that is extremely important in Tseven culture. It means 'a watcher' or 'a sentinel'."

"A . . . watcher?"

"It's a sacred term for a chosen child. A child who will act

164

as a mediator between his people and the spirit world, especially during the hunting season."

Diane repeated vaguely:

"The hunting season . . ."

"Yes. During that period, the child becomes his people's guide. He both attracts gifts from the spirits and decodes their messages in the forest. For example, he's able to detect which areas are favourable for the capture of certain animals. The child heads off, and the group's hunters follow at a good distance. He's a tracker. A spiritual scout."

Diane lay back on her bed. She could see her Paul Klee pastels, lined up on the wall, far far away, in her everyday life devoid of danger. The ethnologist sounded puzzled by her silence. After a few seconds, she said:

"I can just sense that there's a problem somewhere."

Diane, her neck buried in her hair, replied:

"I thought I was adopting an abandoned child in Thailand. I thought I was starting a home with a little boy who'd been unlucky from birth. Now I find I've got a Turko-Mongolian shaman, who watches out for woodland spirits. Where's the problem?"

Isabelle Condroyer sighed. She sounded disappointed. All her planned effect had come to nothing. She returned to her professorial tone:

"Your son must have stayed among his own people long enough to learn his role. Or at least its name. This is an extraordinary story. The ethnologist who deciphered the cassette would like to meet you. Would you agree to see him?"

"I don't know. I'll call you back tomorrow morning. On your mobile."

Diane curtly said goodbye then hung up. She turned towards the wall and curled up, like a gun dog. A vague hallucination was gripping her. She felt surrounded by shadows. She could

visualise the figures of anti-radioactive parkas that were following her, observing her in the rain. Who were they? Why did they
want to kill Lucien, the little "watcher"? What link could there
be between a child shaman and a nuclear site?

To counteract these confused images, she tried to remember
her allies. She summoned up the image of Patrick Langlois,
but she saw nothing. She tried to picture Eric Daguerre, but
no face appeared. She pronounced out loud Charles Helikian's
name, but no echo answered in her mind. She felt alone,
terribly alone. And yet, just when she was about to drift off
to sleep, she was struck by a thought. She could not possibly
be that isolated. Not in a torment of this importance.

Someone, somewhere, must be sharing this nightmare.

CHAPTER 31

Long ago, she had joined a theatre group in the hope of
breaking through her shyness and meeting other people. In
vain. But she had retained a strange nostalgia for the profession.
She remembered sets that smelt of sawdust and neglect. The
almost spooky atmosphere of a theatre plunged in darkness
where, on the brightly lit stage, would-be actors played Greek
tragedies or French farces in practically the same tone. She
remembered the attentive compassion of the other students,
as they silently followed their fellows' efforts. There was something occult or ritualistic in the discipline. As if the aim of the
rehearsals was to conjure up mysterious forces, unknown gods,
which perhaps could be summoned only by such forced speech
and borrowed gestures.

On the ground floor of Block A, the literature department

of the University of Paris X Nanterre, Diane slipped into Room 103 and immediately realised that she had entered a temple of similar quaintness. The room was about 60 feet long, windowless and almost empty, apart from rows of stacked-up chairs leaning against the right-hand wall. At the back, there was a dark stage edged with black curtains on which bits and pieces from a set stood out in the mote-filled air. A table, a chair, vague shapes made of dark polystyrene, suggesting a tree, a rock or a hill.

It was ten o'clock in the morning.

This was the only address that Isabelle Condroyer had been able to give her for her meeting with Claude Andreas, the ethnologist who specialised in Turko-Mongolian dialects.

She asked a few actors who were chatting by the stage. One of them was the man she was looking for. Tall and thin, he was wearing a polo-neck jersey and black leggings. He reminded Diane of a long, rolled-up parchment – which concealed the most esoteric alchemical mysteries. Diane rapidly introduced herself. He apologised with a smile:

"Please forgive the battle-dress, but we're rehearsing *Waiting for Godot.*"

He then pointed to a table to their right. "Come with me. I'll show you a map of the region. Your story is absolutely . . . incredible."

She nodded politely. That morning, she would have nodded at anything. The few hours she had slept had not been enough for her to recover her deep energy – that mix of aggression and nerves which was her surest means of existence.

"Coffee?" the man asked, brandishing a thermos flask.

Diane shook her head. Andreas handed her a chair, poured himself a cup, then sat at the other side of the trestle table. She observed him. His face looked as if it had been coloured in by a child: widely spaced turquoise eyes, an impish nose, a thin mouth formed by a single line – and all surrounded by a solid mass of greying hair that looked like a Play Mobil helmet.

He put down his cup and laid out a map. All the names were written in Cyrillic characters. He pointed out a region at the top of the page, near a borderline.

"I think that your son's dialect comes from this region, in the far north of Outer Mongolia."

"Isabelle mentioned an ethnic group called the Tsevens . . ."

"In fact, it's not easy to be that precise. These regions are extremely inaccessible, and were under Soviet domination for almost a century. But, judging by the pronunciation and the use of certain words, I'd certainly go for the Tseven dialect. They're of Samoyed origin and are an endangered group of reindeer breeders. I'm even surprised that there are any of them left. Where did you adopt your child? It's . . ."

"Tell me about the watchers and hunting."

Andreas smiled at her abruptness. He seemed to sense that today was not his day for asking questions. He gestured to apologise; his curiosity was as smooth as Chinese silk.

"Once a year, in autumn, the Tsevens organise a large hunt. And this hunting party obeys strict rules. The men must follow a young scout. The child fasts the night before, then at dawn sets off on his own into the forest. Only then can the hunters start following the "watcher", or "Lüü-Si-An", in the Tseven language."

The ethnologist's words faded away in Diane's mind. She stared hard at the map. Green. Huge stretches of green dotted here and there by the blue of a lake. These plain-lands of low grasses and endless forests of pine trees, these lakes of limpid water ran in Lucien's veins. She remembered the moments of closeness, with her child sleeping in the crook of her arm, with the magic word "elsewhere" ringing in her ears. Like a distant flood, Andreas's explanations worked their way back into her consciousness.

"There's no doubt about it," he was saying. "If your son really is a Watcher, if he's been chosen by his people, then that means he's a clairvoyant. Somebody with ESP, with perceptions that go above and beyond our normal senses . . ."

"Hang on there."

Diane stared at him coldly.

"You're telling me that people from his tribe think that children like him have supernatural powers?"

The man in the polo-neck grinned. His soothing gesture irritated her.

"No," he murmured. "That's not what I meant. Not at all. I think the Watchers really do have such powers. According to extremely reliable witnesses, they're capable of detecting things which are totally inaccessible to our usual five senses."

Too bad for her. She had landed another nutcase. A man who had spent too long on the other side of the world amid superstitious tribes.

"What sort of things do you mean?"

"For example, the Lüü-Si-An can predict the migration routes taken by moose. They can also foresee other spectacular events such as the appearance of shooting stars or comets. Or else, certain changes in the weather. There's no doubt about the fact that they're mediums. And their gifts can be detected at a very early age . . ."

Diane interrupted:

"You do realise what you're saying, don't you?"

With one elbow leaning on the table and the other hand slowly stirring his coffee, the man simply replied:

"There are two sorts of ethnologists, young lady. The ones that examine the spiritual behaviour of a group in purely psychic terms. To their minds, shamanic powers or possession can be explained by mental problems such as hysteria or schizophrenia. But for the second category, to which I belong, these events remain bound up with the actual world of spirits."

"But how can you believe that?"

A smile. A swirl in the cup.

"If only you'd seen what I've seen during my career ... In any case, it seems to me to be overly simplistic to reduce shamanic events to mental illnesses. It's as if a musicologist were concerned only by the volume level of an orchestra, and not about the music itself. The instruments are the materials. Then there's the magic that they give off. I refuse to write off a people's religious beliefs as pure superstition. I refuse to consider that sorcerers' powers are just mass hallucinations."

Diane fell silent. Her mind was flooding with memories. She, too, had witnessed strange ceremonies and bizarre occurrences, especially in Africa. She had never worked out her own attitude to such matters. But she was sure of one thing: there was a force at work at such times. And this force seemed to be both inside and outside mankind or, even more strangely, on our borderlines. As though it were a sacred contact, or some indescribable threshold that had been crossed.

Claude Andreas seemed to notice her dilemma. He whispered:

"Let's look at things from a different perspective, shall we? Let's forget about the spiritual or religious aspects of paranormal phenomena, and examine their concrete, physical side."

"No problem," Diane butted in. "There isn't one."

The ethnologist's voice deepened:

"You've never had a premonitory dream?"

"Like everyone else. A few vague impressions."

"You've never had a phone call from someone you've just been thinking about?"

"Pure coincidence. Look, I'm a scientist. I just can't swallow this kind of chance occurrence and . . ."

"You're a scientist. Then you know that there's a threshold beyond which chance becomes a probability. And then a second one where probabilities become axioms. You see, I've been interested in such matters for a long time. There are now scientific laboratories in Europe, the United States and Japan where the borders are regularly crossed, and where there are successfully repeated experiments using telepathy, clairvoyance or precognition. I'm sure you've heard of such things."

Diane volleyed straight back:

"Of course. But no matter how rigorous the protocols of these experiments might be, the results are still hard to interpret."

"Yes, that's what most scientists say. But then that's because the implications would be too important. If we admitted that such anomalies were well-founded, then we'd cast doubt over all of modern physics and our current state of knowledge . . ."

"We're getting off the point."

"No, we're not. And you know it. We're talking about mankind's hidden skills. We're talking about abilities that may be highly developed in your child. Abilities that will allow him to defy the normal laws of the known universe."

Such additional heights were too much for her. And yet, something held her back. A suspicion that such forces were perhaps the explanation for the entire story . . . Andreas went on, still in his carefully balanced tone of voice:

"Let's look at this from yet another angle. You're an ethologist, aren't you? You work on how animals perceive the world."

"So?"

"Many such perceptions seemed mysterious or incomprehensible to us for ages, because we misunderstood their morphological source. It was a mystery how bats flew in the dark, until we discovered the ultrasonic frequencies that they use as their guide. Each of these perceptions has a physical explanation. There's nothing supernatural about them."

"You're on my territory now. I don't see any relation between man's so-called psychic abilities and . . ."

"Who says that we know everything about our modes of perception?"

Diane sneered:

"The famous sixth sense . . ." She stood up. "Sorry, Monsieur Andreas. I think that the two of us are wasting our time."

The ethnologist also got to his feet and stood slightly in her way.

"Who says that the children we're talking about don't have an advantage we no longer have?"

"An advantage?"

He smiled – a comma on a sheet of paper.

"Innocence."

Diane tried to laugh, but her throat was choking. Claude Andreas went on:

"In the laboratories I've just mentioned, it has been shown that the best results are always obtained during the initial tests, and especially from children. Because they're more spontaneous."

"Meaning?"

"That our preconceptions are the main block on our psychic abilities. Scepticism, materialism and indifference can be seen as forms of pollution, corruption that eats into our spirit and prevents it from exercising its power. A sportsman who isn't convinced of his strength is always beaten. Our consciousness works in just the same way. A sceptic has no access to his own skills."

She manoeuvred round his long thin form and grabbed her coat. A doubt niggled at her. He asked:

"You don't have any children, do you?"

"I have Lucien."

"I mean, you've never given birth?"

She turned her head away so that he could not see the expression on her face.

"What do you mean by that?"

"All mothers will tell you the same thing: they communicate with their child during pregnancy. The foetus feels the sensations of the woman carrying it. But we're already talking about two distinct entities. Pregnancy is the birth of telepathy."

Diane felt on surer ground at this physiological level.

"Wrong," she said. "What you call paranormal transmission is based on real physical phenomena. If a pregnant woman hears some news that upsets her, then hormones such as adrenalin are produced by her body and are absorbed by the embryo via the blood stream. At this stage, the mother and child can't be considered to be separate. On the contrary, they're in constant physical contact."

"Quite. But what about after the birth? The same communication then carries on. This is a proven fact. The mother perceives her children's needs at the very moment that they experience them. The link hasn't been broken. What do you call that? The maternal instinct? Female intuition? Why not? But how far can intuition go? And where does premonition begin? Isn't this relationship also based on parapsychological communication, which is itself derived from love?"

Diane was wilting like a flower. These allusions to the mother/baby relationship were destroying her. But at the same time, they were filling her with a strange feeling of serenity. She, too, had experienced this. When better had she communicated with Lucien than at those enchanted, magical moments when he had been sleeping in her arms?

"Fine words, Monsieur Andreas, but I don't think I've learnt as much as I'd have liked about my adopted son's identity."

"You'll learn more when he regains consciousness. If he really is a Watcher, then he'll be able to convince you of the fact far better than anybody else can."

Diane nodded to him, then headed towards the door. She felt a knot of sadness tighten in her throat. The ethnologist called to her:

"Wait a moment."

He walked over to her and said:

"I've just thought of someone who should be able to tell you more about Lucien's psychic gifts. I don't know why I didn't think of him at once. He's travelled in the region. In fact, he's the only one of us really to have done so. I must admit that I've never been there. I've only worked on tapes recorded by deported political prisoners and scientists in the Gulag."

Andreas was already looking up this exceptional person's whereabouts in his address book. He jotted down the details on a small piece of graph paper.

"His name's François Bruner. He knows the Tsevens. And he also knows about parapsychology."

She took the paper and glanced at it.

"He lives in a museum?" she asked.

"Yes, he's the curator of his own foundation, out in Saint-Germain-en-Laye. He's immensely rich. Go and see him. He's a fascinating man. It'll only take you a couple of hours to get out there. And those hours will perhaps enlighten the rest of your life."

CHAPTER 32

Things now started to move extremely quickly.

She first visited the hospital in order to see Lucien's new room. Then she contacted the man at the foundation. She got a warm and somewhat excited reception. François Bruner was clearly intrigued by the presence of a Watcher in France. He also sounded impatient to air his memories and knowledge of a region that he had been one of the few Europeans to explore. They made an appointment for seven o'clock that evening.

Diane figured that it would take about an hour to get out to Saint-Germain-en-Laye in the western suburbs of Paris, and as a precaution she set off at 5.30. After crossing Neuilly, she avoided La Défense by taking the bypass and then turned on to the interminably long stretch of Route Nationale 13, which would take her to her destination.

On the way, she stopped asking herself questions about her investigations. Her mind was now entirely taken up by what Claude Andreas had told her, and its conceptual implications. As a confirmed ethologist, Diane Thiberge was also a rationalist. Even if she had been impressed by the strange effects of Rolf van Kaen's treatment, and even if her imagination had been set on fire when reading about acupuncture, she was incapable of forming any profound belief that would disturb her own view of reality.

Like most biologists, Diane thought that the world, no matter how complex it was, could be broken down into a series of physical and chemical mechanisms, composed of concrete identifiable elements, which operated along a scale leading up from the infinitely small to the infinitely large. Of course, she did not deny the existence of the human mind, but she saw it as a separate entity whose job it was to perceive and understand.

It was a kind of spiritual spectator, sitting in the dress circle of the universe.

But she also knew that this was an out-dated and simplistic view of the workings of the universe. It was a vision handed down by the pragmatists of the 19th century, which implicitly rejected the presence of the human consciousness in the logic of reality. But now more and more scientists felt that the mind, no matter how invisible and impalpable it might be, was as intrinsic a part of reality as a molecule or a neutron star. That consciousness would then, in some as yet unexplained way, be another link in the great chain of existence, just as much as any tangible element. Some even thought that consciousness was not a passive observer, but that it was a pure force directly influencing the objective world in a way that exceeded any actions it might directly carry out itself.

Diane concentrated on the road. She crossed Nanterre, where the lines of plane trees modestly concealed the poverty and the usual clutter of suburbia – that miserably dull mixture of old buildings, dreary detached houses and over-modern constructions that were glittering and cold.

In Reuil-Malmaison, the landscape changed. Poplars replaced the plane trees, with their long trembling branches of leaves, which seemed to suggest water and greenery. Near Malmaison, walled enclosures, covered with Virginia creepers rose up on Avenue Bonaparte, and gateways decked with delicate miniature roofs. The high dwellings seemed to be staring down at the flow of traffic beneath their walls like Grand Dukes, as though the haughtiness of the Château de la Malmaison had infected all of the surrounding houses and manors.

The traffic was flowing freely and Diane drove on without difficulty. Her mind now moved back to her inquiries. Was Lucien a Watcher? Did his alleged powers really exist? Were they connected with some hitherto unsuspected dimension of reality? Rolf van Kaen had said: "This child must live". He must have known the truth about Lucien – and what he had known must explain why he had intervened. What had the doctor expected from her son? She had no idea, but she was now sure that she was heading in the right direction. She had to concentrate on this question of psychic abilities – even if she did not believe a word of it all, even if for her such stories were pure mumbo-jumbo. Right now, it was not her convictions that mattered, but those of the killers by the ring-road and of Rolf van Kaen.

In Bougival, she rejoined the banks of the Seine and saw long wooded islands in the distance, reflected on to the surface of the water. A bridge took her over the locks of Bougival, and she stopped for a moment to contemplate the boats, the barges and the ripples of the gentle stream. The air seemed full of an odour of weekends away, of picnics, of quiet days snatched from the tumult of Paris.

She drove on for another 20 minutes and reached the main square of Château de Saint-Germain-en-Laye. The church clock was chiming a quarter to seven. She went up the broad avenues, which still seemed to echo with carriages and royal parades, then turned towards the forest, as Bruner had instructed her to do. She was now in a network of narrow streets, edged by high walls full of gypsum shards and covered with zig-zagging ivy. The sun was going down over the town, and the trees seemed to be trembling with impatience, as though thrilled by the approaching darkness. Diane decided not to turn on her headlamps in order to appreciate the light outside, which seemed to be growing more intense and clear the further night fell.

Finally, she parked in front of a tall black gateway. When she got out of her car, she was struck by the freshness of the air, like an invisible covering that quickened her senses and concentrated her mind. It was seven o'clock in the evening, and darkness was nearing in great folds of shadows. Diane thought once more about her little boy. She suddenly felt certain that, in a few hours' time, she would be in possession of a part of his secret.

CHAPTER 33

She pressed the button on the intercom, which was topped by a CC camera. No answer. She tried again. Nothing. Without thinking, she pushed open the gate, which slowly swivelled on its hinges. She buttoned up her buckskin coat, whose collar rose up in a fleece of fine wool, and walked down the gravel drive. For several minutes, she went on past endless lawns. Everything was deserted. All she could hear was the slight whispering from the automatic hoses, unseen in the gloom. Finally, above a grassy knoll, she saw the dark mass of the museum.

The building presumably dated back to the beginning of the 20th century. It was made up of powerful lines and crude angles, and looked as if it had been melted down from some bulkier materials. Verdigris of bronze. Ochre of brass. Black shadows of steel. Diane approached it. The double front door was closed. The metal-framed windows showed no sign of any light inside. She remembered that François Bruner had told her to walk round the building to the back door, which led directly to his private quarters.

The gardens were surrounded by darkness and trees. Their tips, shaken by the gusts of wind, produced a symphony of rustling foliage. When she reached the rear of the building, she rang at the door. Still no answer. Had the professor forgotten her? She turned back towards the main gate, but then changed her mind. Instead, she headed once more towards the front door, leapt up the steps and tried to pull it towards her.

Quite unexpectedly, it opened.

Diane entered a shadowy hall. Then the first room. She would never have imagined that a menacing façade would conceal such an interior. The walls, floor and ceiling were white. They refracted the moonlight that filtered in through the windows with great intensity. Such bare surfaces were already beautiful to look at, but then there were the paintings. Splashes of bright, radiant colours like openings leading into another world. Diane walked on and realised that the foundation was holding a Piet Mondrian exhibition.

She was far from being an art expert, but she particularly liked this Dutch painter, and she owned several reproductions of his work. As she advanced along the walls, she identified paintings from his early period: the crazed windmills with fantastical wheels, standing out against brightly lit skies, as though auguring the imminent destruction of the physical world in a final conflagration.

In the second room, Diane found more canvases from the same period. But this time of trees – winter trees with sombre, hieratic forms, scattered with reflections, harbouring the most insane shadows in the cracks of their bark. Then there were trees in spring – black and red, as though injected with fire and ready to melt in a pastoral explosion. Diane had always thought that this burning sap and those flaming skies contained a promise of what was to come. They already concealed the utter transformation of Mondrian's art.

She supposed that this transformation would begin in the third room.

She crossed the threshold and smiled as she took in the work of his maturity. As of the 1920s, Mondrian's trees had slimmed out, turning into pure lines, and his skies had become ordered and smooth, thus summoning up the artist's true springtime. But not with flowers and fruit. With squares and rectangles of the most absolute geometrical purity. Henceforth, Mondrian had painted only ascetic compositions, bringing together strict figures and monochrome colours. People spoke of a "break" in his work, but Diane disagreed. So far as she was concerned, this was a natural alchemy. From the incandescent lyricism of his early work, from the backgrounds of his fire-and-earth land-scapes, the artist had extracted the essence of his pictures. The perfect geometry of line and colour.

Diane was so dazzled that the absurdity of the situation never crossed her mind. Here she was, alone, in a private museum, where she was supposed to be meeting a specialist on a Turko-Mongolian tribe. And she was freely strolling around, unwatched, amid paintings that must be worth several million dollars each. She walked into another room, already anticipating the sight of the famous *Boogie-Woogies*, the painter's final compositions, produced in New York . . .

A rustling made her turn round.

Two figures were standing in the room she had just left. She thought they might be watchmen, but then changed her mind at once. The two men were both dressed in black, with night vision devices, and holding assault rifles topped with laser sights. In a flash of certainty, she knew that these were the accomplices of the killer on the ring-road. They had followed her here, and were about to finish her off in this gallery.

She glanced behind her. There was no door, no way out. The men were advancing slowly, their guns sending off red beams. Absurdly, she was struck by the beauty of the scene: the paint-ings reflecting the clear bluish moonlight, the two assailants with their beetle-like masks, and the scarlet dots dancing in the chalky shadows.

She felt no fear. Already another thought had dawned on

her. In some obscure way, she had been waiting for just such a combat for the last 15 years. It was her moment of truth. The chance to show that she was no longer that vulnerable little girl in Nogent-sur-Marne. Once again, she pictured the willows and the glassy lamplight. She felt the cold earth beneath her hips. The two shadows were still approaching. They were now just a few yards away.

Another step.

She saw one of the gloved fingers press the trigger.

It was too late.

For them.

She leapt forward and chopped with the side of her hand – *sao fut shou*. The first man was hit in the middle of the throat and curled up. The second raised his gun, but she had already spun round, shooting out her leg with her foot bent upwards. The killer was thrown backwards. She heard the "phut" of a gun with a silencer tearing out a lump of stone from the wall. Then, all was silent. Nothing moved. Trembling from her head to her toes, she went over to one of the inert bodies.

A metallic blow knocked her flat. A wave of pain shot through her. She tried to raise herself on to one knee, but a second blow hit her in the face. Her glasses were knocked flying. Blood filled her mouth. She collapsed, realising too late that there must have been a third man hidden in a blind angle of the room. Blows started raining on her. Clenched fists, kicking boots, rifle butts. The other two must have come to and were joining in the fun. Her arms wrapped round her head, all Diane could think about was her nose-ring. Don't let them tear out her nose-ring. As if in answer, she felt a warm flood pour over her lips. She bent double and felt for her nose. The skin had been split and her nostril was gaping open. The very thought sapped the last of her strength. She curled up tighter and no longer reacted even to the blows that were still showering down.

There was a brief respite. She crawled, putting out one hand towards the wall. She did not have time to reach it. A toe-capped shoe hit her in the guts, completely taking her breath away. Her entire being craved for air. A moment of suspense, of pure nothingness in time and space passed, then Diane felt herself slump back down, vomiting in spasms. A gloved fist grabbed hold of her hair, turned her over and pushed her shoulders back against the concrete. The man removed a knife from a holder that was strapped on to his thigh. The jagged blade approached, gleaming in the light of the moon. Diane's last thought was for Lucien. She asked his forgiveness. She was sorry that she had not been able to defend him. That she had not understood his secret. That she had not been able to stay alive and so give him all the love that . . .

A shot reverberated.

Distant, muffled, deep.

The killer's expression changed beneath his night vision device.

His features seemed to disintegrate, then freeze.

Once again, a shot broke the silence.

The killer doubled over, his lips curled in an expression of amazement.

It took Diane a moment to realise that she had been the one who had fired. While she had been mentally saying her farewell prayer, physically she had had no desire to die and had been looking for another way out. And so her hands had fumbled around and found the killer's automatic which was slipped into his belt. With her thumb, she had undone the holster strap. Her fingers had then removed it, pointed the barrel upwards and pressed the trigger.

She fired again.

The body juddered heavily. He slumped down towards her, while she was already drawing to one side, her arm out, trying to get a shot at the other two attackers. They had gone. All she could see were the dots from their lasers moving through the room where *Compositions* had been displayed. She shoved away the corpse, picked up the assault rifle and crossed the room diagonally. She crept into a blind angle and pulled the gun back against her. Despite her state of shock, despite the blood staining her clothes, her body was making a firm statement: they weren't going to get her. One way or another, she'd get out of this alive.

She glanced towards the exit, then had an idea.

The paintings.

The paintings were going to save her life.

She had already used night vision devices when observing nocturnal predators in the African brush. She knew that their field of vision was bathed in green light, and provided only a very weak contrast between colours. She thought of the red sights – those dots the killers would have to aim at and which would appear less distinct in that green halo. If she managed to destroy the clarity of those dots by walking in front of red paintings, then she would win a few seconds' respite, which might be enough for her to cross the room.

Without another thought, she set off. She immediately saw the two beams converge towards her, then go past. Just as she had thought, the two killers had taken up position on either side of the exit door. She immediately headed for *Composition Number 12*, which contained a red square, then leapt towards *Composition with Red, Yellow and Grey*. The scarlet points were fluttering around her, like killer flies. She ran on. Her idea was working. The killers could not see a thing. She passed the crimson tones of the next painting and saw the opening into the next room. She had made it.

At that moment, she slipped. Her head hit the concrete. Stars exploded in her skull. Pain stabbed her ankle. She turned round at once. The killers were after her. She bent round on to her right side and pressed the trigger of the rifle which was propped up under her arm. The recoil sent her flying back against the wall but, in the blue gleam of the silencer, she saw a shadowy form twitching in the throes of death.

The second assailant stopped. She fired again. But the miracle did not happen twice – the gun jammed. She dropped the rifle, then with her right hand grabbed the automatic which she had slipped into her belt and aimed at the man, who was now no more than a yard away. Once again a ghastly click resounded, instead of the expected blast. Diane was staggered. It was all over. The killer had her in his sights. She spotted his thigh, remembered the commando knife and leapt at the holder. She pulled out the knife dived forward and plunged it into his throat, screaming to avoid hearing the metal slicing into the living flesh.

Instinctively she jumped to one side, leaving the blade in the open wound. Pale and covered with blood, she stepped back. As soon as her foot touched the ground, she felt a piercing pain. She started hopping, like a huge heron paddling in a reddish pond, then she noticed the door to her right, which now materialised before her as if by magic. She pointed herself in the right direction, hopped over towards it, slipped, fell again, dragged herself up on to one knee then pushed it open. Amid her teeming thoughts, she realised that she must finally have reached François Bruner's private quarters.

CHAPTER 34

She could not hear any noise, not the slightest sound. She came to a halt and leant back against the wood, feeling it press into her coccyx. Had those men with insect heads killed François Bruner, or had he managed to escape?

Diane tried to get up. Just that simple movement was extremely painful. Her body was cooling down. In a few minutes' time, all the blows she had received would deepen and form clots of pain. When that happened, she would no longer be able to lift a finger. She had to act quickly, and find an exit route.

She limped on into the darkness, holding one hand to her nose, which was bleeding profusely. Without her glasses, the world she moved through was made up of vague shapes and indistinct masses. Only the pale night lights over the doors guided her steps. At the end of the corridor, she came across a rectangular room with a shallow pool. To cross this obstacle, it was necessary to take an iron gangway which passed just above the water, then climb up a few steps before entering the next room. Without stopping to wonder about such strange architecture, Diane forged ahead. She crossed the bridge of metal slats, noticing that below her cups of oil with lit wicks were floating on the pool – like burning waterlilies.

She reached another room, this time perfectly square. It was followed by a precise rectangle. The moonlight filtered through a long bay window, lighting up the rows of sketches – sacrificial rites drawn in Indian ink, the paper of which seemed to have been tortured by the pen.

In other circumstances, Diane would have been struck by the beauty and rigour of the place. But right then, she was in tears and struggling not to spread about too many red stains, which fell to the ground as heavily as hot wax. She began to despair of ever finding a way out when, at the end of a corridor, she spotted a door that was ajar, through which a chink of light shone. The mirrors and a dripping tap told her that it was a bathroom. An intermediate solution. She could rinse her face and then move on when she had freshened herself up a little.

The room's decorations were of jade and bronze. Sculpted blocks and plates of these materials were all over the place. Thick stained-glass panels covered the walls, like screens at the seaside. A bath had been dug out from a green, polished stone. The towels on their black rails looked like variously shaded seaweed. And everywhere, by the windows, along the tiles and on the supports of the basin and other porcelain, those pairs of parallel bars of bronze multiplied indefinitely in the infinite play of mirrors.

She spotted the wash-basin and turned on the tap. The jet of cold water felt good. Her bleeding slowed, her aches and pains started to fade. She then noticed that the water at the bottom contained tiny transparent fibres – or minuscule membranes. She looked up and noticed that the dry bathtub to her right also contained a scattering of these diaphanous particles. She thought they might be some sort of plastic film but, when she picked one of them up, she realised that it was organic.

Skin.

Human skin.

She turned back and automatically tried to find the source of this new monstrosity. What she found dragged a scream from her throat. In the middle of the room was a black marble massage table. On it lay a body, covered by an emerald-green shower curtain. Through the transparent folds, she saw that it was a tall thin man. Was it François Bruner? With a trembling hand, she pulled the curtain on to the floor. The body abruptly appeared in all its nakedness.

The man was lying, with his arms crossed on his chest. He

had been positioned like a statue of a knight in a church built in the Middle Ages. But the comparison did not stop there. That old, scrawny body, with its bones sticking up under the skin, seemed to be connected in some aesthetic way with the symmetrical decorations of the bathroom, just as sculpted knights shared an inescapable solemnity with Gothic architecture.

The body seemed quite literally to be peeling. Thin strips of skin hung from its various members, or crumpled up across its torso, revealing new pinkish skin underneath. Diane tried to hang on to the little reason she had left and walked over towards it. She was in for another shock. Now that she was a mere yard away from the body, she could clearly see the abdomen – and it bore a tiny incision, just below the sternum.

François Bruner had been killed in the same way as Rolf van Kaen.

What did it all mean? Who had carried out the execution? The three bastards with rifles? She did not think so. It was not their style. And why would they then have placed their victim on a block of marble?

She drew back and noticed what she should have seen at once, and which shed a new light on all the different elements – the old man's face, his flinty cheekbones, his high bare forehead, his heavy eyelids.

She recognised him. It was the man in the anti-radioactive parka.

The man who had tried to kill her and her son three weeks ago.

CHAPTER 35

Apart from the bed, her hospital room contained no furniture. It was plunged in darkness. Lying down, with one arm shielding her eyes, all Diane Thiberge could see in the light under the door were the feet of the policeman standing guard. She looked at her watch. It was six o'clock in the morning. So she had slept all night. She closed her eyes again and tried to piece her thoughts together.

At the precise moment when she had recognised the snakeskin man in the jade and bronze bathroom, flashing lights had emerged from the entrance to the park. The police. Diane's initial reaction was to feel strangely relieved. It was the first rational thing that had happened all night. So, there were alarms in the museum. The paintings were protected. Of course they were. The fight had set off an alert, a call to the police station in Saint-Germain-en-Laye. She then remembered the dead bodies and her fingerprints on the guns she had left there. Who would believe that a young woman had managed to eliminate three hit-men armed with assault rifles? She could avoid having to admit that she had killed them. After all, she had used their own weapons . . .

With a final effort, she had gone back to the room with *Compositions* and laid out the bodies and weapons in a way that corresponded with how the bullets had been fired. She also found her glasses. They were intact. This discovery had helped to focus her ideas. She pulled off the men's gloves and pushed their hands on to the rifle butts. When the police arrived in the museum, all they had found was a prostrate woman, surrounded by dead bodies and paintings by Mondrian.

The next part had been even easier to act out. In the car, all she had to do was allow her genuine feelings to overflow.

The investigators had answered as many questions as they asked, deducing all by themselves that the three men had killed one another after attacking her. Oddly enough, they seemed convinced that she had not been the reason for their fight. Diane did not press the point, but she sensed that the police had already identified the killers.

At the clinic in Vésinet-Le-Pecq, the night duty doctor had been reassuring. All she had were cuts and bruises. The pain in her left ankle quite simply came from a slight sprain. Her only real wounds had been caused by own jewellery: her nose-ring had been torn out, slicing her nostril as far as the cartilage. As for the pin in her navel, it had been rammed so far down into her flesh that it had taken half an hour of surgery under local anaesthetic to retrieve it.

She was then sedated and placed in a locked room. She had fallen asleep at once but now, drowsy with pain killers, she felt as though she was floating painlessly in space. Just an intense lucidity, which was almost unreal in its clarity, filled her. It allowed her to draw up a list of the facts she had uncovered.

On 22 September 1999, François Bruner, the curator of the Bruner Foundation, seasoned traveller and specialist in the Tsevens and parapsychology, had tried to murder Lucien when he and his accomplices had set up an accident on the Paris ring-road.

On 5 October 1999, Rolf van Kaen, the chief anaesthetist in the paediatric surgery department in the Charity Hospital, had carried out some unofficial treatment on her child, in the hope of saving him by using acupuncture.

These two men knew something about Lucien which remained an enigma to Diane – perhaps the true nature of his power, which meant that the former had wanted to kill him, while the latter had wanted to save him.

What was this power? Diane pushed aside this question that

she had no hope of answering and turned to the concluding fact, which was perhaps the most terrifying of them all.

Another killer was at large.

The man who had crushed Rolf van Kaen's heart in the kitchens of Necker hospital during the night of 5 October 1999. The man who had carried out exactly the same operation inside the body of François Bruner on 12 October 1999, presumably just a few hours before Diane had arrived at the museum.

The bolt clicked open. Two uniformed officers came into the room, illuminated by the light of day. In their wake, a tall figure appeared. Diane grabbed her glasses. She recognised the black pullover and the steely hair. Patrick Langlois looked even more bristly than usual.

Looking at Diane's bruised face, he whistled in admiration, then said threateningly:

"Don't you think it's about time you stopped fooling around?"

CHAPTER 36

In the lieutenant's car, Diane's first instinct was to pull down the sunshade and examine her face in the mirror. A blue bruise ran down from her left temple to her chin. On the same side, her cheek had swollen, but without managing to deform her bony features. The white of her left eye, which was veiled with blood, gave her a strange asymmetrical stare. As for the cut to her nose, the stitches and dark scabs were hidden beneath a haemostatic dressing. It could have been worse.

Without a word, Langlois pulled away and joined the flow of morning traffic. In the entrance hall, he had stopped to give her a long dressing down for her imprudence and for working as a loner. Diane hoped that he was not going to start again – her migraine would not have coped with it. Instead, at the first red light, he extracted a pile of papers from his cardboard folder and tossed them on to her lap.

"Read this."

Diane did not even look down. A few minutes later, keeping his eye on the traffic, the lieutenant asked her:

"What's the matter now?"

She was still staring at the road.

"I can't read in cars. It makes me puke."

Langlois groaned. He seemed to have had enough of Diane's little ways.

"OK," he sighed. "I'll explain. This is your photofit's file."

"François Bruner?"

"His real name was Philippe Thomas. Bruner was just an alias. But that's common practice with spies."

"Spies?"

He cleared his throat, eyes fixed on the road, then launched into his explanations:

"When we put his face into the scanner we immediately got a result, from the DST – the counter-espionage boys. François Bruner, also known as Philippe Thomas, had been on their books since 1968. At that time, our man was a professor of psychology at Nanterre University. A real prodigy. Not yet 30, and an authority on Carl Gustav Jung. I should have remembered his name." He smiled briefly in apology. "I, too, had my Jung period. Anyway, in 1968, Thomas, who came from a wealthy family became one of the main Communist agitators during the student riots."

Diane pictured the man in the green greatcoat, raising his index finger, his face swept by the rain, in the shrubbery bordering the ring-road. Langlois went on:

"In 1969, he vanished. In fact, he was so disappointed by the failure of the revolution that he decided to go over to the East."

"What?"

"He crossed the Iron Curtain. He moved to the land where the people had triumphed – the USSR. I can just imagine his father's face when he heard the news – he was one of the greatest business lawyers of the post-war era."

"And then?"

"We don't know much about what he got up to over there. But it's certain that he travelled to the regions we're interested in, and especially the People's Republic of Mongolia."

Langlois's car was now speeding up the left-hand lane of the Nationale 13. The morning sun was reddening the tips of the trees, seeming to distil a purplish mist in the air. Diane absent-mindedly stared at the park gates, the huge manor houses and the bright buildings behind the screens of foliage. Yesterday's journey now seemed unreal and vague to her. The lieutenant continued:

"In 1974, he reappeared. Thomas knocked at the door of the French Embassy in Moscow. By then, he'd had a belly full of the Soviet system. He begged the French government to take him back. At the time, this was quite possible. And so it was that the deserter to the East ended up demanding political refugee status five years later . . . in his own country!"

Langlois waved the file in the air, as though brandishing an exhibit in court, while holding the steering-wheel with his other hand.

"And I swear, every word of it's true!"

"What happened then?"

"Then things get confusing again. In 1977, Thomas resurfaced again, guess where? In the French army as a civilian adviser."

"In what field?"

Langlois laughed.

"As a psychologist. He worked in an army health centre specialising in aeronautic medicine. In fact, the institute was a cover for interrogating and debriefing Communist dissidents who wanted political exile in France."

Diane was beginning to understand the turnabout.

"You mean he was now questioning Soviet deserters?"

"Exactly. After all, he spoke Russian. He knew the USSR. He was a psychologist. Who else was better qualified to gauge their honesty and credibility? In fact, I don't think he had any choice. He was paying his debt to the French government."

Langlois fell silent for a few seconds. Then, once he had got his breath back, he finished his tale:

"During the 1980s, the ice started to melt between the East and the West. The era of Glasnost and Perestroika began. The military authorities relaxed their grip on Thomas. He was now free again. He wasn't even 50 and he'd just inherited a huge family fortune. So he didn't go back to teaching. Instead, he started investing his money in Old Masters and set up his own foundation, where temporary exhibitions are held – like the one of Mondrian right now. Thomas no longer hid his past as a deserter. On the contrary, he started giving lectures on the regions of Siberia that he had been one of the very few Europeans to have visited and on the tribes that live there, such as the Tsevens, your son's people."

Diane thought this over. So much new information was making her head spin. Names. Facts. Roles. The elements fitted together, and a logical whole was beginning to emerge.

"And what's your opinion about all this?" she finally asked.

He shrugged.

"I'm back with my original theory. This story goes back to the Cold War. It's a settling of old scores. Or scientific espionage. I've had additional confirmation since I started looking into that nuclear power station over there . . ."

"The tokamak."

"That's right. So far as I understand, nuclear fusion hasn't been properly worked out yet, but it's a very promising technique. It's probably even the future of the nuclear industry."

"Why?"

"Because existing power stations use uranium, and there's only a limited quantity of that on earth. Whereas controlled fusion uses products taken from seawater. In other words, it's a limitless source of energy."

"And so?"

"So, there's a lot at stake here in terms of international interests. I reckon this whole business is about some secret to do with tokamaks. Van Kaen worked over there. I'm sure Thomas must have been there, too, while he was travelling in Mongolia. And I've just learnt that the boss of TK 17, Eugen Talikh, also came over to the West in 1978. He then settled down in France, with Thomas's help!"

"This is getting a bit too complicated for me."

"It's getting a bit too complicated for all of us! But one thing's for sure: they're all there."

"Who do you mean?"

"The ex-members of the tokamak. Either in France, or elsewhere in Europe. I've started a search for Eugen Talikh. He worked in the first controlled fusion power stations that were built in France in the 1980s. He's now retired. We've got to get to him as quickly as possible. If we don't, then I wouldn't be surprised if we didn't find his corpse some place, with his heart in ribbons."

"But . . . why are these men being murdered? And why like that?"

"No idea. All I'm sure of is that the past is coming back to haunt them. Something that not only explains the murders, but also pushes these scientists to go back East."

Diane looked surprised. Langlois picked up another xeroxed sheet of paper.

"We found these notes in Thomas's flat. They're plane times for flights to Moscow and the People's Republic of Mongolia. He was planning to go there, too. Just like van Kaen."

Diane felt the effects of the pain killers surge up inside her. Returning to her own worries, she asked:

"And what about my adopted son? What's he got to do with all this?"

"Same answer: I've no idea. Just in case, I looked into the foundation, through which you adopted Lucien . . ."

Diane started.

"And what did you find out?"

"Nothing. They're as pure as the driven snow. In my opinion, this was all organised behind their back. I reckon the child was simply placed near the orphanage so that they'd pick him up."

Langlois suddenly turned left and took the dual carriageway. He changed up and drove at full speed down a long tunnel, punctuated by lines of helixes. Diane no longer felt so sure about her hypotheses. She might have got it all wrong. This whole business might have nothing to do with Lucien's supposed powers, and instead be focused on nuclear research. But then, as if to relaunch the parapsychological angle, Langlois added:

"There's one more thing about Philippe Thomas that bugs me . . . It seems that he was an intellectual with psychic powers."

Diane held her breath.

"What do you mean?" she murmured.

"According to several reports, he was able to move things from a distance, twist bits of metal . . . You know, Uri Geller stuff. It's what specialists call psychokinesis. But if you want my opinion, I reckon he was more of a conman, an artful dodger."

"Hang on. You mean he could influence matter by thought?"

The lieutenant glanced in amusement at her.

"That's funny coming from you. I thought you'd crack up laughing at the idea. As a scientist, you . . ."

"Just answer my question. Could he influence matter?"

"That's what the counter-espionage records say. He's supposed to have undergone several tests, under an extremely strict protocol – for instance, with sealed objects under Pyrex covers – and . . ."

She swallowed the shock. That moment was a turning point in her investigations: either she ignored the paranormal aspect and dropped the entire affair, or she plunged into that obscure world and took a giant leap forwards.

For, if she accepted that Philippe Thomas had such powers, then this cleared up the final mystery about the accident. Using his mental powers, the man in the greatcoat had opened Lucien's belt from a distance.

By clicking open its metal buckle.

Diane was devastated. She refused to believe in such a thing, and yet if she did accept it then everything fell into place. For example, how could a man with such powers fail to believe that a child Watcher was gifted too? And wasn't it now clear that the motive for the murder was Lucien's suspected psychic faculties?

"Diane? Are you listening to me?"

She re-emerged from her thoughts.

"Yes, yes of course I am."

"The Saint-Germain squad have identified the three men who killed each other in the museum."

"Already?"

"They knew them. At the end of August, Thomas had three men brought over from the Federation of Russia. Three former elite soldiers – or *spetsnaz* – who'd started to work as bodyguards. Officially, he took them on to increase security in his foundation during the Mondrian exhibition. But according to our sources, these men had already worked for the Russian mafia. We don't know how Thomas unearthed them, but we can suppose that he still had contacts in Russia."

Diane thought over the violence of the previous night: the steel-capped boots raining kicks on her face, the figures jolting from the force of their own bullets. How on earth had she survived? Langlois went on:

"So we can assume that Thomas actually took them on to organise the 'accident' on the ring-road. But I think he was also scared of something. Or someone. Such as the murderer who managed to infiltrate the museum yesterday afternoon . . ."

He turned towards her, carefully articulating his conclusions:

"I mean *our* murderer, Diane. The one who killed Rolf van Kaen. It's then easy to piece together last night's events. At the end of the day, the three Russians found the body and put it in the bathroom. Then they started arguing, probably about money – they must have been tempted to take a couple of paintings away with them. At that moment, you showed up, which really put the cat among the pigeons. Then they shot each other right in front of you. That's what you told the police, isn't it?"

"Exactly."

"It just about fits."

Diane peered round at him.

"What do you mean, *just about*?"

"We still have to reconstruct the scene, to check the positions of the bodies and the trajectory of the bullets. I hope for your sake that it all stands up."

Langlois sounded distinctly incredulous, but Diane pretended not to notice. Her thoughts were becoming increasingly confused. Amid these dark waters, another memory floated up: Philippe Thomas's ghastly pink corpse, covered with a veil of dead skin. She asked:

"Do you know anything about Thomas's illness?"

Langlois looked astonished.

"You saw the body?"

She had blown it. It was too late to go back.

"Yes, after the massacre," she said. "I went into the apartment and . . ."

"Then you went back into the museum?"

"That's right."

"And did you tell the Saint-Germain police that?"

"No."

"This is a ridiculous game you're playing, Diane."

"But Thomas was ill, wasn't he?"

The lieutenant sighed.

"It's called desquamation. It's a particularly virulent form of eczema, which causes the skin to peel right off. From what I understand, Thomas regularly changed his skin."

Diane suddenly thought that he might have worn that great-coat to protect his mutating body. But her thoughts started to blur. She was beginning to feel sleepy. She noticed that they'd reached Porte Maillot. The traffic had got a lot thicker and Langlois promptly placed his magnetic flashing light on the roof. He then sped up Avenue de la Grande-Armée with his siren blaring. Diane slumped down into the seat and let the feeling of torpor wash over her.

When she woke up, the car was crossing Place du Panthéon. For some strange reason, she liked the idea of having slept while the lieutenant had been driving through Paris at full speed. Patrick Langlois parked at the beginning of Rue Valette and removed a folded newspaper from his coat pocket.

"I've saved the best bit for last, Diane," he said. "Just look at yesterday's *Le Monde*."

She immediately saw the article in question on the right-hand page. The paper gave a detailed report of the murder of Rolf van Kaen on the night of Tuesday, 5 October. The journalist also mentioned Lucien's miraculous recovery and the accident that had happened to Diane Thiberge, the stepdaughter of Charles Helikian, an "important personality" in the world of business and politics. Langlois commented:

"Your stepfather is livid. He phoned the Prefect."

Diane looked up.

"Who leaked this?"

"No idea. The hospital, probably. To be honest with you, I couldn't really give a damn. It might even help us. It'll certainly provoke some reactions."

Langlois rapidly filed away his papers. Diane noticed that he also had a leather pencil case containing yellow highlighters and coloured crayons. She softly remarked:

"You're not very 'high-tech', are you?"

He raised an eyebrow.

"Not so fast. There's a time and a place for everything. For my inquiries, I prefer the old way – with pen and paper. I keep my computer for the rest.

"What rest?"

"My daily existence, fun, and feelings."

"Feelings?"

"The day I have something important to confide in you, Diane, I'll send you an e-mail."

She got out of the car. Patrick Langlois did so too. Above them, the huge dome of the Panthéon looked like a massive sea-shell. The lieutenant came over to her.

"Diane, there's something I wanted to ask you. If I say 'Heckler & Kock' or 'MP5', does that mean anything to you?"

"No."

"What about a 45-calibre Glock?"

"They're guns, are they?"

"Yes, the ones the Russians used to kill each other. And you've never used automatic weapons during your field-trips in the brush?"

"I study big cats. I don't shoot them."

The face below the silvery fringe lit up in a smile.

"Good. Perfect. I just wanted to be sure."

"Sure of what?"

"That you had nothing to do with that carnage. Now, go and get some sleep. I'll call you this evening."

CHAPTER 37

The first thing she noticed on returning to her flat was the red light on the answering machine, which was once again flashing in her bedroom. She was not sure if she wanted to see who had called. The last time she had listened to her messages, a chain reaction had been set off, throwing her as far as the Bruner Foundation and into the ensuing violence.

She crossed the living-room into the bedroom, then sat down on her bed, just as she had done the day before, observing the red light as it beat like a heart. Already she could imagine the messages from her mother, as brief as rifle shots. Or calls from her scientific colleagues, who had seen the article in *Le Monde*, which made her think that she had not set foot in her office since . . . How long had it been?

The phone rang. Diane jumped up from her duvet. Without thinking, she picked up the receiver.

"Mademoiselle Thiberge?" an unfamiliar voice asked.

"Who's asking?"

"My name's Irène Pandove. I'm calling about the article in yesterday's *Le Monde* concerning the death of Rolf van Kaen."

"How . . . how did you get my number?"

"You're in the phonebook."

Diane dumbly repeated to herself: "That's right, I am in the phonebook."

The woman went on, in a calm serious tone:

"You aren't taking enough precautions. That's a big mistake."

The hairs rose up on the nape of Diane's neck.

"Whatever do you mean?"

"I'd like us to meet. I've got some information that might interest you."

"Did you know Rolf van Kaen?"

"Only indirectly. But he's not the person I want to talk about."

Diane remained silent. She thought: "Maybe this woman's nuts, maybe she just wants to toy with my nerves. Maybe she wants money." She then asked:

"So who do you want to talk about?"

"I want us to talk about the little boy I adopted five weeks ago."

Her flesh chilled even more. She pictured her veins – her nervous system filling up with icy sap.

"Where . . . where did you adopt him?"

"In Vietnam. At the Huai Orphanage."

"Via the Boria-Mundi Foundation?"

"No, Pupilles du Monde. But that's irrelevant."

"What is relevant?"

Irène Pandove ignored her question and went on in the same cool tone:

"You'll have to come and see for yourself. I'm stuck here. My son hasn't been very well for the last few days."

In Diane's arteries, the sap hit absolute zero.

"What's the matter? Has he had an accident?" she asked.

"No, he's feverish. His temperature keeps soaring."

She thought of Lucien and his attacks of fever, and of Daguerre reassuring her that everything was all right. Then she suddenly remembered the intuition that had struck her two days ago when falling asleep: someone, somewhere, must be sharing this nightmare. Irène Pandove went on:

"Come and see me. As soon as you can."

"Where are you? What's your address?"

The woman lived over 600 miles away near Nice, in a town called Daluis. Diane jotted down the address and directions. She was already thinking. First flight in the morning. Hire car. No problem. She assured her:

"I'll be there tomorrow, around noon."

"I'll be expecting you."

Her voice was smooth, still full of an off-putting gentleness. Suddenly, Diane had a flash of inspiration. She asked:

"And what did you decide to call your little boy?"

The smiling sweetness sounded even more present.

"If you want to know that, then you obviously haven't worked out what's going on yet."

Diane murmured, as though blowing out a candle, giving up all hope:

"Lucien . . ."

CHAPTER 38

Diane landed in Nice at 8.30 a.m. Half an hour later, she was driving into the hinterland without even having seen the Mediterranean. Along the Nationale 202, rows of houses, shopping centres and industrial areas stretched out up into the hills and down into the valleys. Then, near Saint-Martin-du-Var, the landscape changed, the constructions became more spaced out, darker greens and rock started to predominate, and finally the mountains surged up.

She was now driving in pure high-altitude country: pine trees hugging sheer slopes, black domes poking up into the sky; the deep dark traces of dry streams ... The day was overcast. She was far from softness, sea air and Provençal flora. Stone and cold were now in control of the landscape. Diane followed the same road, as it rose up above the dry bed of the River Var.

After an hour's drive through endless winding lanes, she at last found the place she was looking for: a lake at the bottom of a valley, like a mirror reflecting the light and the storm. Its surface wavered between grey and blue. Ripples ran across it, like steel blades. All around, there was a maze of emerald-green. Tall conifers seemed to slice their way into the clouds. Diane shivered. She could feel the cruelty of each tip, each reflection, each detail, sharpened by the feverish sun that was breaking through the black sky.

Around a bend, she spotted a clearing. A dark, cramped hamlet of log cabins lay a few yards from the bank. Irène Pandove had said: "A U-shaped ranch, by the lake." Diane swerved and took the road that snaked down to the valley.

A sign indicating the Ceklo Holiday Camp loomed up, pointing to a gravel drive leading downhill. At each curve, Diane saw the shapes of the cabins becoming clearer. It was a large collection of brown buildings, surrounded by a fence. To the left, pastures stretched out, presumably used for horses in the summer months. To the right, brightly coloured constructions could be seen in the adventure playgrounds.

She parked her car beneath the boughs of the pine trees, then breathed in the fresh air deeply, full of the scent of resin and the fragrance of cut grass. Silence reigned. Not the slightest bird call, or insect noise. Was it because of the storm? Struggling to fight off her apprehensions, she walked over to the main building.

She went through the log gate and across a covered courtyard with a deal board floor and a row of small coat hooks to the right. Through the bay windows to the left, a large patio could be seen, enclosed between the two wings of the ranch and leading up to a hill bordered by a section of the forest. The smooth waters of the lake presumably lay beyond. The silence and emptiness seemed to weigh even more heavily in this place designed for crowds of kids.

She came across a corridor that led to a series of rooms. Cautiously, she went down it. Blankets woven with naïve designs had been hung on the wooden walls, like paintings. Through the open doors, Diane also spotted tom-tom stools, pink or violet wallpaper and rice paper lampshades. The whole place reeked of the 1970s. Her mother would have loved it.

She went on, through games rooms full of ping-pong tables and table football. In another room, there was a large television and a scattering of cushions. At the end of the corridor, she stumbled over a little cage, flowing over with grain and sawdust. She bent down to examine it. Its occupant – a guinea-pig or hamster – had also packed its bags.

She finally reached a vast office – the ranch's administrative centre. Her apprehensions now turned into certitudes. Once again, she had arrived too late. A hurricane had hit the room. The oak table had been overturned, the chairs flung all over the place, the cupboards emptied, files torn apart and folders scattered across the floor.

Diane thought of Irène Pandove, but dared go no further into her thoughts. At that moment, she noticed some frames fixed to the wall, which had escaped the carnage. The photos showed the same two people: a blond woman aged about 50, and a short Asian man, with a wrinkled face and a devilish grin. In other pictures, they were kissing. In others still, they were holding hands. These images gave off a strangely joyful existence. And a slight touch of humour – the woman was a good five inches taller than the man, who was always wearing a double-breasted Astrakhan coat, with its collar turned up. Without knowing why, Diane grabbed one of the frames, smashed it against the edge of the table and pocketed the photo.

As she looked up, she noticed a framed article. It had been published in the magazine *Science* – a learned journal specialising in scientific breakthroughs – and was signed Dr Eugen Talikh. Diane jumped. Langlois had mentioned that name. He had been the boss of TK 17, before going over to the West in 1978. She took it down from the wall and glanced over the text, which was written in English. She understood very little of it – it was about nuclear physics and hydrogen isotopes – but she was not surprised when she saw the photo of the author: the same as the little slant-eyed man in the lovey-dovey shots. She was standing in the deserter physicist's home.

This discovery led to further flashes of inspiration. Firstly, she now knew that Eugen Talikh was not a Caucasian Russian, as she had supposed, but an Asian probably from Siberia. She also realised, but without grasping the possible implications, that this man and his wife had just adopted a young boy who came from the region of the tokamak. Why? What was he expecting from the child? Diane broke the second frame, and pocketed the article as well.

A further search revealed photocopies of flight timetables to Ulan Bator, via a stopover in Moscow, but with no trace of a reservation. Like Rolf van Kaen and Philippe Thomas, Eugen Talikh was also getting ready to go back to the People's Republic of Mongolia, and without having decided on the exact date.

At that moment, she heard groaning.

Diane spun round. Someone was moving behind the upturned desk. She approached it, then gingerly looked over.

A woman was lying on the floor under a pile of papers amid a dark pool. Diane could not remember having ever seen so much blood – not even at the Bruner Foundation. The body was completely still and turned towards the wall. Diane recalled an old Jewish custom, where dying people were laid so that they were looking at the wall and so would not see death face to face.

She went around the table and gently took hold of the victim's shoulder, turning her head towards her. She immediately recognised the woman in the photographs. Her abdomen had been ripped apart into two folds of flesh. The wound started at her navel and went up to her breasts. Her clothes and skin were stuck together into a nightmarish mush. Diane tried to summon up her compassion, but no feelings were able to allay her own fear.

She thought of the murderer of van Kaen and of Thomas. This wound was not his *modus operandi*. Had he slipped up? Had Irène struggled too much?

What she now saw flung her into even greater terror.

In her right hand, Irène Pandove was holding a knife with a jagged edge, which was dripping with blood.

She suddenly propped herself up on an elbow and murmured:

"He was here . . . I had to avoid . . . I had to avoid talking."

In total amazement, Diane realised that Irène must have cut her guts open in front of her attacker. She had killed herself so as not to talk, so as not to reveal some information which otherwise he would surely have forced her to tell him. Despite her confusion, Diane noticed how beautiful her face was beneath her dishevelled chignon and hair matted with blood. Irène repeated:

"I had to avoid talking."

"Who to? Who was here?"

"Those eyes . . . I couldn't have resisted them . . . I had to avoid saying . . . Where Eugen is . . ."

"Those eyes"? Whose could they be? The heart crusher? Other henchmen despatched by Thomas? Or someone else? But first things first. Diane bent down and asked Irène:

"Lucien . . . Where's Lucien?"

The dying woman grinned. Despite everything, she seemed almost pleased to see Diane and to hear that innocent name. She moved her lips. Her mouth was filling with blood. Diane wiped it away with her sleeve. The gurgling formed into a single word:

"The peninsula."

"What?"

More dark clots flowed out. The lips mumbled:

"On the lake. The peninsula. That's where he always goes . . ."

Forcing back her tears, Diane tried to reassure her:

"You'll be all right. I'll call an ambulance."

Irène grabbed Diane's wrist. Blood spurted from between the clenched fingers. Diane closed her eyes. When she opened them again, it was all over. Irène's irises were staring up into eternal emptiness.

CHAPTER 39

Diane went round the right wing of the ranch, climbed over the fence and went up the winding track that led to the hillock topped with firs. It had started to rain. In the lightning, Diane caught glimpses of the glittering surface of the water. She rushed down the slope and arrived at the bank. A long hedge of trees and reeds lay between the path and the lake. It was impossible to break through. Instinctively, Diane turned to her right and started to run.

Soon the earth became softer. The smell of vegetation grew heavier and, at the same time, more vivacious and sharp. The waters of the lake seemed to have seeped in between the grasses, turning them into a large swamp. As she ran, Diane immersed herself in this transformation. The green clarity of the thickets, the laziness of the lascivious, wild flora which allowed increasingly frequent transparent gaps to appear between the folds of grasses and leaves. It seemed to her that the water here was the fragrance of the earth. A finger on a nape of humus, slipped beneath hair of rampant weeds . . . And she mentally thanked this landscape for its vigour and omnipresence, because it prevented her from thinking about anything else.

To her left, a space appeared between the shrubs: there was a path. Diane took it, moving in below a vault of greenery. She no longer felt the rain, but instead the thousandfold caresses of the rushes, reeds and twigs. Only then, after this long descent, did she reach the bank and discover the surface of the lake. From where she was standing, it looked more like a sea. A glittering grey expanse that was spluttering in the rain, with no apparent banks or limit.

Then she spotted the peninsula.

A few hundred yards to her right, a sandy spit of land extended from the bank, slipping over the waters as far as a rustling grove. A freshwater peninsula, built not even on salt, just on transparency. Could the boy be hiding under the trees?

Diane removed her glasses, then took off her shoes. She tied them together with their laces and hung them over her neck. Then she set off once more. Before her eyes, the world was hazy, green, fantastic. Now she was wading through the waves of the lake, mixed with grasses and earth. She dug her legs knee-deep in the cold maw of its depths, feeling the striking contrast with the lukewarm shower. She was drenched, streaming, saturated. She felt simultaneously sucked in by the lake and oppressed by the rain.

Finally, she reached the bushes of the peninsula. She dived in beneath the willows, pushing aside the grasses, bent double, breathless, feeling each gap, sensing each leaf. Where was Lucien? She elbowed her way forwards. Watery mouths with green greedy lips opened beneath her to trap her. She was submerged up to her hips, rowing with her arms to keep going. Around her, she spotted the furtive scales of fish that wandered into that herbaceous maze. Suddenly, the earth grew firmer again beneath her feet. She had got to the end of the peninsula without seeing a thing . . . She stopped at once.

The child was there.

He was sitting with his back to her, about 20 yards off, at the very tip of the land, facing the heavens.

She could not see him very clearly, but she immediately felt relieved. Physically, he did not look like her Lucien. Without admitting it to herself, she had imagined some strange story of twins, of clones, of the monstrous products of secret Soviet experiments, that had been carried out in the tokamak.

But the two children were quite different. This one had to be a good two years older than hers. She got her breath back and took a step towards him. He remained sitting cross-legged. Diane walked in front of him and saw that his eyes had rolled back and his face was scarlet. He was in a trance. His limbs seemed harder than metal bars. He was trembling, but this movement was an almost imperceptible electric shudder. Like a wave imprisoned in his body.

Diane put out a hand to his forehead. It felt red hot. Never had she imagined that somebody could reach such a temperature.

She stepped even nearer, then stopped. A sanctuary had been laid out in front of him: a circle of white stones with a dense pyramid of twigs in the middle, and some tiny ribbons tied on to them. At the top of these branches, a small narrow skull had been placed. The freshly skinned skull of a guinea-pig or hamster. Diane thought back to the empty cage in the ranch and realised that the boy must have sacrificed the animal in some shamanic rite.

CHAPTER 40

"We have observed an extremely high level of neuromuscular excitation, which causes these fits of muscular spasms and contractions . . ."

The hospital once again.

A doctor's discourse once again.

It had taken Diane only a few minutes to go back to Irène Pandove's house, to wrap the child up in the blankets that were hanging from the walls and then find an old raincoat for herself. She had then driven at full tilt to Nice and headed for the emergency department at Saint Roch hospital. It was only 2.00 p.m., but she felt as though she had aged several years.

The doctor went on:

"He's also running an exceptionally high temperature. It's almost reached 106°. For the time being, we have not found any physical explanation for this. An external examination proved fruitless. The blood test shows no sign of any infection. We'll have to wait for the other results. There is also the possibility that it might be a chronic condition. But these aren't the symptoms of epilepsy, so . . ."

"Is he in danger?"

The man standing by the desk looked as if he had slept in

his white coat. It was completely ruffled. He adopted a doubtful tone:

"Normally speaking, no. At his age, there is not much risk of convulsions. And his fever is already starting to come down. As for his cataleptic state, that seems to be wearing off too. I'd say that the child appears to have had some sort of . . . attack, and that now the worst is over. We'll now have to work out why."

Diane pictured to herself the circle of stones and the skull balanced on the twigs. Should she mention this to the doctor? Should she explain that the boy had presumably been in a shamanic trance? His next question brought her back to reality:

"And what is your exact relationship to the child?"

"I've already told you. He's the adopted child of one of my friends."

The doctor looked at the file.

"Irène Pandove. Is that right?"

She had given the name on arriving in emergency admissions. She wanted them to be able to identify the child after she had gone. He went on:

"And where is this Madame Pandove?"

"I don't know."

"What about the child? . . . You just found him like that? Was he alone?"

Diane went through her story again: a visit to her friend, the empty house and discovering Lucien in the swamp, but without mentioning the dead woman. She had no qualms about such half-truths. In a few minutes' time, she would be out of there. Do you turn round when you have your back to the precipice?

The doctor looked sceptical. He stared intently at Diane's drenched raincoat, the marks on her face and the dark scar on her nose – she had lost her dressing. She suddenly said:

"I have to make a phone call."

She had lost her mobile during her safari round the lake. The man pointed at the phone in front of him.

"Help yourself. I'll . . ."

"It's personal."

"Then go into the next office. My secretary will dial the number."

"Really, I'd rather be alone."

The doctor grumbled and waved vaguely towards the door.

"There are pay phones that way, in the main lobby."

Diane stood up. He frowned and added:

"I'll wait for you here. We still have a few things to discuss."

She smiled.

"Of course. I'll be back in a minute."

As soon as she closed the door behind her, she heard him lift the receiver. "The police," she thought. "The bastard's calling the police." She slipped rapidly down the corridor.

In the main lobby, she bought a phone card at the newsagent's kiosk. Then she took refuge in a phone box and called Eric Daguerre. A fresh worry was bugging her. What if her Lucien, for some strange reason, had also gone into a trance? She sensed that such events must happen simultaneously. There was a system of echoes between the two children and their symptoms.

Diane was put through to the switchboard. The surgeon was operating. As a second best, she asked to speak to Madame Ferrer. Her suspicions were confirmed. Lucien had just suffered a huge rise in temperature, linked with symptoms of catalepsy. But everything seemed to be returning to normal now – his temperature was going down, and his muscles were relaxing. Dr Daguerre had asked for a series of tests to be made. They were now awaiting the results. In conclusion, Madame Ferrer added that Didier Romans was desperately trying to get in touch with her.

"Where is he?" Diane asked.

"Here, in the office."

"Then put me through to him."

A minute later, the anthropologist's voice proclaimed:

"Madame Thiberge, you absolutely must come in to the hospital!"

"What's happened?"

"Something extraordinary."

"Do you mean Lucien's trance?"

"Yes, he was in some sort of a trance. But now there's something else."

"WHAT?"

The man suddenly seemed to realise how much he must be worrying her.

"Don't worry," he said at once. "Your child's not in any danger."

Diane repeated, emphasising each syllable:

"What's happened?"

"It'll take too long to explain on the phone. You'll have to come here. It's very . . . visual."

Diane concluded:

"I'll be there in three hours' time."

She hung up. Suddenly, the overheated hospital air was stifling her. She felt the wet locks of her hair sticking to her temples, her collar soaked with sweat. Another gulf now opened in her thoughts: how had these two children managed to have the same fit at a distance of over 500 miles? And what new phenomenon had the anthropologist discovered?

It was 2.30 p.m. There was no time to lose. She glanced at the main doors. She was expecting a squad of gendarmes to arrive at any moment. Men asking her about where she had found Lucien, and about the death of Irène Pandove, whose body would soon be discovered.

She had to get back to Paris. She had to see her son. She had to tell all this to Patrick Langlois – he alone could cover for her, protect her against the legal system. She called the lieutenant on his mobile. He did not even give her time to speak.

"For Christ's sake, where are you?" he yelled.

"In Nice."

"What the hell are you doing there?"

"I had to see someone . . ."

His voice sounded relieved.

"I thought you'd done a runner . . ."

"Why would I do that?"

"With you, anything can happen."

Diane paused for a few seconds. Suddenly, in that silence, she felt more trusting and close to him than she ever had done before. She said rapidly, to avoid bursting into tears:

"Patrick, I'm in the shit."

"Tell me something new."

"I'm not joking. I've got to see you. To explain."

"How long will it take you to get to Paris?"

"Three hours."

"I'll be expecting you in my office. I've got news for you, too."

"What?"

"I'll tell you when I see you."

Diane sensed a new hint of anxiety in the lieutenant's voice. She pressed him:

"What is it? What have you discovered?"

"When I see you, Diane. Watch out for yourself."

"Why?"

"Because you might be more deeply involved in this business than you imagine."

"What . . . what do you mean?"

"I'll see you at the station."

She left the phone box and headed out through the automatic

doors. Suddenly, she stopped. Outside, the avenue was coated with dry, wrinkled red leaves. When Diane got into her car, she felt as though it was autumn itself that was about to ambush her.

CHAPTER 41

Diane Thiberge reached Necker hospital at about eight that evening. Didier Romans was waiting for her in a highly nervous state. She immediately asked to see Lucien, but the anthropologist replied:

"Everything's fine. Honestly it is. We have something more urgent to deal with."

They walked over to the Lavoisier block, which made her feel extremely anxious. That place was too full of atrocious memories.

When they went inside and headed towards the Computerised Tomography Scanner room, her anxiety doubled. She saw the white walls and blinding strip-lights pass by – and it was like another direct route to violence. As they walked, the scientist told her:

"During my initial investigations, I'd already spotted something along these lines. But I didn't want you to panic."

Diane almost burst out laughing. Everyone seemed to have decided that, no matter what happened, she should never be allowed to worry. It was a sort of peace of mind conspiracy.

They went into a room crammed with computer terminals and monitors. Romans sat down in front of the main console, exactly as the pathologist had done on the night when Rolf van Kaen had been murdered. He clicked his mouse and said:

"Pictures will speak louder than words."

Diane leant on one of the metal bars. She was expecting

to see the German doctor's mutilated innards appear on the screen. But, to her great surprise, what she saw was the contrasted outline of two hands. A child's slim, white hands, looking as though they had been polished by the brilliance of the computer screen.

Without a word, Romans typed in some instructions and the same image appeared again, but this time palms forwards. He then zoomed in on the fingertips, revealing their prints.

"As part of my anthropological study, I had already examined Lucien's dermatoglyphics. I noticed some scars, which looked rather old, under the top layers of the epidermis. As though . . . as though the skin had grown back over them, follow me?"

The image of the grooves enlarged. Diane could now make out some tiny vertical or oblique lines that did not look like the usual patterns to be seen on fingerprints. The anthropologist added:

"Madame Ferrer noticed that, when his temperature rises, these strange marks become more pronounced. The geometric lines remain white, while the fingertips turn red. Daguerre saw this, too, and called me in. I then realised what was happening."

The fingerprints were now filling the entire screen. Their geometric designs were clearly visible. They looked like stripes, or crossings out . . .

"These scars are indeed situated under the surface of the epidermis. And, I reckon that they stay white because they were caused by burns. They're made up of dead skin where the blood no longer circulates. In this way, increases in temperature accentuate the contrast between the irrigated flesh and the cold scars. It's a fairly classic phenomenon. Some marks like this are more clearly visible during a bout of fever."

Diane examined the fine lines once again. They looked distinctly like writing. But at the same time, the letters seemed half erased – and also inverted, as though meant to be read in a mirror. Apparently, the anthropologist was following her line of thought.

"My first idea was that they were letters, which had been etched there with a red-hot nib," he explained. "But they're the wrong way round. So my next theory was that they had to be printed on to a piece of paper, and thus turned back the right way round in the process. I tried rubbing them on an inkpad . . ."

The image on the screen changed. The grooves in the skin were now soaked in ink.

"And here's the result. As you can see, the writing's still inverted. There's no solution to the problem."

Diane gripped the metal frame. A flame seemed to be spreading through her. Romans pressed a key, bringing up a different presentation on to the screen. This time, the hands were completely black so that the tiny white marks stood out clearly.

"Here's an infra-red shot. The writing's much plainer this way, because of the difference in temperature between the living flesh and the scar tissue. It was by using this approach that I finally figured out the answer."

"And?"

"They aren't Roman letters. They're Cyrillic characters."

A blow-up of the signs from each of the child's fingers filled up the screen: figures and letters from the Slavic alphabet.

"And . . . and what do they mean?" Diane asked huskily.

"It's a date, written in Russian. I've had it translated."

Another click. Another image:

20 OCTOBER 1999

The anthropologist concluded:

"The boy was carrying a message."

He then added, his voice trembling with fear:

217

"And a message that was engraved there by fire, and is 'programmed' to appear during bouts of fever, because of the heat being given off by the body. It's ... absolutely incredible. In fact, the only way to read this date is when Lucien has a temperature."

Diane was no longer listening to his explanations. Her own answers were crowding her mind. She was certain that the second Lucien had been burnt in the same way. That the "Lüü-Si-Ans" all had a date on their fingertips that appeared when they were in a trance. They were messengers. But who was this date meant for? And what did it mean?

She rapidly came up with a working hypothesis: there was no doubt but that the date had been addressed to men such as Rolf van Kaen, Philippe Thomas and Eugen Talikh. Men that had been part of the tokamak team, and who had been waiting for this call to return to that distant land.

Her mind was now racing. These children had arrived incognito in Europe, via adoption organisations which, she supposed, were not in on the plot. Such bodies were simply one of the instruments used by the network – just as she had been used when she had adopted Lucien. What is more, if Irène Pandove had succeeded in adopting Eugen Talikh's Watcher, Rolf van Kaen had not been so fortunate. It had fallen to Diane Thiberge, a young unknown woman, to be his recipient. That explained why the German acupuncturist had said: "This child must live." He was quite simply waiting for the message to appear, and it never would have appeared if Lucien had died before having his trance.

Another fact now fitted into the puzzle. By creating the accident on the ring-road, Philippe Thomas, the Marxist spy, had for some mysterious reason tried to exclude van Kaen from the meeting by preventing him from finding out the date. It was crazy, absurd and terrifying, but Diane was sure she was right. Not only were these men linked by their past, but a strange rivalry had made one of them try to blackball one of his fellows by killing his messenger.

Diane now glimpsed a further fact. Somebody else was also trying to stop the members of the tokamak from returning. And in the most radical way possible – by crushing their hearts.

From the bottom of this pit, Diane could nevertheless see two bright lights.

Firstly, she now felt that Lucien – "her" Lucien – was out of danger. They had tried to stop him from delivering his message, but the date had now been revealed. So he was no longer of any importance to them. He had completed his mission.

Oddly enough, the second light concerned the nature of the mutilations that the children had suffered. They were horrible, abject and disgusting – but they were not magical. There was nothing paranormal about them. The Watchers were quite simply little boys who been marked for life.

Staggered and exhausted, she suddenly remembered Lieutenant Langlois and the news he had for her. She felt sure that the revelations awaiting her were going to fit into this vertiginous structure and give it even greater coherence. She mumbled to the anthropologist:

"I'll be back later."

CHAPTER 42

Diane filled in the visitors' register and went through the metal detector. It was 10.00 p.m. and the corridors of the Prefecture were deserted and silent. The smell of leather and old papers was even more striking than usual. These odours were so strong, so heady, that they reminded her of the stench of wild animals. She felt as though she was walking in a whale's belly. The red leather lining the doors made her think of organic walls and the slanting shadows from the stairwell of baleens – those horny blades that stand up vertically in the monster's maw.

Diane reached Office No. 34. A small card was marked with the name Lieutenant Patrick Langlois, but she had already recognised the felt covering of the door. A line of white light emerged from the room. She knocked on the door, but the softness of the fabric dampened the noise. With two fingers, she pushed it open.

It seemed to her that she could no longer be terrified or prone to any other emotion. She thought that she had finally woven a delicate invisible shawl around herself, as impenetrable as those spun by spiders and used to make bullet-proof jackets. She was wrong. In that room bathed in darkness, except for a small halogen lamp that was dipped down lighting up the varnished surface of the desk, a fresh wave of panic seized her.

Patrick Langlois was slumped over his desk, his head turned to one side. His dark eyes still had their wicked charm, but they were no longer moving. Nor did the body in the chair move. Diane's first instinct was to run away. But once she had crossed the threshold, she changed her mind. She glanced up and down the corridor. Nobody. She went back into the office, closed the door and went over to the corpse.

The policeman's face was swathed in blood, which was gradually drying like a layer of tarmac. Diane forced herself to breathe slowly, through her mouth. She grabbed two pieces of paper and gingerly lifted up his head, peering down at the wound which was below his chin. His throat had been slit. The cut opened out like a black beak revealing the dark oozing mush of the larynx. For some strange reason, Diane was managing to keep a certain distance from this ghastly scene – and from what it meant. She was simply counting the seconds, as each one summoned up a fresh question: who had killed the lieutenant? Was she still following in the wake of the solitary murderer – the crusher of hearts? Or was it an accomplice of the Russians from the Foundation? What took her breath away was the audacity of the thing. The murderer had dared kill a police lieutenant in the very midst of the Prefecture.

She remembered his file: those papers which he had always had with him and which contained a part of the truth. She started moving round the blood-stained objects on the desk and flicking through the stained papers. As though repeating a litany, she kept muttering: "Lucien ... Lucien ... Lucien ..." She was doing all this for him. He was her strength, her source of life. She opened the drawers, rummaged through the folders, checked each document and detail. She searched his bag and the two filing cabinets that stood there in the shadows. Nothing. She found nothing. She realised that she was just going through the motions. That the killer must have taken everything. That he had killed him with the intention of destroying all the proof and evidence.

She looked once more at the face of the man whose silvery hair was reflected in the mirror of blood. On the phone he had said: "You might be more deeply involved in this business than you imagine." Whatever had he found out? She felt terrified and lost. She thought of Irène Pandove. Of Rolf van Kaen. Of Philippe Thomas. And of the three men she had killed. What was the explanation for such carnage? And what was she doing in these killing fields? She saw herself as a deadly bloom, destroying everyone that approached her. Burning tears trickled down her cheeks. She fought them back and flitted like a shadow back along the corridor.

As she went, she thought of the visitors' register she had filled in a few minutes before. She was trapped. There, in black and white, she had been the last person to have seen Patrick Langlois alive. She had to run away. And fast.

Diane crossed the inner courtyard of the Prefecture and discreetly left by a side entrance. She strode rapidly along Quai des Orfèvres, then Quai du Marché-Neuf. She then accelerated towards Notre Dame, before stopping in front of Hôtel-Dieu. The hospital was brightly lit. Through its high windows, the lights were casting their halo over the pale façade, thus creating a strange festive atmosphere that was both solemn and frivolous.

The thought of Lucien cut into her. She could not just abandon him, even if she was now convinced that he was out of danger. When he woke up, who would welcome him back to the land of the living? Who would look after him? Who could he talk to until Diane came back – if she ever did? She thought of the young Thai girl she had employed and had had to lay off after the accident.

Then she had another idea. She found a phone box and dived inside. Through the panes of glass, she could see the tarpaulins covering the scaffolding around Notre Dame, like massive screens in the darkness. At the bottom, the gleaming hanging lamps looked like figs stuffed full of light. For a second, she thought of acupuncture, with its points that freed the human body's vital energy. In the topology of Paris, the forecourt of Notre Dame must be such a point. A place of liberty and total absence.

She dialled the number of a mobile phone. Three rings, then a familiar voice answered. Diane simply mumbled:

"It's me."

Immediately, there came an answering deluge of insults and complaints. Sybille Thiberge was firing on all cylinders – anger, indignation, compassion – while mixing in a pinch of indifference to show that, come what may, she was still in control of the situation. What was more, Diane could distinctly hear the sound of a dinner party going on in the background.

She butted in:

"OK, mother, I didn't call to have a slanging match. Now, listen carefully. I want you to promise me something."

"What?"

"I want you to promise to look after Lucien."

"Lucien? But . . . of course, what do you . . ."

"You must take care of him. Nurse him through to full recovery. Protect him, whatever happens."

"What on earth are you talking about? You . . ."

"Promise you will!"

Sybille sounded stunned.

"All right . . . yes, I promise. But what about you? What . . .?"

"I've got to go."

"Go? What do you mean, go?"

"Go away for a while. It's something I can't get out of."

"What, for your work?"

"I can't tell you."

"Look, my darling, Charles told me that you were investigating . . ."

Diane had been mad to trust her stepfather, he had immediately spilt the beans to his wife, and they must have talked long and hard, and with great compassion, about Diane's mental instability. She pictured them as two intertwined vipers. They were pathetic.

Without bothering to explain the situation, Diane mentioned the second Lucien. A little boy aged about seven, who had recently been adopted and who had just lost his new mother. Diane dictated the name and address and made her promise to ask after the second orphan, too.

She should also have warned her mother about what was probably going to occur during the next few days, police suspicions, and a string of corpses left in her wake. But she did not have enough time. She hesitated. Words rose to her lips. Words of apology, to say she was sorry for her aggressiveness, her harshness and hostility, but her jaws refused to release them. In conclusion, she said:

"I'll be banking on you."

She hung up. A taste of ash filled her mouth. She remained there, leaning back against the glass panes of the phone box, asking herself once again the question that had been bugging her since her adolescence: was she right to treat her mother this way? Was that woman really the only person responsible for her broken existence? All she could do in answer was to mutter a few unintelligible insults.

Two police cars were speeding up Rue de la Cité, with their sirens blaring. She jumped. They were like a warning. Langlois's body had been discovered. She dialled directory inquiries and asked:

"Could you put me through to reservations at Roissy-Charles-de-Gaulle airport?"

Diane immediately heard a different ringing tone, then a woman's voice. She examined her left hand. Her nails were black with blood. Her veins were protruding. It was already an old woman's hand. She added:

"Is it possible to book a seat on the next flight to a given destination, irrespective of the airline?"

"Yes, of course. Where do you want to go?"

She looked again at her fingers and palm.

An old woman's hand.

But a hand that was no longer shaking.

She answered:

"Moscow."

III
Tokamak

CHAPTER 43

Cheremetievo 2. The arrivals hall.

Moscow International Airport.

It was five o'clock in the morning, on Friday, 15 October 1999.

Shivering in her parka, Diane followed the tide of travellers towards the luggage retrieval area. She had taken the last Aeroflot flight of that day, at half past twelve, and she was now on Russian territory. All she had going for her was the fact that she knew the Russian capital a little, having already visited it on two occasions. The first time, in 1993, it was to attend a congress on Siberian fauna organised by the Moscow Academy of Sciences. The second, two years later, when she had been in transit on her way to Kamchatka. On her return, Diane had spent a week as a dreamy, fascinated tourist in the city. It was not much, but at least she could remember the name of the hotel where she had stayed: the Ukrainia.

At about six o'clock, the luggage arrived. The hall had a low ceiling, was badly lit and felt like a crypt. Muttering and cursing, the passengers had to bend down over the piles of cases and search for their belongings with the aid of their lighters.

Diane soon found her bag. Before leaving Paris, she had dropped in to her apartment to grab a few things, including a prototype satellite phone that a specialised company had lent her. She also took her special reserve of $800, and emptied

225

her bank account of its 7,000 francs via a cash point. At that moment, she experienced a strange sensation of freedom. Just as someone committing suicide must feel, an instant after throwing himself off a roof.

On leaving the airport, Diane realised that she had taken off in autumn but landed in winter. The cold was no longer an ancillary detail. It was an implacable, bitter presence that clutched her skull and bit into her hands, like upturned claws. Stagnant mists seemed to trap the glittering pavement. On the horizon, the earth and sky joined together in the shadows with a long seal of ice.

There were no cabs, but Diane was not even looking for one. She knew the rules. She moved away from the tourists and, as soon as she saw a normal-looking car, she started swinging her arms around in the air. The vehicle kept going. It was only on the third attempt that a Jigouli, with its headlamps off, stopped beside her. The name of the hotel and the green colour of her banknotes were enough to convince the driver. Diane slumped down on to the worn-out leatherette seat, with her bag on her lap, woolly hat pulled down to her ears, and was whisked away into the darkness of the night.

The car drove down a lonely alley, dotted with ghostly birch trees. Then, after a neighbourhood full of unlit apartment blocks, it turned on to the ring-road. Smoke from fires on the wasteland and the carbon monoxide from the lorries replaced the fog of the countryside. With no headlamps, their visibility was no more than five yards. From time to time, the shuddering din of a juggernaut, its axles clunking above the roadway, burst out. Diane started to feel distinctly uneasy. Anxiety was rising up from the past – the recollection of her accident. The driver, who had not said a word since taking her on board, and whose face was hidden beneath a balaclava, apparently sensed that his passenger was nervy. He turned on the radio. A violent hard rock track joined with the grooves in the asphalt to make the Jigouli judder even more. Diane wanted to scream by the time the man drove up an exit ramp and into the city.

She remembered that from the north, they had to go down Leningrad Boulevard. Myriads of lights appeared, with flashy shop windows displaying their wonders as if they were marvellous caverns. Advertising logos and slogans set about seducing the consumers. The entire city was draped in neon and fluorescence. Such an orgy of electricity was like a nocturnal nod and wink to the unbridled capitalism that was daily encroaching on the scene. A sort of obligatory expenditure or imposed waste, showing that the days of penury and restrictions were over, even if most Moscovites even now did not have enough to eat.

Diane was surprised to notice that the driver was still heading south through the mists. He should have turned east, towards Minsk ... Suddenly, everything was dark once more. There was a proliferation of churches in this neighbourhood, so much so that they even stood next to one another on the same pavement, or else faced each other across a narrow alleyway. In the shadows, she glimpsed their eroded façades, their black arches and cleft gates. Beneath the tarpaulin of the scaffolding, statues held out their cracked, severed arms, their faces creased, their heavy robes petrified like an icy coat. Diane was beginning to feel worried, and wondered if her driver was leading her into a trap down some deserted back road.

The car then swerved and emerged on to Red Square. Another shock for Diane. She saw the Kremlin, with its crimson ramparts and domes sprinkled with gold. Behind his balaclava, the driver burst out laughing. She then realised that he had wanted to show her the jewel in his city's crown. Head down in her parka, with her chin inside her collar, she had to admit that she was pleased to be there. The car drove along the banks of the Moskova. It then took the Kutuzovki Perspective, crossed

Lubianka Square – Diane could still remember the names – before coming to a halt below the glittering street sign of the Ukrainia Hotel, which was twinkling in the night like a huge Alka Seltzer dissolving in brackish water.

Diane thanked the driver as the opening chords of Led Zeppelin's *Stairway to Heaven* were filling the car. Still not a word. Still faceless. At the reception desk, she filled in the necessary form then took the lift up to the eighth floor. In her room, she did not bother to switch on the light. The parliament building, just opposite, was so brightly illuminated that a generous gleam was carried as far as the hotel.

The room was just as she remembered it. Twelve square feet. Curtains and counterpane cut from the same red muslin. An odour that was a mix of burnt fat, mould and dust. Pure Russian chic. Only the bathroom had new porcelain and had clearly been treated to fresh plumbing. She took a hot shower. She really needed one. Then, drowsy from the scalding water, full of aches and pains, she slipped in between the harsh sheets and fell asleep at once.

A dreamless, carefree night.

Which was already quite something.

CHAPTER 44

When Diane opened her eyes, bright sunlight sparkled on the walls of her room. She looked at her watch. It was ten o'clock in the morning. She swore to herself, tripped over her bag, then bumped into the corner of the table, before finally reaching the bathroom. She got dressed quickly and opened the window.

The city was there.

Diane saw the Moskova, its dark waters glistening in the morning sunshine. She also spotted some Orthodox churches, Stalinist skyscrapers and unfinished buildings surrounded by cranes, which seemed to be trying to outdo one another in height and haughtiness. But above all, she absorbed the busy atmosphere of the city. That hazy deluge made up of greyness, noise and acidic smells that is so typical of all megalopolises and which here seemed even harsher and more powerful than ever. She looked down at Kutuzovki Perspective, with its hundreds of cars. Then she closed her eyes and mentally joined up with the trembling mass, experiencing that tingle of pleasure that proved to her that no matter how much she might travel, no matter how much she might love animals, she would always be a city girl at heart.

When she was chilled to the bone, Diane closed the window again and turned her mind to her investigations. If she was sure of one thing, it was that this whole nightmare revolved around the tokamak: the return of its former members; the special role of the Watchers who had been sent out by some mysterious authority to inform the men in question; and even the murders which, one by one, seemed to be striking down the people associated with the nuclear lab.

She had even thought of a way to begin. It was a simple and at the same time realistic strategy. First she ordered her breakfast, then she contacted the French Embassy and asked to speak to the science attaché – all diplomatic units have their scientific specialists, buried among the more traditional posts. After a minute's wait, a firm voice resonated in the receiver. Diane introduced herself. She gave her real name, then said she was a journalist.

"What magazine do you work for?" the voice butted in.

"Um . . . I'm freelance."

"Freelance for which magazine?"

"Freelance for myself."

The man sneered.

"I see."

Diane changed her tone:

"Do you or do you not intend to help me?"

"Go on."

"I'm looking for information about the tokamaks. They're nuclear furnaces which . . ."

"I know what they are."

"Good. So maybe you also know where I can find records dealing with them? There must be an academy in Moscow that . . ."

"The Kurchatov Institute. They have all of the files dealing with controlled fusion labs."

"Can you give me the address?"

"Do you speak Russian?"

"No, I don't."

The science attaché burst out laughing.

"Then what sort of research are you intending to do?"

Diane forced herself to stay calm. In a humble voice she asked:

"Do you know an interpreter?"

"I have someone even better than that. A young Russian who specialises in thermonuclear fusion. His name's Kamil Gorochov and he speaks fluent French. He's visited our country on numerous occasions to study sites working in the same field."

"Do you think he'd help me?"

"Do you have any money?"

"A little."

"Dollars?"

"Yes, dollars."

"Then there won't be any problem. I'll get in touch with him at once."

Diane gave him the address of the hotel, thanked him,

then hung up. One minute later, her breakfast arrived. Sitting cross-legged on her bed, she gobbled down the stale bread and savoured the over-stewed tea. It was served in a glass with a carved silver handle. So far as she was concerned, this detail was worth all the croissants in the world. She was feeling strangely light and calm. As if the night flight had erected an impenetrable wall between her and the events in Paris.

The phone rang. Kamil Gorochov was waiting for her in reception.

The Ukrainia's lobby still bore the marks of Stalinist grandeur. The sunshine through the high windows transformed the net curtains into pure white stalactites, while the marble floor shimmered with iridescent light. Diane spotted a young man, done up in an over-large anorak, who was pacing up and down near the reception desk. He was glancing around like an escaped criminal.

"Kamil Gorochov?"

The man turned round. He had cat's eyes and long black silky hair. In reply, he nervously swept a lock away from his forehead. Diane introduced herself in French. The Russian listened to her in a half-aggressive, half-wary attitude. No longer sure if she was speaking to the right person, she hesitated. But this feline creature immediately asked in his rugged French:

"So, you're interested in tokamaks?"

Diane narrowed the field:

"I'm interested in TK 17."

"The worst one."

"What do you mean?"

"I mean, the most powerful. The only one that has ever reached, for a few thousandths of a second, the temperature of solar fusion . . ."

He sniggered off-puttingly beneath his Cossack's moustache, then looked appealingly around the lobby as though calling all those present to bear witness. His good looks seemed to thrive exclusively on dark ideas.

"Do you know the myth of Prometheus?" he suddenly asked her.

Diane was now past being surprised that a Russian should be referring to Greek mythology while conversing with a strange French woman in a dusty hotel lobby. She decided to play along:

"You mean the man who tried to steal lightning from the gods?"

Another smirk, another flick of his hair. Kamil did not even seem to have noticed Diane's cuts and bandages – he was from another planet.

"For the Ancient Greeks," he went on, "it was a legend. It's now a reality. Men really have tried to steal the secrets of the stars. The archives of the tokamaks are kept at the Kurchatov Institute in the south of the city. Pay for a full tank of petrol and I'll take you there."

Diane beamed at him. He had already spun round and was heading towards the sun-drenched revolving door. She slipped in behind him and pulled on her parka. Her good mood seemed to be unbreakable. She could just sense how productive this trip to Moscow was going to be.

CHAPTER 45

Kamil drove a beat-up R5, which he pushed as hard as it would still go. After a short detour, they reached an eight-lane thoroughfare. Diane remembered the neighbourhood of churches and mists that she had seen the previous night. Everything was quite different now. On either side of the road, cubes with glass façades formed an unbroken chain of skyscrapers stretching endlessly away.

They crossed the river then reached a large, congested square. Dormitory suburbs now replaced the colossal constructions, whose drab colours seemed to absorb the sunlight to nourish their bitterness. They went past casinos, a station with a marble façade, then the Dinamo stadium. They then turned down a different street, punctuated by perpendicular pedestrian precincts.

In amazement, Diane observed the crowd. The surging schapskas, the streams of woolly hats, the floods of scarfs, pelisses, raised collars, of every conceivable warming material: wool, felt, leather, furs ... Through the steamed-up windows, the splashes of colour became more precise, more vibrant, as though crystallised by the cold. In the world of clichés, the inhabitants of Moscow were supposed to be dull, with sad faces. She discovered something quite different. When watching that crowd, she felt thrillingly vivified. A sting of cold and joy, like those tiny frosted glasses that contain a promise of intoxication even before they have been filled.

With his eyes still on the road, Kamil suddenly asked her:

"So, what do you know about the TK 17?"

"Nothing. Or practically nothing," Diane admitted. "It was the USSR's largest thermonuclear furnace. It was a method that the Soviets had invented with a view to eventually replacing nuclear fission. I know that the lab was shut down in 1972 and that it was managed by an Asian physicist called Eugen Talikh. He then went over to the West in 1978."

The young physicist smoothed down his moustache.

"And what's your interest in it?"

Diane improvised:

"I'm researching an article about the remains of Soviet science. The tokamaks are a little known field, so I ..."

"But why TK 17?"

She was unprepared for that question. Suddenly, she remembered the little man in the photograph, with his ancient schapska.

"What interests me most is Eugen Talikh," she replied at last. "I'd like to use him as an example of the Soviet scientists of the period."

They now turned on to the ring-road. In the sunlight, the black fumes and the grimy colours of the vehicles seemed even more sinister than the night before. Kamil replied – without any trace of an accent:

"But Talikh is not a typical example of Russian scientists. He was more like a one-man vengeance of the Asian peoples over the Soviet empire. In the entire history of Communism, there's no other example of such a success. Except maybe for Jugdermidiyn Gurragtcha, the first Mongol cosmonaut. But that was in 1981, and things had already changed by then . . ."

"Where is Talikh from exactly?"

"But he's a Tseven, didn't you know that?"

Diane's ears pricked up.

"You mean he was born in the region of the tokamak?"

The driver sighed with a mixture of irritation and amusement.

"It looks like we're going to have to start from the very beginning."

He took a deep breath, then ploughed ahead:

"In the 1930s, Stalinist oppression reached the borders of Siberia and Mongolia. The aim was to wipe out anything that stood in the way of the Kremlin's authority. The lamas, the great cattle owners and the nationalists were all arrested. In 1932, there was a Mongol uprising. The Soviet army crushed the rebellion using armoured cars and tanks. The nomads were on horseback and had only rifles and sticks to defend themselves. Nearly 40,000 people were massacred. The remaining population was now leaderless, with no ambitions or religion left.

Then, in 1942, a Soviet decree imposed the Cyrillic alphabet and the Russian language.

"From that moment on, all of the children of the steppes and the taiga had to go to school. The idea was to dissolve the Mongols and the surrounding ethnic groups into the great Soviet people. So it was that at the end of the 1950s a typical little boy from the Tsagaan-Nuur region, in the north of Mongolia, was sent with his friends to Ulan Bator to learn to read and write. He was then twelve and the Russian name he'd been given was Eugen Talikh. He immediately proved to be an extremely gifted pupil. When he was 15, he left for Moscow, where he joined the Komsomol – the Communist youth movement – and attended mathematics classes at the university. At the age of 17, he turned his attention to physics and astrophysics. Two years later, he completed a PhD on the thermonuclear fusion of tritium. Talikh had become the USSR's youngest doctor of science."

Diane felt a wave of sympathy for this child of the wilds, who had also turned out to be a child of the atom. Kamil went on:

"In 1965, our prodigy was sent to the TK 8 site in the Tomsk region. At the time, they were using deuterium, another hydrogen isotope, in their fusion trials, but they were beginning to think that tritium might provide better results. And that was Talikh's speciality. Two years later, he was transferred to a crucial site: the construction of TK 17, the largest thermonuclear furnace ever built. At first, he was part of the scientific team, which oversaw the conception and fine-tuning of the machine. Then, in 1968, he personally supervised the initial trials. Don't forget, he was only 24 at the time."

The Russian was driving down the motorway, but it was impossible to guess in which direction. Diane saw signposts, written in Cyrillic characters, pass by. But she trusted this physicist. Beneath his surly exterior, she sensed that he was pleased to share his passion with her.

"But the most incredible part of it," he continued, "is that the chosen site was in Talikh's native region of Tsagaan-Nuur."

"Why there?"

"An additional precaution taken by the Russians. The West had started to identify the secret Soviet research centres in Siberia's industrial and military towns, such as Novosibirsk, which appeared on no maps, but which had millions of inhabitants. By placing the site in Mongolia, they were sure to be out of sight and out of mind. So it was that Talikh, the little nomad, came back home as a great nuclear scientist. He at once became a popular hero."

They were now driving down an ill-made road, cracked by the frosts of successive winters. Black fields, as though hunched up over their furrows, stretched dismally away. Occasionally, women in brightly coloured headscarfs appeared, like odd flowers growing up in the meadows. Kamil suddenly turned down a mud track. An astonished Diane made out a tall gilded gate. On the far side could be seen relatively well-kept paths and lawns. In the distance, a vast violet palace stood, presumably dating to the 19th century. She was amazed to discover that such architecture still existed in post-Communist Russia.

"Don't look so flabbergasted," Kamil said, while parking on the gravel drive. "The Soviets didn't destroy everything."

It was not so much a manor house as a large hunting lodge, with windows framed by white stones, pillared porticos and stucco ornaments decked with curved-roofed turrets. They went up a few steps and reached the terrace which was covered with pale pebbles. To the left, a uniformed guard was standing in a sentry box. Kamil vaguely saluted in his direction, then opened one of the French windows. He had his own set of keys.

A crystal chandelier glittered on the ceiling. The large hexagonal hall had a marble floor. To the left, a broad staircase curved up to the first floor. Upstairs, half-open doors revealed large black-and-white photographs depicting industrial sites. There were also some polished copper turbines, which had been placed on plinths like Venuses. Diane supposed that this must be a museum devoted to controlled fusion.

Kamil immediately turned right. They went through several rooms with cracked walls, decked with panelling and containing statues. Diane spotted alcoves where young countesses used to forget their handkerchiefs, and armchairs where princes put down their butterfly nets . . .

Wrapped up in his anorak, Kamil kept going. He looked like a young cat that had been abandoned by its owners in a large house which he now knew by heart. They went down a narrow staircase. The temperature abruptly dropped. At the bottom, their path was blocked by a padlocked gate. Beyond it, a vaulted room disappeared into the shadows, full of metal shelving which presumably housed the archives. Kamil muttered as he unlocked the gate:

"We carefully maintain a microclimate suited to the preservation of paper. Seventeen degrees Centigrade. Fifty per cent humidity. It's very important."

He lit a shaded ceiling light. There were thousands of files, stacked up on the metal racks, stuffed into filing cabinets and piled on the floor. There were also complete collections of books with gilded letters on their spines that glittered in the dark recesses. Old newspapers, tied up in bundles, mounted up towards the vaulted ceiling.

They walked on into a back room. Kamil felt for the light switch. A bizarre violet halo revealed the interior: a small windowless room, with a row of desks topped with formica. The physicist whispered:

"Don't move."

He disappeared, then was back almost at once, his arms laden with a large cardboard box, which he placed on the table. From it, he removed several mouldy files which were done up with cloth straps. He opened them then, utterly indifferent to the rising dust, dextrously flicked through them. Diane started to feel those scraps of time crunching between her teeth.

Finally, he handed Diane a black-and-white snap, and proudly announced:

"The first aerial shot of TK 17, the machine that rivalled the stars."

CHAPTER 46

It was a circle.

A huge stone circle, whose circumference measured a good hundred yards, at the foot of a rocky slope. Around it could be seen smaller buildings forming a grey, geometric town running as far as the neighbouring forest. To the north-west of the site there was a power station, with huge turbines, beside the mountain streams that were pouring down from the heights.

"Do you know how it worked?" Kamil asked her.

"No, I've told you. I have no idea."

The physicist chuckled, then pointed at the concrete ring.

"Inside this circle," he explained, "there was a vacuum chamber, directly powered by the generator you can see here. Just imagine a massive short circuit, an electric cable swallowing its own tail, then you'll have some idea of what this tokamak was like. A current measuring several million amps arrived, was distributed by tall magnetic arches, heated up and then, in a fraction of a second, the circuit reached a temperature of over ten million degrees. The researchers then injected a gassy mixture of tritium atoms into it. The atoms immediately started moving inside the chamber until they had nearly reached the speed of light. That's when the miracle happened: the electrons left their nuclei and turned into plasma – the fifth state of matter. The temperature got even higher and then it was time for the second miracle: the tritium nuclei joined up and turned into other atoms – helium isotopes. But in fact, as I told you, this happened only once."

"What was the point of the experiment?"

"Normally speaking, this atomic transmutation should have given off an enormous amount of energy – far more than our current nuclear power stations. And the only material used would have come from seawater. Unfortunately, the site was closed in 1972 and the Soviets seemed to lose interest in the technique. So then the West took over, but no-one has as yet obtained really significant results in this field."

Diane tried to swallow her saliva, but the dust was drying her throat. She asked:

"And . . . was it dangerous? I mean, was it radioactive?"

"The chamber was. The bombardment of neutrons made the structure of the machine radioactive – for example all the cobalt that it contained. And that radioactivity could remain there for several years. But outside there was no problem. The walls of the chamber were made of lead and cadmium, which absorbed the neutrons."

Diane found it hard to imagine Rolf van Kaen, a doctor-cum-acupuncturist, and Philippe Thomas, a dissident psychologist, at such a site.

"I have the names of two people who I believe worked there," she said. "Can you check if they were part of one of the teams?"

"No problem."

She spelt their names and mentioned their specialities. Kamil looked through his lists. The papers crumbled between his fingers like parchment.

"No, they're not here."

"Is this a full list?"

"Yes. If they worked in the actual tokamak, then they should be here."

"What do you mean by that?"

"Site TK 17 was a huge place. A real town. Thousands of people worked there. And there were various annexes."

Diane suddenly had a flash of inspiration.

"What sort of annexes? Could the profiles of van Kaen and Thomas fit any of the other activities practised on the site?"

Kamil's fingers were drumming on his files. A wicked look was lighting up his almond eyes.

"An acupuncturist and a psychologist could well have belonged to TK 17's top secret department. The one devoted to parapsy-chology."

"What?"

"The site had a lab for carrying out psychology experiments. And a unit researching unexplained phenomena of perception and influence – telepathy, clairvoyance, psychokinesis, that kind of thing. At the time, there were several other similar labs in the USSR."

It was as if a door, whose existence Diane had never imagined, had suddenly been flung open to reveal brilliant daylight. She asked him:

"And what sort of experiments were carried out in these labs?"

He pouted and shrugged.

"I really don't know. It's not my field. I think that some psychologists and physicists were trying to incite modified forms of consciousness, by means of hypnosis for instance, or else encourage psychic events, such as telepathic communication or cures using magnetism. These were then studied physiologically, but also in terms of magnetics, electricity . . .”

"But why was there a lab like that near a tokamak?”

Kamil burst out laughing.

"Because of Talikh! He was fascinated by the subject. While working on fusion, he also studied what he called 'bio-astronomy'. The influence of the stars on the human body and on our moods.”

"Like astrology?”

"Yes, but more scientific. For example, he was interested in the supposed relationship between the brain and solar magnetism. Apparently, there's statistical proof of a relationship between the Sun's activity and the number of accidents, suicides, heart attacks, and so on. From what I've heard, Talikh himself had strange gifts. He could predict stellar phenomena, such as eclipses. But there we get to the mystical side of the man. And I don't believe in such nonsense. It's enough to make you laugh.”

But Diane was not laughing. She was beginning to perceive a hitherto unsuspected aspect of the affair: Eugen Talikh, the child prodigy of nuclear fusion, was also a Tseven, a child of the taiga, who had grown up in a shamanic society full of inexplicable phenomena. Once he had become a physicist, he must have imagined that he could then study such powers rationally. So he had called in the greatest specialists in various fields, men like Rolf van Kaen, the virtuoso acupuncturist, or else Philippe Thomas, a French deserter interested in telekinesis.

Diane was sure that she was close to the heart of the matter. She now had to explore this lead and get a better understanding of the context that had allowed for such a project.

"There's something I don't understand,” she said in an innocent tone. "The era of Marxism is synonymous with materialism and pure pragmatism. It was a time when churches were closed and history was based on utter realism. So how could the Soviet authorities have taken this business about the paranormal seriously?"

Kamil frowned to show his mistrust.

"Are you really that interested in parapsychology?"

"I'm interested in everything that concerns Soviet science."

The physicist sighed.

"You could write a novel about the relationship between Russia and parapsychology."

"How about a short summary?"

He leant against the old boxes and seemed more relaxed, his sharp features lit by the same violet light.

"You're right. On the one hand, Communism opened an era of complete pragmatic rationalism. But at the same time, the Russians remained Russians. And we're deeply tainted by spirituality. I don't just mean religion, but also ancestral beliefs and superstitious fears. For instance, the Soviets thought that their victory at Stalingrad was due to the shamanic spirits which had been let loose in the region of the Volga. In the same way, they continued to believe that their space programme had been helped along by celestial forces."

Looking resigned, the young man crossed his arms.

"We often say that this is the Asian side of our people. After all, most of our territory is covered by the taiga, the home of the spirits . . ."

Diane butted in.

"But there's quite a long step between popular belief and scientific research, isn't there?"

"True. But our country also has a tradition of parapsychological research. Don't forget that our greatest Nobel prize winner was Ivan Petrovich Pavlov, the discoverer of conditioned reflexes and father of modern psychology. Pavlov thought that there were various distinct states of consciousness. In the 1920s, his institute even had a department devoted to studying clairvoyance."

Kamil seemed to find this subject both fascinating and absurd. He went on:

"In the 1940s, such research disappeared because of the Stalinist purges and the Second World War. But then, after Stalin's death, the fad for parapsychology came back, as though it had never left Russia's inner being. I'll tell you a little story which amply sums up feelings during the 1960s. Do you know the history of our country?"

"Not very well."

The sceptical expression reappeared below his silky hair.

"You've never heard of the 22nd Congress of the Communist Party, which was held in 1961?"

"No."

"It's extremely famous. It was then that Nikita Khrushchev first publicly referred to Stalinist crimes. He suggested that Stalin had not been the enlightened guide he was supposed to be, but a tyrant who had committed terrible crimes. That day, the master fell from his pedestal. Some time later, his mummified body was removed from the mausoleum where he had been lying next to Lenin."

"What's that got to do with the paranormal?"

"During the congress, a female deputy called Darya Lazurkina took the floor. She explained, in the most serious terms, that Lenin had appeared to her in a dream the day before, and told her that he was suffering from having to sleep beside Stalin in his mausoleum. What Lazurkina said was taken down in the official minutes of the congress, and I can assure you that her words were as influential in the decision to move the body as Khrushchev's speech. That's what we Russians are like. Nobody was surprised by the idea that a dead man spoke by reappearing as a vision to an old woman. In a way, Lenin had also participated in the congress."

Diane had seen pictures of the Party's grand masses – a huge auditorium, with rising rows of seats occupied by thousands of Communist deputies, the lords of what was at the time one of the world's most powerful nations. She found it a little worrying that a mere dream could have had any part to play in the decisions of the Party commissioners. As ever, darkness lay in the pit of mankind's consciousness. Beneath the fear of human power lay the dread of the universe, of the unknown, of the spirits that seemed to watch over Russia from their Siberian taiga.

"Go on," she whispered.

"From then on, psychology, and in its wake parapsychology, made a big comeback. Labs were opened all over the country. The most famous examples were the Neurosurgical Institute in Leningrad, where psychic dream experiences were studied, and the Psychiatry and Neurology Institute of Kharkov, where scientists looked for possible psychic particles, which might explain phenomena such as telepathy and psychokinesis. Then there was Department 8 of the Siberian Academy of Sciences in Novosibirsk, where some scientists tried to communicate telepathically with the crew of a nuclear submarine. It was all a bit silly, really."

Diane returned to the central point.

"What do you know about TK 17's activities in the field?"

"I've neither read nor heard anything about it. There hasn't been a single article published about that department."

"Why the silence, in your opinion?"

Kamil shrugged.

"It could mean anything. Either that the researchers didn't find anything at all, not even enough to write a report. Or, on the contrary, that they found out something important.

Something so important that it had to be hidden."

Suddenly, Diane realised that she had the answer to the question. Yes, something vital had been discovered. Something that not only concerned the nature of psychic gifts, but perhaps allowed them to be developed.

She had not forgotten the extraordinary events that had marked the last few weeks. An acupuncturist had saved a child who had been written off by traditional medicine. A psychologist had opened a metal belt using nothing but mental power. And now there was Eugen Talikh, gifted with clairvoyance when it came to cosmic phenomena. What if these men had, between 1969 and 1972, discovered in their laboratory some way to isolate and harness mankind's occult powers? What if, for the past 30 years, they had shared this extraordinary secret?

She remembered the date marked on Lucien's fingers: 20 October 1999. She was now sure of something else. Those men had decided to meet at the tokamak. And their meeting had something to do with this new mystery – the inexplicable acquisition of psychic powers.

Diane looked at the date on her watch. 15 October. There was only one way to find out the real reason for that appointment. She heard herself ask:

"You wouldn't mind dropping me at the airport, would you?"

CHAPTER 47

From Moscow, it was necessary to travel 5,000 miles east to Ulan Bator, the capital of the People's Republic of Mongolia. There was a night flight, with just one stopover at Tomsk in Western Siberia. The journey was over a uniform forest landscape. A frozen infinity of aspens, elms, birches, pines and larches, either in ordered plantations, or else in impenetrable jungles. Diane remembered Claude Andreas's map, and its huge monochrome expanses. The taiga was a hermitage as big as a continent which, at the frontier of Mongolia, opened out on to the adjacent immensity of the steppes.

Since he had never been to Mongolia, Kamil had not been able to tell her anything of interest about the journey. His knowledge of TK 17 was purely theoretical, which gave him even greater admiration for Diane's perseverance. At Cheremetievo, he volunteered to deal with buying the tickets.

Meanwhile, she chose some warm clothing at the main boutique in the airport, while mentally drawing up a list of what she already possessed. When trying on a fur-lined schapska in front of the mirror, she noticed that her bruises were starting to fade. She felt strong, energetic and invigorated. In fact, her plan was making her heady, and this headiness was dangerous, given that it prevented her from gauging just how much danger she was putting herself in.

"Great."

Kamil's almond eyes were smiling in the mirror. The physicist seemed to appreciate the sight of Diane's face, bordered by her unruly hair and topped by a fur visor. He did not seem to notice her cuts, scars and plasters. Brandishing a wad of faded blue notes, he warned her:

"Get a move on! The last flight to Tomsk leaves in 40 minutes."

Kamil slipped into the departure lounge with her. When she saw her fellow passengers, she started to have some misgivings. They looked mortified. They were just standing there, stock still, clutching their bags, and glancing from time to time with resignation towards the plane that was taxiing outside.

"What's up with them?" Diane asked.

"So far as they're concerned, Mongolia's the end of the world."

"Why?"

Kamil frowned again, his eyebrows forming an inverse echo of his smiling moustache.

"Don't you realise that Mongolia is even worse than Siberia? It's further away, and not even under Russian control. All these people can expect from Ulan Bator is loneliness, cold, destitution – and hatred. The country was a Soviet colony for nearly a hundred years. Now the Mongols are independent, they hate us more than the rest of the world put together."

She observed the crowd going past the check-in desk: weary figures, exiled stares. Then something occurred to her:

"And why aren't there any Mongols?" she asked.

"Because they've got their own airline. A Mongol would drop dead rather than fly Aeroflot. Do you know what real hatred is?"

She smiled wearily.

"Sounds promising."

"Goodbye, Diane. And good luck."

She found it hard to believe that, in a few seconds' time, this young cat would vanish and she would be alone again. And alone to a degree that she had difficulties imagining. He turned on his heels, then said over his hood:

"And don't forget: the gods don't like it when we try to imitate them."

The old Tupolev was juddering like a steam train. Diane abandoned herself to the night flight's strange lassitude. Oblivious to the lack of comfort in the plane, the biscuit crumbs that stood in for a meal and the brilliant lights that would not turn off, or else would not turn on depending on the seat, she did not even feel the cold that seemed to penetrate inside the trembling fuselage.

At Tomsk, they were made to leave the plane then herded through the darkness to a warehouse at the end of the runway. The place looked like a lazaret, where they were going to be quarantined. They all sat down without a word on the benches against the walls. Under the naked light bulb, Diane noticed some large black-and-white photographs hung on the walls. Miners in hieratic postures, pick-axes in their hands. Mining valleys that looked like canyons. Electrical installations full of towers and cables. An entire dream world of production and planning depicted in snaps that seemed themselves to be ingrained with coal and filth.

She looked at her watch: 22.00 p.m. in Moscow, 3.00 a.m. in Ulan Bator. But what time was it here in Tomsk? She turned to her neighbours and asked them in English. But nobody understood her. She asked some other passengers. The Russians did not even lift their faces from their collars. At last an old man answered in pidgin English:

"Who interest time in Tomsk?"

"Me. I'd like to know where I'm at."

The man lowered his eyes and did not look up again. Diane noticed her own long, slender shadow standing out against the photos of the miners. She sat down again, suddenly feeling a sharp pain in her chest, as though she had just been hit by a stone.

An image of Patrick Langlois had just surged up into her memory. His eyes of dark lacquer. His small silver-grey fringe. The mild scent of over-clean clothes. Grief hit her. She felt alone, lost, adrift in an endless land. But even more lost inside . . .

She wanted to cry. To cry as though she was vomiting. While thinking about that man who could have loved her – even her – his death seemed doubly ridiculous, even more pointless. Because if he had lived, he would have soon seen that Diane was impossible. His advances would have slipped off her skin like water on a pool of petrol. She would never have echoed his desire. Her own desire would never settle on a single object. It was like a wild beast, an underground blaze which raged beneath her skin without ever finding the way out.

Diane looked again at the hands of her watch, which were turning in a vacuum. "Don't play at being Miss Sherlock Holmes", that was what the lieutenant had told her. A smile rose up against the current of her tears. She was no Sherlock Holmes. She was not even a detective.

Just a young woman lost in a forest of time zones.

On her way to the monster continent.

CHAPTER 48

It was the light that woke her.

She sat up in her seat and leant her hand against the window. How long had she been asleep? As soon as they had got back on board she had collapsed. And now she was being dazzled by the dawn. She put her glasses back on and stared outside. Then, in the bright morning light, she saw what surely existed nowhere else on earth, and which takes the breath away from every traveller who breaks through the clouds on the way to Mongolia: the steppes.

If fires were green, then they would produce just such a colour. A flaming, shimmering verdure. A light bursting up from the earth, tousled with vegetation. A brazier as large as the horizon, but with the closeness of a sigh in each of its unfolding details. It was a fever full of dew and chlorophyll.

The sun could blaze for all its worth, but never would it alter such freshness.

In order to get a better look at this richness, Diane searched for her sunglasses. She had the strange impression that she had always known that endless abundance of wild greenery. Those hills leapfrogging across each other in their wondrous solitude. Those gleeful plains, as though drunk on their own sap, moving towards an eternal appointment with the horizon.

She leaned over to the window until she was touching it with her forehead. Despite the distance and the din from the motors, her thoughts drifted to the ground and she could almost hear the rustling of the pastures, the buzzing of the insects, the tiny hum of nature when the high winds fell. Yes, this was a land to listen to. Like a sea-shell. A land that revealed all its subtleties on its surface, then, underneath, could be heard the distant gallop of short-maned horses. And perhaps, deeper still, the muffled heartbeats of the world . . .

Ulan Bator airport was a building made of rough concrete, where suitcases were marked with chalk, and where the arrivals and departures desks were combined into a single wooden counter topped by the terminal's one and only computer. Through the windows, Diane noticed a few horsemen among the cars. They were all wearing brightly coloured traditional robes done up with a silk belt.

Diane had no idea what to do next. To buy time, she followed the other passengers and picked up a form. Leaning it against the wall, she started to fill it in. It was only then, when she noticed something written in English on the top of the document, that she realised how foolish she had been.

A voice behind her asked:

"Are you Diane Thiberge?"

She jumped. A young Westerner was smiling at her. He was wearing a British parka, corduroy trousers and Timberland boots. Diane said to herself that this surely couldn't be a cop. Not here.

She drew back to get a better look at him. He had a baby face, with curly brown hair, glasses with narrow golden frames, and three days' growth that emphasised his sunburnt appearance. Despite the beard, his features, brown skin and impeccable clothes gave off an impression of cleanliness and neatness that immediately made Diane jealous – she felt so wan and shabby in comparison.

He introduced himself, a slight accent cooing across his tongue:

"My name's Giovanni Santis. I'm an attaché at the Italian Embassy. I come here to welcome all our Western visitors. I spotted your name on the passenger list and thought I'd . . ."

"What are you after?"

He looked taken aback by her aggressive tone.

"Nothing . . . To help you, guide you, give you advice," he answered. "This is no easy country and . . ."

"Thanks anyway. I'll get along just fine."

Diane started filling up her form again, while observing him out of the corner of her eye. At the same time, the young attaché was staring at the marks on her face. He softly insisted:

"You're sure you don't need anything?"

"No, really. My trip's been carefully planned. No problem."

"What about a hotel?" the Italian tried again. "Or an interpreter?"

She turned round and cut him off:

"You really want to help me, do you?"

Giovanni bowed, like a Venetian gentleman. Diane waved her form at him and grinned ironically.

"Well, I don't have an entry visa."

The Italian's eyes opened wide and he stared at her in pure astonishment.

"No visa?" he repeated.

His eyebrows continued to rise, into two hanging arches. He

251

looked so surprised and full of such intense innocence that Diane burst out laughing. She realised that the funny face he had pulled depicted what their future relationship was going to be like.

CHAPTER 49

Giovanni was driving flat out along the straight road that led to Ulan Bator. He had managed to sort out Diane's administrative problem in under an hour. She realised that she was in the presence of a red-tape wizard, and a man who could speak Mongol as fluently as he also spoke French and Italian. She was now under the responsibility of the Italian Embassy – as a sort of surprise guest – and this new situation did not bother her in the least. Or not yet.

She opened the window and leant out. The white dust from the road dried her throat. She felt her lips chapping and her skin drying as rapidly as the wind hit her. In the distance, a town could be seen, as flat and as grey as a shield, topped by a power station's two massive chimneys.

Diane closed her eyes and breathed in that arid breeze deeply. She yelled over the din of the cross-country vehicle:

"Can you feel the air?"

"What?"

"It's so . . . so dry."

Giovanni laughed into his parka. He shouted in reply:

"Have you never travelled in Central Asia before?"

"No."

"The nearest sea must be about 2,000 miles away. There's never the slightest sea breeze or trade wind to temper the variations in temperature. In the winter, it goes down to minus 50° Celsius. And in the summer, it bounds up to the 40s. In just one day, there can be a shift of up to 40 degrees. This is a super-continental climate, Diane. A pure, hard climate with no shaded nuances."

He laughed merrily:

"Welcome to Mongolia!"

She closed her eyes again and let herself be rocked by the bumps in the road. When she opened them, they were entering a town. Ulan Bator was a city with Stalinesque architecture, criss-crossed by wide avenues, which were sometimes tarmacked, but often made of clay, dotted by huge buildings full of windows that were as sharp as razor blades. Beneath these giants, small dull monotonous estates shared out the rest of the land. Everything seemed to have been conceived, designed and built all in one go by architects intent on applying the grand principles of socialist town-planning: grandeur and power for the government offices, symmetry and repetition for human existence.

But the people wandering through the streets made a complete contrast with that over-weaning scheme. Many of the inhabitants wore the traditional *deel*, as Giovanni put it: a quilted robe buttoned obliquely, secured by a cloth belt. Others were on horseback, trotting along among the Japanese cars or the black Chaikas, which seemed to have come back from the distant past. This contrast epitomised the essential duel that had taken place: Stalin versus Genghis Khan. And a comparison between the cracked walls and the immaculate robes left little doubt as to the winner.

Diane noticed a large hotel, with several vehicles already in its car park.

"Why not stop here?" she asked.

"We're not going to the hotel. It's fully booked. There's

some sort of congress going on. But don't worry. I've got another idea. We'll put you up at the Gandan Buddhist monastery at the edge of town. The monks have a few guest rooms."

A few minutes later, they reached a vast concrete block, surrounded by a weather-beaten red fence. There was nothing special about the building, except for the roof with its upturned edges, in the purist Chinese tradition. However, once inside the enclosure, each detail became more and more charming. The stone walls were covered with an ochre sheen. The plain cement surface of the courtyard was covered with dead leaves, which rustled like flames across the ground. The brown, flaking surrounds of the windows looked like mysterious frames inviting the visitor to lean inside and examine the monastery's secrets. A few seconds after the imposing pillars of the gateway had been passed, the entire place was transformed into a golden cradle, bewitching the eyes and casting a precious shimmering powder over the heart.

Diane walked on and saw some prayer wheels to her right, below a canopy. These huge vertical barrels were constantly spinning on their own axes. She had already seen some in China, on the border with Tibet. The very idea of those bits of paper, written by the faithful, then placed in these kegs to be churned, mixed and shaken fascinated her.

Some monks appeared. They did not look like the shaved, shining bonzes of Ra-Nong in Thailand. They were wearing red cowls and leather boots, turned up at their tips. They grinned at Giovanni, but seemed to have trouble deserting the natural gloominess of hardened horsemen, isolated for too long on the steppes. Finally, the Italian winked at her to tell her that everything had been arranged.

They showed her to a small room, with wooden panels, where she was delighted to be left alone once more. Giovanni promised to get the necessary official permission for a trip to the north of the country. She had had to explain her plans a little. This time, she said that she was researching a book about the remaining vestiges of Soviet science in Siberia and Mongolia. The idea appealed to her intellectual guide.

"I see," he said. "You mean it's contemporary archaeology."

And he immediately volunteered to go with her. At first she refused, but then she allowed herself to be talked round. Alone, she would have had no chance of getting to the tokamak in time.

At around four o'clock, she went down into the monastery courtyard. She felt like savouring the calm of the place. There were no smells, except for the fragrance of burnt grasses coming from the neighbouring steppes. No noise, apart from a few distant galloping hooves thundering behind the yellow-brown walls. No faces, unless she stared at the few monks that passed by under the shade of the veranda, wrapped up in their brick-red robes.

There was a stunning feeling of clarity and purity. Sunlight. Cold. Wood. Stone. Nothing else. Only the tall barrels moaned occasionally as they turned slowly, cradling that essence of sensations. Diane smiled. Everything about the place was strange to her, and yet, at a lower level of consciousness, she felt extraordinarily familiar with that ground scattered with crimson leaves and that sun stretching out the shadows. She pictured to herself her school playground, and the earth and the rocks she had dug into with a stick, as though trying to expose the world's secret textures. Here, there was just the same mix of hardness and intimacy, cold and softness, that had so captivated her during break times when she was young.

Suddenly, some pigeons took wing. Their beating wings resonated inside her, like some paper skylight that had abruptly been flung open. This moment seemed so crystalline and intimate that it was as if it had sprung up from her own expectations and desires.

Footsteps. Coming up behind her.

Wrapped up in his parka, Giovanni was standing on the steps, stroking his three days' growth with the back of his hand. There was something decidedly sweet about him. He made Diane think of a little boy who had been given too much candy. Or those Italian bakeries where gaudily coloured cakes glitter in the almost unlit shop windows. His whole being suggested mild abandon, a toothsome treat to be gobbled down at tea time . . .

She hoped that he would make some wonderful pronouncement – words that would instantly engrave themselves in stone. But, not one for lyrical gushes, the Italian put his hand to his belly and said:

"I don't know about you, but I could do with a bite to eat."

CHAPTER 50

Giovanni led her straight to the monastery refectory. According to him, the monks here made the best *booz* in the capital – a Mongolian speciality consisting of ravioli stuffed with mutton. During the afternoon, he had amassed all the necessary authorisations and organised their departure for early the next morning. To save time, he had even decided to sleep in one of the cells on the first floor. He completed his explanations with a firm smile. He seemed to have decided not to let Diane make a move without him.

She was in no mood to respond. Their growing intimacy bugged her, even annoyed her. She still felt imbued with Patrick Langlois's presence – his deep voice, his squeaky-clean fragrance, his gestures tinged with humour. This Italian's intrusion was disturbing her reminiscences and, in a way, desecrating his memory.

In the canteen, she sat down at the other side of a large table, so that she was not quite facing Giovanni. It was hard to imagine a situation in which they could be dining together so far apart. The diplomat made no allusion to this point – he had apparently formed his own opinion of Diane and her mysteries. Instead, he plunged his hand into his dish of *booz* and gobbled up his ravioli hungrily. As for her, she ate only the accompanying rolls and refused even to touch the large greasy main course.

The Italian kept talking. In fact, he was an ethnologist. In the 1990s, he had written a thesis about Communist persecution of Siberian ethnic groups, and in particular the Tunguses and the Iakutes. Then he had tried to travel up to the Arctic tundra, but the permission had never materialised. So he had then turned to a diplomatic career and got a job in Ulan Bator which nobody else wanted. The peoples living in this new territory had then become his field of study.

Diane was only half listening to his explanations. Something else was bothering her: the other person who was eating in that room lit by dim lamps. Apparently he was a Westerner and was wearing sunglasses. He looked to be in his 60s, but his brushed-back yellow hair did not seem to correspond to any particular age group. Giovanni had apparently not noticed this odd figure. When he had finished eating, he pushed the plates to one side and produced a laptop from his rucksack.

"I've drawn up our itinerary on my computer. Want to have a look?"

Diane went round the table and leant over the gleaming screen. A map of the People's Republic of Mongolia stood out clearly. All of the names were spelt in Cyrillic letters. With his mouse, Giovanni indicated a black circle in the midst of the area.

"We're here," he said.

Then he pulled a line up towards the north, which reached a blue point, which was presumably a lake near the border with Russia.

"And that's where we're going. To Tsagaan-Nuur. The White Lake."

The path had crossed almost the entirety of the map.

"Is . . . is it really that far?" she asked.

"Yep, just over 600 miles north-west. We'll start by flying to Mörön, which is there. Then we can take a second flight to the village of Tsagaan-Nuur. Then we'll have to buy reindeer if we actually want to get to the lake."

"Reindeer?"

"There aren't any roads. No vehicle can get there."

"Why . . . why not horses?"

"We'll have to cross a pass at an altitude of over 9,000 feet. It's tundra at that height. The only things that grow are mosses and lichens. Horses can't survive up there."

Diane was beginning to get a clearer idea of her coming journey. As though trying to reassure herself, she searched for at least one familiar detail. Her eyes fell on the thermos flask on the table. A red lacquered pot decked with Chinese flowers. She poured herself some more tea and stared down at the spindly brown leaves that were floating in the reddish liquid. She tried another question:

"How long will it take us to get from Ulan Bator to the village of Tsagaan-Nuur?"

"One day. If the flights fit together nicely."

"And then how long to get to the lake?"

"Another day, more or less."

"And from the lake to the tokamak?"

258

"Only a few hours. The lab's nearby, in a valley just beyond the first mountain in the Khoridol Saridag range."

She thought of the fatal date – 20 October – and calculated. If they left tomorrow, 17 October, then she could get there on time. She would even have a day to spare. After a sip of tea, she went on:

"Have you ever been there?"

"Of course not! It was a restricted zone until the middle of the 1990s and . . ."

"What do you know about the tokamak?" she asked.

Giovanni pouted.

"Not a lot," he replied. "So far as I know, it was a site where they did nuclear fusion. But I can't tell you any more than that. It really isn't my field."

"Did you know that there was a parapsychology lab at TK 17?"

"No. That's news to me. Does that interest you?"

"Everything about that place interests me."

Giovanni suddenly stared into space. A few seconds later, he mumbled:

"Funny you should mention that."

"Why?"

"Because I worked on other similar labs while I was writing my thesis."

Diane was amazed:

"But I thought you'd studied the persecution of the Siberian peoples."

"That's right."

"What's right?"

The Italian looked conspiratorial. He glanced across at the man in sunglasses then grinned.

"There are Slavic spies everywhere!"

He leant over towards her, both elbows on the table.

"Listen," he said. "One part of my thesis was about the

religious persecutions in the 1950s and 60s. Most people think that the Khrushchev era was more liberal, but when it comes to religion that's totally wrong. In fact, the main targets of oppression were minority faiths: Baptist Christians, for instance, or else Buddhists, or yet again the animists of the tundra and taiga. Khrushchev had all the lamas and shamans locked up, then burnt their temples and sanctuaries."

"But what's that got to do with parapsychology labs?"

"I'm coming to that. In 1992 my research led me to the archives of the notorious Gulag Archipelago: Norilsk, Kolyma, Sakhalin, Chukotka and so on. That's why I was able to record all of the shamans who had been imprisoned in the labour camps. The work was time-consuming, but easy. Each prisoner's origins had been recorded, as well as why they'd been locked up. That's when I stumbled on a quite incredible discovery."

"Which was?"

"After the end of the 1960s, many Iakut, Nenet and Samoyed shamans were transferred."

"Where?"

The Italian looked once more over at the motionless yellow-haired man.

"That's where things start getting interesting," he said. "I found out that they hadn't been transferred to other camps, but to labs."

"What sort of labs?"

"Ones like Department 8 of the Siberian Academy of Sciences in Novosibirsk. Labs specialising in parapsychology."

He seemed to be wallowing back into the thrill of his research. The gleam from the lamps and the glints from his eyes were ricocheting from his glasses. He said in a whisper:

"You do follow me, don't you? These scientists needed psychic subjects for their experiments. People who were supposed to be telepathic, or gifted with paranormal perceptions. And, sure enough, the Gulag was full to the gills with Asian sorcerers."

This was one tale too many for Diane.

"What's to say these shamans weren't just frauds?"

"Nothing. But even if they weren't, I don't see why they'd tamely reveal their secrets to a load of Russian scientists. All the same, these people were experts in trances, hypnosis, meditation and so on . . . In fact, all of what are called altered states of consciousness. That's why they were perfect specimens for parapsychological experiments."

Diane felt the blood drain from her face. She thought back to the TK 17 and wondered once again if the researchers had been able to tame and take on the powers of the shamans who had been studied in their lab.

"What have you found out about these experiments?" she asked.

"It's one of Soviet science's best-kept secrets. Nothing I've read mentions the slightest real result. But who knows what really went on in those laboratories? One thing's for sure. I certainly wouldn't have liked to be in those shamans' shoes. The Russians must have treated them just like guinea-pigs."

She thought of those men who had been abducted from their homes, locked up in freezing camps, then manipulated in occult experiments. A dark wave of nausea rose to her throat.

"I suppose they used Tseven shamans in TK 17, didn't they?" she asked him.

Giovanni looked surprised.

"Where did you hear that name?"

"I've read up about the region. So, did they use Tsevens or didn't they?"

"Of course they didn't."

"Why not?"

"Because the Tsevens have been extinct since the 1960s."

"What?"

"It's the truth. An established fact that has recently been proved by several Mongol ethnologists. The Tsevens didn't survive collectivisation."

"Can you explain why in detail?"

"The work of collectivisation only really hit Outer Mongolia at the end of the 1950s. In 1960, an assembly decreed that there would no longer be one single private landowner in the country. The entire territory was parcelled up and reorganised into kolkhozes. The nomads were forced to settle down. Their tents were destroyed and houses were built for them. Their livestock was confiscated then redistributed. The Tsevens didn't take this lying down. Instead of giving their herds to the Party, they slaughtered all of their animals with their bare hands. This was during the winter. Most of them died of starvation. So, to repeat what I just said, that ethnic group no longer exists. There are probably a few descendants still left today, but they will have lost their culture and be married to Mongols."

She pictured the plains covered with slaughtered reindeer. A massacre of their own resources. A sort of collective suicide. She imagined the Tseven women and children dying of cold and hunger. Each step she took brought her nearer to the heart of Evil.

But, at the same time, this information did not fit in with what she had found out. Diane had proof that the Tsevens – and their traditions – were still alive. The existence of the "Lüü-Si-Ans" was ample testimony. They were of Tseven origin. They spoke the Tseven language. They were Watchers, who had been initiated by shamans. So Giovanni was mistaken. But she refrained from contradicting him. This was just one more mystery to add to the legion of enigmas and impossibilities that already scattered her route.

The Italian was now looking for a telephone plug so that he could get his e-mail. This brought back to Diane a distant, buried, almost forgotten memory, which blazed out like a cut diamond. When Patrick Langlois had dropped her off at her apartment after the massacre in Saint-Germain-en-Laye, he had said: "The day I have something important to confide in you, Diane, I'll send you an e-mail".

And what if the lieutenant had sent her an e-mail the next day, given that he thought she had run away for good? She nodded towards Giovanni's computer and asked:

"Could I consult my e-mail via your laptop?"

CHAPTER 51

They got to work in one of the monastery's studies. The walls were panelled with deal boards and the floor was a parquet of broad slats laid on joists. The desks provided further shades of wood, while an anaemic light bulb cast a hazy illumination over those brown surfaces. The tiny room seemed to be still occupied by the monks' patience and concentration where, like suns of pure meditation, they bent each day over their books.

They plugged the computer into the one and only phone line. Giovanni gallantly let Diane check her e-mail first. Since they both used the same mail and navigation software, she was soon able to access her provider and open her mail box. There was a list of messages with familiar names and titles.

A few seconds later, she discovered that one of the messages she had received on 14 October was from Patrick Langlois. It had arrived at 13.34, in other words about an hour before she had phoned him from the hospital in Nice. She had guessed right. The lieutenant had supposed that she had fled and had sent her this e-mail in the hope of being able to inform her of his discoveries.

She clicked on the icon and the message opened. She could hear her heart pounding.

From: Patrick Langlois
To: Diane Thiberge
14 October 1999

Diane,
Where are you? All of my men have been out looking for you for the last few hours and I'm about to issue a wanted notice. What has got into you? Still, whatever you have decided and wherever you are, I must tell you the latest. Call me as soon as you've read this message. What matters now is mutual trust

Diane clicked again to move down the text.

The German investigators called this morning. They have discovered that van Kaen made several bank transfers to a young couple in Potsdam, near Berlin. Apparently, the woman, Ruth Finster, had an operation performed on her Fallopian tubes at Berlin's Charity Hospital in 1997, where she met van Kaen. It seems that he then became her lover.

But that isn't the main point. What matters is that she became sterile after the operation and last September adopted a little Vietnamese boy from an orphanage in Hanoi, the adoption being to a large degree financed by none other than van Kaen.

Diane had to restrain her entire face to stop herself from screaming. Another click. Another page of text:

This was just too much of a coincidence. So I immediately looked into Philippe Thomas, alias François Bruner. An hour later, I had what I was looking for: also in 1997, the ex-spy had taken under his wing a 35-year-old Fauve specialist called Martine Vendhoven. Of particular interest is the fact that she was suffering from an ovarian insufficiency and couldn't have children. At the end of August, she adopted a little Cambodian boy from the Siem-Reap centre, near the temples of Angkor. The adoption was organised by the Cambodian Foundation, of which Philippe Thomas was one of the main benefactors.

Each word was like a nail being hammered into her flesh. Diane soaked up every line:

It's obvious that all of this can't be a coincidence. These former Communists, with a shared past related to Mongolia and toka-maks, managed to organise the arrival of Asian boys at around the same date. They must all have been Watchers, from the region of the nuclear lab.

Diane, it seems obvious that you adopted your son unwittingly on behalf of somebody you know, probably an oldish man with a Soviet past. Who is it? That's for you to find out and for you to tell me.

But above all, contact me as soon as possible.

Carl Gustav Jung said that it wasn't the author that chose his characters, but the characters that chose the author. I think the same applies to destinies. When I close my eyes I try to picture you happily married with several children and a quiet life. Don't take it badly, but I just can't see you like that. It's a compliment, in fact. Phone me.
Love,
Patrick.

With a flick of a key, she wiped out the message. Giovanni, who had been standing at a discreet distance behind her, came over and asked:

"Good news?"

She could not even raise her eyes to him. She just said:

"I'm going to bed."

CHAPTER 52

It had all happened in his villa in the Lubéron, at the hour when the insects finally fall silent. What Diane remembered most were the colours, which deepened as night fell. The ochre of the quarries above the elms and pines. The mauve of the sky, gradually becoming iridescent as the dusk gathered. And the over-bright, artificial-looking blue of the swimming-pool which was lapping a few feet away from them.

The man spoke in his deep voice, between two puffs of his cigar, while she watched the whirls of smoke fade into the gloaming. It made her think how dreams of power and symbols of authority vanish into nature's indifference.

It was August 1997, and he had advised her to adopt a child. Diane had already considered the possibility, but that evening she made up her mind.

Almost a year later, in March 1998, he had volunteered his personal assistance in making the application go through the mill more quickly. He would call the head of the social services in person. He could pull strings for her. Diane had refused at first but, when she realised that her application had no chance of being accepted, she agreed to his help on one condition – that he said nothing to her mother about it.

A few months later, she had received official authorisation and could now start exploring the international adoption associations. He had then directed her towards an organisation that he funded himself – the Boria-Mundi Foundation.

In September 1999, Diane had gone to Ra-Nong where she collected Lucien. Another clear memory came back to her. On the evening of the accident, when she had taken the little boy to her mother's, he had joined them on the landing and observed the child. He had seemed deeply moved and, quite unexpectedly, had kissed her. At the time, she had not understood why. She simply could not believe that he had just been trying it on with her, and she had been right. That kiss concealed a quite different reality. That kiss revealed the excitement of a man with a double life, who had just received his Watcher. A man with a murky past who, from behind his inscrutable smile, was waiting for the exact date when he should return to the dark landscape of his youth.

Charles Helikian was 58. He owned several offices specialising in company psychology. He was a personal adviser to several of France's captains of industry, and the strategic consultant of various ministers and public figures. A man of image and influence, who moved in the corridors of power, but who had never lost his altruism and humanity.

Diane knew nothing about his past. Except for one fact, which might be a connection: Charles had once been an extreme left-winger, in a Trotskyite group. At least that was what he always claimed, with his eyes shining as he spoke of his tormented youth. But what if he had in fact been a hard-line Communist, faithful to the Party and fanatical enough to take the plunge and cross the Iron Curtain, just as Philippe Thomas had done in 1969? Helikian was sufficiently intelligent to admit a half-truth now, thus knocking on the head any exploration of his past.

She could certainly easily picture him, young and slim,

screaming out his fury on the barricades in Paris in May 1968. She could also imagine him meeting Philippe Thomas at his psychology lectures at the University of Nanterre. After the failure of the Paris uprising, the two of them must have united their fervour in one crazy scheme – to go over to the heart of the red continent. Presumably they also shared an interest in psychic powers and hoped to be able to research the subject more thoroughly in the USSR.

The picture was beginning to come into focus in Diane's mind. Once they had reached the Soviet Union, the two deserters had joined the parapsychology lab in the tokamak. They had then taken part in the TK 17 experiments. They had belonged to a circle of men on a quest for the impossible.

Diane had not turned on the bedside lamp in her tiny room. She had just slipped in beneath the duvet, still fully dressed, and curled up with her knees against her chest. For the last three hours, she had lain there thinking. And she was increasingly sure that she was right. She had been tricked and used by her stepfather, for whom she had been the ideal prey. The perfect godmother for his Watcher.

She now tried to work in all the other events that had occurred after Lucien's arrival in Paris. For some strange reason, Philippe Thomas and Charles Helikian had now become enemies. This explained why the museum curator had tried to eliminate Helikian's messenger – thus stopping him from finding out the date and being able to go to the tokamak. Why? Was Charles a danger to him? If, like the others, he had paranormal powers, what were they? Diane imagined that her stepfather had then contacted Rolf van Kaen, another member of the circle, so that he could use his acupuncture. In this way, she started to perceive the alliances and rivalries between the former members of the laboratory – but what was their objective?

Was Charles Helikian still alive?

And if he was, was he now heading towards the stone circle?

That was easy to find out. Diane sat up in bed and looked at her watch. In the darkness, the fluorescent hands indicated that it was three o'clock in the morning. So in Paris it was eight the previous evening.

She got up and felt for the wall. When she had located her satellite telephone, she pointed it towards the small blue square of the window, with the light still off. But when she looked at the quartz screen, she saw that no connection had been made.

Without even putting on her shoes, she went out into the corridor.

CHAPTER 53

Everything was quiet. She felt the uneven planks wobble beneath her feet. Her eyes gradually got used to the dark. At the far end of the corridor, she noticed a large moonlit window. Exactly what she needed.

She went over to it, grabbed the handle and pulled it open. The icy wind slapped her face, but this made her feel that she was re-establishing contact with the far-off world of satellites. She pointed her set outside and stared at the screen. It was now capturing a signal. She rapidly dialled the number of the flat on Boulevard Suchet. No answer. Then she tried her mother's mobile. There were several electronic screeches and three rings, then she heard a familiar "Hello?"

She remained silent. Sybille asked again:

"Is that you Diane?"

"Yes, it's me."

Her mother started firing on all cylinders:

"What the hell are you doing? Where in God's name are you?"

"I can't tell you. How's Lucien?"

"You disappear, the police start looking for you, then you just phone up out of the blue like this?"

"How's Lucien?"

"First you tell me where you are."

The miracle of technology was working overtime. At a distance of nearly 6,500 miles, the two women were rowing as if they were in the same room. Diane articulated firmly:

"We won't get anywhere like this. I repeat that I can't tell you anything. I did warn you about what was going to happen."

Sybille sounded out of breath.

"The policeman in charge of the investigation is . . ."

"I know."

"They say you're involved, and also in the death of a young woman, I just . . ."

"I told you to trust me."

Her mother's voice cracked:

"I mean, do you really understand what's happening here?"

Sybille was starting to run out of steam. Diane repeated her question once more:

"How's Lucien?"

"Fine. Better and better. You can see smiles on his lips. According to Daguerre, he'll regain consciousness in a few days' time."

A wave of warmth ran through Diane's veins. She pictured the corners of his tiny lips rising with a surge of merriment. One day, perhaps, they would be together again, sharing those smiles in peace and quiet. She asked:

"What about his temperature?"

"It's gone down. He's stable now."

"And . . . what about the hospital? Has anything odd happened?"

"What do you imagine might happen? Haven't you had enough strange events yet?"

It seemed to Diane that her hypotheses were all being confirmed. The trances and the fits were over. The Lüü-Si-Ans were now out of the picture and out of danger. The focus had moved to the tokamak. Her mother yelled:

"How can you do this to me? I'm worrying myself sick."

Diane glanced out at the shadowy, chaotic town. She noticed the broad avenue that ran alongside the monastery and the headlamps of a few Japanese cars as, white with dust, they drove through the chill night air. At the other end of the line, she could hear the hum of traffic behind her mother's voice. She pictured to herself the gleaming bodywork and the modern lighting of Paris's streets. Now it was time for the crucial question:

"Is Charles with you?"

"I'm just about to join him."

Eight o' clock. Time for the evening's activities to start. Diane now realised why her mother sounded out of breath. She was presumably rushing towards some appointment, a dinner party; or else a theatre. She asked:

"And how is Charles?"

"He's worried. Just like me."

"And there's nothing special?"

"Whatever do you mean?"

"I don't know . . . he's not planning a trip or anything?"

"No, not at all . . . What's this all about?"

Her new hypothesis had just disintegrated. Her ideas always led her down blind alleys. She now weighed up her vain suppositions. How could she have thought that her stepfather was involved in this chaotic adventure? How could she have fitted that calm, tranquil Parisian existence into her own nightmare?

She heard a noise behind her to her left. She peered down the corridor that led away from her. Nobody. But the noise came again, even clearer this time. Before hanging up, she mumbled:

"I'll call you back."

At that very moment, a shadow appeared at a distance of about 20 yards. A small man, seen from behind, wearing a long coat and ill-fitting schapska. In a flash, Diane thought of the photograph of the Tseven physicist, wearing just the same sort of hat. She whispered: "Talikh . . ."

She followed him. The man was swaying slightly, steadying himself on the walls from time to time. One detail intrigued her: his right sleeve had been pulled up to his elbow. When the man reached the end of the corridor, he bent down over the water pump, which each floor had and which made for a sort of communal bathroom. Diane approached him. The shadow was using his left hand to work the pump, while holding his right arm below the metal spout. The water had not yet arrived.

She froze. Intuitively, she turned to her right and saw a mark on the wall – the bloody print of a tiny hand. At once she glanced back at the shadow and at the dark gleam from its outstretched right arm. Dumbstruck, she suddenly understood that the murderer was there, just a few yards away from her. And that he had just killed again, in the midst of the monastery.

The man in the schapska turned round towards her. He was wearing a balaclava over his face. Diane stared at his eyes, or rather at the way they gleamed through the openings in the wool like two drops of varnish in the night. It felt as though he were reading her mind – and that, mirror-wise, he had just encountered his own identity as a murderer in the young woman's stare. A second later, he had gone. Without any idea what she was doing, Diane sprinted after him. She rounded the first corner of the corridor and found nothing. It stretched away across a distance of a good 50 yards. The killer could not have covered it in just a few seconds. What about the bedrooms? Maybe he had hidden in one of the cells on that storey . . .

She slowed to a cautious walking pace and peered round at the doors to her left and to her right. Suddenly, the cold intensified and she looked up. A skylight had been left half-open. To the left, the wall was covered with irregular slats and formed an ideal ladder. Leaping up, she emerged through the hole, leaning both hands on the wooden frame.

The splendour of the night overwhelmed her. The sky was indigo and dotted with stars. The roof tiles ran down in a gentle slope. The upturned edges then rose up in front of the darkness like the prows of ancient ships. It felt as though she had just crossed a panel of rice paper and had broken through to the far side of Asia's image. She was now moving like a black ink brush on a sketch – the very essence of grace.

Nobody was there. The only place of shelter was the chimney, so Diane clambered up the slope towards the ridge of the roof. Despite her fear, despite the cold, the spell did not wear off. It felt as though she was walking over a sea of terracotta with red ripples. She reached the top and headed for the chimney. She slowly moved round it. Nobody. Not a sound. Not so much as a rustle.

At that instant, she saw the figure of a man, crouching on top of the chimney right in front of her. Once more, it felt as if the killer was reading her mind and that, in return, she could fathom his resolution: he had to kill her to stop her from talking. By the time she had realised this, the figure had stretched up into a black line. Then a terrible weight crashed down on her. Diane fell, but a hand stopped her at once. She looked up. There he was, holding her by her pullover, crouching down over the roof like a wild animal. His turned-up schapska stood out against the bright blue of the night.

Diane did not have the strength to fight. Even more than

the terror, weariness and despair were dragging her down. But also something more indistinct and confused, which was now starting to crystallise: the feeling that she had already experienced this scene. She half-opened her lips, perhaps to groan, perhaps to plead, but the man jerked her up and dragged her to the top of the roof. She was now lying on her back.

The monster leant over her and opened its mouth horribly wide. Slowly, as though in a ritual movement, its dry, blood-stained fingers drew near to its lips. Then Diane suddenly saw what the hand was after – beneath the tongue glistened the blade of a carpet cutter. She forced herself up. She just could not die like that. The tiles slid away under her feet. She was then gripped by a crazy hope. She could slide down the roof and launch herself into the void. Exchange one death for another. Bending both legs, she kicked out at the killer's belly. He dropped her, and she rolled to her right, slithering down the earthen surface. Seconds were transformed into jolts. Her speed increased. All she could feel now were the bumps of the tiles, the chill of the night and the abyss that was waiting for her, drawing her in. Death. Peace. Darkness.

She fell over the edge and felt her body tumble.

But she did not fall. Something inside her had grabbed on to the edge. With splinters beneath her fingers, with the icy wind blowing her to and fro, her hands refused to let go ... Her conscious mind was now powerless. Her body had decided for her. It was a coalition of her muscles and nerves. A fight for survival.

Suddenly, hands gripped her wrists. When she looked up, she could not believe what she saw. Above her, standing out against the sky, was Giovanni's face, with that expression of amazement that he did so well. He vanished from view once more. Then she heard his breathing as he panted under the strain. Suddenly, she was hiked up straight back on to the roof again. Broken, exhausted and annihilated, she slumped down like a sack of potatoes.

"Are you OK?" Giovanni asked.

She just managed to murmur:

"I'm cold."

He took off his pullover, put it over her shoulders then asked her:

"What happened?"

Without answering, Diane doubled up. He knelt down and spoke just by her ear, his voice resonating in the darkness:

"The monks . . . they called for me. They've found . . . a corpse in one of the bedrooms."

Squeezing her knees into her armpits, she slowly rocked backwards and forwards.

"I'm cold."

The Italian hesitated for a moment, then said:

"We'll have to go back down. The police are on their way."

She stared at him, as though amazed about him being there. She examined those chubby, round features of a spoilt child, and that astonishment of a normal man living in a normal world. She finally whispered:

"Giovanni, you're going to have to learn . . ."

"To learn what?"

She felt her tears glisten on to her cheeks.

"To learn about me."

CHAPTER 54

The sleepy monks were sitting side by side along the ill-lit corridor. The police – or soldiers, Diane was not sure which – had decided to round everyone up, thus emptying the monastery and taking its entire population to some governmental building somewhere in Ulan Bator. It was a huge cube of concrete criss-crossed by long corridors and dotted with small rooms with bare walls and broken windows, patched up with cardboard. The parquet had potholes gouged out of it and the other surfaces were so cracked that, in the shadows, it looked as though they were tracing out fossilised trees.

Diane and Giovanni had been given privileged treatment. They were waiting in an officer's room, beside a dark wood stove, which was unfortunately unlit. The two of them shivered beneath their hoods, unable to get warm. For some mysterious reason – or because of some strange mistake – they were alone in the office with the suitcase and clothes that had been found in the victim's room. Diane peered rapidly through the slit in the door, then went over to them.

"What are you doing?"

In the icy darkness, Giovanni's voice sounded unreal, almost magical. Without looking at him, she answered:

"What does it look like? I'm snooping around."

She stuck her hand into the pockets of the black woollen coat, where she found an olive green passport. The gilded symbol and letters engraved on the cover stood for the Czech Republic. She opened it and read the name: Hugo Jochum. As for the photograph, she recognised the face at once: it was the old man with dark glasses who had been sitting behind them some hours ago in the refectory of the monastery. A bronzed, wrinkly face with brown blotches on the forehead.

He was presumably another member of the tokamak, on his way to the stone circle.

She searched through the other pockets, but found nothing. Giovanni came over to her.

"Are you crazy, or what?"

Diane was now opening the suitcase. It was not locked. With a flurry of gestures, she went through its contents: pricey clothes, cashmere sweaters and designer shirts. Apparently he had been far wealthier than most other Czechs. She carried on looking. Two cartons of cigarettes. An envelope containing $2,000. And, among the clothing, a book written in German by Hugo Jochum and published by a university press. Giovanni was stammering:

"Stop . . . stop . . . You're mad, we'll . . ."

"Can you read German?"

"What? . . . Yes, a bit, I . . ."

She threw him the book.

"What does the blurb on the back say? Who's the author?"

The Italian glanced round at the door. Beyond the threshold, complete silence reigned. Nobody would ever have thought that a good 30 people were waiting there to be questioned. Trembling, Giovanni concentrated on the book.

Diane searched on. No weapons, not even a knife. Nothing. He clearly had not felt in danger. And he knew the country. Because there were no guide books or maps. Giovanni blurted out:

"It . . . it's incredible!"

She turned towards him. Credibility would have astonished her. She nodded to him to explain.

"He was a professor of geology at the Charles Polytechnic Institute in Prague."

"What's incredible about that?"

"He was also a water diviner. According to the blurb, he

could detect streams deep under the earth, as though he had a supernatural power. As a scientist, Jochum studied these sorts of phenomena in his own body."

Diane mentally filled out the list of parapsychologists at TK 17: Eugen Talikh and his bio-astronomy, Rolf van Kaen and acupuncture, Philippe Thomas and psychokinesis. And now Hugo Jochum and dowsing.

A form appeared in the doorway.

Diane just had time to close the suitcase, as soon as Giovanni had slipped the book back inside. The two of them turned round, with their hands behind their backs.

The man standing there was the person who had organised the rounding-up of the monks: a colossus with a black hat and a capacious leather coat. The chief of police, or something along those lines. He was holding the two Europeans' passports, as though showing them that he was the cat and they were the mice.

He spoke to Giovanni in the sharp syllables and guttural counterpoints of Mongol. The embassy official nodded rapidly. Then, manoeuvring his glasses on his nose, as though they were a piece of precision surgical equipment, he whispered to Diane:

"He wants us to go and see the body with him."

CHAPTER 55

It was not a morgue. Not even a hospital.

Diane imagined that it must be Ulan Bator's medical school, or perhaps the science academy. They reached a dazzlingly bright amphitheatre. The floor was made of clay, while the rows of seats, topped by desks, formed a tiered arc that ascended up towards the ceiling. To the left, above the blackboard, huge painted panels still bore the profiles of Karl Marx, Friedrich Engels and Vladimir Ilyich Lenin.

In the midst stood an iron table that had been bolted to the floor.

And on that table lay the body.

Two male nurses stood motionless, one at either side. Their traditional robes were covered by long plastic aprons. Beside them, policemen in quilted, Chinese-style coats and caps embroidered with gold and red were stamping their feet on the ground and blowing into their hands in an attempt to warm themselves up.

The police chief, followed by Diane and Giovanni, approached. She had no idea why they had been brought there. They surely could not be suspected of the murder, nor be witnesses – she had mentioned nothing about her clash with the killer. She imagined that the leather-clad officer naturally associated them with the victim for the simple reason that they were the only three Caucasian people in the monastery.

With a rough sweep of his hand, the man unveiled Hugo Jochum's face and torso.

Diane stared at his thin face, with its jutting features and halo of yellowish hair. The old yellow skin, stretched out over the bones, looked like fossilised amber. But a bizarre detail had already caught her attention. The body was dotted with brown marks. On the torso, these signs of aging had proliferated. Dark and granular, they covered the body with their untiring geography. For an instant, they made her think of a leopard's skin.

Then she noticed the slight incision below the sternum – the killer's mark. Clenching her hands in her pockets, she bent down and examined the cut. The man looked slightly pigeon-chested, as though his torso had been raised up from inside. It still bore the traces of that arm which had slipped in under the ribs, reaching for the heart amid the living organs.

She looked up. All the men were staring at her. What she read on their worried faces told her something new. The murderer's technique might mean nothing in Paris, or else be seen simply as a sign of a pathological condition. But in Ulan Bator, things were different. Everyone recognised that scar. Everyone knew the method. Here, the technique had not been chosen at random and was not a symptom of some inexplicable madness. The murderer was intentionally killing his victims as he would slaughter cattle. By doing so, he was reducing them to the level of beasts. She thought of Eugen Talikh and the conviction that had gripped her in the corridor of the monastery. If he really was guilty, then why had an inoffensive physicist become a savage murderer? Was this revenge? What wrong had these men once done to deserve to be slaughtered like animals?

The officer stepped forwards and stood in front of Diane. He was still holding their two passports. Staring at her, he spoke to Giovanni. Then the Italian came over to her and asked:

"He wants to know if you knew this man."

Diane shook her head. What worried her now was that they might be kept there to help with the inquiry, or because of some administrative procedure. And she had just three days left to get to the tokamak. She whispered her fears softly to Giovanni. He then launched into a brief discussion with the giant, who, quite unexpectedly, burst into laughter, then answered with a quick rejoinder.

"What did he say?" she asked.

"We have our official authorisations. There's no reason to keep us here."

"Why is he laughing?"

"He thinks that, whatever happens, we won't be able to escape."

"Why?"

The Italian grinned even more broadly for the policeman's benefit, then peered round at Diane.

"According to him: 'You can always escape from a prison. But who can escape from freedom?'"

CHAPTER 56

The Tupolev did not even have any seats or a cabin. It was a freight plane with grey sides, about 300 feet long, decked with nets for hanging on to, or for stashing parcels. Crammed in, several hundred Mongols were sitting side by side on the floor, bent over their bags, boxes and bundles, while trying to control their children and sheep.

Diane was crouching among the crowd. She was now so feverish that she was almost hysterical. She had not slept, but did not feel at all tired. She did not even feel any pain from her rooftop fight. The violence of the previous night seemed to have passed straight through her, leaving no visible mark, except for an intense excitement, an inner vibration throughout her body.

Despite the murder, despite the mysteries in the monastery and despite the fact that Diane had clearly told him only about ten per cent of the truth, Giovanni had not held back – he wanted to lead this expedition as far as the border with Siberia. The two of them had just had time to pack and drink some scalding tea before heading off to the airport to catch the weekly flight to Mörön, a small town about 300 miles to the north-west of the capital.

The plane had now been flying for over an hour. The

humming of the jet engines was stinging their ears and deadening their limbs. Even the sheep were now as motionless as figurines. Only Diane remained agitated, constantly getting to her feet then sitting down again between the passengers and bags. At other times, she tried to calm herself by observing the men and women around her.

The faces were already different from those she had seen in Ulan Bator. The men had yellowish-brown skin with deep wrinkles, while the women and children were diaphanous and spotless. Diane also examined the brilliant colours of the *deels*. There were shades of blue, of green and of yellow, splashes of white and of red, shimmerings of orange, of pink and of violet . . .

Diane took the hand of a little boy, sitting on a crushed cardboard box next to her, and then asked Giovanni:

"What's his name?"

He asked the mother, listened to the reply, then translated:

"Khoserdene, or 'double gem'. In Mongolian, names have a meaning."

"What about him?"

She was now looking at a younger boy, sheltering in the arms of a woman with a blazing indigo turban.

"March sunshine," the attaché interpreted.

"And him?"

"Iron armour."

Diane stopped asking questions. She was now staring at the women's headscarfs, which enveloped their black hair. Among the printed patterns, she noticed some animals. Majestic reindeer, eagles whose wings were tipped with gold, or bears whose paws stretched out into dark designs. Taking a closer look, she noticed something else. In the reflections from the silk, the antlers, wings and paws became human arms, forms and faces . . . In fact, on each fabric, both interpretations were possible. It was a sort of double-faced secret, revealed by the light. Diane sensed that this optical effect was intentional – and highly significant.

"In the taiga," Giovanni explained, "there's an identification between man and beast. To survive in the forest, hunters take their inspiration from animals and devise their own ways to adapt. The fauna is both the prey and a model. An enemy and an accomplice."

The Italian was yelling over the din of the freight plane.

"And this goes even further when we come to the shamans. According to the ancient beliefs, they had the power to transform themselves quite literally into animals. When they needed to talk with the spirits, they went into the forest and stopped living as humans – they gave up eating cooked meat for instance – before undergoing the final transformation and entering the world of the spirits."

The attaché fell silent for a few seconds to get his breath back. Then he leant over to Diane, as though he was about to whisper a secret in her ear. The grey sides of the fuselage were reflected in his glasses, turning them into gilded vessels.

"There's a famous Tseven tradition. In the days before they disappeared, the shamans from each clan had to meet up at a secret location and fight each other in the forms of their fetishistic animals. These combats terrified the Tsevens and were of vital importance."

"Why?"

"Because the winner took over the losers' powers and thus – in a way – brought them back to his clan."

Diane closed her eyes. For the last ten years, she had been studying predators, analysing their behaviour and observing their reactions. There had been just one basic objective in her research: to fathom out these animals' violence and, perhaps, to reveal their inner secrets.

Such shamanic traditions were extremely close to her own interests. And the idea of a fight to the death between two human animals fascinated her. She, too, had taken refuge in the minds of animals for her psychic survival after her teenage accident.

She opened her eyes again and, in the pale light of the plane, observed the passengers in their brightly coloured *deels* and the women's shimmering headscarfs. In some strange way, she felt that she too had an appointment in the depths of the taiga.

An appointment with herself.

CHAPTER 57

At the end of the afternoon, aboard the second aircraft – a tiny biplane, wobbling through the winds and clouds – the steppes suddenly became covered by an immense forest. Hills rose up with red and golden slopes, clearings mined out darker shades, while the earth scintillated with the hundreds of white veins formed by streams. They were now at the northern border of the country, just beside Siberia.

Instead of receiving an energy boost from such beauty, Diane felt exhaustion slide over her. But Giovanni was clearly ecstatic at the sight of this landscape.

"The lake district! It's Swiss Mongolia!" he yelled, leaning over to the window.

He produced a map, settled down at the back of the aircraft and proceeded to broadcast a commentary at a high enough pitch to drown out the din from the propellers.

"This is going to be an incredible journey! We're pioneers, Diane!"

At six o'clock that evening, they touched down on the plain.

Tsagaan-Nuur boasted only about 30 buildings: isbas painted with pastel shades. While the passengers in the freight plane from Mörön had shown no interest at all in these European travellers, the population of the town became fascinated by them, especially Diane, whose blond locks trailed from her schapska.

While Giovanni was talking to an old reindeer breeder, Diane walked over to one of his enclosures. His animals were small, dotted with black and white, and looked like scale models, somewhere between cuddly toys and stone statues. Only their antlers gave them a certain nobility. Each animal's head was crowned with branches covered by a sort of grey velvet, which peeled off at that time of year.

The ethnologist came over to Diane to explain the situation. The farmer was ready to hire out six or seven mounts but there was one condition: he wanted first to see them in action, and to judge their ability to ride reindeer. His pride stung, Giovanni tried to mount one of them immediately. After his third fall, he seemed to be getting tired of the laughter of the Mongols, who had gathered round to enjoy the show. After the fifth, he examined his equipment. Why wasn't the saddle fixed properly? After the seventh, he began talking about the possibility of going there on foot. Finally, the owner was good enough to offer a few explanations. The reindeers' hide was so smooth that nothing adhered to it. So it was impossible to use harnesses. Instead, the saddle remained loose and the rider had to follow the animal's movements – floating on its spine and changing direction by holding on to its neck. To demonstrate, the breeder leapt on to one of his charges and rode it around the pen.

Diane and Giovanni began their apprenticeship. There were more tumbles and more laughter. Soaked and covered in mud, the two travellers abandoned themselves to the village's jovial atmosphere. When Diane did not use the stirrups, she was so tall that she could mount her reindeer straight from the ground. This caused much amusement among the spectators. In this explosion of hilarity, the two travellers seemed finally to attune their moods.

But, above all, after each fall and each burst of laughter, a feeling of melancholy gripped them. They looked up to stare at the high walls of the Khoridol Saridag chain which blocked the horizon in a silence of quartz. The gilded twilight wind suddenly blew up again, beating against their hot faces. Diane's eyes then met Giovanni's, and they suddenly noticed, as the grasses were being blown flat in languid waves, what each blast was carrying: sad songs of broken hearts and journeys with no return. When night fell, and they at last could manage their little grey mounts, they had also discovered another secret: the unnerving nostalgia of the taiga.

CHAPTER 58

Their trek started at dawn.

The breeder and his son had finally decided to accompany them. Their convoy was made up of seven animals, with three carrying their supplies: guns, mess tins, the canvases and pegs of Soviet army tents, quarters of mutton wrapped up in cloth and various other items Diane had failed to identify. They advanced slowly. The reindeer plodded across the surging plains, slipping on the reddish foliage and gripping on to the first outcrops of rock, causing showers of loose scree. It was easy, there was no danger, and it could well have been dull had it not been for the constant torment of the cold.

It infiltrated the slightest gap in their clothing, wrapping an icy membrane over their skin, petrifying their limbs, freezing their fingers and toes. Every hour, they had to stop to walk a little, to move, to drink tea, anything to revive themselves. While the Mongols were scratching the insides of their eyelids with their knives, Diane and Giovanni remained motionless, shivering, unable to speak, stamping on the ground with their numb feet. Taking their gloves off was out of the question, for the slightest contact with a frozen rock would have stripped the skin from their palms. They also had to avoid drinking anything that was too hot, since the enamel on their teeth would have cracked because of the huge contrast in temperatures. When they mounted their reindeer once more, their bodies scarcely less rigid, their hearts were filled with a sense of defeat, of the invincibility of death. The cold had not left them.

On other occasions, the sun beat down on them. The travellers then had to put up their hoods as a protection against its torrid beams, as though out in the middle of the desert. The burning wind became so intense, so voracious that it seemed almost to have started blowing in reverse, sucking the skin from their faces in charred flakes. Then, suddenly, the blinding disc vanished and the mountain was plunged once more into a profound gloom. The cold clamped itself again around their bones, like a frozen vice.

By the beginning of the afternoon, they had reached the pass, which stood at an altitude of some 9,000 feet. The landscape altered. Beneath the clouds, the entire scene became black, lunar and sterile. The grass gave way to mosses and lichens. The trees became scarcer and more gaunt, before finally disappearing completely, to be replaced by verdigris rocks, stony gulches and grim shafts. Sometimes their path took them through dull marshes, dotted with a sprinkling of conifers. While on other occasions the country seemed quite literally to be bleeding, turning up blocks of turf with heather whose violet flowers

287

looked like drops of gore. The tundra, the frozen entrails of the earth, inaccessible and forgotten, had enveloped them like a curse.

Diane observed the migrating birds in the sky, all flying in the opposite direction to them – towards warmth. She watched them winging their way in haughty silence. With her lips white from her protective cream and with sunglasses wrapped round her skull, she felt more resolved than ever to overcome these mountains. She absorbed each sensation and each moment of suffering, even drawing a strange ambiguous pleasure from them. This trek seemed to her to be a sort of justified test. She had to confront this country. She had to cross its rocky flanks, bear its cold, its heat and this bitter desert of granite.

Because this was Lucien's country.

It was as if she were returning to the source of her child. The barriers around her, the obstacles in her path and the cracks marking her skin were all necessary steps in bringing him to life. Her physical links with her adopted son were growing stronger in this granite corridor. This terrible, pitiless journey was her giving birth. A delivery of frost and fire, which would result in a total union with her child – if she survived.

She suddenly realised that the landscape was gradually changing. A softness and a rustling were now taking the edge off the harshness of the environment. Flakes were floating gracefully in the air and progressively covering the tundra. An immaculate whiteness sprinkled the branches, rounding off their angles, reshaping each form and contour into a soft, personal, intimate architecture. Diane smiled. As they reached the top of the slope, they were now moving through the sacred world of snow. The convoy was crossing an increasingly pure and transparent clarity, at the precise border between earth, water and air.

The convoy slowed slightly, growing languid as the reindeers' hooves became silent. The Mongol breeder started yelling. His weary beasts belled back at him and speeded up, crossing the white frontier and finally starting the descent on the far side of the mountain. The land levelled out, seeming to hesitate between gentle slopes then abrupt drops, which were now sweeping downwards amid snowdrifts and layers of moss. Grass reappeared and trees multiplied. Suddenly, they reached the mountain side that led down to the final valley.

The tips of the larches swayed in the gilded mists. The leaves of the birches shimmered in ochre or purple tones, or else, already dry, twisted into grey shavings. The fir trees seethed with shadows of green. Below them, the pasturelands glittered with such freshness that they evoked an entirely novel sensation – a childlike wonder that stirred the blood. But, most importantly, at the bottom of that huge cradle lay a lake.

Tsagaan-Nuur.

The White Lake.

Above its clear waters, the blue and white mountains of the Khoridol Saridag range surged up, while below, on its utterly still surface, the same peaks were reflected upside down, as though prostrating themselves before their own models, while at the same time surpassing them in majestic purity. Joined in this peaceful, warm embrace, the real mountains and their watery roots merged together in a vague, mysterious line.

Dazzled by the scene, the convoy stopped. All that could be heard was the clicking of the stirrups and the hoarse breath of the reindeer. Diane had to make an effort not to lose her balance. She slipped a thumb under her sunglasses to wipe away the drops of condensation that were misting her view.

But she couldn't.

Because there were tears running from her frozen eyelids.

CHAPTER 59

That evening, they camped beside the lake. The pitched their tents beneath the fir trees then ate outside, despite the cold. After praying to the spirits, the two Mongols prepared a traditional meal: boiled mutton and tea flavoured with animal fat. Diane would never have believed herself capable of swallowing such food. But that evening, like the day before, she moved nearer the fire and devoured her share without saying a word.

The sky above them was absolutely pure. She had admired many night skies, especially in the deserts of Africa, but she could not remember ever having seen such violent clarity and proximity. She felt as though she were sitting directly beneath the primordial explosion. The myriad stars in the Milky Way danced away in an endless saraband. Some clusters of stars shone with such intensity that they rippled with dazzling fire. Others, meanwhile, were lost in iridescent mists, like mother-of-pearl. And all of the time, the extreme edges of the circle faded away in sparkling shimmers, as though about to evaporate into the interstellar immensity.

When she looked down, Diane saw that their guides, who were sitting a few yards away, were talking to a newcomer, who was invisible in the darkness. It was presumably a lone breeder, who had spotted their fire and had joined them for a hot meal. She listened. It was the first time that she had been so attentive to the Mongol language, which sounded to her like a succession of raucous syllables, strangely dotted with Spanish jotas and undulating vowels. The newcomer pointed up at the sky.

"Giovanni?"

The Italian, immersed inside his anorak, lifted up the side of his woolly hat. She asked him:

"Do you know who he is?"

He put his hands back into his pockets.

"A local, I imagine. He's got one hell of an accent."

"Do you understand what he's saying?"

"He's telling some old legends. Tseven tales."

Diane sat up.

"Do you think he's a Tseven?"

"You can't get that out of your head, can you? I've already told you, they don't exist any more!"

"But if he's telling stories that are . . ."

"They're just part of the local folklore. By crossing the pass, we've entered the territory of Turkish ethnic groups. Everyone around here has a few drops of Tseven blood. Or at least, everyone knows the old stories. It doesn't mean a thing."

"You could still ask him, couldn't you?"

The Italian sighed and stood up. He went over to the three men. Giovanni started by introducing himself. The visitor was called Gambokhuu. His face was like an old wrinkled mask which, in the starlight, seemed to throw off disturbing shadows. The ethnologist translated his answers:

"He says he's Mongol. And that he's a fisherman on the White Lake."

"Was he here in the days when the tokamak was working?"

Giovanni interpreted question and answer:

"He was born here. He remembers the circle perfectly."

Diane's skin prickled with a new flame. This was the first time that she was face to face with a man who had been near the stone circle when it was still operating. She went on:

"What does he know about what went on in the tokamak?"

"Really, Diane. He's only a fisherman. What do you expect . . . ?"

"Ask him!"

Giovanni did as she wanted. The fir trees were swaying in the icy blast, filling the night air with a fragrance of resin that was so strong and deep that it rasped their throats like smoke from a fire. Diane felt surrounded, penetrated by the texture of the taiga. The old Mongol was shaking his head.

"He doesn't want to talk about it," the Italian explained. "He says the place is cursed."

"Why is it cursed?" Diane raised her voice. "Insist on that point! It's of vital importance!"

The ethnologist looked at her suspiciously. Diane calmed down a little.

"Please, Giovanni."

He then resumed his conversation with the fisherman, who had produced a pipe – a sort of bent metallic tube – which he was now patiently stuffing with tobacco. It was only when he had lit its tiny bowl that he got round to replying. Giovanni provided a simultaneous translation.

"What he remembers best is the parapsychology lab. He recalls convoys of trains arriving from the Siberian border, full of shamans who were taken to one of the buildings in the compound. Everyone was talking about that because, for the Tseven workmen, this was an unspeakable outrage. By imprisoning the sorcerers, they were defying the spirits."

"Ask him if he knows what went on exactly in the lab."

Giovanni asked him, but the visitor made no reply. His burning pipe flashed back and forth like a distant lighthouse.

"He refuses to answer," the Italian concluded. "He just says that the place is cursed."

"But why? Because of the experiments?"

Diane was practically yelling. Suddenly, the old man's voice rose up once more, between draws on his pipe.

"He says blood was spilt," the ethnologist explained. "That the scientists were madmen, that they conducted horrific experiments. That's all he knows. He repeats that blood was spilt and that is why the spirits took revenge."

"How did they avenge themselves?"

Gambokhuu now seemed to have made up his mind to tell the whole story. He spoke without waiting for Giovanni, who was now summarising the flow of words.

"The spirits caused an accident."

"What accident?"

In the darkness, Giovanni's face hardened.

"In the spring of 1972, the circle exploded," he whispered. "A lightning bolt went through it."

It seemed to Diane that this bolt of lightning had torn her apart, too. She had been focusing exclusively on the parapsychology lab, with the idea that the origins of this drama lay in the research into altered states. But the real tragedy had sprung from the infernal machine itself. She asked:

"Were there any victims?"

Giovanni asked him and, sallow faced, listened to his reply.

"He says that there were at least 150 casualties. Apparently, all of the workers were inside the circle when the machine blew up. They were doing some kind of maintenance work when the plasma broke through the wall and burnt them."

Gambokhuu was now constantly repeating a single word – a word Diane recognised.

"Why is he talking about the Tsevens?" she asked.

"All of the workers were Tsevens. They were the last ones in the region."

So Diane and Giovanni had both been right. That solitary tribe had almost been wiped out by the Soviet oppression, but some of its members had survived. Now sedentary and living in a kolkhoz, they had been turned into obedient slaves doomed to a nuclear death. The ethnologist went on:

"He says that some of the survivors were holding their intestines in their hands, that the women refused to nurse their husbands because they no longer recognised them. He says that, despite their wounds, the dying were crying out that they were thirsty. When they died, their jaws broke like glass. There were so many flies on the injured that they couldn't see if their bodies were covered with burns or insects . . ."

Diane thought of the other survivors, of those who thought that they had escaped from being burnt. She was not sure about the exact after-effects of tritium radiation, but she knew all about the consequence of being irradiated by uranium. During the weeks after the bombing, the survivors of Hiroshima had begun to understand that survival meant nothing in the world of the atom. First their hair fell out, then they started suffering from diarrhoea, vomiting fits and internal bleeding. Then irreversible diseases appeared, such as cancers, leukaemia, tumours . . . The Tseven workers must have suffered in the same way. Not to mention the women who, months after the explosion, had given birth to monsters, or those who could no longer become pregnant, because the radiation had destroyed their reproductive cells.

Diane stared up at the sky. She refused to give in to compassion. She just could not allow herself to give way or to collapse, because she had to keep all of her deductive faculties in order to extract more information from these terrible revelations. The thought of Eugen Talikh suddenly crossed her mind. Indirectly, by organising those nuclear tests, the physicist had caused the doom and destruction of his own people. The scientific genius, the great Tseven hero, had brought about the annihilation of his own tribe . . .

Then another idea gripped her. What if Eugen Talikh had not been personally involved in that last fatal trial? If the accident had not been his fault, then wouldn't it have given him a perfect reason for such terrible retribution? Diane now framed a new hypothesis. What if, for some reason that escaped her for the moment, it was the staff of the parapsychology lab that had been responsible for the explosion? Wouldn't Talikh, the peaceful deserter to the West, then turn into a vicious killer when he heard that the researchers were about to return to the scene of their crime?

CHAPTER 60

Diane awoke with the first beams of daylight. She got dressed, putting on some watertight leggings and her parka before slipping under a waterproof poncho. Then she packed her rucksack: halogen torch, ropes, snap hook and spare batteries. She had no weapons, not even a knife. For an instant, she considered the idea of stealing a gun from one of the Mongols who were sleeping in the neighbouring tents, but immediately decided that it would be too risky. She zipped up her bag and emerged into the light of dawn.

Everything was frozen. The grass was white and occasionally dotted by bluish puddles. The dewdrops glistened in the stillness of frost. In the foliage, brittle stalactites hung from the branches. All of this scintillation seemed even brighter because of the surrounding mists which wrapped everything up in a light, playful opacity.

Further off, she sensed the presence of the reindeer. She could hear their hooves crunching into the layers of ice and their harsh breathing digging out zones of warmth in that world of total cold. She pictured them, grey and invisible in the fog, looking for salt among the stones, the lichen and the tree bark. Further off, she could just make out the regular lapping of the waters of the lake. Diane breathed in the chill air and looked round the camp. Not a movement. Not a sound. Everyone was asleep.

She plunged into the undergrowth, being careful not to smash the crystal bushes. A hundred yards on, she had to stop to relieve herself, cursing herself for not having thought of doing it before she had dressed completely.

Behind the trees, she pulled off her leggings as best she could and crouched down. The reindeer immediately smelt the salt in the urine and rushed over towards her, crashing through the frozen branches. She just had time to get dressed again then run off. At a safe distance, she slowed down and burst out laughing. Her laughter was nervous, edgy and silent, but it did her good. She stuck her thumbs under the straps of her rucksack and marched off. Once she had reached the lake side, she looked round to her right at the hill behind which, according to the guides, lay the tokamak. This meant a walk of a little over a mile. She slipped in under the larches and started her ascent.

Her breathing soon became painful. She was covered with sweat. Condensation from the fog was glistening on her poncho. Her breath was causing a crystalline rain to fall. She noticed darker shadows in the grasses. She went over. The verdure had been pressed into three distinct beds. Diane went to look. Some deer had slept there that night. The beds were still warm from their presence. She took off a glove and ran her fingers around them. Then her eye was caught by the dark roots that ran beneath her feet. She touched them, too, savouring their rugged texture.

Diane continued to climb. Only then did she recall what Gambokhuu had said. His description of the atomic catastrophe and the death agony of the victims. At the same time, yesterday's conclusions seemed more likely than ever. For some strange reason, the parapsychologists shared the responsibility for the disaster at the tokamak. One way or another, they were involved in the accident. She was suddenly struck by a succession of memories. She pictured Hugo Jochum's dark mottled skin. The pink epidermis of Philippe Thomas, whose bouts of eczema made him quite literally moult. She also recalled, from what seemed like a distant niche in her memory, Rolf van Kaen's strangely atrophied stomach, which meant that he had to ruminate red fruit . . .

Why hadn't that occurred to her last night?

The parapsychologists must also have been irradiated.

Each of them still bore the trace of that atomic blast, which must have hit them at a greater distance, and thus not so hard. Radiation stigmata could appear decades later, as deformities or illnesses. The probable explanation for the strange nature of those men's side-effects lay in the novel nature of the experiment. No-one before had ever been exposed to tritium radiation.

Diane started developing the idea. What if the explosion had not only upset their metabolisms, but also altered something in their minds? Perhaps the atoms could augment the power of consciousness and develop paranormal abilities.

In this affair, it was hard to believe in coincidences. So why not instead posit the idea that the researchers had intentionally exposed themselves to the radiation? That, while they had been carrying out their experiments, they had detected signs of possible mental transformations in the Tseven workers that had been caused by being exposed to tritium? Then the parapsychologists had set off the atomic blast as part of an incredible experiment. Something had gone wrong, men – a people – had died. But these sorcerer's apprentices had got the result that they wanted. Their powers had increased from the radiation. These men were Magi. Magi of the nuclear age.

As Diane strode on through the forest, her blood warmed up and the scenario became clearer and clearer. Everything fitted. The accident had happened because some scientists in search of the impossible had sabotaged the apparatus. This explained why Talikh was now hunting them down and intentionally reducing them to the level of wild beasts at the moment of death.

And this also no doubt explained why the men were coming back to the stone circle. They wanted to repeat the experiment, expose themselves to radiation and so renew their powers . . .

Diane stopped. She was now at the top of the hill and, through the fog, she could make out the descent into the next valley.

And, in the midst of that clearing, stood the huge crown of the tokamak.

CHAPTER 61

It looked like a town. All around the stone circle, a maze of buildings and rusty equipment stretched out, covering several hectares and disappearing into the mist. By the mountain to the right were the turbines of the power station that fed the thermonuclear circuit. She continued her descent. Beyond the buildings could be seen the half-obscured traces of roads and railways. It was thanks to this infrastructure that the Russians had managed to transport the men and materials needed for the construction of the site. Diane felt giddy. How many engineers, builders and roubles had been swallowed up by this project which had ended with a murderous lightning bolt?

She rounded the west side of the ring. Beneath her feet, the grassy soil was gradually being replaced by concrete slabs. She clambered over the fallen rock and lumps of old iron, then went inside the first building. It was partitioned by fitted panels, whose windows had all been smashed.

At the end of a corridor, Diane emerged on to a bare concrete patio, which had been fissured by the cold, and was covered by rubble and pine needles. As she approached, some red-beaked terns took off. The clacking of their wings echoed off the concrete walls and cast a red contrast against the green paint. She felt no fear. This place was so huge and so abandoned that it seemed unreal to her. Turning to her left, she went inside a block with large windows that let in the dawn light. As she advanced, she noticed that the walls were covered with fungi and that heather and whortleberries had taken root.

She came across other rooms containing torn straw mattresses, massive pieces of equipment and strange machines. Further on, she found a stairway leading down to a lower floor. She turned on her torch. At the bottom of the steps, a line of metal bars blocked her way. She pushed open the gate, which was not locked. Ignoring her apprehensions, she went down the dark corridor. It was as if her own breathing were filling up all the available space.

She had apparently stumbled on the prison. Her torch beam revealed the rows of cells at either side of the room. They were basic compartments, separated by low walls, where chains could still be seen bolted into the ground. Diane thought of the shamans that had been "imported" from Siberian prisons and camps. She thought of the Russian psychiatric asylums where thousands of dissidents had been "treated". What had gone on in this secret site? The jail still seemed to be echoing with the screams and groans of the terrified, shivering sorcerers as they waited in the darkness to find out what fate was in store for them.

Suddenly, her torch beam revealed an inscription that had been dug out in one of the walls. She went over to it and immediately recognised the same Cyrillic characters that she had seen in the Kurchatov Institute. They spelt the name: TALIKH. Beside it was another word, which she did not understand, then some figures: 1972. A white noise, a terrifying echo, rang out in Diane's consciousness. Eugen Talikh, the big boss of the tokamak had also been imprisoned here. He had shared the other shamans' suffering.

She tried to imagine why. In fact, this new piece of information solved more problems than it created. If TK 17 had been used to carry out sadistic experiments on the sorcerers, then Eugen Talikh would certainly not have approved of such practices. On the contrary, he must have stood up to the perpetrators, and threatened to report them to the Party. The roles had then been reversed. The parapsychologists, no doubt in league with the soldiers on the site, had imprisoned the physicist on some trumped-up charge of unpatriotic behaviour. After all, once a Tseven, always a Tseven. The Russian army must have been delighted to crush the pride of that little Asian. Diane ran her fingers over the inscription. It was almost as if she could sense the physicist's anger, engraved in the rock. Even though she was incapable of deciphering those scratches, she was sure that they must spell out a date not long before the accident in the spring of 1972.

So, she had guessed correctly. When the explosion happened, Talikh was no longer in charge of the tokamak – he was in jail as a simple political prisoner.

Astonished by her discovery, Diane went back upstairs and wandered around aimlessly. It took her a while to notice that the architecture was becoming grander and grander. The doors were getting higher and the ceilings were rising up to extraordinary heights. She was now nearing the tokamak.

She finally came across a leaded door, framed with steel, which was opened and closed by means of a wheel, like the airlock in a submarine. Above it, a faded red sign had been painted: the helix which in every country in the world announces the presence of radioactivity.

Diane put her torch between her teeth and clutched the wheel in her gloved hands. After a deal of effort, she managed to unblock it. With another yank, she opened it completely and, muscles at full stretch, pulled it towards her, breaking the seal of lichens around the frame. The door abruptly lurched out, then slid sideways along a rail. She was amazed. Made half of concrete and half of lead, it must have been over a yard thick.

There was a surprise awaiting her over the threshold: lamps had come on in the corridor. Fluorescent tubes were sending out a harsh, white light. How could the electricity still be working there? She thought of the other members of the tokamak. Had they already reached the circle? But she could not possibly turn back now. Not now that she was so near her goal.

Gingerly, she stepped inside the stone circle.

CHAPTER 62

Diane was now in a circular corridor whose width was a good 15 yards. At the centre of this passage ran a cylindrical conduit forming a circle within the circle, covered over with wires, coils and magnets. Above this apparatus stood magnetic archways which looked as though they were steel supports for this strange pipeline. Everything seemed to have been conceived in terms of circles, rings and curves.

She approached. The tangled cables were drooping down like creepers. Copper coils stood at regular intervals along the circuit. They shone with an antiquated pinkish gleam, as though redolent of the taste of a sucked sweet. Below, geometric structures of black metal held up the entire apparatus. Diane was now just a few paces away from the conduit. Amid the complex equipment, she could now see a smooth shell of black steel, the vacuum chamber, where plasma had once neared the speed of light and reached the temperature of stellar fusion.

She walked on cautiously, being careful not to make any noise or disturb the gravel that was covering the floor. She had never felt so tiny and pathetic. This machine came from another scale, another logic. She felt strangely uneasy inside this edifice, forged by mankind's megalomania, by that will to violate earthly laws, to disturb the very heart of matter and to surpass the primitive state of things. Kamil had mentioned Prometheus who had stolen the gods' fire. Gambokhuu had spoken about spirits that had taken revenge because of mankind's audacity. Whatever had really happened in that ring, Diane sensed that the tokamak had been the scene of a profanation, of a forbidden assault against superior forces.

She walked on like this for a few minutes, following the curve of the corridor. Then she decided to turn back. There was nothing to be discovered in this circle. Its technological hubris did not provide her with the slightest lead . . . The scream rose up like a metallic roar.

Instinctively, she clamped her hands to her ears. The cry of rebellion at once became even shriller. It was a piercing wave. An unbearable vibration. In shock, Diane suddenly realised that this was not a scream, but an alarm signal. The tokamak was coming back to life.

In sinister confirmation, a lead-coated door to her right slammed violently into the wall and bolted itself, as if by magic. She saw its wheel turn, while a red light came on above the frame. It was as if the entire edifice was switching itself back on. But, as in all high-risk sites, the first thing that happened in an emergency was that the danger area had to be isolated, the exits had to be closed, even if some human life was lost.

That was why the Tsevens had been burnt alive. And that was how she was going to die.

She thought of the airlock that she had left open. She turned round and sped towards it as fast as she could. She ran, and ran, and ran, her eyes dazzled by the flashing lights and her ears exploding from the alarm. She came across several doors, which all swung shut at her approach. Did she have the slightest hope of being able to run faster than the security system?

Suddenly, a purring started up beneath her feet. The circuit was heating up. Her mind raced. Would it set off a wave of electricity? Was there still some tritium gas in the vacuum chamber? How long would it take the atoms to turn into an arc at a temperature of several million degrees? Her heart aflame, she kept running down the corridor. The humming grew louder. The vibrations were now making the walls, floor and cables tremble and sending waves of terror through her body. At last she found the door she had come in through. It was still open. At that very instant, it started to slide along its rail. Diane saw the black pulleys turning, the hinges moving across laterally, then the thick lump of lead and concrete lining itself up with the opening.

She made a superhuman leap forward through the doorway, feeling the edge of the concrete brush against her ribs. She stumbled over the steel threshold, fell over, then immediately shrank back against the block that had just locked itself. Out of breath, her mind blank, she just kept on screaming, kicking with her feet and banging on the floor with her fists. She was letting off her panic – a panic caused by all of the trials she had confronted.

The shaking reached a pitch, taking her breath away. The wall seemed to be pounding against her, like the surface of a loudspeaker. Diane curled up more tightly, her muscles stiff, her jaws clamped, feeling the ground rise upwards in a tidal wave.

It lasted just a second. A fragment, a fraction of a second. Then silence fell, pushing away the deafening wailing of the alarm. It grew quieter. The floor became stable once more. She stayed there motionless, prostrate, staring into space.

Slowly, thoughts began to form in her mind again. A fact, a rumour quivered far, far away in the pit of her consciousness: it was all over. The tokamak's rebirth had lasted only a few seconds. The security system from another age had stopped the mechanism in its tracks. Diane realised that she was thinking of the thermonuclear circuit in terms of an independent entity – like a beast, or a volcano. But that was far from the case. A man had generated that new electric arc. Who was it? And why? To kill her? She was too exhausted to answer. Too worn out for any more questions.

She braced herself and got to her feet. It was then she noticed that the left half of her poncho had melted. She tore it off. Her parka, too, had been blackened and ripped into a long opening. Diane put her hand inside the gap and felt the wool and polyester fibres. They were also burnt. She rapidly pulled up her clothes. From her groin to her armpit, her skin was still crackling from the effects of the fire. Red crinkles ran across her flesh, as on anatomical prints of flayed people. Diane did not understand. And the absence of any pain was terrifying.

She leant down and examined the lead-coated wall where she had slumped down. There were tiny vertical cracks in it. Freezing winters and scorching summers had finally undermined the lead's hermetic seal. The atomic rays had filtered through the cracks and hit her, burning her to the very core. Horrified, she stumbled backwards. She thought that she had escaped from death. She had been wrong. Absolutely wrong. Because she had not just been burnt.

She had been irradiated.

And was virtually dead.

CHAPTER 63

The sun was now climbing over the valley. The verdant plains seemed to be rising up against the horizon, framed to the right by the forested hills and to the left by the foothills of the mountain which were still veiled in mist. A hundred yards further on, Diane noticed a form standing out. She screwed up her eyes and saw that it was Giovanni, who was advancing towards her, a gun slung over his shoulder. The long, languid grasses came up to his knees.

"What's going on?" he yelled. "I felt the earth shake and . . ."

A gust of wind carried the end of his sentence away. Diane staggered over to him. The burn was still numb, but she could distinctly perceive the wind beating into her face, the grass stroking her legs and the fresh fragrances rising up in heady streams to inebriate her soul.

"You might have waited for me," the Italian grumbled as he approached. "What happened?"

"The tokamak switched itself back on. I don't know what . . ."

"What about you?" he asked. "You look OK."

Diane smiled so as to curb her tears.

"How observant can you get?" she said.

She dug her fingers into her hair and effortlessly pulled out a handful. The radiation was already at work. The billions of atoms that composed her were beginning to break up, setting off a chain reaction which would stop only once she had been totally transformed. How much longer did she have? A few days? A few weeks?

"I was inside the machine, Giovanni," she murmured. "I've been irradiated. Irradiated to the core."

The ethnologist at last noticed the dark split in her parka. With two fingers, he pulled aside the material to reveal the

305

reddish burn. The skin was beginning to crack and peel off in strips.

"We'll . . . we'll get you looked after, Diane," he stammered, "just . . . just don't panic."

She was not listening to him. She did not want to slump into either despair or hope. All that interested her was how much time she had left. She had to live long enough to be able to unmask those demons, to reveal the truth and be certain that her adopted son would be let alone for good.

"We'll get you looked after," the Italian obstinately repeated.

"Shut up."

"I promise, we'll get you sent back to France at once and . . ."

"I told you to shut up."

Giovanni stopped. Diane went on:

"Can't you hear that?"

"What?"

"The earth's trembling."

Was the tokamak working again? She imagined the valley disappearing in the flames of an atomic blast. Then she realised that the vibrations were not coming from the site, but from the other side of the valley. She stared straight in front of her, between the hill and the rocky cliff. A huge cloud of dust, a sort of mist made of earth and blades of grass, was blocking the horizon.

Then she saw them.

She recognised them at once.

Tsevens.

Not ten of them.

Not a hundred.

But thousands.

A horde of riders steering a herd of reindeer whose countless backs were shimmering beneath the mirroring clouds, making a constant oscillation of spines and reflections. An endless flood was pouring down into the plain, then spreading out in a splendid mass of vigour, tumult and beauty. All that was missing were the colours: the men wore only black *deels* and the reindeer around them were all white or grey. On they galloped, rubbing against each other's spotted, mottled flanks and clashing with each other's velvety antlers, like animated branches, fantastic coral or concrete images of wind and of life.

Diane was so stunned, delighted and overwhelmed that she no longer knew where to look. She was trying to find a precise point where she could focus her attention when, abruptly, she found one. If she had to die at that instant, then it would be with this image printed on her irises.

The women.

It was the women, and they alone, who were controlling the herd at either side. Most of them were on horseback. They were yelling, with their cheeks on fire, their feet firmly set in their stirrups. Diane imagined that the designs on their clothes must also depict those magical metamorphoses that she had noticed on the aircraft. It now seemed as if those legendary creatures had leapt out of silk to walk the earth and redraw this clearing by ripping out clods of it and casting up grasses with their hooves.

They spun round on their horses, turned back and moved off again. With their bellies and thighs clamped to their mounts, they seemed almost to have passed directly through the animal and to be bounding back off the earth with rage and joy, an explosion of vitality that rose up to the sky.

Giovanni shouted over the din:

"What's happening now? We're going to get trampled to death!"

Flicking her hair to one side, Diane replied:

"No, I don't think so ... I think they've come to fetch us."

Then she strode off into the high grasses covering the plain.

In front of her, the lines of snowy, ashen reindeer galloped on through the vegetation. Diane kept walking. Behind the riders, she could now see some children on wooden saddles, straddling smaller animals. Their crimson faces popped out occasionally from behind the twisting antlers. Impassive, wrapped up in furs, they sat like princes on their stormy mounts.

The troop was now just a hundred yards away. Diane noticed a man who was ahead of the others. His posture and splendour had a special edge, which seemed to imply that he was in charge of the herd. And yet, he was very young – almost still a child – wearing a wide black hat. She suddenly felt sure that this Child King was a Watcher, a Watcher now maturing into a man and venerated by his tribe. She thought of Lucien. A confused mass of images passed in front of her, the theft of children, messages burnt into their flesh, the crossing of the frontier between life and death, the murders, the torture . . . all of it would finally fit together. But, right then, she could not give a damn. For, from the depths of this tumult, from among these people who had risen from the shadows, she saw a light beam out.

If they were still alive then, maybe, there was hope for her . . .

Like an ocean slowed by the beach, the entire herd stopped in a single movement just 20 yards from Diane. She approached them. The first reindeer were already sticking out their necks for the salt they could smell on her tear-stained cheeks. Staggering from exhaustion, she wondered what she could say to establish contact and in which language.

But that was not necessary.

The teenage king was already pointing her towards a harnessed mount, which was staring at her with its big gentle eyes.

CHAPTER 64

The massive cortege now headed for the slopes of the mountain. The herd was trotting with a docile elegance. Soon, it was crossing the stony terrain and pouring through the undergrowth, past the thickets and by the last trees until it had reached the pale lands of the tundra. It now manoeuvred on to a broad plateau covered with dense grasses and ringed by granite blocks, which looked like high altitude safety barriers. Dozens of men and women were pitching tents and placing military camouflage tarpaulins over their ridges.

Giovanni, who was alongside Diane, murmured:

"They're yurts, Tseven tents. I never thought I'd see such things."

Other groups were putting up pens of birch trunks, while the reindeer were already gathering inside. Animal cauls, the organic membranes that enclose the intestines, were drying like flags on the wooden poles. Diane allowed her mount to guide her. Her skin was prickling with static electricity and drying into bloodless rashes, while the burn started to ache beneath her skin, its bitterness mingling with the biting cold.

But she was almost too fascinated to care. She gazed at this tribe, which had sprung up from nowhere and which had presumably escaped observation from the air thanks to the mountain mists. Their faces were broad, hard and wrinkled. These were features that had been chiselled by the wind and the cold. Traits that had been sharpened and toughened by the bitter climate, but also worn down by atavistic characteristics and too much inbreeding. All of them – men, women and children – were wearing sombre *deels* with violet or indigo tints. But what most made the difference was the variety of their headgear: gaucho hats, fur schapskas, Phrygian caps, fedoras, balaclavas ... a veritable carnival dancing on their heads as they capered up and down on their mounts.

When they reached the centre of the camp, several women made Diane get out of her saddle. She put up no resistance. She just had time to whisper to Giovanni: "Don't worry." Then they led her to an isolated tent standing a hundred yards away by the outlying rocks. It enclosed an area of several square yards, with nothing on the ground except for the grass and a few stones dotted with moss. Diane looked up. Lumps of frozen meat had been hooked on to the frame of the yurt. To her right, some ritual objects were hanging up, or else laid on bark tablets: strings of horsehair, birds' nests, a chaplet of tiny jawbones, probably from baby reindeer. She could also see some black wrinkled shapes, which looked like the dried feet and penises of animals.

Two of her "escort" undressed her, while the third threw some horsehairs and drops of vodka on to the fire of the stove. A few seconds later, she was lying naked on a leather cover, which was as hard as an iron plate. She shivered, her eyes staring at her own body, which now seemed too tall, scrawny and pallid on that black bed. Three men entered the yurt. Diane curled up, but they did not even glance at her. They threw off their hats – a ski bonnet, balaclava and fedora – and picked up some drums that had been placed near the sanctuary. Immediately, their hammering began. Hard, dull blows with no resonance. Diane remembered something that Giovanni had told her: the ritual drums of the taiga were always sculpted from trees that had been struck by lightning.

A progression now appeared in the rhythm: a death-like rattle could be heard between the beats, as a muted echo of the drums. The men – three rock-like faces, dressed in black threadbare *deels* – started swaying from one foot to the other as they lifted their sticks. They looked like gloomy bears, still muddy from the woods.

The women forced Diane to lie out flat. She resisted for a moment to hide her nakedness, but quickly realised that the smoke from the stove had grown so thick that her body was now invisible. One of her escort sprinkled talc over her body, while a second one made her drink some scalding beverage. Sensations ran through her body, without any of them managing to dominate – cold, panic, suffocation . . . She laid her head on the leather and told herself that it was too late to turn back now. With her eyes closed and her shivering hands on her shoulders, she caught herself starting to pray. Hoping that the miracle was really going to happen. That Tseven magic was going to whisk her away and save her . . .

The drumming intensified. And the counterpoint of sighs grew louder, too, bursting out from their closed lips, producing an obsessive beat. Diane opened her eyes again in spite of herself. She was running with sweat. The men, mere hazy forms in the dense smoke, were moving sideways, bending their legs at each drumbeat. The women were now sitting on their heels, just beside Diane. With their eyes closed and palms placed upwards on their knees, they bent down, sat up, then bent down again. Their earrings caught her eye – they were made in the shape of migratory birds.

Suddenly, the fabric of the ceremony was torn in half. The women had produced flutes made of horn from the sleeves of their robes and were now blowing into them in unison. Their trills were so high-pitched and heady that it seemed that they might even overcome the drummers in the fieriness of their playing. Although still sitting, the flautists arched over, spinning round like tops made of sound, silk and fire. It was as though their lips were soldered on to their terrible instruments. Their puffed-up cheeks were like censers concealing sacred embers.

Then, amid this din, through the smoke, she appeared.

Her hat was stuck with eagle's feathers and its rolls of cloth were dangling down over her face. Her tiny form was wrapped up in a coat covered with heavy pieces of metal. As tense as a fist, she advanced in short rhythmic steps, clutching a mysterious object in her hands. It looked like a sort of fur purse. Petrified, Diane watched her approach. An indescribably shrill sound drowned out the beating of the drums and wailing of the flutes. She quickly realised that it was a cry. At first she thought that it was the sorceress, who was chanting beneath the folds of her hat. Then she caught on. It was not the shaman that was screaming, it was the furry pouch that she had in her hands.

It was alive.

A rodent, with long black hair, was wriggling with panic in the old woman's bony clutch. Diane shrank back against the edge of the tent, terrified by such compulsive images: the men swaying furiously back and forth, the women bending over their flutes and that sorceress fringed with feathers like a bird, holding out a small screaming mammal.

She just had to get away from this nightmare, to forget . . . Her shoulders were violently pressed back against the mattress. Her escort had dropped their instruments in order to pin her down. She tried to scream, but the smoke billowed into her mouth. She tried to struggle, but she was paralysed with terror. The musicians' faces had changed. Their eyes were now shot through with blood, like red lacquer. Diane understood that this ceremony was reducing their bodies to primal chaos, to the outpouring of primitive vigour. Each heart was now pounding, each vessel bursting.

The shaman was now right in front of her. The creature in her hands was still squealing and snapping with its curved, vicious teeth. The old woman moved the monster towards the burn. Diane looked down at her belly, which was sprinkled with talc.

Beneath the white marks, her skin was swelling, puffing up and in places already cracking under the irreversible push of putrefaction. With a final burst of energy, she decided to break away, but sheer stupefaction stopped her.

The sorceress had just placed the animal on her wound and was crushing its furry body into her rotting flesh. Instantaneously, the rodent's eyes were veiled by a curtain of blood. The shaman moved the bundle of fur up and down over the wound with an obsessive perseverance, a crazed application.

Diane fathomed the obscure logic of this act. The sorceress was trying to use the rodent to wipe out the effects of the atom. She was using the animal like a sponge of suffering, a curative magnet, which would smooth away the marks of the fire and suck out its lethal sting.

Suddenly, the animal started to sizzle and splutter. Sparks shot out from its fur. Diane could not believe her eyes: when the creature touched her burn, it burst into flames. Its body was now smoking between the witch's hooked fingers.

The rest happened in a few seconds.

The shaman brandished the blazing creature over her head. Then, with a rustling of feathers and metal, she spun round and crushed it on to a rock, its claws in the air. In the same sweep of her hand, she removed a sword from her sleeve and sliced the body open from its genitals to its neck. Diane watched as the steaming innards spilled out from its guts. She saw the shaman's bent fingers rummaging around inside the entrails then, amid the dark shapes of the organs, a darker movement appeared, a generation of malignant cells eating into the fibres and tissues. Seeds of fear. Marks of suffering. A caviar of death.

Horrified, Diane grasped what had happened before passing out.

It was cancer.

The atomic cancer had been transferred into the animal's body.

313

When Diane woke up, the day was coming to an end. She stretched, feeling her muscles unwinding to their very extremities, then she savoured the warmth from the stove which was humming in the middle of the tent. In the distance, she could hear the sounds of the camp. Everything was so pleasant, and familiar . . .

She was in a yurt, otherwise occupied only by a few wooden saddles, a loom and those omnipresent grey rocks that stood in for furniture. There was no trace left of any shamanism, except for some hanging figurines dressed in robes of hide, and some small muzzles for rodents. Looking up, she could see the sky through the opening at the top of the tent. She remembered how Giovanni had told her that Mongol tents always had open roofs so the occupants could stay in contact with the cosmos.

She sat up on her mattress and pulled aside the felt blanket. She had been dressed in new underclothes. Her jeans and roll-neck sweater had been carefully folded and laid next to her. She saw two splashes of reflected light among the thick grass. Even her glasses were to hand. She put them on with an automatic gesture, then pulled up her tee-shirt to have a look at her burn. What she discovered came as no surprise. She felt overcome by gratitude and shot through with a beam of love as a river is lit by the sun. She finished getting dressed and went out of the yurt.

They had finished setting up camp. A good 40 tents were now standing in the clearing. In the low light of evening, the landscape of the tundra looked more lunar than ever. All of the nomads were going about their business. Women were preparing food in the yurts. Men were escorting the last of the herds into the pens. Children were running about left, right and centre through the smoke, ripping apart the dismal air with their laughter.

A smile rose to Diane's lips when she spotted Giovanni, sitting next to a lonely fire. She went and sat down beside him, amid the saddles and bundles. He handed her a goblet of tea.

"How do you feel?"

She took the cup, sniffed at the steam, but did not reply. He refrained from asking again. Hunched up in his parka, he was poking at the fire with a dead branch.

"We're never going to be the same again, Giovanni," Diane whispered.

The Italian pretended not to hear. He asked once more:

"How do you feel?"

Her eyes on the flames, Diane went on:

"In the West, people think that shamanic wisdom is just pure superstition and foolish beliefs. People think that such ideas are a weakness. But they're wrong. Ideas like this are a strength."

To save face, the diplomatic attaché bent down to blow into the embers. The flaming grasses were crinkling up into orange filaments, creating a tiny incandescent ballet. She repeated:

"It's a strength, Giovanni. I understood that today. Because when the mind believes, then it has already gained a certain power. It is perhaps that very power itself. The human part of a force shared by all of the elements in the cosmos."

The Italian abruptly sat up. He was covered in whiskers, as though hiding behind his beard.

"Diane, I can quite understand how you feel, but I really can't believe that . . ."

"But this is no longer a question of believing or not believing."

She pulled up her sweater and tee-shirt, baring her stomach. Her skin was white, smooth and almost unmarked. All that was left was a slight blush where, just a few hours before, crevasses of fire had been dug out. Giovanni gaped.

"The sorceress managed to cure my burns," Diane continued. "She succeeded in wiping out the effects of the radioactivity. Using a burning rodent, she tore out the heart of the cancer. Call it what you want – witchcraft, psychic powers, the intercession of spirits . . . But here the spiritual force I'm talking about exists in an incredibly pure form. And it was that force which saved me."

She felt no fear of sounding ridiculous. Such fears were irrelevant there. Giovanni opened his mouth to reply, then, suddenly, surrendered:

"OK. Anyway, who cares? I'm just delighted for you, Diane."

He picked up a few bark shavings and threw them on to the fire. The dance of the filaments started up again.

"But now," he said, "you must tell me everything. And when I say 'everything', I mean it."

Diane sipped at her tea, spent some time gathering her thoughts together, then she began. She told him about how she had adopted Lucien, the ambush on the ring-road and the intervention of Rolf van Kaen. About her child's origins and the people who were interested in him. Then about the tokamak and the parapsychology research lab there. She told him how the Watchers had been given the job of communicating the date of some mysterious meeting on their fingertips. She explained her idea that the researchers in TK 17 had uncovered a secret that had allowed them to acquire and develop psychic abilities. Then she closed on the final certainty: those men were coming back that very day because of their secret. They had an appointment at the tokamak on 20 October 1999, in other words in a few hours' time, to replenish their powers.

Giovanni heard her out. He did not look surprised, or incredulous. When she had finished, he simply asked:

316

"But how did they manage to acquire their powers? How could they have developed such . . . impossible faculties?"

Diane felt the sting of the blaze on her face while, behind her, the chill of the dusk was biting into the nape of her neck. She imagined her blood in fusion. She pictured it becoming as orange as burning resin.

"I don't really know," she murmured. "All I can say is that, until now, I had it all wrong."

"What do you mean?"

She breathed in again. The bitter smoke filled her throat like a mouthful of incense. She thought back to the ceremony that had cured her and said:

"My first hypothesis was that the parapsychologists had made an important discovery while studying and questioning shamans from Siberia."

"That sounds reasonable enough."

"But not in the way I first thought. It wasn't their research that gave them their power."

"Why not?"

"For several reasons. Firstly, just picture to yourself those exhausted shamans who had already spent years in various camps and prisons. How could they have taught the scientists anything? How do you imagine that they were able to inspire them into special mental states, such as trances or waking sleep?"

"Maybe they just asked the right questions."

"But the sorcerers wouldn't have replied."

"The Soviets had some very persuasive techniques."

"True. But I must insist on the point that these shamans must have been finished, emptied of their powers. Far from their culture and their faculties, they couldn't have taught the parapsychologists anything. Even if they'd wanted to."

"So, what happened?"

317

Diane drank a sip of tea.

"This morning, I thought of a new hypothesis. Maybe they acquired their powers via an external event. Something that had nothing to do with psychic research."

"What sort of event?"

"The explosion of the tokamak. If radioactivity can transform the structure of the human body, then maybe it can also alter the conscious mind and its mental forces."

"You mean that the researchers were irradiated too?"

"I'm not sure about that. But the ones who are dead all had strange deformities, such as skin diseases, atrophied organs and other deformities that might have been caused by radiation. I even thought that they might have set off the accident on purpose and exposed themselves."

"And now you've changed your mind?"

"That's right. The explosion of the tokamak played quite a different role. It was a revelation."

"I'm not with you."

Diane leant over the flames and stared into Giovanni's eyes.

"The 1972 accident indirectly revealed the astonishing powers that reside in this valley."

She looked round at the camp and the Tsevens busying themselves in the clouds of smoke that were now joining up with the gloaming to blacken out the countryside.

"Look at these men and women, Giovanni. Where have they sprung from? How can this tribe have survived persecution, collectivisation and famine? One thing's certain, in the 1970s there were two sorts of Tseven. The ones that had managed to hide out in the mountains, and the ones that had remained in the valley to become sedentary, acculturated slaves. The latter worked on the site of the tokamak and accepted the most dangerous jobs. They were the people who were burnt in the circle in the spring of 1972. I can even imagine what happened . . ."

318

Giovanni grimaced.

"I'd rather not," he said.

"Just try. Imagine those burnt workers dying of radiation. Imagine their desperate wives, who were quite sure that no help would ever come from the Soviets. So what do you suppose they did? They saddled up their reindeer and went into the mountains to look for the Tseven shamans, people who still possessed extraordinary powers as healers."

"Are you kidding?"

"Not at all. The Tsevens in the valley of course knew that a part of their people were living in the heights in a traditional way, and that they were still in close contact with the spirits."

"I think this whole business is sending you round the . . ."

"Just hear me out! The women went up into the hills. They explained to the sorcerers what had happened. They pleaded with them to come down into the valley and carry out a rite to save as many people as possible. The shamans accepted. They took the risk of being spotted and arrested, and organised a ceremony to heal their brothers. And this shamanic rite worked perfectly, because most of the men were indeed cured."

"How can you be so sure?"

Diane grinned broadly, her eyes ablaze.

"If I survived the radiation today, that means things went just the same way back in 1972."

The ethnologist's face was relaxing into agreement. He was starting to believe Diane's story.

"So what do you reckon happened then?" he asked.

"Then the real nightmare started for the Tsevens. One way or another, the parapsychologists must have found out about the miracle cures. They then realised the incredible truth: the powers that they had been trying to locate for the past three years by studying shamans that had been sent from the Gulags could in fact be found just a few miles from their lab! They were within reach! And unimaginably so! I'm certain that they then realised that they were in the very cradle of the powers that they had been after for so long."

"And they arrested the shamans?"

"Definitely. They captured the virtuosos. The real gems. Then they started their experiments all over again and, this time, they succeeded. They managed to rob them of their shamanic wisdom."

"But how?"

"That piece of the puzzle is still missing. But I'm sure they did seize their powers. That explains why they now have such extraordinary gifts. It explains why my own investigations have been surrounded by such inexplicable events. And that also explains why they're coming back now. They mean to conduct their experiment again, the experiment that allowed them to acquire their faculties."

The Italian was slowly shaking his head.

"That's over the top."

"You could say that, yes. But there's one more point that I'm now sure about. The theft of those secrets is the real motive for the murders. Eugen Talikh is avenging his people, but not in the sense I first thought. He isn't so much avenging the slaughter of the workers in the circle, but more the pillaging of their culture in general. He's taking revenge for a profanation. Those bastards stole the Tsevens' gifts. They're now paying for that very dearly."

"But why 30 years after the event? Why wait for their return to the tokamak?"

"I guess the answer to that also lies in the missing piece of the jigsaw – how they managed to capture their powers. And the appointment given by children with burnt fingers . . ."

She got to her feet. The diplomat stared up at her.

"So? So what happens now? What are we going to do?"

Diane was zipping up her parka. She felt drunk on life and truth.

"I'm going back to the site. I've got to find their old lab. That's where it all began."

CHAPTER 66

Night was falling. Giovanni had brought along two acetylene storm lanterns, equipped with reflectors, which they were now holding at arm's length. They looked like two miners from a distant era, lost in a maze of forgotten galleries. When they changed their fuel cartridges, they realised that they had been wandering around like that for over three hours. They set off again without exchanging a word, coming across more machines, more reactors and more corridors. But still not the slightest sign of the sort of place they were looking for.

At around midnight, they came to a halt in a totally empty room with bare walls. The cold hit them, while fatigue and hunger were beginning to make their heads spin. Exhausted, Diane slumped down on to a heap of rubble.

Giovanni mumbled:

"There's just one place we haven't searched yet."

She nodded. Without another word, they set off towards the stone circle. After a fresh series of corridors and more patios they reached a room that Diane recognised at once: the ante-chamber of the tokamak. To the left, she spotted an area that looked like a changing-room. It contained some great-coats like the one Bruner had been wearing on the ring-road in Paris. There were also some masks, gloves and Geiger counters. The two of them slipped on the protective clothing and picked up the measuring equipment.

They went inside the ring. This time, the neon lights did not come on. Giovanni went over to a large switch and motioned to turn it on. Diane seized his arm and whispered through her mask:

"No. Just our lamps."

They moved on, clutching their torches, which swayed to the rhythm of their steps, breaking through the clouds of dust that were deepening the obscurity. They edged round the ghastly curved wall, looking for an opening that might lead to a secret chamber.

"There."

Giovanni pointed his gloved hand towards a door set in the inner wall of the circle. It took both of them to open it. Diane hesitated for a moment in front of the mouth of darkness it revealed. So the ethnologist went in first, holding up his lamp to scout. Soon afterwards, she followed him and closed the door behind her. She was now in another airlock. She looked down at her counter, but the needle was still. All radioactivity had been absorbed. So she pulled off her mask and then saw a spiral staircase, which Giovanni was already going down. The steps followed the curve of a huge supporting pillar. They were now descending below the floor of the tokamak, into its foundations.

At the bottom, they found some double doors. They were made not of iron or lead, but of copper. Giovanni shoved them open with his shoulder and slipped inside. Diane followed. In the shifting beams of their storm lanterns, a circular room appeared containing instruments of a now human dimension. These brutal, complex machines were reminiscent of those used in experimental psychology research. Diane felt certain that they had finally arrived. The spirit circle was to be found below the atomic circle. In this place where no-one would ever have dreamt of looking: right underneath the infernal ring.

They took off their greatcoats and advanced. The curved wall was covered with fluorescent lichen, revealing the oblique shadows of chains hanging from the ceiling. The links clicked together with a sinister regularity, as though being rocked on a ghost ship. Giovanni was looking for a light switch.

This time, Diane let him. They just could not examine such a place in the half-light. After a hesitant crackling, the neon lights came on and the room appeared in all of its immensity. There were no openings in the circular wall, apart from the door they had entered by. Among the cables dangling from the ceiling, neon strip-lights had been arranged in an arc, thus leaving everything that was out of their range in the shadows.

Nothing seemed to have been touched; it was as if no robbers had ever dared come in. The first pieces of equipment that Diane noticed were some Faraday cages: rectangular copper boxes, measuring six feet by three, which provide complete protection against electrostatic energy. She knelt down and examined the inside of one of them. Electrodes lay on the bronze floor. Men had been placed inside. She stood up again and, a few yards further on, discovered some high-backed chairs, like cathedral thrones, equipped with iron bracelets and copper straps. Beside them, some black counters were connected to suction pads, suggesting that sessions of electroshock treatment had been carried out. On the floor, she noticed some tufts of hair, stuck down among the fungi and dust. People's heads had been shaved so that the electrodes could be placed correctly.

Diane's next discovery were some sensory isolation tanks – six-foot coffins full of salt water. She bent down over them. Tiny bones were floating on the surface. The remains of very small men or else children. She thought of Lucien and nearly fainted – her mind went blank for a moment and her blood beat in her eardrums. Behind her, Giovanni suddenly said:

323

"I can't stand any more. Let's get out of here!"

"No," she said firmly. "We've got to keep looking. We've got to understand what happened here."

"There's nothing to understand! A bunch of sickos tortured some poor bastards! That's all there is to it!"

Diane licked her lips. The air was full of salt, as though laden with bitterness. She noticed another area at the back of the room, marked out by metal screens. She strode over to it and found a stainless-steel table and iron shelving containing jars whose contents had frozen, causing them to break open. She went over to look. Her feet crunched on the shards of glass. Vapour flowed from her mouth, creating an unreal halo around her. All that was left at the bottom of the jars were dark pools and brown organs, embalmed by the cold and the solitude.

She was beginning to grasp the logic of the place. Each machine, each tool had been perverted and turned from its initial use into techniques for torture. Once these bastards had failed to get anywhere using normal research methods, they had turned into inquisitors in their attempts to tear out the truth through suffering, to track the reality that eluded them in pain and dissection. Was that how they had finally succeeded in obtaining the secrets of the Tseven shamans? This seemed improbable. The parapsychologists had surely never acquired their psychic powers by such violent and grotesque means. Even here, the final link was still missing.

Beside the operating table she saw a chest on wheels, containing pointed tools, blades and hooks. These objects seemed half way between surgical instruments and weapons. Their curved handles were coated with precious materials – ivory, mother of pearl and horn – and finely engraved with arabesques.

Diane froze. It is said that sometimes when a man is struck by lightning, the phenomenon is so swift that combustion does not have time to take place. The victim is not burnt, but simply transfixed by fire. In that case, the very fibres of the flesh will always remember that flash of possession. That was just how Diane felt. Once upon a time, she had been struck by lightning full of latent power, and now that bolt had re-awoken in the depths of her being.

She had just recognised those carved instruments. They belonged to her own past. She almost fainted, catching the edge of the table at the last moment. Giovanni ran over to her.

"Are you OK?"

Diane leant with both hands on one of the metal chests. The steel tools smashed down on to the floor, among the remains of the jars. A crashing of metal on shards of glass. Sparks were dancing beneath her blinking eyelids. The Italian automatically stared down at the blades on the ground and asked:

"What's wrong?"

"I . . . I recognise those instruments," she stammered.

"What!? What do you mean?"

"They were used on me."

Giovanni gave her a stare that was full of both horrified astonishment and utter exhaustion. Diane hesitated for a moment, but it was too late to turn back now.

"It was in 1983," she said. "A hot June night. I was 14. I was walking home from a wedding through the streets of Nogent-sur-Marne in the suburbs of Paris. I was going along the riverbank when I was attacked."

She stopped and swallowed hard.

"I hardly saw anything," she continued. "I was on my back. A man in a balaclava was pressing his hand over my face, shoving grass into my mouth, undressing me. I was choking, I tried to yell, but I . . . all I could see were the willow trees in the distance and the lights from a few houses."

Panting, she took a deep breath of the salty air, which dried her throat even more. And yet she felt strangely relieved. Before, she would never have imagined being able actually to say those words. The Italian risked asking:

"And, what did he do to you? Did he . . . ?"

"Rape me?"

Her face broke into a smile.

"No, he didn't. All I felt was an intense burning sensation. When I looked up again, he'd gone. There I was, by the river, in a state of shock. Blood was pouring down my thighs . . . I managed to get home. I disinfected the wound. I dressed it. I didn't call the doctor. I said nothing to my mother. And I healed up. Much later, with the help of an anatomy book, I figured out what the bastard had done to me."

She came to a halt. She was now weighing up the awful familiarity of the memory. Despite all of her efforts, despite all her furious attempts to wipe out the horror, she had lived with that trauma every minute, every second of her life. Then she pronounced the forbidden words – words like white-hot pebbles in her mouth:

"He excised me."

She looked up to see that the diplomat had frozen, as though petrified by his own amazement. He finally said:

"But . . . but what's that got to do with the tokamak? And with these instruments?"

Diane went on in a hoarse voice:

"All I really saw that night was the weapon which my attacker was holding in his gloved hand." She placed her foot over one of the bistouries lying on the floor. "It was one of these instruments . . . the same ivory handle, the same engravings . . ."

Giovanni's reason seemed to balk at this last enigma.

"But . . . but that's impossible," he proclaimed.

"Not at all. It's quite possible and perfectly logical. My whole part in this story starts with that attack. Unless of course that attack was just one more link in the story, in the role I had to play in this circle of stone. My life as a woman began with that atrocity. And it's just that atrocity which might provide a key to the whole puzzle."

Diane fell silent.

Discreet applause could be heard in the half-lit room.

CHAPTER 67

The man who now walked into the halo of light was completely hairless.

His temples were bare beneath his large brown schapska, nor did he have any eyebrows or eyelashes. All that could be seen in the neon lights were the harsh features of his face: his arching brows, the curved line of his nose and the startling whiteness of his skin. The fluttering of his hairless lids was reminiscent of the terrible blink of a raptor.

"You do have a most marvellous imagination," he said in French. "But I'm afraid the truth is rather different . . ."

The man was holding an automatic revolver, half black and half chrome-plated. Among all the possible reasons for surprise, Diane was struck by just one: the perfect French that the intruder spoke, with just a hint of a Slavic accent.

"Who are you?" she asked.

"Evguenei Mavriski. Doctor. Psychiatrist. Biologist." He bowed ironically. "Member of the Novosibirsk Academy of Sciences."

The Russian took a step forwards. As small and stocky as a block of wood, he was wearing a grey jacket with a fur collar, done up over his thick neck. He must have been about 60, but his smooth face gave him a sort of terrible agelessness. Diane asked a purely rhetorical question:

"And you were a member of the parapsychology lab, weren't you?"

Mavriski nodded with his fur visor.

"I ran the department specialising in healers. The influence of the mind over human physiology. What some call bio-psychokinesis."

"And were you a healer yourself?"

"At the time, all I had were a few minor, indefinable gifts that came and went. Like all of us, in fact. In a way, that's what caused our downfall . . ."

Diane shivered. Her mind was teeming with questions.

"So how did you manage to acquire your true powers?"

Instead of an answer, fresh footfalls could be heard crunching over the shards of glass. A deep voice said:

"Don't worry, Diane. You deserve a full version of the story."

She immediately recognised the voice of the man who had moved out of the shadows. It was Paul Sacher, the hypnologist of Boulevard Saint-Germain.

"How are you, young lady?"

She tried desperately to adjust her thoughts to the speed of the events. But in fact, his presence there was not that surprising. Sacher had the perfect profile to be one of that circle of scientists. He was Czech, a political refugee, a specialist in hypnosis, the occult side of human consciousness. She also realised that it had been he who had got to Irène Pandove before her, while presumably looking for Eugen Talikh. When she had said: "Those eyes . . . I couldn't have resisted them", she must have been talking about the hypnologist's irresistible stare.

He stood next to Mavriski. He was wearing a closely knit woollen hat, a dark-blue parka and Gore-Tex gloves. It was almost as if he had just stepped off the slope of a fashionable ski resort, were it not that he, too, had an automatic gun in his right hand.

Diane started to tremble again. Sacher's presence obviously

made her think of Charles Helikian. Her old hypothesis came back to haunt her. Did the old cigar smoker belong to this infernal circle after all? Had he made the journey in just 48 hours? Was he there? Or was he already dead?

The Czech doctor went on, in his neutral tone:

"I suppose that you now know at least the bare bones of our story . . ."

Diane felt oddly proud at revealing what she had found out. She told them everything, certitudes and suppositions mixed together. The site consecrated to parapsychology that Talikh had set up in 1968. The recruitment of specialists from the entire Eastern Bloc, including one or more French exiles. The perversion of the lab's aims, as it started to be used for torture and suffering. Talikh's protests and his arrest, carried out with the help of the Soviet army. Then the accident at the tokamak, probably brought about because Talikh was no longer in control. Then how the healing of the workers by their brothers had revealed the mountains' secret: the presence of a pure tribe, which had in its ranks shamans possessed of a quite extraordinary power.

Out of breath, she came to a halt. Mavriski was slowly nodding his head, making his ivory face gleam under the lamps. His lips curled up in an admiring grin.

"Congratulations. Your investigations have been quite . . . remarkable. Give or take the odd detail, that is indeed what happened."

"What details?"

"The accident in the tokamak, for instance. That's not how it occurred. I agree that our engineers do sometimes lack rigour, but not so much that they would accidentally set off such a machine by mistake. Even in the USSR, we had numerous reliable security systems."

"So, who switched the machine on?"

"I did." He then pointed at Sacher. "Or should I say, we did. We absolutely had to get rid of those Tseven workers."

"You . . . you did that? Why?"

Sacher took over, in a headmasterly tone:

"You have no idea of the place Talikh occupied in their hearts. He was their master. Their god. When they heard that we'd imprisoned him, they decided to try to free him, by force. We really didn't want a rebellion on our hands at that time. How can I put it? We sensed the presence of a power, here, in this laboratory. We felt that we were on the verge of an incredible discovery. We simply had to be able to continue doing our research . . ."

"And so you were scared of a few unarmed workers?"

Mavriski grinned.

"Let me tell you a little story. In 1960, the Red Army reached the borders of Mongolia and forced each tribe to accept collectivisation. As you know, rather than give up their animals, the Tseven chose to slaughter them themselves. The Russian officers were flabbergasted. One morning, they found thousands of gutted reindeer lying across the plains. As for the Tsevens, they'd vanished. The Russians sent out their troops to search for them, but they didn't find a soul. So they assumed that the nomads must have fled into the mountains. In other words, that they had chosen death. It was winter, and nobody would have been able to survive for long at that time of the year without meat or livestock. The soldiers went home, thinking that the mountains would be the Tsevens' collective grave. They were wrong. The nomads hadn't run away. They'd quite simply gone into hiding right under their noses."

Diane's heart started pounding faster.

"Where?"

"In their reindeer. In the bodies of the gutted animals. The men, women and children had slid in among the intestines and waited for the 'white men' to leave. Believe me, there's much to be feared from a people that's capable of such things."

Each word had the ring of truth. Diane thought of how the slaughter had been carried out – arms plunged into the creatures' guts. Everything was connected. Each detail contained all of the others. Another point occurred to her.

"In 1972," she exclaimed, "you used the tokamak to kill. And yesterday, you did so again, to get rid of me."

The Russian slowly nodded.

"We just had to open the dam to make the turbines and alternators work again. Then, when the electricity arrived, I simply liberated the tritium residue. The chamber still contained a vacuum, so you were sure to be irradiated."

"But why didn't you just shoot me?"

"Our entire story has been written under the sign of this circle. As we had once killed with the tokamak, it seemed logical to me to do so again."

"You're just common murderers."

Diane glanced over at Giovanni. He was looking completely devastated, but at the same time fascinated by this flow of information. They both knew that they were going to die. But both of them wanted only one thing – to know the rest of the story.

The hypnologist continued:

"The day after the accident, we closed off the contaminated area and continued with our research. That's when the miracle happened. The soldiers guarding the warehouses where the survivors had been placed noticed a number of strange cures."

Diane took over:

"That's when you realised that by setting off the accident you'd forced the Tseven shamans to come out of hiding. You realised that there were forces in this valley whose strength you'd never dreamt of. That the powers you'd been chasing in old shamans brought in from all over Siberia could be found just a few yards from your lab, and to quite an unexpected degree."

Sacher deigned to smile.

"That's the great irony of our story. We had the sorcerers arrested, as they were heading back up to the mountains with their 'patients'. We were certain that, thanks to them, we were finally going to be able to unveil the secrets of another reality. The secrets of the psychic universe."

Diane closed her eyes. She was now on the final threshold.

"So how did you rob them of their powers?" she asked.

It was Mavriski who answered, his voice trembling with excitement:

"It was the two Frenchies."

She opened her eyelids. This answer was totally unexpected.

"Which French?"

Sacher went on, his voice softer:

"Maline and Sadko, to give them their Russian names. They were two exiled psychologists, who shared our ideas. Until then, they'd followed us in our blood and guts explorations, though with little enthusiasm. When the Tseven sorcerers arrived, they suggested a different approach."

"Which was?"

"It was Sadko's idea. Since the shamans' powers were purely mental, then there was only one way to uncover their secrets: to penetrate inside their minds, to study them . . . from the inside."

"But how?"

The Russian waggled his head.

"We had to become shamans ourselves."

Mavriski chuckled – he looked like a crazed sailor who had abandoned the shores of reason. Sacher went on, in a more measured tone:

"That was our French colleagues' idea. We had to initiate ourselves into the Tsevens' rites. We had to become sorcerers, and thus pass over to the other side of consciousness. Sadko was extremely insistent. If we didn't attempt the great leap now, then we'd never have the same opportunity again."

Diane was ready to accept this madness. In some ways, it was the most reasonable explanation. But she still hadn't grasped the logic of what had occurred.

"But how could you hope to be initiated by imprisoned shamans?" she asked. "How could you hope that they'd reveal their secrets to you?"

"We had someone to intercede for us."

"Who?"

"Eugen Talikh."

Diane burst into hysterical laughter.

"Talikh? After you'd locked him up? After you'd murdered his brothers?"

Mavriski took a step forward. He was now just a few inches away from her. She could make out every detail of his eagle's face.

"You're right," he said, his voice suddenly going strangely calm. "That bastard would never have agreed to negotiate with us. So we had to use a different technique."

"What sort of technique?"

"A gentle technique."

"What do you mean by gentle?"

The man was following his own line of thought.

"That's what Sadko did for us."

"What are you talking about? You mean Sadko set about sweet-talking Talikh?"

Mavriski drew back. His eyes suddenly arched in an expression of surprise. He said, in amusement:

"Apparently I have omitted to reveal an important detail."

Diane yelled, her anger fighting against the cold, and her reason against insanity:

"WHAT DETAIL?"

"Sadko is a woman."

Voiceless with stupor, Diane repeated:

"A . . . a . . . woman?"

Footsteps could be heard to her right. Diane turned round towards the zone of shadows, beyond the neon glare. During her adventure, she had proved herself to be strong, intelligent and cool-headed. But, at that moment, she turned back into the gawky, clumsy, hesitant girl she had been in her teens.

She said, to the figure that was now emerging into the light: "Mother?"

CHAPTER 68

Never before had she looked so beautiful to Diane.

She was wearing a white après-ski suit by a top Italian designer. There was not a single shadow or fold out of place in that acrylic elegance. It was only in her face that Diane detected some imperfections. Beneath her red woollen hat, her blond locks looked almost white, as though emptied of colour and life. And her eyes, which had always been so bright and blue, now looked like two lumps of ice. Diane would have so liked to come up with a remark suitable for the occasion, but all she could say was:

"Mother? Whatever are you doing here?"

Sybille Thiberge replied with a smile:

"But this is the true story of my life, my darling."

Diane saw that she, too, was carrying an automatic in her right hand. She now recognised the model: it was a Glock, just like the one she had used at the Bruner Foundation. For some reason, this detail gave her fresh strength. She told her mother:

"Out with it. You owe me the truth."

"Oh, do I?"

"Yes, you do. For the simple reason that that's what we've come to hear."

A smile. That smooth familiar smirk which Diane had hated ever since her adolescence.

"How true," Sybille agreed. "But I'm afraid it's going to take rather a long time . . ."

Diane stared round the room at the chains, sarcophaguses and operating table.

"But the night's young, and I suppose that your experiment won't start till tomorrow morning."

Sybille nodded. The two Slavs were now standing either side of her. Their breath was freezing into tiny crystals. Their brown schapskas and white hats were now glittering with frost. The sight of those two motionless men either side of her mother reached an almost terrifying perfection. But that wasn't what amazed Diane. It was the adoring way that these two torturers were looking at her.

"I'm not even sure if you really understand the essence of my existence," Sybille replied. "Its motivations and its underlying logic."

"Why shouldn't I?"

Sybille glanced absent-mindedly over at Giovanni, then stared back into her daughter's eyes.

"Because you know nothing about the period. You have no idea about the thrill of it. Your generation is just a dry husk, a dead root, with no dreams, no hope, not even any regrets. Nothing."

"How can you be so sure?"

Her mother continued, as though talking to herself:

"You live in the era of consumerism, of gilded materialism.

All you're interested in is your own navel." She sighed. "Then again, this lack of imagination might well be due to our fire. After all, we were so passionate, so exalted, that we took it all!"

Diane felt a familiar anger start to rise.

"What are you on about? What's this dream we're supposed to have missed out on?"

There was a moment's pause. A silence filled with astonishment, as though the mother were gauging the daughter's profound ignorance. Then, her lips rounded into a curl of respect, she replied:

"The Revolution. I'm talking about the Revolution. The end of social inequalities. Power to the People. Property at last being given to those who control the means of production. Man no more exploiting man!"

Diane was speechless. So the keystone to this edifice, the golden section of the nightmare, was contained in those four syllables. Her mother's voice was picking up speed:

"That's right, my little darling. Revolution. It was no illusion. It was built on fury and certainty. We could overturn the system that had structured our society and alienated our minds. We could free mankind from its social and mental prison, thus creating a world of justice, generosity and clarity. Who would refuse to admit that this dream was the greatest, the most magnificent one that has ever existed?"

Diane found it hard to believe that this speech was being delivered by an upper-middle-class woman who lived on Boulevard Suchet in Paris. Still she tried to connect her words with some memories which she might not have paid attention to at the time. But never had she heard her mother talk about politics, let alone about Communism. She gave up searching. The answer would soon be revealed. The answer was the entire story.

"In 1967, I was 18 and studying psychology at Nanterre University. At the time I was just a *petite bourgeoise*. But I devoted my body and soul to my era. I was fascinated by Communism and by experimental psychology. With the same excitement, I hoped to be able to go to Moscow and soak up the socialist system, and also to the University of Berkeley in the USA, where chemists were probing unexplored zones of the brain using LSD and meditation.

"My hero was Philippe Thomas. He was both one of Nanterre's most prestigious psychology lecturers and a leading member of the Communist Party. I went to his classes. I thought he was wonderful, immaterial, inaccessible . . .

"When I heard that he was looking for volunteers to undergo tests in his experimental psychology lab at Villejuif Hospital, I put my name forward. At the time, Thomas was working on the subconscious and the emergence of paranormal faculties. He'd set up a series of parapsychological tests, like the ones being carried out in certain American hospitals. At the beginning of 1968, I started going regularly to Villejuif. It was a let-down. The tests were boring – in general you just had to guess the colour of hidden cards – and Thomas never came to the lab.

"And yet, a few months later, the master sent for me in person. My results were statistically interesting. Thomas asked me if I'd agree to undergo a series of more thorough tests, with him as the tester. Right then, I don't know which was the greater shock: the fact that I was apparently a medium, or that I was going to spend weeks side by side with my idol.

"I threw myself into the work. It was wonderful being with Philippe, as I now called him. But I found his attitude worrying. I had the feeling that he was trying to track down inside me some sort of force or phenomenon that fascinated him. Soon I learnt that he, too, thought that he possessed a faculty. Not the extra-sensory perceptions that I had, but psychokinesis. He thought that he could influence matter at a distance – and especially metals. In fact, he had had results of this sort once or twice, but was incapable of willing it to happen. It slowly occurred to me that he was jealous of my abilities.

"Then the May 1968 revolt started. Philippe and I became lovers on the barricades. I had the sensation of caressing the flesh of a dream, of an ideal that in fact had a body. But a wave of terror rose up between us. In an instant, during those century-long seconds when he came inside me, I saw hatred burning in his eyes.

"It was only later that I worked out what was happening. Thomas was a man of theory. Someone who dreamt his own existence in a flow of ideas, superior desires and spiritual forces. But I had brought him back to sordid reality: he was just a man, and he had been possessed by my body. To his mind, I had become the instrument of his fall and of his failure. I was an envoy of the Devil.

"The great rebellion was over in just a few weeks. The workers went back to their jobs and the students to their studies. Thomas had drawn a line under any more revolutionary activities in Europe. Some of our comrades were so disgusted that they gave up politics, while others joined the armed struggle of terrorism. Philippe had quite a different idea: he would desert to the East. By going to true Communist countries, he would at last experience at first hand the system he had defended. In fact, what he really wanted to do was work in the Russians' para-psychology labs. He was sure that, once there, he'd be able to harness his psychokinetic abilities. But his problem was that he had nothing to offer the Soviets. In those days, if you wanted to cross the Iron Curtain, you had to prove that you had something to give the system. That's when he realised that he already had what he needed to open the door: me.

"Claiming that we were going on some sort of official visit to Moscow, we visited the Russian Embassy on several occasions.

Thomas knew some of the diplomats there. So it was that in a grimy office with filthy net curtains we underwent some parapsychological tests. Thomas failed, but my results were exceptional. The Russians tried to uncover the trick, then they realised that they were in the presence of the strongest case of psychic ability that they'd ever seen. From that moment, things started to move quickly.

"I was obviously going to follow Philippe, even if his mental state did continue to decline. In just one year, he had to be taken to a clinic on two occasions. He kept alternating between phases of mania and depression. He was obsessed by pain, violence and blood. Despite that – maybe even because of it – I loved him even more.

"In January 1969, we went to a cognitive science congress in Sofia, Bulgaria. Some KGB agents contacted us and gave us Soviet ID papers under the names Maline and Sadko. It was sudden, dark and disturbing. It was what we'd been hoping for. Forty-eight hours later, we were in the USSR.

"It was an utter disappointment right from the start. We thought we'd get a hero's welcome, but instead we were treated like spies. We'd dreamt of an egalitarian society. All we found was a world of injustice, treachery and oppression.

"I soon became the target for Philippe's bitterness. He grew increasingly irascible and cruel. He desired me more than ever and, for him, that desire was a permanent humiliation. When I woke up in the morning, I used to find cuts in my skin. While I slept, Philippe used to wound me with the needles and blades he used in his psychokinetic experiments.

"I went into a complete decline. Thomas's torments, the cold, malnutrition, solitude and the psychic tests that I had to undergo on a daily basis in their filthy laboratories all worked together to break me. I was losing my mind. I was losing my body. And I didn't even have what had, till then, identified me as a woman: I no longer bled. For several weeks, I'd known that I was pregnant.

"In March 1969, the Party told us that we were being transferred to a lab 5,000 miles from Moscow, somewhere in Mongolia. The very idea terrified me. But it gave Philippe his confidence back. When I told him that I was expecting a baby, he hardly even listened to me. The only thing that interested him was that we were being sent to the Soviet Union's most secret institute. We were finally going to be able to work on paranormal phenomena and benefit from the Russians' experience in the field.

"I'd suspected that giving birth in Moscow wasn't going to be a cutting-edge experience when it came to technology, but I just wasn't ready for that degree of barbaric violence. I was too exhausted to give birth naturally. I couldn't even contract the muscles of my diaphragm or my abdomen. The neck of my womb refused to dilate properly. The nurses panicked and called in the night duty doctor, who turned up completely drunk. The vodka on his breath stank more than the ether that was filling up the room. Then that trembling pisshead started using the forceps on me.

"I felt those metal instruments pulling me apart, cutting into me, slicing into my guts. I screamed and struggled, while he was pushing down into me with his metal hooks. He finally decided that he'd better do a Caesarean. But the anaesthetic was past its use-by date and had no effect at all on me.

"So the only way out was to operate without anaesthetic. They cut open my belly while I was still conscious. When I felt the terrible burn from the blade and saw my blood spurt up over their white coats and the walls, I fainted. When I woke up again twelve hours later, you were lying there beside me in your plastic crib. I didn't yet know that the operation had made me sterile, but if someone had told me, I'd have been delighted. Right then, if I hadn't been too weak to move, I'd have smashed your head against the floor."

Her mother's words tore into Diane. So, that was how she had arrived in the world. In blood and hatred. Here at last was one truth that concerned her: she was the daughter of two monsters called Sybille Thiberge and Philippe Thomas. She felt a strange warmth, a sort of well-being. Through all this chaos, she realised that she had managed not to be like them. She had passed through genetic determinism like a veil of smoke. She might be unbalanced, weird, a bit odd. But never would she be like those two wild beasts.

Her mother had picked up her story again:

"We left for Mongolia two months later, during the autumn of 1969. I then discovered absolute cold and stinking people. I discovered the immensity of this continent, where you can travel through the same forest for 24 hours, without seeing anything or anybody. The stations cracked by the frost that look like military camps. Everything was khaki, hostile, full of greatcoats and Kalashnikovs. Everything seemed strapped up by telegraph lines or barbed wire. It felt like I was entering one long endless Gulag.

"I can still hear the wagons clashing together, those blocks of iron bouncing up and down and the continual screeching of the rails. It was like a steel respiration, that was linked to my own breathing. I'd become a metal woman, made of an indestructible alloy. The metal of the instruments that had dug into my womb. The metal of the tools Philippe used to scratch me with each night. And the metal that I would now carry with me to protect myself against him and others. All I wanted now was revenge. And I knew – I knew from my psychic intuition – that there, in the midst of the taiga, I'd be able to enact my vengeance."

CHAPTER 69

The heat from the neon lights was now powerless against the bitter cold. Diane felt her limbs grow numb and stiff. Could she last until the end of this story? Until dawn?

Mavriski and Sacher remained totally still. They were listening to Sybille Thiberge's words, as though she were recounting Genesis. Their faces were as solemn as statues. But their eyes still glistened beneath the frozen tips of their hats. They reminded Diane of stone animals guarding the entrance to a Chinese temple.

Her diabolical mother continued:

"When we got to the tokamak, the parapsychologists had already gone off the rails. Thomas was immediately fascinated by the cruelty of the experiments. But all I saw in them was another step in my own damnation. I went through it all with a cold indifference.

"But then, when they arrested the Tseven shamans, I decided to intervene. During those two years, there had been a total shift of power between the other researchers and me. Despite their madness and cruelty, one after another they had all fallen in love with me. I taught them French. I listened to their drunken confidences. I portioned out the scraps of tenderness they so badly needed. They adored me, worshipped me and respected me more than anything else in that hell-hole."

Diane pictured those Slav torturers. Her mother seemed to her to be some sort of mad Gorgon.

"I convinced them that their butchery wouldn't get them anywhere, and that the only way we were ever going to gain access to those powers was by initiating ourselves. I also knew how to persuade Talikh to . . ."

Diane suddenly butted in:

"I don't believe you. You kill all the Siberian sorcerers, you throw Talikh in jail, you burn his brothers, then all you have to do is go and flutter your eyelashes at him in his cell for him to jump up and obey your orders? Pull the other one."

Sybille's face hardened.

"You underestimate my charms, my dear. But you're right. I was mistaken and Talikh had already made another plan."

"What sort of plan?"

"Patience! Everything in good time."

Paul Sacher, with his usual attention to detail, then added:

"At the end of April, we freed Talikh and the Tseven shamans. There were nine of them. We met here, in this very room. I can still see them, with their thin faces, their skin as hard as bark and their old black *deels*. Then we closed the circle together and the council could begin."

"What council?"

Sybille explained:

"The *iluk*, as they say in Tseven. It's a religious council, like the bishops meeting at the Vatican, except here it's with shamans. The most powerful shamans in Mongolia and Siberia. We held it in a circle of stone, and so the Tsevens decided to call it 'the stone council'."

The ethnologist in Giovanni suddenly came back to life:

"And how did the initiation ceremony work?"

Sybille stared scornfully at the Italian.

"When you acquire a secret, you go from one side of a line to the other. If you reveal it, then you go back. We were led by the forest shamans. Little by little, we left aside our human habits, we abandoned speech and we ate raw meat. The taiga then entered into us, tearing us apart and destroying us. The experience was one of death but, after the trial, we returned to life with our hands charged with power."

"What sort of power do you mean?" Diane asked.

"The initiation allowed us to develop the faculties we already had to the greatest possible degree."

She started shaking again. The cold and the truth were filtering into her blood. She knew that in conditions like this, the body loses one degree every three minutes. Were they all going to die of cold? She asked another question:

"What did you do to the Tseven shamans?"

Mavriski bowed his head, adopting a tone of mock repentance.

"We killed them. Our story is one of infamy. A story of boundless power and ambition. We wanted to be the only ones to possess such secrets."

"What about Talikh?" Diane cried.

"This was no time for in-fighting," Sacher replied. "The Party Commissioners were on their way with fresh troops to investigate the nuclear accident. Only Suyan, the sorceress who saved you, managed to escape."

Diane turned to her mother:

"How did you and Thomas manage to get back to France?"

"That was child's play. We lay low for a while in Moscow, then we contacted the French Embassy. All we had to do was play at being sorry for having made such a terrible mistake."

"And the Russians just let you go?"

"Who cared about two French parapsychologists from a lab that hadn't produced the slightest result of any interest? Believe me, in Brezhnev's Russia, they had other fish to fry."

Diane was thinking aloud:

"So you all went back to your various countries to live anonymous existences, like van Kaen, Jochum, Mavriski, Sacher . . . And during all those years your psychic abilities have brought you all power and riches."

Sybille sneered. Her eyes looked as though they were veiled with fever.

"You will never understand what we possess, what lies inside

344

us. Material reality has no importance for us. All we have ever been interested in are our own faculties. Those marvellous mechanisms that are at work in our minds, that we can examine, observe and manipulate at will. Don't forget. The only way to study psychic faculties is to possess them. And you could never even imagine such a vista."

Diane replied wearily:

"Well, yes, who cares really? But there is just one final mystery."

"Which?"

She opened her hands. Frostbite was beginning to inch into her fingertips. This meant that her heart was now slowing down and was no longer making her blood reach her skin and her limbs.

"Why have you come back here today?"

"Because of the duel."

"The duel?"

The woman in the red hat advanced a few paces. She seemed not to feel the cold at all. With the tip of a gloved finger, she stroked one of the surgical instruments that remained on the metal table, then said:

"The council gave us its powers. In return, we must follow its rules to the letter."

"What rules do you mean? I don't understand."

"Since time immemorial, the Tseven sorcerers have confronted one another here and put their powers at stake. The winner of each combat takes away the loser's powers. We have always known that sooner or later we'd have to fight one another and gamble with our powers in this valley. We finally got the signal. So we came here to fight."

Diane and Giovanni stared at each other. During the flight in the freight plane, the ethnologist had told her that the shamans from each clan had to meet up at a secret location and fight each other in the forms of their fetishistic animals.

Astonishment.

Fear.

These initiates were Fausts.

They had made a pact with the spirits and now they had to pay the price of their initiation and submit themselves to the law of the taiga. The law of combat.

CHAPTER 70

Once this idea of combat had been accepted, then everything fitted together. If these shamans were preparing to fight one another in the symbolic forms of animals, then their duel was rather like a hunt, and as a result it must be conducted on the ancient Tseven hunting grounds.

The duel had to be announced and ushered in by the Watchers.

That was why these modern sorcerers had taken in children from the taiga. That was why they had waited for the fatal date to appear on their burnt fingertips during a trance. Such was the rite. Such was the law. The Watchers had to tell them the date of the duel, the date of their return.

Another factor perfectly coincided with this animal symbolism. Eugen Talikh killed his victims by crushing their hearts inside their chests. His method was the same as the one used in Central Asia for slaughtering beasts.

Suddenly, a fresh train of thought started. She remembered each initiate's peculiarities. Patrick Langlois had told her that Rolf van Kaen used to seduce women by singing opera arias. He had even told her that his voice bewitched the entire female staff in the hospital. And then she remembered what Charles

Helikian had said about Paul Sacher: "Watch out. He's a bit of a ladies' man. When he was a teacher, he'd always make off with the prettiest girl in the class. The other students just had to shut up and look on. He's a real leader of the pack."

A man's attitude to sex was an extremely reliable sign of his true personality. And these apprentice sorcerers were no exception. Diane was now sure that they had adopted the behaviour of certain animals in the course of their possession.

And not just any animals.

In the case of van Kaen, Diane as an ethologist could recognise the behaviour of the cervidae and their troating. Reindeer and caribou were the only mammals to provoke sexual excitement in females by their voices. No matter how astonishing it might sound, the German had behaved like a reindeer.

As for Sacher, Helikian himself had provided the key to his behaviour: a pack leader. A man who made off with the prettiest girl in the class and dominated all of the others could be compared to a wolf. Or to an "alpha", as the dominant male in each pack was termed, the one who fertilised the females and demanded respect and submission from all of the others.

Then Diane thought over the trap laid by Philippe Thomas. A trap that had been prepared with infinite care, based on hypnosis and dissimulation, extraordinary patience and imagination. Such a technique reminded her of another sort of animal: snakes that captured their prey while standing erect on their tails, thanks to their staring eyes and motionless lids.

Since their initiation and "death", they had been reborn into a wild life, governed by the spirit of the fetishistic animals that these shamans had chosen as their "masters". They were possessed by their own totems.

The reindeer for van Kaen.

The wolf for Paul Sacher.

The snake for Philippe Thomas.

She suddenly had a flash of inspiration. Other facts, other details sprang to mind. Physical signs that she had mistakenly put down to being symptoms of irradiation, but which she could now analyse from quite a different point of view.

Rolf van Kaen had suffered from an atrophied stomach, which meant that he had had to ruminate his food. The police lieutenant had presented this as a handicap, or a strange mal-formation. Diane now pictured the situation the other way round. For years, van Kaen had no doubt forced himself to regurgitate what he ate until his body had finally adapted itself to this bizarre practice. His stomach had changed and the rest of his body with it. Even in his very guts, he had started to be like his wild mentor: THE REINDEER.

Diane could also remember a particular point about her hypnosis session with Paul Sacher. In the half-light, she had noticed an unexpected, sparkling flash in his eyes, like that produced by a wolf's retinae, which are equipped with a light-intensifying plate. How could such a phenomenon be explained? Was he wearing contact lenses? Was it a natural evolution caused by constantly staring into the shadows? Whatever the truth, it was Sacher's attribute, his point of resemblance with his totem: THE WOLF.

The case of Philippe Thomas was even plainer. She had certainly not forgotten his peeling, dead skin in that bronze bathroom. By force of will, the curator had managed to contract a psychosomatic condition: eczema that dried his skin so much that his entire epidermis was regularly renewed. His will and obsession had turned him into: THE SNAKE.

Flabbergasted, she continued along this line of thought. She pictured to herself Hugo Jochum's ghastly body, covered with countless dark blotches. The old geologist must have brought on this dermatological disease by over-exposing himself to the

348

sun, the aim being to give himself the colourings of a wild cat: THE LEOPARD.

Which were the wild idols of Mavriski and Talikh? What had they made themselves look like? A glance towards the Russian provided the solution. His glabrous face emphasised his hooked, beak-like nose. His lash-less eyelids accentuated the blinking of his eyes. By depilating his face, he had brought out his natural resemblance to a raptor. Evguenei Mavriski was THE EAGLE.

Suddenly, her mother's voice recalled her attention:

"I see that Diane's no longer with us. Are you daydreaming, my darling?"

Diane shivered, but she felt her blood surge back into her limbs. She managed to stammer:

"You . . . you all think you're animals."

Sybille brandished the blade with its mother-of-pearl handle, making it glisten in the light. She put on a childish voice, as though reciting a nursery rhyme:

"You're warm, my little one, very, very warm. So if I'm an animal, have you guessed who I am yet?"

Diane noticed that, despite herself, she had left her mother out of that infernal circle. She now thought over her memories of Sybille's private life. She saw nothing significant. No gestures, no habits, no physical indications that might be more or less reminiscent of an animal. Nothing that gave away the identity of her idol, except . . .

All at once, a series of clues filled her mind.

Her mother licking her fingers drenched in honey.

Her mother patiently putting away her apiculture supplies.

Her mother and her eternal royal jelly tablets.

Honey.

She had the taste of honey in her blood. In her body. In her heart.

Diane remembered the strange way her mother had of kissing

her when she had been little, during which her harsh, rough tongue had always come out. In fact, Sybille had never really kissed her daughter – she had licked her, just as a certain animal licks its young. Diane steadied her voice then proclaimed:

"You're THE BEAR."

CHAPTER 71

Their masks had fallen. They were three survivors. Three animals. Three fighters. She glanced down at her watch. It was four o'clock in the morning. The sun would be up in an hour's time. In an hour, the duel would begin. What would it be like? Using their bare hands? With those weapons with ivory hafts? With their automatics?

Diane's mind now turned to the Lüü-Si-Ans. She could easily imagine how they had kidnapped these children from the Tsevens, who now revered them like shamans. She could also form a vague idea of how they had then dispersed them around various orphanages that they themselves financed. She could even see why they had chosen the end of August, when adoption centres are emptied by parents, who have taken advantage of the summer holidays to make the journey in their search for children.

But an essential point was still missing. How had they all decided simultaneously to organise their network? How could they have known, at least two years ahead, that it would soon be time to collect the Watchers, and that the date on their fingertips would be in the autumn of 1999? Sacher replied:

"It started with dreams."

"Dreams?"

"In 1997, we all started dreaming about the stone circle. Night after night, the dream got clearer and clearer. The tokamak was filling up our minds. So we knew that this was a message. It was time to act. The duel was in the offing."

Could she really accept such an explanation? Swallow the idea that seven people, spread out all over Europe, had all had the same dream at the same time? The hypnologist went on:

"In the spring of 1999, the dreams became so intense that we realised that the duel would happen very soon. So it was time to gather the chosen children, and time to receive the exact date on their bodies . . ."

"Why didn't you adopt the Watchers yourselves?"

"The Watchers are taboo," Sacher answered "We aren't allowed to touch them. And scarcely even to look at them. We had to wait discreetly for the sign to appear in a household that was close to us."

She remembered how her mother had observed and examined Lucien, but had never kissed or hugged him. During her visits to the hospital, she had quite simply been waiting for the arrival of the sign. Diane walked over to Sybille.

"Why did you think of me as your Watcher's adoptive mother?"

Sybille Thiberge jumped, but in a way that seemed calculated and false.

"Why? . . . But I chose you right from the beginning."

"You mean you always knew that I'd play the part for you?"

"Yes, from the moment I knew the rules of the council."

"How did you know that I'd agree to adopting a child? How did you know that I'd be prevented from having a normal . . ."

Diane came to a horrified halt. She had just seized the final crux of the nightmare. It was her mother who had attacked and mutilated her on that June evening on the banks of the Marne. It was her mother who had brandished those engraved instruments from the tokamak. She fell to her knees amid the shards of glass.

"Jesus Christ, mother, what did you do to me?"

The shaman leant down over her. Her voice had become as sharp as a blade:

"No more than what was done to me. I've never forgotten the way I suffered when they were trying to rip you from my womb. So, with you I killed two birds with one stone. I took my revenge and prepared you for your future role. I wanted to be sure that you'd never sleep with anyone. That no-one would make you pregnant. Not only does excision remove any pleasure from having sex, but if the labia have been closed due to infection, then it also makes intercourse sheer physical torture. That was the result I aimed for when I sliced you up. I was hoping that the trauma would destroy any interest you might have in sex. And I must say that I succeeded beyond my wildest dreams."

Diane was now sobbing, but no tears came. At that instant, Mavriski raised his voice:

"It's time."

Completely drained, Diane looked up at them as, holding their guns, they retreated towards the stone door. She screamed:

"No, wait!"

The sorcerers looked at her. Her mother had not budged. She yelled:

"Just let me understand the final details! You owe me that much!"

Sybille stared at her daughter.

"What now?"

She forced herself to concentrate once more on the chronological order of each fact. It was the only way to avoid collapsing. She said:

"Nothing went to plan when the Lüü-Si-Ans arrived in Europe."

Her terrible mother chuckled:

"That's putting it mildly."

"Thomas tried to stop you taking part in the duel by killing your Lüü-Si-An."

"Thomas was a coward. Cowardice is the only possible explanation for such a violation. He wanted to break the circle."

"After the accident, when you realised that there was no chance of saving Lucien, you called in van Kaen. You contacted him telepathically. That's why there's no trace of any phone call."

"It was all I could do."

"Then Talikh put his oar in," Diane went on. "He decided to eliminate you one by one . . ."

Sybille's voice shook with anger:

"Talikh had been manipulating us right from the word go. He knew that we'd kill the other shamans. So he realised that the only way to save his exclusively oral culture was to initiate us. During all those years, we were his guarantors, the receptacles of Tseven magic. Meanwhile, Talikh just had to wait for the sacred duel, in which he would vanquish us and recover all of our powers."

Deep down, Diane felt a wave of satisfaction. At last, she knew what had motivated Talikh, the man who had wanted to save his people. But there was still a snag.

"But there's still something that doesn't fit," she declared "Talikh didn't wait for the duel, because he killed van Kaen and Thomas in Paris, then Jochum in Ulan Bator. Why?"

There was a moment's silence, then the sorceress whispered:

"The answer's easy. Because it wasn't Talikh who killed the shamans."

"Who was it then?"

"Me."

Diane yelled:

"You're lying! You can't possible have killed Hugo Jochum!"

"Why not?"

"I was there in the monastery. I saw the killer when he came out of Jochum's room."

"So?"

"So, I was talking to you on the phone. You were in Paris!"

"Who says I was in Paris? That's the miracle of modern technology, darling. I was only a few yards away from you. In Jochum's bedroom."

Bewildered, Diane remembered her mother's breathless voice and the traffic noise that had matched that of Ulan Bator. They had quite simply been the same cars. Then there had been that strange feeling of déjà vu on the roof, and for a perfectly good reason: the same woman had attacked her 16 years before. She said, her voice breaking:

"And it was you . . . you who killed Patrick Langlois."

"He'd found out about van Kaen's and Thomas's Watchers. He'd been nosing around in Thomas's past and discovered that a certain 'Sybille Thiberge' was one of his old students. So he called me in straight away. When I got to his office, I slit his throat and made off with the file."

"But . . . but what about their powers? By killing the others like that you couldn't get their . . ."

"I don't give a damn about their powers. My clairvoyance is quite enough so far as I'm concerned. All I wanted to do was stay alive and know they were dead. Today, there are just three of us left in the circle, and the taiga will decide who will be the absolute winner."

"It's time."

Mavriski opened the lead door. A ray of light was coming down the stairwell. The sun had risen. She shouted once more:

"And where's Talikh now?"

"Talikh's dead."

"When?"

"Talikh had the same idea as Thomas, but rather earlier. I was the only adversary in the council that he really feared. So he decided to kill me, and so eliminate me from the combat. He tried to take me by surprise. I felt his presence long before he even got near me. I read his mind like a book. And I used my hidden blade." A smile crept over her face. "If you see what I mean . . ."

Diane pictured the blade beneath her mother's tongue. Then she thought of those bear's kisses, those little pecks that she had been given when she was young, and which had already contained their lethal potential. Everything had already been written. Mavriski moved off towards the stairs, then turned round on the threshold:

"It's time."

"No!"

Diane was now pleading. She turned to her mother:

"Just one more thing . . . the most important thing for me." She stared hard at that slim figure in the red hat. "Who burnt the children's fingers? Who summoned you all here?"

Sybille looked surprised.

"Why . . . no-one."

"What do you mean? There must have been someone who marked the dates on the children!"

"No-one touched their fingers. They're sacred."

A last abyss was opening in front of her. She pressed the point:

"Who fixed the date of the duel?"

Sybille shook her head.

"Have you really not understood a word we've been telling you? We made a pact with higher forces."

"What forces?"

"The spirits of the taiga. The forces that control our universe."

"I don't understand."

"That was the secret of our initiation. The spirit is older than matter. The spirit dwells in each atom and each particle. The spirit is the music of the universe. The immaterial force that forges concrete reality."

"I don't understand."

Her mother's voice grew softer:

"Think of the Watchers' fingers. Of the physical deformities of van Kaen, Thomas and Jochum . . . Of the cancer that leapt from your belly into an animal . . ."

The world grew hazy before Diane's eyes. She pictured the researchers' deformities, their atrophied bodies which she imagined had been marked by their obsessions and sick imaginations. She now knew she was wrong. Her mother repeated:

"The spirit controls the flesh. Such is our misfortune. We stand outside matter. And we have returned for the final transformation."

"What sort of . . . transformation?"

The woman's laughter echoed around the huge circle.

"Have you not understood the law of the council, my child? Have you not understood that it's *all* true?"

CHAPTER 72

The slender tips of the tall grasses seemed to be stroking the grey wind, while dawn was slowly making them glow as though with crimson sap. The three shamans walked into the clearing, or *alaa*, then moved back, keeping a close eye on one another, their bodily movements gradually shimmering with wariness, until they formed the points of a perfect triangle. Diane and Giovanni had remained on one of the tokamak's concrete mounds. They had been abandoned there by the three adversaries, who were now interested only in the coming combat.

Diane tried to keep her eyes on each of them. But across the plain, all she could see were the bending stalks and verdant shoots that seemed to be drinking them up, absorbing and dissolving them. When they were standing at about a hundred yards from each other, they stopped and stood as still as rocks. Suspense hung over their flesh and the dawn's light.

The three shamans undressed. Diane made out their pale skin and bony bodies. Instinctively, she concentrated on her mother. She saw her curved, muscular shoulders blending in with the surging vegetation. She saw her white locks fluttering in the gusts of the wind. Then she realised that all of her mother's body was now swaying to that motion in the clearing. She was falling asleep. She was slipping into that veiled intermediate state, which stretches out a bridge of communication to the spirit world . . .

Diane was still refusing to understand when the impossible truth materialised.

She felt a shadow pass over her. When she looked up, a huge eagle was flying a good 30 feet above her. Its vast cross of feathers seemed to be lying on the sky, in a perfect attack position. A second later, a deep roaring broke out, whose bass notes seemed fit to tear the entrails from the earth. Diane stared back at the grass bed that her mother had made as she swayed herself to sleep.

A huge bear was standing amidst the vegetation. It was a brown bear, a grizzly, and it stood over seven feet tall. Its tawny hide shone with a thousand sparkles. The brush across its back looked like a fortress wall and its dark, gloomy, imperious snout, with two even darker eyes, was inscrutable. "A female," Diane said to herself without a moment's hesitation. The beast bridled up and roared, as if every shred of the taiga would now have to face its fury.

Diane felt no fear or panic. She had left such feelings behind. Turning towards the third point of the triangle, where Paul Sacher had vanished into the grasses, she was now no longer looking for that old dandy, but the bristling back of a wolf, *Canis lupus campestris*, the native species of the taiga.

She saw nothing, but as frequently happened to her on expeditions, she sensed an unusual quality in the air. A smell of the hunt, full of hunger and tension, seemed to be filling every instant. There was a rustling to her left. Diane immediately saw the wolf's black and white head, thrusting forward rapidly, its sharp nose cutting through the undergrowth, and its eyes, rimmed with black and shining, which seemed to be ready to pounce ahead of its body.

Diane grabbed Giovanni's arm and dragged him after her. They skirted the clearing and moved away from the lab buildings. Suddenly, the ground gave way beneath their feet. They slid down a long slope, cutting themselves on the ridges of flint, before finally coming to rest on a sandy surface. Diane immediately started fumbling around. She had lost her glasses. A few yards away, Giovanni was in the same predicament. The very idea of their situation almost finished her off: two grimy, vulnerable, short-sighted humans up against three incredibly powerful animals. When she at last found her glasses she saw that the wolf had gone. It had apparently abandoned its prey for the time being. Giovanni was putting his own glasses back on and stammering:

"What . . . what's going on? What's going on?"

Diane was already mentally measuring the distance from there to the clearing where her mother had crossed over the final threshold. She reckoned it was about 400 yards, due west. It would be risky, but it was the only chance they had.

"Wait for me here," she ordered.

Then she clambered back up, using the roots to help her.

"No way," replied Giovanni, following her.

They re-emerged together and plunged back on to the surging plain. Diane's sense of orientation was far from perfect, but she had a very clear mental image of that bear. They crawled through the grasses until they had reached the site of the metamorphosis. Diane found her mother's clothes. She rummaged through them and soon located the Glock. It was a 45 calibre. She pulled the magazine out from the grip and counted. Fifteen rounds, plus one in the breech. Then she thought of the other two guns. Was it worth trying to get them, too? No, it was too dangerous. Trying not to disturb the slightest blade of grass, they silently retraced their steps and slipped back down the slope.

Diane tried her best to think through the situation. There were three of them. Three predators, guided by their hunting instincts. Three powerful, destructive animals. Intuitive, sensitive creatures, full of all-perceiving receptors. Fighters that were perfectly attuned and adapted to suit their environment. Even that idea was wrong. They had not adapted to nature, they *were* nature. They shared its laws, its forces and rhythms. That very vibration was their reason, their raison d'être.

She turned to her companion:

"Listen to me carefully, Giovanni. The only chance we've got of getting out of here in one piece is by no longer perceiving our environment like humans do. Understand?"

"No."

"There's not one kind of forest," she went on. "There are as many forests as there are species of animal. Each creature perceives, divides and analyses space according to its own needs and perceptions. Each animal constructs its own world, and can see nothing beyond that. It's what we ethologists call an umwelt. So if we're going to save our hides, then we're going to have to think how our enemies think. The umwelts of the bear, wolf and eagle. Because those will be our battlefields, and not the terrain we usually perceive with our five human senses. Got that now?"

"But . . . but . . . we know nothing about . . ."

Diane could not resist a smile of pride. How long had she been studying such mechanisms? How well had she understood such systems of perception and combat strategies? In the burning cold of the wind, she described each of their adversaries in detail.

THE EAGLE: A bird that could see everything. Its tubular eyes meant that it could zoom in on tiny details. When flying over a forest at an altitude of 300 feet, it could focus on a minuscule rodent to such an extent that its prey occupied the entire surface of its retinae. At that instant, it could pull off a second miracle, by using its extraordinary sight in two different directions at once. While still concentrating on its target, which was directly in front, it could also look downwards towards its talons and position them correctly for the kill.

It was then that its huge wingspan – of about nine feet – came into full effect. The eagle dived on its prey at a speed of 50 miles an hour but, when it had almost arrived, it slowed down in a fraction of a second to a man's walking pace, without making the slightest sound. The victim did not even feel that it was dying. The beak and claws had pierced through its spinal cord before it had had time to jump.

This raptor's only weakness was its reliance on light. Its eyes' great depth darkened its field of vision so that it could see properly only on a clear day. It would thus attack before night-fall. The first shadows of dusk would mean that the combat was over for it. This was only a slight consolation given that, until then, nothing and nobody could escape its gaze.

THE WOLF: In contrast, it was the night that provided this predator with its favourite hunting conditions. The wolf's vision was monochrome, but this was compensated for by a special tissue on the retina, called *tapetum lusidum*, which provided it with perfect eyesight, even in pitch darkness. Its perception of movement was also extraordinary. It was able to detect the movement of a hand at a distance of over half a mile, and even to gauge its degree of agitation. The slightest sign of panic or weakness immediately launched its attack reflex. Meanwhile, its sense of smell allowed it to analyse particles produced by perspiration and thus to detect fear.

The wolf would almost certainly wait for nightfall before attacking. That, at least, was what Diane kept repeating to herself so as to lessen the task ahead. In fact, she was not that sure. After all, it had already picked up on their vulnerability. This immediate aggressiveness had shown that the beast in question was an alpha, the leader of its pack, which would have no hesitation about attacking again, at the slightest sign of fear, fatigue, or after the slightest wound. Diane looked at Giovanni, who was trembling from his head to his toes, and realised that *Canis lupus campestris* would follow them all through the forest on a wake of panic.

THE BEAR: The bear could see nothing, or practically nothing, and its hearing was not exceptional. On the other hand, its sense of smell was unrivalled. The mucous surface designed to capture odours was a hundred times larger than mankind's. A grizzly could find its way home from a distance of almost 200 miles just by using its sense of smell, or else it could follow a tiny fragrance in the wind while swimming down a stream.

But the bear's main danger quite simply lay in its physical strength. The grizzly was the strongest animal in the world. It could break a moose's spine with one blow, or smash a caribou's limbs with its jaws. The bear was the enemy most to be avoided. This solitary creature was so unused to social behaviour that its face never betrayed its mood. It was powerful, cruel, implacable and accustomed to lording it over its territory, fearing no rival except its fellows. The females of the species knew this well. Each spring, they had to fight against the males to stop them from devouring their young.

Giovanni listened to Diane's lecture. He was pallid and looked crushed by fear. And yet, when she had finished her explanations, only one question came to his mind:

"How do you know all that?"

Diane's throat was dry, her palate streaked with earth.

"I'm an ethologist. I've been studying predators for the past twelve years."

The Italian was still staring at her. She leaned over to him.

"Look, Giovanni. There are at most ten people alive who could get out of this shit. So look cheerful. You just happen to be with one of them ..."

"But ... what about the Tsevens ... won't they help us?"

"No-one's going to help us. And especially not the Tsevens. Don't you realise that this is a sacred combat? There are just two outsiders in this clearing: us. And the animals are going to begin by wiping us out. They'll even remain allies until they've done so. Only when the land has been purified will they turn against one another."

She zipped up her parka and got to her feet.

"I'm going to try to find a stream. I need to check something."

Lower down, the slope led to a different part of the forest. They slid down as far as the first thicket, then slipped in among the trees. A few minutes later, they had reached a mountain stream that was frothing up into white foam. Diane knelt down.

The water was so clear that she could see the silvery pink forms of salmon in it.

"What are you looking for?" Giovanni asked.

"I need to know which way the salmon are migrating."

"Why?"

"Because I think the bear will instinctively head that way. It'll go to where there are fish in plenty."

"Are you sure?"

"No. It's completely impossible to predict an animal's behaviour."

"And especially with creature such as these," Diane said to herself. How much animal instinct did they have? And how much was still human? What role did the shaman play in each of them? Turning round, she whispered:

"Giovanni, you should . . ."

The shock took her breath away. He was bent double, his face livid, his chest streaming with red. The eagle was wrapping him up in its huge wings. Its talons were firmly planted in his shoulders and its beak was ripping greedily into the nape of his neck. Diane drew her gun. The man and the bird swung round. One of its wings struck her hand. The revolver flew into the air and landed several yards away. She dived after it. When she aimed again, the Italian was swaying by the riverside, his arms flailing. She tried to find a direction to shoot in, then screamed out absurdly:

"Put your arms down!"

Giovanni fell, head first. The bird had still not let go of him. Suddenly, it tore a lump out of his flesh. The wound opened into a gaping red stream. All that Diane could now see was the bird's back. It was too dangerous to shoot.

She dived into the fray. Sliding below the raptor's wing, wriggling in among its feathers, she managed to work her arm up next to its pulsating torso. She then turned the gun round and fired. The bird reared up. Giovanni screamed. Diane pressed the trigger again.

Everything came to a standstill. Silence settled. The black remiges were flapping gently. She fired again and again, feeling her hand forcing its way up into the wound. Finally, the eagle collapsed, dragging both the man and woman over with it. Their three bodies rolled down to the riverside. When she heard its heavy wings hit the water, Diane knew that it was over.

The raptor's round iris was staring at her. A dead bull's-eye. But its talons were still stuck in Giovanni's back. The bird was beginning to be caught up by the current. Diane pushed her gun into her belt and tried to extract those horny claws. Giovanni no longer reacted. When she had finished, she saw that the scratches were not as deep as she had feared, but the wound in his neck was fatal. Blood was pouring out in gentle pulsations. Diane felt choked with grief and disgust. But then she stood up and tensed her muscles again. She could not think of anything now except the coming battles.

What most preoccupied her now was the fact that the smell of blood, the clearest possible sign of weakness, was soon going to attract the wolf. She had to stop it at its source. Twenty yards upstream, she noticed a wooden surface that stood out from the line of the bank. She readjusted her glasses and headed towards it. She discovered a hollow nine feet long, covered by five dark beams of wood.

She managed to heave up one of the planks. The interior was about three feet deep and was covered with a layer of dried branches. The fishermen of the White Lake presumably used it to dry their catches. It made for a perfect shelter. Then she went back to Giovanni, grabbed him under his armpits and started dragging him. He screamed. His face veiled with sweat, he started reeling off whole litanies of staccato words. For a moment, she thought that he was praying in Latin, but she

364

soon realised that he was quite simply agonising in his native language. Trying not to listen to his cries, she pulled him as far as the hide-out. Slowly and surely, she was forging her own umwelt. A world of perceptions and reflexes that depended on each momentary situation and which were all geared towards one objective – survival.

She pulled up a second beam, went into the dugout, then dragged his body inside. When she had moved the roof back into place above them, darkness descended. Only the tiny gaps between the beams let in a little light. It was a good place to wait. For what? Diane had no idea. At least she would now be able to think up a new strategy. She lay down next to him, put one arm round his neck, then held him against her, as though he was a little boy. With her other hand, she stroked his face, petted and cuddled him – it was the first time that she had willingly touched a man's skin. There was no room left in her heart for her usual demons. She kept whispering in his ear:

"Everything'll be fine . . . everything'll be fine . . ."

Suddenly, a light pattering of feet could be heard above them and the panting of breath. The alpha was there. He was walking on the wooden beams and running his snout along the gaps to snuffle up the stench of blood.

Diane held Giovanni even more tightly. She was now speaking baby language to him, trying to drown out the wolf's padding, which was becoming faster and more frenetic. It was now scratching at the bark with its claws, just a few inches from their faces.

Suddenly, between the beams, she glimpsed its black and white face, with its attentive, avid stare. She could even see the flash of its green pupils.

Giovanni stammered:

"What is it?"

Diane continued mumbling words of reassurance while

gauging the resistance of the beams: how long was it going to be before it forced its way inside?

"What is it?"

The Italian's body was now shuddering. She hugged him with all her strength, feeling his blood ooze over her. With her other arm, she drew the Glock.

It was impossible to fire. The wooden beams were too thick. The bullets would never pass through, and might even ricochet back into the cavity and hit them. A different noise now opened a fresh possibility. There was a regular scratching coming from the other side of the excavation. Diane looked round. The wolf was now digging up the earth and trying to force its way inside. In a few seconds, it would be there, in front of them. Its supple body would work its way under the beams and its fangs would rip into their flesh.

Daylight now shone clearly into the dugout. The animal's claws appeared, still frenetically digging.

"Diane, what's going on?" Giovanni tried to lift up his head but, hand on his forehead, she held him down.

A kiss, a caress, then she tensed herself and crawled towards the side where the wolf was still nearing. She was now just a foot away from her opponent. She could see the white flecks on its paws and its nails that were digging, digging, digging. She breathed in its heavy, threatening, heady fragrance. Never had a smell seemed more distant from mankind, more foreign to her own body odour.

Nine inches from the opening, she put down her elbows, tightened her grip on her gun and raised the safety catch with both thumbs.

The clashing of two worlds.

Umwelt versus umwelt.

The wolf scraped, nosed and moved aside the clods quite openly, without taking the slightest precaution. The smell of blood was driving it crazy. When she saw its besmirched snout push its way in, she closed her eyes and pressed the trigger. A warm spray hit her face. She instinctively opened her eyelids and, against the daylight, saw the monster's gory head. She aimed at one of its eyes, turned her head round and fired again, feeling the cartridge case bounce off her face.

She was expecting a blow from its claws or for its fangs to sink into her. But nothing happened. Once more, she risked a glance. The smoke was now blowing away. As the light filtered through the hole, the body could be seen lying there, its back legs sticking out as though it was stretching itself. The creature was motionless. Its head blown away.

Diane pushed it away, filled up the hole again, then turned back towards Giovanni's face. She kissed him and whispered:

"I got the bastard . . . I got the bastard . . ."

She was laughing and crying at the same time, while removing the magazine from the gun to see how many rounds were left.

"I got the bastard . . . I got the bastard . . . ," she repeated obsessively, thinking that so far it had not really been her knowledge as an ethnologist that had saved them.

That was when the sun broke through.

Everything appeared all at once. The sky. The light. The cold. And the slanting shadows of the wooden beams as, one by one, they were being hurled aside. Diane screamed, dropping the gun and magazine. But her screams were nothing in comparison with the roaring of the bear, which was standing at full height above the dugout, and knocking away the last beams as though they were matchsticks. The animal bent down towards the ditch, stretching out its black snout and roaring once again, puffing up its bronze fur and digging into the wind with its fury.

Diane and Giovanni sank back into the hole. The beast was

still leaning forwards, clawing at the air. With his back against the side of the hole, Giovanni managed to get to his feet. She looked up at him in terror. He grabbed her by her collar and yelled:

"Run for it! Run for it! I'm dead anyway."

The next moment, he was staggering across the branches towards the monster. Diane was aghast. It took her a few seconds to realise that Giovanni, the easy-going ethnologist, the young man with the sweet and sugary looks, was sacrificing himself for her.

She saw him stagger in front of the animal, then, with both hands, she pulled herself up to the surface. By the time she had done so, another roar had echoed out. She looked up. At the other end of the pit, the bear's claws had thrown him two yards further on. Bent double over the edge of the pit, Diane could not make herself run. In a fresh arc of claws, the grizzly tore open its victim's chest. In convulsive slow motion, she saw blood bubbling and spewing out between her friend's lips.

It was her turn to roar:

"NO!"

She leapt back down into the pit, grabbed the Glock and slipped the magazine back into the grip. The bear was now eating into the Italian's face. She ran across the trench and, with her feet together, launched herself off the beams to find herself beside the animal.

The bear reared up, a mask of flesh dangling from its mouth. She grabbed hold of its fur then, with her legs apart, she seized the nape of its neck with her left hand. With her right arm, she stuck the gun into its maw, smelling the burning pit of its throat and the scraps of human features. She pressed the trigger. She saw the top of the skull explode in a red rain of splinters. She fired again. Its brain splashed against the sky. She fired again and again and again, until the gun made no sound except for tiny clicks, which were drowned out by the creature's groans. She felt as though she was still firing when the dying bear bit off her arm as it fell, and carried it away into the depths of the river.

Epilogue

The sun beamed into the room like warm milk.

The wooden desk gave off chocolate-coloured reflections, while the parquet glittered in bronze tones, as though it had been painted with tea. The perfect place for breakfast, where there was still that morning sweetness, fed on dreams and vague emotions.

"I don't understand," the woman said. "You want to change your son's first name, is that right?"

Diane just nodded. She was in the registry office in the town hall of the 5th *arrondissement* of Paris.

"That's rather an unusual thing to do."

The civil servant could not stop peering at the dressings on Diane's arm and the scars on her face. She opened the file and muttered:

"In fact, I don't even know if it's possible . . ."

"Forget it then."

"Sorry?"

Diane got straight to her feet.

"I said, just forget it. I'm not even sure any more. I'll call you back."

On the steps outside the building, she stopped to breathe in the chill December air and look at the little fairy lights that were decorating the Place du Panthéon. She liked the old-world fragility of Christmas decorations when set against the grandeur of that mausoleum.

She went down Rue Soufflot and returned to her thoughts. For the last few days, she had been obsessed by the idea of giving

Lucien the names of the two men who had died to stop the stone council. But then, when facing that town-hall clerk, she had realised how absurd the idea had been.

Lucien was not a piece of marble to engrave dead heroes' names on. And, to be quite honest, she did not even like the names Patrick and Giovanni. Above all, she had no need of symbolic acts to remember the friends she had lost in this tumult. They would stay for ever in her mind as the tokamak's only innocent victims – apart from Irène Pandove.

On returning to Paris, Diane had had no difficulty in getting herself cleared of the murder of Patrick Langlois. In fact, she had never even been suspected of having killed him, any more than she had been suspected of the massacre at the Bruner Foundation or of faking Irène Pandove's "suicide". They had quite simply been amazed that she had run away to Italy, as she had claimed. The entire case had now been closed. The investigating magistrate had settled for a rather confused story of ex-Communists settling old scores against a backdrop of nuclear research.

Despite the fact that she had vanished, nobody had hit on Sybille Thiberge's central role in the affair. At first, Charles Helikian had been extremely worried, before assuming that his wife had run away with one of her lovers. Diane saw him off and on. Together, they discussed her mother's curious disappearance. At such times, she suggested that Sybille might have been leading a double life. Such theories plunged him into the depths of despair. But, to Diane's mind, this was the lesser evil. There were other forms of despair and other truths that she would not have mentioned for the world.

She crossed Place Edmond-Rostand and went into the Jardins du Luxembourg. Passing by the railings around the main lake, she went up the steps leading to the puppet theatre, the refreshments stand and the swings. Beneath the bare branches of the chestnut trees, she spotted a stone circle. It made her think of the tokamak, of the circular lab and the seven shamans who had made a pact with the spirits and had paid with their souls. But it was just a sandpit, with well wrapped-up children shivering inside it. Suddenly she saw him in his fleece hat, concentrating hard on building his dams, moats and fortresses.

She retreated behind a tree and, just for pleasure, observed him through the condensation from her own breath. At the beginning of November, Lucien had regained consciousness. Then, on 22 November, he had been discharged from Necker hospital. During the first two weeks of December, he had started playing again as usual. Then, on 14 December, he had for the first time pronounced the word she had so desired and so feared: "mummy". At that instant, Diane knew that she was safe from the past for good.

She swore to herself never to go back over the staggering cruelty that she had had to face and the unimaginable world that she had discovered, where her own universe had been ripped from its hinges right in front of her. But as the weeks went by, a fresh conviction took shape. An idea that provided her with real comfort. She had been thinking of Eugen Talikh, the man who had wanted to reconquer his people's powers. It seemed to Diane that she had established a sort of spiritual continuity with him. Since her return, she was possessed by a new clarity and wisdom. Despite the blood and the madness, she had been initiated by the trial of the circle. Thanks to that, she would be a perfect mother for Lucien. So she contacted the other parents who had adopted Watchers, including Irène Pandove's relations who had taken in the child of the lake. She had promised to help and advise them if their children started to show signs of having strange powers.

She emerged from her hiding place and walked over towards

the sandpit. Lucien was once more being looked after by the young Thai girl from the France-Asia Institute. He spotted her and ran towards to her. She stifled a cry when he leant with all his weight on the stitches in the stump of her arm, and looked for the coolness of his cheeks. If Diane was sure of one thing, it was that she was still convalescing, and the best filter for her recovery was this child's presence, this mesh woven from his own carefree desires. Each detail purified her. Even the size of his hands, of his feet and his clothes were a new texture for her, a particular, light, diaphanous essence that purified her soul.

Suddenly, she burst out laughing and they span round together beneath the tops of the trees. The only mission she now had left was to adjust herself to that clearing of innocence, that slope of tenderness which now formed her destiny's one and only circle. She closed her eyes and saw nothing but particles of light.